Justice Be Done

Carla Damron's
Caleb Knowles Mysteries

KEEPING SILENT

SPIDER BLUE

DEATH IN ZOOVILLE

JUSTICE BE DONE

Justice Be Done

A Caleb Knowles Mystery

Carla Damron

JUSTICE BE DONE
ISBN 978-1-62268-181-5

This book is a work of fiction. Names, characters, places and incidents are products of the author's imagination or are used fictitiously. Any resemblance to actual events or locales or persons, living or dead, is entirely coincidental.

Also available as ebook: ISBN 978-1-62268-182-2

Printed in the USA on acid-free paper.

10 9 8 7 6 5 4 3 2 1

A Note from the Author

This novel was (literally) born in a dream. The character Caleb Knowles wasn't done with me, so he knocked on the door of my unconscious brain with another story for me to tell.

As a writer, I explore issues that are important or troubling to me, which is why *Justice Be Done* is set against the backdrop of race riots that follow a hate crime. Please understand, I'm white. My perspective is both white and Southern. Racial issues infuse much of our life down here in South Carolina as they have for centuries. While we've made strides regarding racial justice, we still have so very far to go.

I strived for an honest portrayal of the characters who are Black, so I consulted with sensitivity readers and made changes guided by their input. My goal was to capture how racial issues get out of control and explore all the ways we must work harder to understand each other. This is the only way healing will happen.

I also want this work to honor the work of Senator Clementa Pinckney. This amazing man was the pastor at Mother Emmanuel AME Church in Charleston, South Carolina, where he was assassinated along with eight other churchgoers in 2015, a pivotal event in recent South Carolina history. His assassination led to the removal of the Confederate flag from our Capitol.

Senator/Reverend Clementa Pinckney must NEVER be forgotten.

Content warning: contains mention of racist ideology and scenes of racial violence.

Acknowledgements

I wish to thank Tim Conroy, Beth Johnson, Ed Damron, Pam Knight, Sheila Athens, Gabi Coatsworth, and Michele Montgomery for their help with this project.

This book is dedicated to the memory of social worker Keitha Whitaker, a champion for social justice who never stopped believing in the power of kindness.

"The Lord teaches to love all,
and we pray that over time,
that justice be done."

–The late SC Senator Clementa Pinckney

Chapter One

As the heavy metal door clanged shut, social worker Caleb Knowles felt the grim vibrations in his teeth. The stainless steel sliding bolt engaged with a bang as loud as a gunshot. How final it must sound to most of the men confined in the jail, including the kid Caleb had come to see.

The officer escorting Caleb said, "Hands at your side. Walk in the center, out of reach."

Caleb knew the drill. He passed cell after cell and tried not to react to the cacophony of shouts from inmates celebrating this smallest interruption to their routine.

"Well, well, well. A redhead! I want me some of that!" A baritone voice boomed.

Caleb kept his face neutral as he stared ahead, gripping his notepad.

The officer smirked. "Moved the kid to the suicide watch cell yesterday. We got eyes on him all the time via video camera. That pen in your pocket—don't let him get his hands on it."

Caleb understood the danger a pen could pose: a weapon that might be used on others or himself. They passed the spartan "suicide watch" cell where the boy spent his second night: a bare light that never turned off. No bed except a thin plastic pad on the floor. No sheets or blankets. A urinal that hadn't been cleaned since the Clinton administration. Loud. Cold. The child shouldn't have been in the adult jail but that was South Carolina for you.

Hell on earth.

"We agreed I'd meet with him in the interview room, right?" Caleb asked.

The officer halted, giving Caleb a skeptical look up and down. "Yeah. He's waiting for you in Room 1. You got ten."

Caleb didn't reply. He knew the kid would be handcuffed, a guard right outside the door. But getting him away from the relentless clamor might make him more likely to talk.

Caleb entered the tiny cell at the end of the unit and dropped into a seat bolted to the floor. The kid, Laquan Harwell, dressed in an orange jumpsuit, leaned forward, the shackles chaining his wrists to his waist clacking against the metal tabletop.

"Hi, Laquan. I'm Caleb Knowles. I'm a social worker." Caleb didn't reach to shake his hand because that was against the rules. Jails come with a lot of rules.

Laquan cocked his head, saying nothing. He had short black hair and big ears, as though he hadn't grown into them yet. His brown eyes looked crusty from lack of sleep.

"You understand why you are here?" Caleb had no time for relationship building. They only had ten minutes.

"Because of Friday," he muttered, his gaze fixed on the scarred tabletop.

"Because Friday you . . ." Caleb needed the kid to speak the words. This would determine what he remembered about his crime and his level of self-awareness.

"Because I beat up somebody at a store." He voiced no pride, just resignation.

Awareness and memory intact, Caleb scribbled on his notepad, then added: *Blunt affect,* which meant his blank expression didn't match the situation.

"And why did you beat him up?" Caleb leaned forward, hoping for eye contact.

The kid shifted again. His hands, folded on the table, lay still. Calm. His nails were neatly trimmed, his fingers pudgy. Not that the kid was fat, he just looked boyish. He was only sixteen. "He pissed me off."

"Can you tell me how he pissed you off?"

A half shrug. Lip curling in a sneer that did not look genuine. "Wouldn't wait on me. I'm in line to buy my mama some soup and crackers behind a white guy. He waits on the white guy. Skips me and rings up a white girl with cigarettes she ain't old enough to buy. So yeah, I was pissed." He faked a no-big-deal tone, as though he was some bully used to assaulting people. Caleb didn't buy it.

Still. The victim, Palmer Guthrie, age sixty-nine, owner of Guthrie's Stop and Shop, had three broken ribs, a sprained wrist, and a fractured orbital. Yeah, Laquan had been pissed all right.

"You thought he was being racist?"

Laquan wiped his upper lip where tiny beads of sweat had gathered. "Know he was. It ain't exactly a new phenomenon."

Caleb leaned back and wished that for a moment, he could step outside his own whiteness. He understood the damage done by generational racism. The anger and pain handed down after centuries of abuse and maltreatment. But he understood it as a Caucasian, not as someone who'd lived it, who felt it roiling in his DNA. Being Black in South Carolina came at a cost.

"You've dealt with Mr. Guthrie before?"

"Only store within walking distance so yeah. Been dealing with him my whole life."

"Does he always treat you like that?"

Another shrug. "Sometimes better. Sometimes worse. Once I got myself a fountain drink and he tipped it over so it splashed all over my jeans. Made me clean it up."

Caleb felt his jaw tighten. He'd want to punch the man, too.

"What happened yesterday? What made you react like you did?" Caleb needed to determine if this was an act of impulse or something Laquan had been planning.

Another shrug. "Last straw, I guess. Stupid. Look, I admitted what I done. Do we need to keep talking about it?"

"I suppose not." Caleb felt for the kid. One bad decision, an impulse, had derailed his life. "You told one of the guards that you wanted to hurt yourself. That's why I'm here."

The kid didn't look suicidal, but Caleb knew from experience how good males could be at hiding it.

He nodded, rubbing his thumbs together.

"You feel depressed?"

"I'm in jail, so yeah."

"Have you ever been depressed before?"

"No. I'm not crazy. I don't need a shrink. Hell, I don't even need whatever it is that you are."

"Clinical social worker," Caleb said. "I specialize in mental health. Now tell me more about wanting to hurt yourself."

"I know what's going to happen. Black guy beating up an old white guy. They're gonna lock me up forever. That's my future. Who'd want to live like that?" He looked up at Caleb, eyes wide and beseeching. And so very young.

Caleb spoke softly. "You're not an adult. That may not be your future."

His laugh had a sardonic edge. "Yeah. Right."

"Do you still feel like hurting yourself?"

"I couldn't do anything here if I wanted to. But now I don't want to."

"I'm glad to hear it. What happened to change that?" Caleb's smartwatch buzzed—a text coming in from his brother Sam. About time. He hadn't heard from his older sibling in over a week, but Caleb never responded to texts when he was with a client.

"I talked to Mama. She was crying and all." He paused, drawing his lips in tight, emotions threatening to surface.

"That must have been hard for you." Caleb wished he had more time, that he could let Laquan feel what he needed to feel, but that wasn't how it worked.

Tears moistened Laquan's eyes and he wiped them and muttered, "She's been through a lot. I don't want to put her through anymore."

Caleb's wrist vibrated again. Sam usually wasn't this insistent.

"I messed up. I don't want her to have to deal with a trial and all. But she said losing me would be worse."

"I'm sure it would be. You love her very much, don't you?"

He nodded, taking in a breath. "You got any more questions?"

"Just a few." Caleb followed up with the typical mental status exam, not surprised that his client was fully oriented and displaying no signs of voices, paranoia, or any other symptoms of psychosis. "Is there anything else you want to tell me? I'm here to help you."

Laquan's gaze flitted from the table to Caleb's face, his voice softening. "Can you get me out of that cell? I can't spend another night there. Let me go back to the other one. Please."

Caleb saw it then, in his eyes. The vulnerability. The boy pretending to be a man. No way he should be stuck in an adult jail. "I'll do what I can."

Caleb motioned to the officer waiting outside the doorway. He entered the room, unlocked Laquan from the table, and shoved him roughly out the door.

Caleb hurried behind them, eager to get to his phone to see what was up with this brother.

The guard asked, "We need to keep him on suicide watch?"

"I don't think so. He can return to general population unless he makes another threat or gesture. He needs to be transferred to a juvenile facility."

The guard laughed at that.

"Seriously. He's underaged. No way he should be here." Caleb looked him dead in the eye, hoping to sway him.

"Yeah, well, he shoulda thought about that before he went off on an old man. Likely to be tried as an adult for that."

Caleb sighed out his frustration.

Caleb's phone had been secured in a locked cubby—a new jail policy—so as soon as he got it back, he scanned the chain of texts.

Need a favor. Interpreter fell through. MD appt at 4. Can you sit in? Then, *Sorry to bother you at work. If you're busy, I'll figure something else out.*

Caleb checked his calendar app. His four p.m. appointment had canceled. He replied. *No problem. Send address.*

TY. Thank you.

Caleb jogged out to his Subaru. A macramé ornament made by his thirteen-year-old daughter, Julia, hung from the rearview mirror. Julia lived in Charlotte with her mother, but the tasseled jute thing helped keep her with him.

Early fall in Columbia meant bipolar weather: some days Hades-hot like July, others chilly enough to warn of winter. Today was in-between: warm and dry, with the trees beginning to hint of reds and yellows. Caleb turned on the AC and tapped the address Sam had sent into the GPS.

He hadn't interpreted for Sam in over a year. Now that his deaf brother's success as an artist had exploded, he had the resources, and the reputation, to command the best sign language experts in the area. At first, Caleb had been a little insulted. He'd been interpreting for his older brother since he was deafened in a motorcycle accident at age sixteen but understood Sam wanting this independence.

Sam had laughed when he brought it up. "How about you just be my brother for a while? God knows being yours is a full-time job." Which was probably true. When they were kids, and Dad had one of his outbursts, older brother Sam had always been the one to absorb the blows. As adults, Sam was his go-to whenever he had a problem, and Caleb served the same role for him.

As he followed the GPS instructions, he tried to determine what kind of doctor Sam was seeing. Dentist? Dear God, don't let it be a proctologist.

He put in a call to the office to let Janice, their sainted office manager, know he wouldn't be returning. "Any messages?" he asked.

"Detective Briscoe called about your meeting with Mr. Harwell."

"Yeah, yeah. I told the staff he could stay in general population. Can you let Claudia know I'll email her later?" Detective Claudia Briscoe had arranged for the consult with Laquan. She'd probably want details he wasn't prepared to give.

"I'll see you tomorrow, Caleb," Janice said, and clicked off.

Sam's directions led him to a large medical building near the hospital, one of those holding twenty different suites with twenty different practices. Sam hadn't been specific about which floor. As soon as Caleb parked, though, a wide hand rapped knuckles on his car window. Sam.

"Hey," Caleb signed.

"Hey. And thanks." Because Sam lost his hearing later in life, his speech was remarkably clear. He worked with a speech therapist to keep it that way.

"So why are we here?" Caleb signed. "Broken tooth? Mammogram? Hemorrhoids?"

"Not exactly." Sam pushed forward, checking his watch.

Caleb tapped his shoulder. "We're not late yet."

"I know. I just . . . Come on."

"Okay then," Caleb said to his brother's back, wondering what had his brother in such a hurry. They entered a crowded elevator and Sam pushed the button for the eleventh floor. Caleb stayed close, watching him. Sam was the larger, more handsome of the two: Chiseled features. Thick waves of brown hair. Even thicker wallet. Annoying bastard.

But now there was that tension knotting his jawbone and Caleb started to feel a tinge of worry.

They entered the door marked "Palmetto Orthopedic Associates" and Caleb relaxed a little. Sam's back was probably acting up again because the damn fool refused to take better care of it. Since he'd been working on larger scale works of sculpture, he'd haul massive hunks of wood up ladders without asking for help or using proper equipment. Maybe Caleb could talk the doctor into giving Sam the lecture he was tired of giving. Sam was two years older than Caleb—almost fifty. Time to take better care of his body.

Sam checked in and pointed to two chairs in the waiting area. He sat forward, elbows on knees, his eyes on the door to the examining area.

Caleb tapped his knee. "Your back bothering you?"

Sam squinted at him, then smiled. "Just a little."

"Yeah. Right."

Sam leaned back, studying Caleb. "When we go in there, I need you to be an interpreter. Not a meddling brother. Okay?"

Sam must have figured out Caleb's lecture plans. "Okay," Caleb signed.

"I mean it. This may . . . get complicated. I hope it won't, but it might."

"I get it. Don't worry, Sam. I'll save the brothering for when we leave."

Sam's answering smile had an edge of sadness to it and Caleb's tinge of worry amped up.

A nurse came for them and Caleb liked how she walked right up to Sam rather than beckoning from the door which is meaningless for a deaf person. They went to an exam room, and the nurse sat Sam on a gurney to take his vitals, which were, as always, disgustingly strong.

When Dr. Gabrick entered, he motioned for Sam to get off the table and sit in a chair. He rolled a stool over close to him.

"You're the interpreter?" he asked Caleb.

"Caleb Knowles," Caleb held out a hand, which the doctor shook.

"Knowles?"

"My brother," Sam said quietly.

Gabrick nodded. He looked to be about forty, small-framed, with short dark hair and close-set, hawk-like eyes. "How are you feeling, Sam? Any pain?" he asked, and Caleb signed.

"Just a little."

"Good. Can I take a look?"

Sam rolled up his right pantleg, which confused the hell out of Caleb. His leg and his back were hurting?

Gabrick ran a hand along the back of his calf. "Looks like the incision is healing nicely."

Incision?

Sam cleared his throat and Caleb remembered to sign for him.

The doctor lifted an iPad and swiped the screen. "Sam, I wish I had better news for you."

"It's . . . cancer?" Sam whispered.

"The mass—lump, as you call it—it is a soft tissue sarcoma as we feared."

"What?" Caleb asked.

Gabrick showed him the screen. "A large cancerous mass on the calf muscle here."

Caleb blinked. Cancerous? Cancer? Sam had cancer?

Sam gripped his still hands. "Caleb! You've stopped signing."

"I can start over," Gabrick said.

"It's okay. I got it." Caleb drew in a deep, calming breath and willed his hands to speak. He letter-signed "cancer" and "sarcoma" words he had never wanted in their vocabulary.

Sam nodded slowly, his face going a little pale.

"I'm referring you to an oncologist, Dr. Pamela Simm."

Oncologist was another word Caleb hated to finger-spell. Crap. This was bad.

"I suspect she'll want to take the tumor out, but she may want to treat it first. She's the best in the business, Sam. She'll take very good care of you."

"Treat it?" Sam asked aloud.

"To shrink the mass."

"Do you think it's spread? I mean, beyond the lump?" Sam asked, and the fear in his voice nearly broke Caleb's heart.

Gabrick gave him a sad smile. "I wish I could tell you something definitive. That the cancer was completely contained and would be gone with surgery. But honestly, I don't know. That's for Pamela to determine."

Caleb didn't mean for his hands to shake as he signed this.

He wanted to be strong. Steady. Whatever his brother needed him to be.

"Do we call to set up an appointment?" Caleb asked the doctor.

"I've already done that. She's working you in tomorrow at ten a.m." He handed Sam an appointment card.

Sam studied it. "I'm supposed to meet with the installation committee at ten."

"What?" Caleb asked. "The installation committee? Christ, Sam. That can wait." His brother had been working like a fiend with another artist on a sculpture to honor the memory of a state senator who'd been assassinated. That had to take a backseat to this new reality.

"Sam," Dr. Gabrick tapped Sam's knee. "This is a lot to take in, I know. But seeing Dr. Simm tomorrow is important. Dealing with this tumor as soon as possible needs to be your priority." He glanced over at Caleb as though making sure he'd signed every word.

"He'll get there." Caleb turned to Sam and signed: "We'll get there, right?"

"Yeah." Sam pocketed the card and stood.

Gabrick stopped him at the door. "You're going to be tempted to get on your laptop and google the hell out of 'soft tissue sarcoma.' My advice? Don't. But if you must, stay with these websites." He handed Sam a sheet of paper with five website addresses. "These are reputable and might even be helpful. But the real answers will come from Pamela. Good luck, Sam. And reach out if you need anything from me."

Caleb followed Sam to his pickup, wishing his brother would say something. Sam fished out his keys and unlocked the door. Caleb lingered as Sam climbed in, then tapped his shoulder. "Where are you going?" he signed.

"Home."

"I'll follow you."

"Not now, Caleb. I need some time."

Caleb didn't like it but expected it. Sam tended to pull inside himself when things got tough. He'd give him some alone time, then check on him later. In the meantime, he had his own research to do.

He held up his phone and wagged it at Sam. "You stay in

touch with me."

Sam reached for Caleb and pulled him into a quick, unexpected hug. "Thanks for coming today."

Caleb backed away as Sam started the truck. Thanks for coming? Where else on God's green earth would he be when his brother needed him?

And it looked like Sam needed him now more than ever.

Chapter Two

Mary Beth Branham tightened the duty belt on her uniform. Next came the Taser, bright green, which she inserted in the left (non-dominant side) holster. Her service weapon, a nine-millimeter Luger semi-automatic, belonged on the right, and she checked that the safety was secure before strapping it in. The radio pouch and pepper spray fit behind the Taser, and she positioned the handcuffs to the left of the side arm. After eighteen months on the force, she'd grown used to the bulk and weight of the gear but donning her Kevlar vest and body camera made her wish she could lose the stubborn fifteen pounds from college. The added gear wore her down as the day went on.

She never let it show, though. Not to her best friend and roommate Paloma Sanchez, suiting up beside her, and certainly not to her recently assigned partner, Lt. Al Fuller.

"Don't forget you got that Taser." Paloma used the locker mirror to touch up her lip gloss. "Use it on Fuller if he gets out of hand."

"Wish I could." Mary Beth adjusted her hat, sharing the mirror with her friend. They were a study in contrasts: Paloma's glossy black hair and golden-brown cheeks beside Mary Beth's mousy blond waves and too-pale complexion.

"They should assign that asshole to me." Paloma, a proud Puerto Rican, slid her straightened black hair behind her ear. She took pride in her appearance that Mary Beth never felt, and envied. "I'd give him hell."

"And probably live to regret it." Mary Beth could picture Paloma in the squad car with the lieutenant. Yeah, she'd sass right back when he started his shit, but she had no idea how bad he could be. How racist Fuller was, how he hated anyone who didn't match his skin tone. She never wanted her friend to be subjected to that kind of hate.

"Branham! Get the lead out." Fuller stood in the doorway of the women's locker room, his mass filling it. He had seven inches on her in height and about the same in breadth—the man's shoulders nearly reached the sides of the doorjamb.

"Coming." She clicked her locker shut, drew a breath, and prayed this day would go better than the last.

"I didn't see you at the gym yesterday," Fuller said.

Mary Beth rolled her eyes at Paloma. "Took a one-hour class at nine."

"Good. Might help you shed some of that spare tire you're wearing." Fuller spotted someone he apparently found more interesting and moved away from the locker area.

"You didn't mention that class was flow yoga," Paloma said with a laugh.

"Namaste," Mary Beth replied, and the two headed out to their respective cruisers.

Mary Beth didn't mind that the afternoon patrol with Fuller stayed busy. A break-in at a local jewelry store. Fender-bender on Sumter Street. The current call was a drunk and disorderly in front of the bus station that Fuller found very entertaining. "You're wasted. And wasting my time." Fuller got in his face.

The old man, propped against the gritty wall, eyes rheumy and unfocused, tried to pull away.

"Where you think you're going?" Fuller shoved him hard against the brick.

"Hey! No need for that." Mary Beth stepped between them. She eyed the drunk man. He had to be over seventy, worn hard by life. Dark skinned, which accounted for Fuller's attitude. "You got somewhere to go? Where you bunking tonight?"

His hand wove through the air then pointed vaguely toward North Main. "My daughter. She got a room for me."

"How 'bout we get you there?"

Fuller stepped closer to her, peering down like she was a bug he needed to stomp. "You forgetting who's in charge here? Read the stripes, Branham."

No, she wasn't forgetting. How could she when he reminded her a dozen times a day? "Of course, Lieutenant. But the way I see it, we have two choices. We arrest him, we have to take him to booking and do a bunch of paperwork that keeps us busy till six. Or we drop him off at his daughter's and get on with our lives. But it's your call, of course." She kept her face neutral. This could go either way. Fuller might agree to an easy resolution, but the satisfaction of throwing another Black man into a cell might be too hard to resist.

Their radios crackled. "10-32, all available please respond."

"Copy that," Fuller said.

"Captain requests a 10-98."

10-98 meant a private channel. Fuller switched to the requested frequency and motioned Mary Beth closer to listen. "What's going on, Phil?"

"Someone tossed a pipe bomb inside the home of assault suspect Laquan Harwell at six a.m. this morning. The mother was badly injured. A crowd of protesters started gathering downtown around five this afternoon, then marched to police headquarters. They're growing. And getting loud. We need all available units back here."

"Laquan Harwell?" Mary Beth whispered.

"Harwell's that black punk who almost killed the old guy who owns the Stop and Shop on Fairfield Highway. Guess someone wanted payback," Fuller said.

Black punk. Fuller had no problem serving as cop, judge, and jury when the suspect wasn't white. Fuller said into the radio, "Ten-four. Got a drop-off then we'll head back to the station."

"Hurry before this turns into a powder keg."

Mary Beth helped the old man into the back of the car but getting an accurate address proved impossible. Following his vague hand gestures and instructions like, "turn by where the preacher used to live," they stumbled upon the modest blue clapboard house. Mary Beth opened the door for their passenger and whispered, "Sleep it off. And stay away from downtown. Next time, you might not be so lucky."

The old guy cocked his head at her. "You be careful, child. Be careful out there."

The drive back to the station took eight minutes with Fuller at the wheel and sirens blaring. Sixty or so Black people stood on the sidewalk, fists raised, chanting something. A barricade blocked the entrance to the station and on the stone steps, the captain and five officers in riot gear made a human wall.

"Jesus. Got ourselves a race war brewing." Fuller sounded almost jubilant. "Get the helmets from the trunk."

Mary Beth rushed to the back of the squad car and pulled

out the helmets and other gear while Fuller hurried over to the commander, a pink-skinned man with a bulldog face. Fuller shifted over so she could hear the update: "According to reports, a pipe bomb was tossed through the window and started a fire. The victim, Pearl Harwell, age fifty-nine, recently suffered a stroke and has limited mobility. This made it hard for her to escape. She suffered burns and smoke inhalation. House is a total loss. A rental."

"Any suspects?" Mary Beth asked.

He shook his head. "Neighbor saw an unmarked van speed away. White male driving. No plates. We've been flooded with calls demanding an arrest. Then the crowd showed up, all fired up. We expect it to get worse. It's trending on social media. Black Lives Matter is calling in reinforcements. Tonight's going to be rough."

"What's the prognosis for Mrs. Harwell?" Mary Beth asked. If the woman didn't survive, the protest could turn into a deadly riot.

"Not sure. She was medically fragile before, so . . ." He punctuated his sentence with a shrug.

Fuller surveyed the crowd. "Strategy?"

"Prevent escalation." The commander moved closer to Fuller. "Am I clear on that? Whatever your personal views are, keep them to yourself."

"Sure thing, Captain. Here to do my job." The two men gave each other a long look, communicating something without words. The "fraternal order of police" didn't leave much room for officers of the female persuasion.

Soon they were in front of the gathering crowd, a line of blue standing in neutral postures, but ready to grab weapons should the need arise. When any of the Black people made eye contact with her, Mary Beth offered a sympathetic smile, hoping it said, *I understand why you are here. Just keep it calm.*

But beside her, Fuller seemed to communicate something else entirely. His hand rested on his gun. He wore an expression of contempt and excitement, conveying a message of *Just give me a reason.*

Paloma joined the line with her partner, Kyle. Mary Beth once called them the "Odd Couple." Paloma stood six feet tall with dark tanned skin and squared, broad shoulders. Kyle barely met departmental height requirements, a freckled ginger who looked even younger than his age of twenty-five. But they worked well together. Trusted each other, something Mary Beth envied.

"Check out the BLM sweatshirt guy on the right," Fuller growled. "Keeps reaching for something in his pocket. Could have a semi-automatic in there." His gun belt creaked when he adjusted his grip.

"Or a pack of gum," Paloma said.

"Or a cellphone," Kyle added.

Mary Beth appreciated their efforts to distract Fuller but knew it wouldn't work. He stepped out of line and approached the protestor.

"Shit," Mary Beth muttered as she followed. Fuller had the guy off to the side, away from the prying eyes of his friends. He was as tall as Fuller but not as wide, with medium brown skin and thick, fully arched eyebrows. He wore a Gamecocks ball cap and looked to be early twenties. A kid.

"What are you packing?" Fuller demanded.

"Nothing. Not a damn thing." The guy scowled down at Fuller's grip on his shirt.

"Could be nothing. Or could be you were reaching for a pistol to take out some of my comrades."

The guy laughed. A stupid move because that would only inflame Fuller. "Comrades? What are you, Gestapo?"

Fuller jerked open the man's jacket and grabbed the pocket, pulling out a small water bottle.

"Not a gun, Lieutenant," Mary Beth stepped closer. "He's not armed."

"Let's just be sure." He slapped the water bottle into her hand and frisked him more roughly than the situation merited. The man looked at Mary Beth, his eyes narrowed. Assessing.

"I'm not packing," he said. "Because if I was, no way I'd let you manhandle me like this."

"Easy, there." Mary Beth fought an urge to call the captain over before this escalated. If she did, there'd be hell to pay from her partner.

"Was that a threat? Did I just hear you threaten a police officer?" Fuller's face was inches from his, redder than a stop light.

"No weapons. Looks like he's clear," Mary Beth patted Fuller on the shoulder. "Captain wants us to keep things from escalating, Lieutenant. We arrest him, that's exactly what we'll be doing."

"Check his ID." Fuller kept his gaze on the man's face. Neither blinked. Mary Beth could almost smell the roil of testosterone in both.

She took his wallet from a back pocket and pulled out a driver's license. "Simon Madigan. Got a USC ID, too."

"Law school. And I know enough to know the law says you'd better let me go," Madigan said.

Fuller's finger came up again. "I want no trouble out of you, Simon Madigan. You got that?"

Madigan took his wallet from Mary Beth and put it in his pocket, then held out his hand again. "My water bottle?"

Mary Beth started to hand it to him but Fuller took it. He made a show of uncapping and emptying it.

"So you can't use it as a projectile." He shoved the empty bottle against the man's chest. Madigan didn't take it, but let it drop.

"Have a nice day, officers," he said with a smirk, and rejoined his friends.

Mary Beth returned to her spot beside Paloma.

"Being his usual ass-wipe self, I see," her friend said.

"I think he wants a race war." Mary Beth wished she was exaggerating.

Paloma scanned the growing crowd. "He may well get one."

The rest of their shift passed without further incident, though the increase in the number of protestors led to the mayor holding a press conference and promising a "thorough" investigation and "Prompt, aggressive prosecution of whoever bombed the Harwell home." When one of the reporters asked, "Will this be classified as a hate crime?" He'd looked dead into the camera and said, "It damn well better be."

By the time she clocked out at midnight, Mary Beth felt weariness deep in her bones. She couldn't wait to get home, scarf down some food, and sleep for twelve hours. Just as she secured her gear in her locker, Fuller approached. "In a hurry, are you?"

"Ready to crash."

"Not just yet. Come over here."

Shit. She approached him, still fully decked out in his riot gear, badge gleaming on his chest as though just polished. "Something you need?"

"Didn't want to say this in front of the other officers and make a scene. But you stepped out of line today when you questioned my actions in front of a suspect."

"Suspect? The guy with the water bottle?"

"You know damn well what I'm talking about. That comment about the captain and not arresting the punk." He pushed in closer, his favorite bullying technique. He had fifty pounds on her and liked to use his mass. She could smell his aftershave—some citrusy shit that made her stomach uneasy.

"I just wanted to calm things down, Lieutenant. You know how you get when you're riled up."

"Who the hell do you think you are? I don't need you analyzing me. And you NEVER disrespect me or my rank in front of scumbags like him. Got it?"

Mary Beth swallowed. She was used to his wrath, to these little lectures, but she wasn't deadened to them. Behind Fuller, a few other officers had arrived to watch. They nudged each other, smiling. The fraternal order liked a bit of drama.

"Yes, sir," she said, like she always did, and returned to her locker.

Chapter Three

When Caleb got home, Shannon's car wasn't in the driveway. He checked his cell to find a text from her saying that she'd be working late. Again. But he couldn't complain—his partner finally had a job that didn't pay well and worked her to death, but one that she loved. Shannon McPherson was a typical damn social worker. Were they all masochists?

Caleb unlocked the front door and thought about getting supper started but couldn't work up the energy. Instead, he dropped on the worn sofa. Cleo, his elderly sheepdog, rose from a nap and lumbered over to him. He stroked her head as he stared at the empty fireplace and thought about his brother and this horrifying new word that had inserted itself into their lives.

How the hell had this happen? Sam had enough to deal with. Since the accident that deafened him at sixteen, he'd struggled to adjust, putting himself through school, starting a career as a woodworker then an artist. He'd lost the love of his life years ago in a horrific murder for which Sam was falsely charged. It broke him for a while, but he'd rebounded because that's what Sam did. While he'd had several steady girlfriends since then, nobody had been "the one." Not that Caleb and Shannon hadn't tried fixing him up. God knew, they had tried.

But now Sam had to face this, and it made Caleb angry. And more than a little terrified.

Caleb squared his shoulders. Brooding wasn't going to help. For distraction, he snagged the remote and found the local news. The lead story was a pipe bomb tossed into the home of Pearl Harwell. Laquan's mom had been seriously injured. He leaned forward, suddenly alert.

"Damn it." Caleb pictured the young man in the jail cell who'd gone to a store to buy his sick mother some soup, only to be harassed for the color of his skin. He'd let his rage loose, a powerful thing that could have killed a man.

But he was still just a kid, and now his mom might not make it. Caleb grabbed his cell and clicked on Dr. Matthew Rhyker's number. Matthew answered on the third ring. "Everything go okay at the prison?" Not surprising that his former boss, mentor, and friend knew about Caleb's visit. Matthew tended to know everything. He worked at the same clinic as Caleb, but in a new high-falutin' role of researcher/administrator. Caleb missed having him as his boss, especially since his new supervisor, one Lonzo Petrocelli, could drive anyone to drink.

"Yeah. Kid's not suicidal. Not psychotic. Just a Black teen who lost his temper dealing with a racist asshole. It's going to devastate him to hear that they tried to kill his mother."

Matthew didn't say anything. Caleb could almost hear his cognitive wheels turning. "You going back to the jail?"

"I'll check on him tomorrow. Claudia Briscoe wants information. What do I disclose?" Fending off the detective, who was also a friend and colleague, rarely worked well. Claudia was too persistent. And stubborn. And determined.

"The answer is simple. Your contract with the jail was for a mental status exam, so basically, he's our patient. He's not making a direct threat, so we don't really have anything to offer the police. Anything else?" Matthew asked.

"Yeah. I'm afraid so. I went with Sam to see a doctor. He's got a lump on his leg. It's a soft tissue sarcoma." It was the first time he'd said those words out loud and somehow it made it all more real. "I'm trying hard not to freak out here."

"I'm sorry to hear this. How's he handling it?"

"Stoic as hell when they told him. Then he left. Wants to be alone for now. Guess he's got a lot to process."

"Yes. So do you." Matthew grew silent.

"About that. Any guidance? What do I need to read? What do I need to do to help him?" Matthew was a psychiatrist who used to lead a cancer survivor's support group.

"I have a few books I can bring to the office. In terms of helping him, do what you always do. Be there for him."

A knot of emotion clawed its way up Caleb's throat. "His oncology appointment is tomorrow at ten."

"Want me to let Lonzo know you'll be in late?"

"I'll take care of it. Thanks." Caleb clicked off. For the one thousandth time, he wished Matthew was still his boss.

The next morning at the kitchen table, Caleb sipped latte from their new fancy coffee maker. This was one of his favorite spots in the old brick bungalow. He liked the picture window that looked out over the yard and the veined granite countertops Shannon had picked out. He loved this old table he'd inherited from his mom, with Sam's and his initials carved into one of the legs. The kitchen was the perfect marriage of the old and new.

He sent a text to his brother. *I'll come pick you up at 9:40.*

I can drive myself. Lisa is going with me, was his response.

Lisa was Sam's favorite ASL interpreter: always animated, easily communicating nuance through expressions that others missed. But Lisa wasn't his brother.

I'd like to be there.

Thanks for yesterday, but no. I'll talk to you after the appointment.

Sam . . .

Don't worry. I'll be in good hands.

This was his own fault, Caleb knew. He'd frozen at Dr. Gabrick's office. Completely stopped doing his job. Let his own emotions take over. A stupid-ass mistake he hoped he never made again. Now Sam didn't need him there when he would find out more about his treatment.

Shannon stumbled in, headed for the coffee pot, poured a cup, and dropped in the seat across from Caleb. A chaos of brown curls circled her face, which held a few more lines than it had when they'd met. Still damn beautiful though, even in the ancient sweatshirt she wore. They'd been together for eight years, and sometimes talked of having a wedding, but both felt married in every way that mattered. "How are you feeling?" she asked.

"Sam fired me. Guess I won't have to cancel my appointments."

She reached over and took his hand. "I'm not surprised. He needs someone objective. Your being there makes it harder for him."

Caleb nodded, sipped, and mulled. "One thing I can't figure out—why didn't he tell me about the biopsy? It's not like him to keep something like that from me. I hadn't heard from him for over week!"

Shannon moved to the coffeemaker and refilled his mug. "I asked him that last night."

"What? You texted with him?" Great. Sam chatted with Shannon while ignoring Caleb's five hundred texts.

"He said he wanted to tell you after he had seen the doctor and gotten a clean bill of health. He wanted to tell you that he'd had a biopsy on his stupid lump, and it turned out fine. He can't seem to turn off the big brother switch."

"I'd better hear from him after the appointment." If he didn't, Caleb would spend his lunch hour hunting down his brother.

When Caleb's phone buzzed, he didn't recognize the number. "Caleb Knowles," he answered.

"Caleb? Oh, that makes sense," a woman's voice said.

"Excuse me?"

"Oh, sorry. But Sam gave me his card and it said that if I needed to leave a voice message for him to call this number. I've texted him and he didn't answer so I decided to call." Whoever she was, she sounded nervous. Rattled.

"Who is this?" he asked.

"Oh, sorry," she repeated. "I'm Amanda Stockdale. We met at the project site. I'm helping Sam with the new installation."

"Right. Amanda." Caleb could picture her: early forties, long brown braid. A few freckles, no makeup, pixie nose, wearing overalls like a farmer might. "How can I help you?"

"It's just that we're meeting with the Equality Foundation people this morning and Sam said he couldn't make it. And I'm just an intern and Jace, well, Jace is over this whole project but he's so nervous he says we have to cancel, but Sam insisted we go ahead. Only now he's not responding to my texts, which isn't like him. Is he okay?"

How to answer that one. Sam was a private guy. If he didn't tell his colleagues about his situation, it wasn't up to Caleb to share the news. "He's fine. Just got busy with some important stuff. I say go ahead with the meeting, and if they have questions Sam needs to answer, tell them he'll be in touch tomorrow. I'm sure they'll understand."

"Okay, okay. I'd better go change clothes then."

Caleb laughed. "Got a business suit?"

"Hell no. But I'll find something better than these paint-spattered jeans. Jace can clean up good if he tries."

Caleb had met Jace, too. A dread-locked, well-muscled artist who taught at the university and made quite a name for himself in metalworks. He'd been given the grant to construct the new mixed-media project and contracted with Sam to oversee the wood elements. The two of them worked beautifully together. "Good luck, Amanda. And tell Jace he'll do just fine."

Chapter Four

Caleb sat in his office at Midlands Counseling Center with his ten o'clock appointment, Lenore Saddington, and sipped lukewarm coffee. Lenore had coffee, too, and stared into her cup as though it held the answer she'd sought for years. The answer wasn't in the beverage. It wasn't in the medicine Lenore took, though the pills helped keep her out of the hospital. The answer was inside her, and it was Caleb's job to help her discover it.

The office held a bit of a chill. One of many things he didn't like about this clinic was how he'd lost thermostat control—management determined the temperature. And everything else: like the boring tan wall color, the mundane, corporate furnishings, and the motivational BS sayings posted in the hall: *Follow your dreams. Life is about creating yourself.*

"It's nice to have a few hours away from the classroom," Lenore said. "The kids have been wild lately."

Caleb offered a small smile. His client taught fifth grade at an under-resourced inner-city school. A tough job made tougher by funding cuts and overcrowded classrooms. "How's the job going?"

She shrugged. "If I didn't love it so much, I'd hate it."

"It's a tough gig." Sometimes she wanted to talk about work. Sometimes, it was her family life that filled their sessions. He always let her decide.

With careful movements, she placed the coffee on the table beside her. She was mid-forties, with highlighted brown hair that brushed her shoulders and an attractive pale face wearing a little too much make-up. She wore a knee-length dress and sensible, on-her-feet-all-day flats. "I spent the weekend scrambling to fill the school's food pantry. More and more kids are using it. One little girl took home two cans of Dinty Moore beef stew and thanked me like it was a Christmas present. Christ, Caleb. We shouldn't have that kind of hunger in South Carolina."

Preaching to the choir, he wanted to say, but didn't. "It's good that you're keeping the pantry full for them."

"Not just me. I hit up James and everyone in his campaign office," she said with a coy smile. "He's worried I'll snag his donor list and go door to door."

"Not a bad idea," Caleb said with a laugh. Lenore and her husband, James, were an interesting mix. While James, a candidate for South Carolina Senate, had polished good looks that made him charismatic on camera, Lenore had no interest in that kind of attention. Caleb had seen her on TV at press conferences, standing behind her husband, looking like she'd rather be in a dentist's chair getting a root canal.

Lenore glanced out the window. "I have a little boy in my class. A sweet, sensitive kid, but he doesn't talk. Not to his classmates. Not to me. I referred him to the school counselor, but he didn't talk to her, either."

"Has he been that way the whole semester?"

She nodded. "And now his mom wants to come see me. She called the principal, very irate that I made the counselor referral. Nothing like getting yelled at by a mom. Especially when the mom's wrong."

"Maybe Mom is in denial. Doesn't want to admit there's anything wrong with her son."

Lenore laughed at that. "Well, we know all about that, don't we?"

He didn't answer, but she was right. He'd met Lenore when she came for therapy eighteen months ago. She'd been struggling with depression for months, but her husband didn't realize, or accept, the severity of her symptoms. Suicidal thoughts landed her in the hospital, and she'd returned to Caleb after discharge for intensive out-patient treatment. "We don't want to think that our family members may be struggling. And when it comes to mental health symptoms—those can be even harder to face."

"It's nothing to be ashamed of. At least, that's what my therapist keeps telling me." She smiled, cocking up an eyebrow.

"That therapist is smart!" Caleb replied with a grin.

"Maybe I can make the mother believe it, too. Or maybe I'll be subjected to thirty minutes of mom-rage. It's happened before," she said with a shrug.

Caleb took another sip and wished he hadn't. Cold coffee

wasn't his thing. Lenore stroked the arm of the chair.

"Something weird happened this morning," she said suddenly.

"What?"

"I took the whole morning off because of this appointment. Which meant I got to sleep in a little instead of getting up at six. Anyway, around seven, a reporter showed up at our door. I was in a robe, and the ridiculous pink fuzzy bunny slippers my son Brian got me for my birthday, and I peek out the door and there she is, with a TV van behind her."

"That's awfully early."

"Right? She wanted a statement from James about some stupid thing his opponent Tommy Doyle said last week about a farm bill. At seven, Caleb."

Caleb noted her hand gripping the chair arm. Blue veins bulged. "How did it feel, having the reporter show up like that?"

"Picture it. My bedroom slippers have ears. My hair looks like a macramé experiment gone wrong. No makeup. Teeth not brushed. And I'm supposed to let this woman in my house?" She sounded outraged now.

Caleb leaned back, picturing the scene. Lenore liked to have control of all things: her schedule. Her home. This kind of intrusion must have felt like a violation.

She went on: "At least they didn't film me. James threw on real clothes and met with them in the front yard. I wished we'd cut the grass, but—" She lifted a hand and dropped it.

"Good. He handled it. But still, what was it like having the media show up that early?"

"Truthfully, I didn't want to answer the door, but James said we had to. Is this what life will be like? Do I have to wear lipstick to bed just in case I have to be 'on' at some ungodly hour?"

Caleb watched the anxiety swell like a wave inside her—she spoke faster, huffing out breaths. Eyes wide and focusing on nothing. The woman normally in control was definitely not. He remembered an early encounter with her, when she'd first come from the hospital, and anticipated returning to work. The *what will people think?* panic had grabbed her by the throat, and they'd worked an entire session on skills needed for 'reentry.'

"That seems very unfair, if that's the expectation," he said softly, monitoring in case this bloomed into a full-out panic attack. "Lenore? Slow down a little. Take a deep slow breath for me."

Her gaze found him and nodded. Like an obedient child, she complied.

"Better?"

"Sorry. I get . . . upset."

"With good reason." He offered a small smile.

"Here's the thing. The reporter wasn't there to talk about Laquan Harwell or what happened to his mom. She didn't even mention it. Of course, James did. He's stood in front of the camera focused on our need for racial justice. He's good at it."

She paused, shaking her head. "But I'm not. And I'm not sure . . . I'm not sure I can do it. I mean, I want James to win. It's crucially important to him so it's important to me. And when he gets in office, he's going to work on racial equality, and improving our schools, and making sure kids don't go hungry. I believe in that. I believe in him. But I didn't realize how demanding the campaign would be. What it would do to our lives."

Caleb leaned back and let silence settle between them. Silence is a powerful tool in therapy, sometimes nudging secrets to the surface. Sometimes opening a door the client doesn't want, but needs, to be opened.

The way she was working her throat, he suspected something was banging on that door.

He kept waiting.

"He . . . he never asked me."

"Asked you?"

"If I wanted this. If I wanted him to run. He never asked."

"Really? Wow." If Caleb tried something like that, Shannon would shave his head in his sleep. "It's a big decision for all of you. It changes all of your lives."

"Exactly. Brian—he's only nine, but it affects him, too. He rarely gets to see his dad. And he has less of my attention because between school and helping James I'm gone so much. It's not fair to him."

Caleb shifted forward. "It's not fair to you either, Lenore." It seemed he said that a lot.

Her lips parted, a puff of air coming out. "I . . . no." She shook her head. "James needs this. What's good for him is good for all of us."

"What if that's not true?"

"What are you saying?"

"What if his running for office isn't good for you? It's a lot of stress. You've come so far in your recovery, and I don't want anything to push you backwards." He didn't have to say the rest, that stress is what brought her here the first-time last year, that it had led to weight loss, sleeplessness, and, disclosed after considerable prodding, suicidal thoughts. After her hospitalization, therapy and anti-depressants had helped, but the recovery was young and vulnerable. He didn't want to see her relapse.

"It has to be," she said quietly. "I have to make it work, Caleb. James's mission is too important."

Her voice quaked. He decided not to push the point any more during this session. She wasn't ready.

"How are you sleeping?" he asked gently.

"Not enough. The hours . . . it's a lot."

"Appetite?"

"I've dropped a few pounds."

He didn't like that. These were all signs of worsening depression, brought on by stress. "Okay. How about this? How about we develop a strategy to help you survive the next two months?"

"Strategy?"

"Yep. You have a crazy schedule, but we're going to find some holes in it for you to do some good, quality self-care. We're talking regular meals—the balanced nutrition kind—breaks during the day, and eight hours of sleep a night."

"It sounds wonderful. And impossible."

"It's not impossible unless you let it be. Maybe we treat this campaign-wife gig like a job. Assign it hours. If the door rings after say, eight p.m., or before nine in the morning, it's up to James to respond. He's the one who's running. And you have a demanding job, yourself. You won't be any good to anyone if you get rundown."

"You're right. He's the one they want, anyway."

"Can you talk to him about it? Or bring him to the next

session so I can?"

"I'll talk to him."

He reached in his drawer for a small notebook. "Here's where you report on your homework assignment. Every day, you record what you ate, when you rested, how much you slept. You bring that back to me next week."

She took the pad and stroked its cover with her crimson-nailed hand. "Like I'm back in school?"

"Exactly. You were a straight-A student, so I expect nothing less with this. We don't want this campaign to worsen your depression. This may help prevent that. And another thing. I'm counting on you to be diligent and honest in your reporting. Deal?"

She cocked her head, studying him. He kept his gaze steady, expectant.

"Deal," she finally said.

Chapter Five

Shull Lassiter leaned back in his leather recliner, skimming through a spreadsheet on his laptop that outlined recent sales. Lassiter Munitions was having a lackluster month: sales of the Honey Badger short-barrel rifle weren't where they should be given their latest promotion, and they'd ordered a hundred more of the damn guns. Shull had to get them off the shelves.

In the background, his TV aired the replay of Representative Tommy Doyle's press conference about the punk who attacked Palmer Guthrie at that store and the bombing of the punk's home. Shull had a lot invested in Doyle, who was in the middle of a reelection campaign for the SC House. So far Doyle was keeping to the script Shull had provided. "Terrible tragedy" and "we will seek justice" were the key phrases, and Doyle hadn't faltered when a reporter mentioned the pro-Confederate flag stance he'd taken a few years ago. "That was about heritage. This is about hate," Doyle said, and it was absolutely beautiful, especially considering last month's oyster roast fiasco when Doyle called a popular Black US senator a "boy." Shull had to pay off the lone reporter covering the event. He liked it that Tommy Doyle was malleable and obedient but wished he had more intelligence than a cucumber.

Shull picked up the phone and called the candidate. Doyle answered on the second ring—just as he'd been taught. *"Never keep me waiting,"* was rule one. Shull's massive donations to Tommy's campaign kept him in charge and led to Tommy sponsoring pro-gun legislation that Shull needed to get passed. "Good job, Tommy, with that presser."

"Thanks. James Saddington's on WXYK right now if you want to take a look."

Shull switched channels and found the broadcast. Saddington, Tommy's opponent in the re-election campaign, stood in the front yard of his modest brick home, no necktie, but still looking sharp in a blue polo and khakis, as he discussed the pipe bomb incident that occurred yesterday. "This isn't just a tragedy for the Harwell family. It's a tragedy for South Carolina. The attack on the Harwell home—which nearly killed a disabled woman—is an attack on all of us and what we believe." He looked dead-eye into the camera and added, "And it will not be tolerated."

"Guy looks kinda rabid, don't you think?" Doyle asked.

"He looks passionate." Shull frowned. Passion could buy votes.

"Gotta say, though, I wish he wasn't so damn good looking. Looks like a damn TV star." No kidding. Saddington looked sincere and personable. Artful silver streaks in his thick dark hair. Blue eyes that seemed to twinkle under TV lights. Strong jaw, symmetrical lines on his face exuding wisdom. The camera fucking loved him. And Doyle? He was jowly and red-faced, sparse hairs doing a poor job of covering his bald spot. Somehow his suits always fit like they belonged to someone else.

"Shhh. I'm listening," Shull answered.

". . . We have a race problem in our beloved state. And this violence—motivated by hate—must stop. I'm not just talking about different laws. I'm talking about different values. About teaching respect and cultural humility in our schools. About each of us accepting our duty to address this horrific problem." Saddington lifted a hand and dropped it.

"Dude is going off the rails now," Doyle said with a snicker.

"Maybe." Shull kept watching, hoping Saddington would push too far.

He didn't. Instead, he smiled into the lens and said, "But this we can fix. Working together, South Carolinians can accomplish anything." The camera pulled back, taking in the small porch, the white rockers, and a planter bulging with pansies. The door opened and a golden retriever bounded out, all wavy fur and awkward limbs and limitless glee. It sat beside Saddington and looked up at him with complete adoration.

The interview ended there.

"Crap," Shull whispered. The guy looked too good. And Shull had invested way too much money in Doyle.

"I have a dog, too, Shull. I can bring my champion bulldog to the next rally if you want," Doyle said, like any good cucumber would. Shull almost laughed.

"Saddington's looking more and more like he's gonna be a

problem for us." Shull didn't want to think what would happen if Saddington won the seat. The gun bill ("Protecting our Families") wouldn't stand a chance. All his hard work—and financial investment in Tommy—shot to hell.

Doyle didn't say anything for a minute, then spoke with an unusual hesitancy. "I . . . you think I'm gonna lose the seat, Shull?"

"Not if I have anything to say about it. You stick to the script and let me do my job. Besides, I've got a secret weapon."

"A secret weapon, huh?" He let out a nervous laugh. "Then I guess it's all gonna be okay."

Shull hung up the phone and wandered into the kitchen, the one they'd renovated for the second time last spring. His wife Glenna (number three, twenty years younger than him at age thirty-seven) had chosen the pale granite with red veining that looked like arteries. The dark oak cabinets made for a striking contrast. He had to admit it, Glenna had a strong sense of style. She was in her backyard yoga studio according to the note on the counter, and the makings of some God-awful kale smoothie disaster waited in the blender. Shull ignored it, grabbed a bagel, and reached for his cell.

May be time to escalate, he texted. *Are we ready?*

These fools were born ready, came the reply.

Chapter Six

Caleb wheeled his Subaru into Sam's driveway, relieved to find Sam's truck in its usual spot. His brother lived on the lake in a two-story cabin with vaulted ceilings and expansive windows looking out at the water. Behind the house, Sam had built a custom workshop that held his tools, worktable, and wood—imported timbers from all over the world. Caleb could see the light on inside and entered to find Sam bent over his drafting table, an elbow lamp splashing a wide beam over his drawing. Caleb flicked the light switch off and on, signaling that he'd arrived.

Sam squinted up at him. "Hey."

"Hey yourself," Caleb signed. "You were supposed to text me after the doctor's appointment."

Sam dropped his pencil. "Sorry."

"No problem. It's not like I've been checking my phone every fifteen seconds or anything." He signed with short, clipped gestures, just in case his face didn't adequately convey his irritation.

Sam came around the table and leaned against it, arms crossed. "I already apologized."

"I know." Caleb signed. "I'm just . . . worried. So tell me what the doctor said."

"She was very nice. Thorough. Reviewed all the scans and the biopsy report. What I have is undifferentiated pleomorphic sarcoma, or UPS. You know, like the delivery service." Sam's forced smile held no humor.

Caleb splayed his fingers sideways then drew them together, signing, "And?"

"And she wants to remove the mass. It's growing fast, so that seems to matter."

Growing fast. Those words smacked Caleb in the belly. "When will they take it out? You'll come stay with us after. No arguments, Sam."

"Here's the thing . . ." he glanced over at the plans displayed on the table. "We have to finish this project. The unveiling is in two months and we're behind. Once I have the surgery, there may be an involved recovery period because they'll be cutting into muscle. It's unlikely I'll be back to work anytime soon."

"So the Equality Foundation pushes back the date for your installation. No big deal."

"It is to me. That's what I told the doctor."

Caleb stared, his mouth dropping open. He probably looked like a guppy. "Let me get this right. You want to postpone the cancer surgery you need so you can finish a sculpture?"

Sam wiped his hands against his jeans, saying nothing.

"And the doctor says it's fast growing. That it needs to come out," Caleb's hands flew through the air.

"But—"

Caleb made a V with two fingers and smacked it against his forehead. "That is the stupidest thing I've ever heard!"

Sam winced.

"Jesus, Sam!" He stepped closer, his face inches from his brother's. He flashed back to years ago, when Sam's fiancée was found murdered in his studio, when Sam was the main suspect and refused to do anything to help himself. Caleb was as afraid for him now as he had been then.

Sam cocked his head as though confused. "My work is important. You know that. And this project isn't just about me. It's about Jace. I can't—won't—let him down. And Amanda. We're making an important statement about racism at a time when this state needs to hear it. And Jace promised the Foundation we'd meet the deadline."

"The Foundation would understand. Hell, *anyone* would understand!" Caleb swallowed, hoping to calm down because he felt almost—not quite, but almost—like punching Sam. "For Christ's sake, they'll understand."

"We need to finish the project." Sam turned as though about to return to his plans. "I can delay the surgery for a few months."

Caleb grabbed him and spun him around. "Sam. You're scared of the surgery. I get that. But—"

"But nothing. I've made my decision. Dr. Simm said we'll go with Plan B. I get some radiation in the meantime to prevent it from growing more—and maybe even shrink it—before she takes it out."

"Radiation?"

"It's often done with this kind of mass."

"But it's plan B," Caleb clarified. "Wouldn't it be better to get this thing out? Before it spreads or—"

Sam let out a loud sigh. "The decision is made. I'll have my first treatment Friday. Targeted intensity-modulated radiation therapy. If it actually shrinks the mass, it'll be an easier surgery. The doctor agreed to this so you should, too."

Caleb studied the lines of Sam's face. The wrinkles fanning out from the sides of his eyes. The worry-dent that appeared between his eyebrows a few years ago. Was Sam afraid of what the surgery would find? Afraid that the cancer had spread?

Afraid of dying?

He glanced over at the plans for the installation. Did Sam think it would be his last work of art?

Caleb couldn't let that idea take root. He had read on one of the cancer sites that this kind of mass could be fatal. He'd shut off the computer and considered hurling it against the wall. Truth was, he couldn't let any of this new reality in too deep.

"What?" Sam asked.

"I didn't say anything." Caleb felt pinned under Sam's scrutiny.

"You look twisted up like a pretzel."

Caleb shook his head. He couldn't give voice to what terrified him. "I know you're dealing with a lot. But this—" he pointed at Sam's leg. "This isn't just about you."

Sam continued to watch him. Caleb had nothing else to say. Like Sam said, the decision was made and apparently, Caleb had no say in it. He fished his keys from his pocket, eager to be gone.

"Caleb, wait."

He turned, feeling antsy to get the hell out of there. Sam stepped closer. "I know this isn't just about me. I don't want you to be scared about this."

"Yeah. That ship already sailed."

Sam nodded. "I figured."

Caleb pressed a finger against Sam's chest and signed, "You better know what you're doing."

Sam reached up and gripped Caleb's moving hands. "I do.

I'm pissing off my little brother. I've always been too good at that."

"True," Caleb said aloud, because Sam still held his hands.

And then Sam slid arms around him and pulled him close. Caleb felt Sam's strong muscles, maybe shaking a little, and that made him scared all over again.

"Don't you dare die," Caleb whispered, knowing Sam couldn't hear it.

"Mr. Petrocelli is looking for you." These words from Janice greeted Caleb when he arrived at the office that morning. The last words Caleb needed to hear. His boss Alonzo Petrocelli, called "Lonzo" by those pretending to be his friends, was the Chief Operating Officer for Midlands Counseling, the shiny new, expanded practice where Caleb worked. His former supervisor, Matthew Rhyker, had no choice but to merge with the larger organization as it spread its tendrils throughout central South Carolina because remaining in the smaller, more intimate practice was no longer practical. Billing was too complicated for Janice to manage by herself. Access to inpatient psychiatric care for their clients meant Matthew needing privileges and Midlands Counseling had the lock on that. Plus Matthew's research grant to expand his new treatment modality for patients with depression and addiction required more infrastructure, more staff, more everything. So, Westville Counseling Center was absorbed by Midlands Counseling, and they left the lovely Victorian house and moved into boring offices in a boring office building. And Caleb now answered to Lonzo Petrocelli instead of Matthew.

It had been a hellish transition. New rules. New productivity requirements. A dress code that made Caleb want to punch someone. And, worst of all, Lonzo.

"Is my nine o'clock here?" Caleb asked Janice.

"Not yet. You have time to stop by his office," she replied. He read between the lines. Lonzo wanted his immediate attention, and it would be wise, in Janice's view, to comply.

"Lucky me," he growled, and headed to the plush executive suite.

Lonzo sat at his desk—a steel and glass modern monstrosity

with no pictures, no pencil holder, no clutter at all—clicking away at his computer. He had black hair, meticulously styled back, a clean-shaven, angular face, and dark eyes set deep under sparse brows. Some of the women at the practice found him handsome, in his crisp suits and polished shoes. Caleb fought a compulsion to muss up his slicked-back hair whenever in his presence.

"Janice said you wanted to see me." Caleb didn't sit because he hoped to keep this visit short.

"Yes. I'm reviewing the case notes from last week. I'm missing—let's see—one, two, okay, five of yours."

"Just five?" Caleb saw that as success. He took comprehensive notes on his sessions but did it long hand. Getting them logged into the computer for Lonzo's scrutiny never made it to the top of his "to do" list.

"I'd like them entered by the end of the day. You're out of compliance with Quality Assurance."

"Okay." He turned to approach the door, but Lonzo wasn't done.

"About the jail consult—did you run into any media?"

"At the jail? No."

"Good. That's good." Lonzo's expression was impossible to read. "If you hear from the press, please send them to me. This case is getting a lot of attention and that's only going to get worse if racial tensions escalate. We have to be careful with how we handle the press."

Caleb drew a breath and mentally counted to ten. "First of all, I won't ever divulge information about a client. Period. The way to 'handle' journalists is to ignore them and walk away."

"I understand you went home after the consult?"

Shit. Janice wouldn't have said anything unless pressed.

"Family emergency," he said.

"Oh? Everything okay?"

Caleb searched Lonzo's face, looking for any sign of concern or sympathy. He found none. "For now. I'll turn in a leave slip." Because heaven forbid there be any flexibility in scheduled work hours.

"That would be good. Also, if you have to leave unexpectedly, you should clear that with me. Not with the administrative specialists."

"Janice is more than an admin. She's an office manager, remember?" This had been part of the deal with the merger. Janice got a raise and supervised the other office staff.

"Nevertheless. Clear departures with me."

"Okay." Caleb felt a knot forming in his jaw from gritting his teeth. He did that a lot when he was in Lonzo's orbit.

He left the glossy office and headed to his more modest one, the one with crayon art on the walls, the philodendron plant with vines stretching from the window to the desk, and the beautiful, abstract coffee table (a Christmas gift from Sam). He checked voicemail messages (three from the same anxious client he'd see later that day), then went to collect his first appointment.

Chapter Seven

"Got a second?" Detective Claudia Briscoe appeared in Caleb's doorway, dressed in a tweed suit, black pumps, and a black top with a bow that almost feminized her. Almost. Claudia was far too bad-ass to pull off dainty.

"How is it that you always get by the front desk with nobody stopping you?" Caleb asked.

"It's all about attitude. Didn't even have to flash my badge."

"Seriously? Because they don't let me back here if I don't have my name tag." Not that he hadn't tried. Many, many times, rebelling against the photo ID attached to a lanyard that every staff person was required to wear. Another infuriating reminder that Caleb was up to his earlobes in corporate bullshit now.

"Oh Caleb. What fresh hell is this for you?" Claudia helped herself to a seat, like she always did.

"Don't get me started."

She smiled. He'd known her for twelve years, first as a client, later—much later—as a colleague and friend. After being promoted to sergeant with the Westville Police Department, Claudia accepted a transfer to the much larger Columbia precinct about six months before Caleb and Matthew moved their offices. She often grumbled that Caleb was following her. "Stalking" had been a word tossed out over a beer, but she'd been quick to demand a contract between the police department and the counseling center, similar to what they'd had back in Westville. Jail consults quickly became a regular piece of his practice and introduced him to clients like Laquan.

"You saw the Harwell kid," she was saying, sipping coffee she'd apparently helped herself to in the employee break room. "Thoughts?"

"I told them to take him off suicide precautions but after what happened at his house yesterday, they should keep an eye on him. He's close to his mom, and this will devastate him. Do y'all have any leads on who bombed the place?"

"Happened before dawn. One witness saw an unmarked van drive from the house. No license plate." She took a sip from her cup. "Did Laquan Harwell talk to you about why he attacked Palmer Guthrie?"

Caleb sat back, studying his friend. Her face was a mask of neutrality, something she'd mastered years ago as a cop. But he could see beyond it. "First off, aside from the risk assessment, anything he tells me is confidential, which you already know. Second: what's going on? There's something you aren't telling me."

She sipped again. Smacked her perfectly lined crimson lips. Swiped a stolen napkin across her brown chin. The stall made him nervous.

"Claudia?" Caleb bent forward, closing the distance between them. "What?"

She placed the coffee on his desk. "The Harwell kid was attacked. Happened around six p.m. last night. Several stab wounds in the abdomen."

The news hit him in the solar plexus. "Oh my God. How bad is he?"

"They took him to Columbia General. Lost a lot of blood. They nicked his spleen. Could be liver damage, too. Kid's a mess, but I haven't heard an update this morning yet."

Caleb fell back, picturing a terrified kid and imagining the horror of the attack. "Who did it?"

"We don't know yet. They operated gang-style—a coordinated attack. We think three or four inmates mobbed him as he left the dining room but of course, no witnesses."

"Which gang? Arian Nation?"

"Could be, though this attack had some different markers."

"What do you mean?"

She gave him a long, sober stare as though deciding what to tell him. Finally, she pulled an iPad from her mammoth purse and clicked it until an image appeared: a close-up of Harwell's chest. A fork-like design had been sliced into the skin.

Caleb pictured Laquan writhing as a blade cut him. How terrified he must have been. The pain must have been excruciating. He was just a boy. "What is that?"

She arched her perfectly trimmed brows. "We're not sure. It's not a symbol any of our gangs use, at least not that we know of. Did Harwell mention anything about being threatened when you were with him?"

"No. He'd been in solitary, remember?" Caleb's cell vibrated, a message from the front desk that his next appointment had arrived. "Does Laquan know about what happened to his mother?"

"Not yet. He's been too sedated."

"I want to see him."

"I figured you would. But if he tells you anything that may help find who did this, I'd better be your first call."

Caleb had an eleven a.m. cancellation, so he drove to the hospital, parked, hurried by the front desk, and rode the elevator to the fourth floor. He followed a woman pushing a meal cart. It clattered up the hall, reeking of overcooked cabbage and sadness. At the nurse's station, several medical staff glared at a computer screen while a lone woman stood off the side, sipping from a coffee cup. She was tall, with long, dark unkempt curls, and she eyed him warily as he approached. "I'm looking for Laquan Harwell's room," he said.

She removed purple bifocals and took a step towards him, her stance protective. "You know it's secure, right? We have cops right outside the door."

"I'm Caleb Knowles. Social worker. Police gave me clearance."

"Let me check on that." She moved to a free computer and pulled up what looked like a medical record. "Yep, you have permission. Caleb Knowles . . . I think I've heard of you. I graduated a few years after you did. Quinn Merrick." She reached for his hand and shook it.

Not a nurse then, but a social worker like him. He should have guessed from the cardigan and Birkenstocks. "How's Laquan doing?"

"It was touch-and-go yesterday, but he's stabilized. Don't want him getting an infection. I tried to get him moved to a room beside his mom, but my bosses don't want him to have any special treatment."

"Is Mrs. Harwell doing okay?"

She shook her head. "She has me worried. I can't go into

details—HIPAA and all—but both of them need some luck and prayers, if you're into that kind of thing."

Caleb was into it. Sometimes. He was more of a *I'll beg for help* kind of Christian, but Sam's new situation had him mentally on his knees.

Quinn rounded the nurse's station counter and cocked a thumb up the hall. "Laquan's gotten some threats since he's been here. Can you believe it? Poor kid's fighting for his life and some bigoted A-hole keeps calling the hospital and spouting off a bunch of racist expletives. Sometimes I don't get people."

"Me neither." Caleb found himself liking this Quinn Merrick and her no-nonsense candor. "Are the police doing anything about the threats?"

"The guy doesn't stay on the phone long enough for a trace. I had the room phone number transferred to me so I can monitor." She waved a cell at Caleb. "Last call, I got a few comments in myself before he hung up."

"Crazy times."

"At least we don't have protesters in our parking lot. Yet." She let out a sarcastic laugh. "Come on. I'll take you to Laquan. He might not be too responsive though. Pretty sedated."

"He knows about his mom?"

"Yes, but we're not sure he grasped it too well. Like I said. Good drugs."

She led Caleb down the hall and they both flashed their name badges at the two officers flanking the door. Caleb entered, freezing at the foot of the bed.

Laquan looked boyish, barely taking up half the width of the narrow mattress. Tubes snaked from both arms to fluid suspended above him. An oxygen cannula pinched his nostrils and his skin had an almost grayish pallor that alarmed Caleb. "Jesus," Caleb whispered.

"He lost a lot of blood, but he's young. That's key. Go ahead and talk to him. Stay a while if you can. He could use a friend."

"Can he even hear me?"

"I think so. Of course, I'm not a doctor. I'm just a low-paid, overworked, overstressed, tired of the BS social worker."

"Welcome to my world." Caleb pulled a chair closer to the bed and sat as Quinn exited. "Laquan? Hey, it's me, Caleb."

No response.

"It's okay if you want to keep sleeping. You probably need it." Caleb continued to talk in a soft, gentle voice. He rambled on about the weather and the Gamecocks football team. He told Laquan about his daughter, Julia, a wild-child pre-teen who had caused each of the gray hairs sprouting on Caleb's head. He told him about Sam and his latest project: the anti-racism sculpture installation across from the statehouse grounds. He didn't say that this was the project that caused Sam to delay his surgery, though that issue never strayed far from his mind.

Through the window, gray clouds hung low, the sun barely visible behind them. It looked oppressive. Caleb leaned closer to his patient. "I wonder what you're feeling right now. You probably hurt, or maybe the drugs have erased the pain. You may be confused, wondering what's going on. Hospitals can be disorienting places. I know, I've seen my share of them."

Laquan's hand, small and ashy from the dry air, quivered a little. Caleb was glad he wasn't cuffed to the bed, but that may come later.

"Hey. You trying to wake up?"

The boy's eyes blinked open, scanned the room, and fixed on Caleb's face.

"There you are. I'm Caleb. We met at the jail."

No answer for a moment, and then a plaintive, "Mama?" God, he sounded so young.

Caleb flashed a sympathetic smile. "She can't be with you right now."

"Mama?" He repeated, his voice scratchy. "She . . . she got hurt?"

Caleb nodded, filling him in on the basic details: fire, smoke inhalation, being treated here at this hospital.

Laquan stared as he took it all in. "They . . . hurt her."

"Yes. I'm sorry and I wish it wasn't true, but yes."

"Because of me?"

"No, Laquan. Not because of you. Because of hatred and fear and ignorance. That's the awful truth of it." Caleb kept his gaze on Laquan's face, gauging his reaction.

A tear slid down the kid's cheek. Caleb snagged a tissue and handed it to him. "She's strong," Laquan whispered. "Tough.

But after the stroke . . ."

"Tell me about the stroke."

He took his time responding, still climbing out of the fog in his brain. "Happened . . . a month ago? She recovered some. Still weak. Right side. Hospital let her out too soon. Tried to make them keep her but we have crappy insurance, so they tossed her out."

"Of course they did." Caleb didn't hide his disgust. "Did she get any outpatient treatment?"

"We went to the doctor last week. He said she needed more therapy. But Mama doesn't . . . we don't have the money." Anger now, just below the surface.

"That must have been frustrating for her. And for you." Puzzle pieces clicked into place. The hopeless frustration of seeing his mother not getting better. Knowing that if she had insurance or the funds, she might get back to normal, but that wasn't the card they'd been dealt. Going to the store to be harassed by the racist shop owner. What had Laquan said during Caleb's first interview? *The last straw.*

Laquan pointed to a cup and Caleb lifted it and placed it against the boy's lips. As he drank, he winced.

"Want me to get a doctor for you?"

He shook his head. "Them guys got me good."

"Tell me about 'the guys.' What do you remember about the attack?" Caleb felt a tinge of guilt. He wasn't there to get information about the crime, but it might help him to talk about it.

"Three of them. Followed me out of the dining area. White guys. One had a tattoo on his forearm. One had a shaved head and a scar across his chin. The other I didn't see very well, just felt him come up from behind. He held me while they cut me."

Caleb suppressed a shiver, imagining the terror of Laquan's experience. Just a kid at the hands of armed, racist goons. "You mentioned a tattoo. Can you describe it?"

"I don't have to. They carved the same damn thing into my chest."

"The weird fork-like design?"

Laquan looked puzzled. "It's a pitchfork. Like farmers use on hay."

A pitchfork. Caleb sat back, mulling that. Wondering what the symbol meant. "Would you mind if I tell that to the police?"

"Like they'd do anything." He let out a sarcastic laugh, then his mouth twisted in pain.

"Easy there. Whatever you tell me is between us—but this might help them find your attackers. I won't say anything without your permission, though."

"Tell them."

A light rap sounded on the door, and it opened. Quinn reappeared. "He's awake!"

"We've had a nice visit," Caleb said.

"I'm glad to hear it. But you'll have to cut it short. The doc's on his way for rounds." Quinn cocked her head for Caleb to join her in the hall.

"You take care, Laquan."

"Will you . . . will you come back to see me?" Again, sounding so young.

"Absolutely. In the meantime, you focus on getting better."

Quinn walked Caleb to the elevator. "Good news. I'm getting him moved to the room beside his mom's after all," she said.

"How'd you swing that?"

"Told administration that she needed protection. Laquan comes with his own cops, so the hospital won't have to pay for special security."

"Is she getting threats?"

Quinn shrugged. "I may have stretched the truth a little. But it worked, didn't it?"

He laughed and entered the elevator. This Quinn Merrick might prove to be a useful person to know.

After calling Claudia and relating the details Laquan had given permission to share, Caleb drove straight to Sam's installation. He found the three artists—Sam, Jace, and Amanda—in the garage they'd converted to a workshop behind where the art installation would be built. They were huddled over what looked like a blueprint, Jace pointing at something on their design.

"The burled oak, I think," Sam said.

Amanda tapped his arm to get his attention. "Will that be strong enough to hold the chains?"

Sam, reading her lips, nodded. "Should be. If not, we'll reinforce it."

When Jace straightened, he noticed Caleb's arrival. "Company," he said to the others.

"I brought Sam lunch." Caleb set the bag in a chair and touched his chin then positioned his elbow on the back of his hand, signing the noonday meal.

Amanda smiled at him. "Hey, Caleb."

"Nice to see you, Amanda. How did it go at the Foundation meeting?" he said and signed.

She shot a nervous glance at Sam. "We did okay, I think. Jace even wore a tie."

Jace Bennett made a grunting noise that Caleb had no clue how to sign. Jace was mid-forties, with coppery skin and hair twisted into short dreadlocks. He worked mostly in metals while Sam's medium was wood. This project merged the two mediums. "Would have been better if Sam was there," he said. "He can stand the bullshit better than me."

Caleb signed "bullshit" with the appropriate enthusiasm.

"I think I've just been insulted," Sam said, then motioned Caleb over to the slab of wood. "Look at this beauty. We salvaged it from an old furniture plant. It's perfect for the supporting beam."

Caleb looked down at the intricate grain of the wood and tried to see it as Sam did. What was it Michelangelo said about his work? *Seeing the angel in the marble and setting him free.* That had to be what it was for Sam.

"Can't wait to see what you'll do with it," Caleb signed.

"What *we'll* do with it," Sam corrected, circling a finger to land on his chest.

Amanda approached. Her brown hair was gathered in a fraying braid, her pale hands streaked with what looked like varnish. She wore overalls with a peace patch on the front pocket. "We have a name for the project. Did you tell him, Sam?" Amanda had learned to speak slowly and clearly so that Sam could read her lips, something he did exceptionally well.

"Well?" Caleb eyed him expectantly.

"Should I tell him?" Sam cocked his head at her and the others.

Jace lifted a chisel in a mock menacing way. "If you swear him to secrecy."

"And we mean pinky-swear," Amanda added.

"Up to you, Jace. You're in charge here," Sam said.

Jace set down his tools and wandered over. "This is about honoring Reverend Clementa Pinckney's memory. I looked over some of his quotes and we liked, 'Justice Be Done.'"

Caleb considered it. Justice be done, for a beloved state senator gunned downed in Charleston at the Mother Emanuel church where he preached. Justice be done, after Dylan Roof slaughtered nine innocent Black people who tried to help him. Justice be done, for Daniel Simmons, the social worker, who perished with the others during that needless 2015 tragedy. Four years had passed, but little had changed. The late Clementa Pinkcney would not be proud of his state.

"Senator Pinckney called out 'Justice be done' after Walter Scott got killed by the policeman in Charleston. You remember that? Kind of hard keeping up with all the different racist attacks." Jace didn't hide his sarcasm. "Guess we're still waiting on the whole justice thing to kick in."

"We're a long way from it, especially after they hurl a pipe bomb that almost kills a disabled woman," Amanda commented. "Or they gang up on a young Black kid in jail and stab him. Just saw that on the news."

Sam watched the exchange, which Caleb signed. "Justice Be Done is an important message," Sam said.

"Even if most won't hear it," Jace grumbled. He looked across the street at the Statehouse, his gaze fixing on the statue closest to them: Governor Benjamin Tillman, who'd served in the 1890s after campaigning on a racist platform, a man who'd committed horrendous atrocities to control Black citizens that Tillman believed to be subhuman. Fitting—or ironic—that the piece honoring Reverend Clementa Pinckney would stand across the road from his statue. The two legacies couldn't be more different.

"This is a great spot for it," Amanda said. "Lots of people will see it. It may have more of impact than you think, Jace."

"So. Can I see the design?" Caleb signed and said.

"Absolutely not!" Sam replied.

"No way," Amanda said as Jace shook his head and muttered, "Nope."

"Y'all like being mysterious, don't you?"

"We do," Amanda said. "But I'll tell you this. It's going to blow you away when this baby's unveiled."

"May ruffle a few feathers that need ruffling," Jace added.

Sam wiped his hands. "I'm having lunch with Caleb."

"Good. We can use a break. Let's meet back here in an hour." Jace slipped off the canvas apron he'd been wearing.

Jace and Amanda headed out the door, leaving Caleb alone with Sam. Caleb unpacked their sandwiches and chips while Sam retrieved cold sodas from a minifridge.

"Thanks for this," Sam said. "It's nice to have a break. They're working me under the table."

"Oh, to be young again."

"Jace's my age and he never tires. Ever. It's intimidating." Sam bit into his brie, fig, and apple sandwich and let out a contented sigh.

Caleb was beginning to regret his ham on rye. Envying something his older brother had was familiar turf. "So. How are you feeling?"

"Pretty good. The leg doesn't hurt much. First radiation treatment is tomorrow afternoon."

Caleb eyed him over the sandwich. "Did you give any more thought to going ahead with the surgery? Getting it over with?"

Sam frowned. "Let it go, Caleb. I've made my decision."

"Okay, okay." He knew better than to push it. He'd let it go, for now. "So radiation starts tomorrow. You nervous?"

He shrugged. "A little."

"Want me to tag along?"

Sam smiled. A bit of fig visible in the corner of his mouth. "They actually have a technician who signs, so I should be fine. I'm taking an Uber in case I don't feel like driving."

"At least let me pick you up. Come on, Sam. I can swing by after work."

Sam wiped his lips and studied his brother. "You gonna eat your sandwich?"

"You gonna let me be your ride home?"

Sam nodded. "I'll call you when I'm done. Now eat."

Chapter Eight

Shull Lassiter loved it when his wife Glenna dressed up. Those long, lithe legs. The cobalt blue satin dress that rode her curves like a second skin. The pearl necklace perfectly placed at her collar bone. Her blond-streaked hair pulled up, a few strands free to frame her exquisite face. Her hand tucked around his arm as they entered the country club banquet hall made him feel like royalty. Glenna was his crown.

The large hall of the exclusive country club had been decorated for the political fundraiser: red, white, and blue balloons at every table. Twinkling lights on the ceiling like a private constellation. Country music over the sound system. A well-stocked bar and attractive wait staff attending to the wealthy patrons.

Shull scanned the crowd. Across the room, the mayor and his dumpy wife. Over by the bar, the head of a steel company. The pastor of the largest Baptist church stood next to the candidate, Tommy Doyle, the star of this event.

Tommy even looked presentable. Nice suit, though it could be a size larger. Shoes polished. Clemson Tigers necktie hanging straight. He spotted Shull and lifted a champagne glass in acknowledgement.

Glenna leaned closer. "I'm going to need a drink for this."

Shull smiled. "I hear ya. Wait here."

He made his way to the bar, pushed through the crowd, and ordered bourbon for himself and chardonnay for Glenna.

Tommy sidled up beside him. "Shull. Looks like a good turnout."

Shull nodded. At a hundred a person, the event should pad Tommy's campaign coffers, but the real money came in the backdoor deals. "How's it going with the pastor?"

"You tell me."

Shull checked his phone as a message from Butch Foulks, his off-the-books business partner, arrived.

Don't waste time on Titus Steel. Earnings down 30% last year and they're facing a big lawsuit.

Shull shook his head. Butch had probably positioned himself outside to watch who entered the building. Butch was most comfortable in the shadows.

Baptist pastor? Shull typed.

Dude's loaded. Family money. Doyle should work him.

"Shull? Everything okay?" Tommy looked concerned.

"Butch suggests that you spend more time with the pastor."

"You got it, boss."

"Would be great if you can get him to support the gun bill. Even better if he'll mention it from the pulpit."

"I can't work miracles, Shull."

"You'd better try," Shull chastised him. "The 'Protecting Our Families' legislation polled well among the evangelicals. Tell him that."

When he returned to Glenna, the cell in Shull's hand vibrated.

Meet me out front.

"What now?" Glenna frowned.

"Work. I'll be back in five." He squeezed her arm as he slipped out the French doors to the patio. A few smokers spoke in hushed tones between planters bulging with ferns and pansies. Floating candles flickered in the vivid blue pool. Behind a palmetto tree, a man waited, dressed in jeans and a trucker's hat like one of the grounds crew.

"Butch. Everything okay?" Shull asked.

"Sure thing." Butch was a scrawny man, with a scrawnier beard that grew too long, and sideburns that had been popular in the 1970s, which was when Shull first met him. "Tommy should work Henry Whitmore," Butch said.

"Whitmore?"

"White-haired guy just walked in the door. Owns Whitmore Automotive Group." Butch handed Shull an iPad that displayed some kind of contract. No, it was a "Request for Proposals" from the Department of Transportation. "He wants the contract for the state fleet. Doyle's on the oversight committee. A few well-placed calls . . ."

"Gets Whitmore the contract and gets Tommy a big fat donation. Nice work. I'll talk to Tommy."

"One more thing." Butch flicked through a few screens on

his device. "Message board is active."

Shull hadn't checked the underground site in a few days, but Butch lived on it. He navigated the dark web better than Shull navigated his own house, setting up less-than-kosher gun deals that earned Shull a fortune. "What's the chatter about?" Shull peered down at the string of comments on the secure server, recognizing some familiar names.

"The downtown protest. Folks are fired up. We're recruiting from other towns."

"Don't want it to get too out of hand."

"We don't?" Butch's smile was an unexpected flash of crooked teeth. "Good for the gun business."

Shull's gaze flicked to a car pulling up. A young couple emerged: his daughter Beryl, dressed in a knee-length pink shift, and her husband, police lieutenant Al Fuller, in his Sunday-go-to-church suit.

"I better say hello," Shull commented, but Butch had already slipped away. "Like a damn ghost," Shull whispered.

Ten minutes later, he stood with Beryl, Al, and Glenna, pretending to listen as Al explained his cop's view of recent tensions in their town. "We've given them too much leniency. Now Black Lives Matter thinks it can come to town and destroy shit. They'll soon see where that gets them."

"Shhh, Al," Beryl said.

"Why shhh? Everybody here agrees with me. Hell, this is the one place where I can say it out loud."

"Still. Best to be cautious. And we're not here about that. We're here to support Tommy," Shull said as he looked over the crowd, spotting Whitmore by the bar. His hair glowed white as typing paper and his hawk nose overpowered his face, but he carried himself with that air of the well-moneyed. Beside him, a thin gray-haired woman who looked like she'd had too much plastic surgery wore a tight pale pink dress. Shull lifted a beckoning glass at Henry, who led the woman over to them.

"Nice to see you here, Henry. And Mrs. Whitmore."

"Shull." Henry's handshake vibrated his entire arm.

"Henry, I'm getting tired." Mrs. Whitmore looked more bored than tired, her gaze scanning the room with little interest.

"Just a little longer, hon." He slid an arm across her shoulders.

"Have you had time with Tommy?" Shull asked. "Let's go have a chat with the candidate." He cocked a thumb toward the stage and Henry followed him to Tommy Doyle, who shook Henry's hand with too much enthusiasm.

"I think Henry here may need your help with something," Shull said.

"I do?"

"The Request for Proposals for the state fleet? You want that contract, don't you?" Shull eyed him over his glass, assessing.

Henry tried to don a poker face, but Shull could see beneath it. Henry definitely wanted that deal. "Every car dealer in South Carolina wants that contract."

"But every car dealer doesn't have the capacity you have. You're the biggest dealer in the Midlands," Tommy said. "And that's what I'll argue in the committee meeting. I mean—if you really want the bid."

Henry's eyes widened. A tell that showed his desperation for the deal.

"And to show your gratitude, Tommy could use your campaign support. We need him to stay in office. We need his vote on things that matter," Shull commented.

"And how much 'gratitude' do you expect?"

Tommy looked at Shull and licked his lips. *Down boy*, Shull wanted to say. Instead, "Gratitude is a subjective thing. You do what you can, and let Tommy do what he can. We're just happy to have you in our camp, aren't we Tommy?"

"Yes. Yes, we are."

"Keep your hands to yourself!" A female voice pealed out over the crowd.

Shull spun around to see Mrs. Whitmore inches away from Al Fuller, her face redder than a beefsteak tomato.

"What the—" Henry hurried over, with Shull close behind. "What did you do to my wife?" Henry demanded.

"I'm sorry. I didn't mean—" Al looked horrified. Beryl had a napkin pressed against the front of Mrs. Whitmore's dress where a red stain spread like blood across the middle.

"Beryl?" Shull asked his daughter.

"Al was talking about his police work—you know how passionate he can be. His hand hit my glass and, well—" She pointed to the red blotch on the older woman's dress.

"Careless. He's a buffoon," the woman muttered.

"Honey, it's just a dress," Henry said.

She snorted. "That cost a small fortune. He's a careless troll." She snatched the cloth from Beryl.

Glenna grabbed a stack of napkins and dipped one in her chardonnay. "Here. I've heard white wine is good for red wine stains. Let's go to the restroom and see what we can do."

As the two women hurried away, Beryl clutched Al's arm. "You didn't mean to."

"I didn't." Sweat dotted Al's forehead. "I'm sorry, Shull. It was an accident."

"Of course it was." Shull frowned. Al's ingratiating tone always annoyed him. He hoped this incident didn't dampen Henry's generosity. "We will gladly pay for the dress to be cleaned. Or replace it, if necessary."

"I think I'd better get my wife home. It's been a long evening and she's clearly tired," Henry said.

"Clearly." Beryl rolled her eyes.

"I'll send my contribution tomorrow." Henry moved to the entryway just as Glenna and Mrs. Whitmore emerged from the restroom. The Whitmores made a quick exit through the front door.

When Glenna rejoined them, she said, "It may not be a total loss."

"That woman's a bitch," Beryl whispered.

"She had a right to be upset," Al said. "I'm sorry, Shull."

Shull shrugged, tired of the drama. He'd look for Henry's donation tomorrow. If it didn't come, he'd make a call. If Henry wanted a favor, he damned well better come through.

Chapter Nine

On Thursday afternoon, Officer Mary Beth Branham popped another antacid into her mouth as her friend Paloma parked the car. They'd met for a late lunch before the evening shift, but that wasn't the cause of Mary Beth's turbulent stomach. It was the massive pick-up truck parked across from them and the equally massive man climbing out of it: Lt. Al Fuller.

"The damn truck's big enough without those giant wheels. Overcompensating much?" Paloma checked her mascara in the rearview mirror.

"Check out the bumper."

She closed her mascara. "Heritage not hate. Confederate prick. Talk about a walking cliché."

"He'd be smart to get rid of that. Could get him in trouble."

"So what?" Paloma climbed out of the car. "I hope everybody who meets him knows exactly where he stands."

"God knows, I do," Mary Beth whispered, wishing the Rolaids would kick in. She'd gone to her doctor about the burning in her stomach and been lectured about the stress level of her work and referred for counseling. She'd seen a therapist as a teen and it helped, but she worried about going as an adult. As a police officer. What if the Al Fullers of the Department found out?

As they approached the building, Paloma halted. "Look. My brother got wind of another protest tonight. It's going to be a big one. Beginning in the north Main area and marching to the state house."

"How big?"

She shrugged. "Folks coming in from out of state. A bus from Charleston. Black Lives Matter and a few other groups got a permit to speak on the statehouse steps when they get there. Rolando's worried things might get rowdy."

Mary Beth nodded. It had been four days since the attack on the Harwell home and the brutal assault on young Laquan Harwell, and Columbia wasn't anywhere close to settling down.

Tonight there could be five hundred good people trying to make a peaceful statement, but a couple of hotheads could turn the calm into havoc. The trick would be to find and contain them before they did too much damage. And of course, Mary Beth's other job: keeping Fuller from overreacting. "Be safe, Paloma."

"You too, amiga. See you on the other side."

An hour later, Mary Beth sat in the cruiser passenger seat as she listened to Fuller babble on about a reception he'd attended with Beryl, his stay-at-home housewife, daughter to some rich gun dealer in town. "All the big players were there. The mayor. Business leaders. The wealthiest people in Columbia," he boasted. "They held it at that fancy country club just northeast of downtown."

"You mean the one that only lets white people join?"

He shot her a look. "That's not true anymore. They integrated a few years ago."

"Good to know."

"Anyway, it was a fundraiser for Tommy Doyle."

Mary Beth would vote for a dead slug over that idiot.

"Of course Beryl made me wear a suit. And schmooze with her dad's rich friends. But the bourbon was the good stuff. Probably a hundred a bottle."

"Sounds fun," she said with fake enthusiasm.

His voice lowered. "Yeah. Until I spilled wine all over some millionaire woman."

"You didn't!" Mary Beth laughed.

"I did. And she flipped out. Made quite the scene. I felt bad about it." He actually looked sheepish. She felt a little sorry for him.

"Poor Beryl," she said.

"Why poor Beryl?"

"Here she is, trying to get culture into you and this happens. She must have been horrified."

"But the woman was a real witch. Acted like I'd scalded her. Rich people can be so damn entitled. I think Beryl decided she deserved her ruined dress."

She thought about Al becoming a part of a wealthy family. How out of place he must feel. Maybe that accounted for some of the anger always roiling in him.

Fuller made a turn on Taylor toward downtown. "Guess we should check out the protest."

Mary Beth knew it was inevitable, as soon as the rally had been mentioned during report. As Fuller headed north on Main, the setting sun gleamed against the Truist building so that it glowed, and the dusky light shadowed the sidewalks. Shadows could hide people. And danger. Fuller parked the squad car close to where a small crowd had gathered, and they climbed out without donning the riot gear. Fuller hesitated, responding to something on his phone. He often got texts that distracted him from the job.

The crowd carried signs with messages like "Justice for Laquan" and "Hate Kills," sentiments with which Mary Beth agreed. Laquan Harwell deserved to be arrested for assaulting the storekeeper—even if the man was a racist—but he didn't deserve getting swarmed and stabbed. He didn't deserve the strange image carved into his flesh.

She scanned the crowd and recognized one protester: Madigan, the law student Fuller had harassed at the last rally. Fuller saw him, too, but said nothing, just eyed Mary Beth with a lift of his brows. "Everything looks calm right now," Mary Beth said.

"Yep. Let's hope it stays that way."

They made their way up Main, Mary Beth mentally assessing crowd size. About seventy folks, but further up the road she could see more coming, and a bus rumbled toward the Capitol. Several other officers flanked the crowd on the other side, but the slow march to the Statehouse halted, and the numbers quickly swelled.

As did the agitation. Rhythmic chants of "Black Lives Matter" devolved into random shouts and banging on makeshift drums. Mary Beth tried to gauge the emotion. Anger. Frustration. And exhilaration, the kind that happens when you've been alone in a fight and suddenly, you're a part of something big.

It scared her.

Over the next sixty minutes, the crowd ballooned, emotions intensifying. Not a protest but a mob. So many of them. Too many of them, hard to see in the dark, particularly after someone shot out the streetlights. They rushed back to the squad car and donned riot gear, just in time to watch someone smash a store window with a brick and run off with something he'd grabbed from inside.

Mary Beth started after him but Fuller stopped her, pointing to a new commotion up the street. A different crowd arrived. Not Black people, but white men, marching up the street like a band, all wearing what looked like matching red T-shirts with an insignia across the middle. "Who are they?" she yelled at Fuller.

"Reinforcements," Fuller answered, gripping his cellphone.

"Are you sure?" She wasn't. She didn't like the way they approached the Black crowd like a giant animal seeking prey. She clicked on her radio to call it in and heard other officers on the com chattering about the newcomers.

"Who the hell are they?" "Anybody see weapons?" "We need reinforcements!" "We need the damn National Guard."

Fuller had vanished. He'd been right across from her but now she couldn't see him. "Lt. Fuller? Come in, please," she said into the radio.

"Lost your partner?" The voice with a Hispanic accent came from behind her. Paloma.

"He was just here." Mary Beth felt a flash of anger. Her partner, such as he was, had no right to disappear like this, not in the middle of this bedlam.

Paloma moved closer. "You okay?"

She eyed the white men as they advanced on the Black crowd. "Pray to God they didn't bring guns."

"Those white pricks? We'll be lucky if they don't have explosives. Idiotas." Paloma checked Mary Beth's vest. Mary Beth did the same with hers.

Minutes later, the chief summoned all the officers and lined them up in riot formation. Still no sign of Fuller. When county deputies arrived for support, they made a police wedge between the two groups of protesters. Skirmishes happened despite them—brawls between the groups, a car set afire, and a few buildings vandalized, but nobody seriously injured. The mood softened—less unbridled rage, more synchronized passion, especially when the Black crowd finally reached the statehouse, and the planned rally began. The white guys lined the sidewalk, watching. Menacing. Like vigilantes looking for a reason to strike.

Paloma stayed at Mary Beth's side. "What's with the T-shirts?"

Mary Beth stared at a graphic on one of the shirts. "That's the same pitchfork design that they carved into Laquan Harwell's chest. It has to mean something. Some Arian Nation thing?"

Paloma shook her head. "Not according to the gang task force. Besides, they don't look the part. You'd see more tattoos and piercings. These look like good old boys hyped up on testosterone and racism."

Out of the corner of her eye, Mary Beth caught a glimpse of an officer standing behind the white men: Fuller lurking in the shadows with two others.

"I'll be right back," she said to Paloma.

Mary Beth worked her way through the line-up of blue—her brethren, keeping the peace. She sidled behind the commander, relieved when he didn't notice her, and reached the sidewalk where Fuller, a protester, and another man—not wearing the T-shirt—looked to be in serious conversation.

"Lieutenant? I've been looking for you." Mary Beth didn't try to hide her irritation.

He shot her an annoyed look. "Why aren't you in formation?"

"Why aren't you?"

He turned to his colleagues: a hard looking white man in a long, scraggly beard and a younger, skinny guy who looked wild-eyed and sweaty. "Give me a minute," he muttered to them.

Mary Beth didn't jerk away when Fuller grabbed her elbow and pulled her off to the side, though she wanted to.

"Who do you think you are, questioning me?" he demanded.

"I'm your partner. The one you're supposed to keep in the loop. You disappeared. I didn't know what had happened. You could have been hurt."

"Or I could have been calming down some tempers. I'm trying to de-escalate the counter-protesters. Now you get back where you're supposed to be and let me do my damn job."

She looked into his face, wanting to believe. Wanting to think Fuller might do something good, but not trusting it for a second. She glanced over at his friends.

“Get back in line. I’ll be there in a minute.”

Reluctantly, she nodded and wound her way through the group and back to Paloma.

“What’s the idiot up to?” Paloma whispered.

“Wish I knew,” Mary Beth replied. “Wish I knew.”

Chapter Ten

"Meet the Red Shirts." Detective Claudia Briscoe thunked an iPad onto Caleb's desk after entering without knocking and sitting without being invited. She looked well-dressed, well-coiffed, and self-satisfied, as was her way these days.

Caleb had watched the riots on the news the night before, had seen the army of men dressed in matching tees. Terrifying to imagine that kind of violence in his town. "You could call or text before showing up. What if I had a client?" Caleb had already had a long day. Four sessions done, and it was only two p.m.

"Your next appointment is in ten minutes, I checked. Take a look." She clicked a nail against the screen. "It took a while for our computer guys to find this stuff. The group is using a server on the deep web. Lots of layers of security. Anyway, they call themselves the Red Shirts after a group in the 1800s. Folks that never got over losing the war, so they formed a paramilitary group. Governor Benjamin Tillman was their leader for a while."

Caleb shook his head, picturing the monument to Tillman on the statehouse grounds, across from where Sam and his group were building the sculpture. Tillman espoused racist doctrine like "white domination or extermination." It infuriated Caleb that this level of racist hatred still thrived in their state over a hundred years after Tillman's death. Sometimes, it seemed it would never end.

Claudia went on. "The 'Red Shirt' incarnation began about six months ago. This message board is getting more and more active, particularly after Laquan assaulted the old man. They see it as a call-to-arms, beginning with last night's counter-protest."

Caleb lifted the tablet for a closer look. The webpage was basic—no fancy graphics, just a string of messages and some photos. He clicked on one grainy photo to enlarge it. "This is a shot of Laquan in his cell. Whoever posted it was likely one of his attackers."

Claudia replied with a sober nod. "And we're hoping to figure out who that is."

"How the hell does an inmate have a camera and this kind of computer access?"

"Jail admins are trying to answer that right now. But honestly, you wouldn't believe what they get away with inside." She reached for the iPad. "You told me about the men Laquan described. The ones who attacked him. You said one had a pitchfork tattoo. Just like what the Red Shirts have on their shirts. Guess they have members inside."

"What's next with these Red Shirts? Are they escalating?" Caleb thought about the footage from last night's news. The rage on the Black protesters' faces. The cars set on fire; the store windows smashed. The arrival of the white counter-protesters, the so-called Red Shirts, with their synchronized movements that looked militaristic. How the whole thing could have exploded into a full-out race war had the police not quickly intervened.

"We're monitoring the site and yes, they are escalating. Black Lives Matter has another protest permit for tomorrow night and the Red Shirts site is abuzz about it." She showed him the latest post on the message board: "End the barbarism now! OUR lives matter! The White Way is the right way!"

"Crap." Caleb scowled at the message. "How do you stop it?"

"Reinforcements. Somebody steps out of line, we bust them."

"Do we know how big they are? Are they just local?"

"Another excellent question. We have a lot to learn about these Red Shirts." She paused, angling her head to the side as she gave Caleb a thorough study.

"What?"

"You talked to Sam lately?" Her question took him off guard.

"Had lunch with him yesterday. Why?"

"He mention a press conference today?"

"No." Caleb had read the paper online that morning and seen nothing about Sam's project.

"The Equality Foundation held a press conference this

morning about the sculpture installation. Sam was there with some of the other artists," Claudia went on. "They're getting mileage out of recent events. The foundation director talked about the importance of this project, given the racial tensions. Got on a real soapbox about the evils of Benjamin 'Pitchfork' Tillman. I don't think he realized he was inciting the Red Shirts."

"Good coverage?" Caleb asked.

"Every news station had it on their noon broadcast. They'll likely be a big feature for the six p.m. We're monitoring the Red Shirt site to see if they're going to respond."

"Respond? How would they do that?" Caleb's voice rose in alarm.

"Don't worry. Honestly, your brother's comments were quite impressive. He focused on all the good Pinckney did. Definitely calmed down the rhetoric."

"Good for Sam." He could only imagine how much his brother hated having anything to do with a press appearance. Caleb would set his DVR as soon as he got home.

"What about Laquan Harwell? He's not getting out of the hospital any time soon but when he does, won't there be a target on his back?" Caleb asked.

"Hopefully we'll ID the Red Shirt hitmen that are in the jail by then. You going to visit him again?"

"Plan to."

"Good. You can bill us for your time, especially if he gives you any pertinent information that will help find his attackers."

Caleb's boss, Lonzo "Bill More" Petrocelli, would be happy to hear that. "You know I'll only tell you what Laquan gives me permission to tell you."

"Yeah, yeah." Claudia approached the door. "But you can be persuasive. And we're all just trying to keep the kid safe."

"All of us but the Red Shirts," Caleb replied.

Chapter Eleven

Shull Lassiter sat with a gloating Tommy Doyle in his campaign office—a squat brick building on Main Street that Lassiter had rented from an old school chum. A few volunteers assembled voter packets in the front while Tommy and Shull claimed the small room in the rear, door closed. Nobody needed to hear their business. In the corner, a mounted TV aired the evening news.

Doyle's massive oak desk dwarfed the candidate, who wore wireframed glasses that made him look smarter than he was. He described the campaign schedule to Shull, who couldn't have cared less about Doyle's appearances. Victory wouldn't come from the candidate's less-than-golden-tongue; it would come from Shull's pocketbook.

"While I don't like doing these senior centers," Doyle said, "the old ladies love me. I just have to ask about their health and their grandchildren and I. Am. In."

"They're important voters." Shull's gaze returned to the TV which showed clips from a press conference giving an update about the status of the new Clementa Pinckney memorial. Some Black guy hogged the mike and preached about the horrors of Ben Tillman, how terrible and insulting it was that his statue remained on the Statehouse grounds. Shull smiled, picturing how those words were gonna piss off many of his friends. He'd check the Red Shirts message board later to measure the response.

"Tillman is so misunderstood," Tommy said to Shull. "People don't remember what he did for our state at a time when we needed leadership."

Another man was summoned to the mike. He looked reluctant. A tall, muscular white guy with blondish brown hair and the kind of handsome chiseled features that pissed Shull off. He was introduced as Sam Knowles, the other artist leading the design and installation.

"What's with the hand signals?" Doyle pointed to a woman

beside the artist, dressed in black, signing the question asked by one of the reporters.

"The guy's deaf!" Shull exclaimed, fascinated.

But Sam Knowles didn't sign his answer. He spoke. The voice had that odd, monotone tenor that deaf people often had, but he was very articulate. "We are honoring the life of a great man. Clementa Pinckney's fight for justice continues to this day, and that's the spirit we hope to capture in our project." He paused and looked at the assembled reporters before continuing. "More than that, though, we want to respect his love for this state and its people. His belief that we can do better. And we must. He would not want to be remembered with violence, but with change. What better way is there to honor such a great man?"

Damn, this guy had great camera presence. His being deaf made him even more appealing though Shull didn't understand it. He'd make a great candidate, except for that liberal BS he was spouting off. Plus, he didn't look like the kind of guy who could be bought. He was no Tommy Doyle.

But he might be useful to Shull. He needed to get on the message board and work his magic. "Tommy, I need your office for a moment. Why don't you run along and help some of your volunteers?"

Tommy flashed a look of annoyance, but Shull lifted his brows in warning. A few seconds later, the office was all his.

Shull retrieved his laptop from his briefcase. He opened the special, untraceable web browser and signed into the Red Shirts message board. Responses to the press conference popped up.

ZION: *Another barbarian we need to shut up!*

REBEL SON: *How dare that idiot mouth off about Governor Tillman!*

ZION: *He was a great man. Ahead of this time.*

WARRIOR ALPHA: *We know what we need to do.*

But did they? Shull enjoyed the testosterone-fused threats, the passion of these men, but they needed direction. Which was why he was there.

He strategized for a moment. His mission was to stoke fear, and that took time. Sudden, rash actions didn't do it. Momentum needed to build, fueled by raw emotion. An idea came to him, and he began typing under his username of "Pitchfork":

We should give them a warning first. Let them know what they're in for.

ZION: *What kind of warning?*

PITCHFORK: *One that will be heard.*

WARRIOR ALPHA: *Right. Of course.*

PITCHFORK: *What comes after will take some careful planning. It needs to be . . .* Shull hesitated, mulling what to say. Finally, he added: *comprehensive. And merciless.*

REBEL SON: *Merciless! Eradicate the barbarians!*

Shull smiled. This Rebel Son guy always quoted Tillman, his hero, and Shull wasn't sure he was capable of independent thought. Rebel Son might prove useful as Shull's plan continued to evolve.

A different messenger requested to enter the "room". Zion granted him access.

VICTORY IS OURS: *We striking tonight?*

WARRIOR ALPHA*: I'll be at the protest with the rest of the brothers.*

ZION: *I'm in. And this time, I'm packing.*

That made Shull Lassiter smile. Any mention of guns meant he might make a sale.

Chapter Twelve

Caleb entered the large medical practice building attached to the hospital and rode the elevator to the seventh floor. Sam's radiation treatment was supposed to last thirty minutes, which meant Caleb was twenty minutes early to pick him up.

A TV in the corner aired coverage of last night's riot. Everything was escalating. The violence. The bloodshed. The camera focused on a Black police officer who looked frazzled, her eyes red and swollen from the tear gas. Caleb thought about Claudia, knowing she'd probably been in the middle of the fracas. He hoped she was safe.

He was grateful it was Friday, though he dreaded what the weekend might bring. Would the riots escalate? More violence and arrests? When would it all end? From what he'd read, the Red Shirts had grown in number and in the extremism of their rhetoric. Well-funded and well-armed, they generated a fervor that frightened him. Caleb worried what their actual agenda might be.

A patient came through the door—a skeletal-thin woman with pale hair wisping over a mostly bald scalp. She smiled at him, and he smiled back, trying not to imagine Sam getting that weak. Caleb had read about "intensity-modulated radiation therapy." He knew the machine they used was the size of a car. He knew they'd mark Sam's skin where the radiation would go—like a tattoo or something—and that it should be painless. Some side effects could be expected—swelling. Soreness at the site. Exhaustion. Sam might lose hair on his leg, and Caleb would tease him about that one day if they ever felt like joking again.

Sam wasn't supposed to use ice or heat on the treatment area. He'd come back in a week or so for treatment number two. And maybe the mass would shrink. Maybe. Caleb understood his own role in this. He would no longer complain about Sam's decision to delay surgery because that strategy had gotten him nowhere. Maybe he'd raise the point later, when Sam was in a receptive mood. For now, he'd be supportive and strong, even when he didn't feel that way, and resume his job of being the irritating younger sibling. Normalcy would be good for Sam. Still, Caleb had studied all he could find on "undifferentiated pleomorphic sarcoma." He knew it was aggressive. It might be removed and never recur. Or it could spread, and . . . and he shouldn't think about that.

If only Sam would go ahead with the damn surgery. This thought never strayed far from Caleb's consciousness. If only Sam wasn't so stubborn.

When the door opened, they brought Sam out in a wheelchair. He wore sweatpants and a hoodie that somehow made him look small when he was anything but. The wheelchair made Caleb's breath catch.

As soon as Sam spotted him, he stood, wincing a little. "Hey."

"Hey," Caleb signed, splayed hand waving in front of him.

The technician who'd wheeled him out signed, "You have the aftercare forms?"

Sam waved a few sheets of paper at her.

"Anything I need to do?" Caleb signed.

"Get me home. I'm supposed to take it easy for the rest of the day."

"I'll make sure of it."

Sam made annoyed growling sounds that made Caleb smile. Yep, normalcy was good.

Thirty minutes later, Sam lay on his leather sofa, his leg propped on pillows he swore were unnecessary, the remote to the TV in his hand. Caleb sat across from him, trying not to stare at Sam's leg. "Is it sore?"

"Not too bad. Feels like it got hit by a baseball."

It had been hit by a "linear accelerator" that fired targeted radiation at the mass. Might as well be magic, as far as Caleb was concerned. High tech voodoo.

"You heard from Julia?" Sam asked in a not-so-subtle attempt to change the subject.

"Talked to her the other day. She wants me to join the protest."

"Said the same thing to me when we Zoomed yesterday." He laughed. "You're raising my niece to be a radical."

If only Caleb was raising her. He'd love it if she stayed with him all the time instead of a few weekends a month. His ex-wife was a good mother, and her husband an acceptable stepfather, but Caleb missed his kid. She was growing up so fast and he needed to be a bigger part of her life.

"I told her about the cancer," Sam said. "I probably should have warned you, but I can't lie to that kid, and she could tell something was up."

Caleb nodded. He wanted to shield her from anything that might hurt, but understood the importance of honesty, especially now. "How'd she handle it?"

"She was upset at first, but I told her that it was treatable, and I had faith that the doctors would beat it. She seemed to believe it."

Caleb wanted to believe it, too. He hated the part of himself that always expected the worst.

"Then she said she didn't want me to go to the protests. But that if she could get a ride to Columbia, she'd be on the statehouse steps until Laquan Harwell was free. I told her that was a very bad idea." He laughed. "She's a piece of work."

"My hair will go from gray to gone if she keeps this up."

"Imagine in three years when she's sixteen. Dating some vegan jerk who drives a car running on compost." Sam laughed. "You'll be buying toupees. I can't wait."

"I sent her the clip of you at the press conference yesterday. She loved it."

"I hated doing it, but Amanda made me."

Amanda. The overalled woman with the long braid. Nice looking, Caleb had thought. "I didn't think anyone could make you do anything."

"She's . . . persuasive."

"And pretty." Caleb wagged his brows.

"Yeah, I guess she is." Sam turned on the TV and settled on a detective show, closed captioning in bold yellow. Soon, his eyes drifted closed.

Caleb sat across from him, watching him sleep. They'd get through whatever came next.

They had to.

Chapter Thirteen

Mary Beth stood next to Paloma as they prepared to join the line of police officers dressed in full riot gear: ballistic helmets. Tactical vests. Gas mask pouches. Riot shields. Some wore flash-bang and teargas grenades in special holsters.

Their city was on fire. The crowd from the night before had quadrupled. Small fires erupted along Main Street—fingers of flame from piles of scrap wood. Smoke billowed from a few cars that had been torched.

The mood of the rioters wavered between rage and exhilaration. Teens jumped on top of police cruisers parked to cordon off the precinct station. Shouts of "Justice for the Harwells!" pealed between "Black Lives Matter" chants. Storefronts had been boarded up after a group of revelers shattered windows, leaving broken glass glistening under the few working streetlights.

Loud pops pierced the night. "What was that? Gunfire?" Mary Beth felt for her weapon.

Paloma touched her shoulder. "Fireworks. Like we need those in all this bedlam. Come on."

Mary Beth followed her friend to the large group of officers in riot-control stance. Kyle Drake, Paloma's partner, stepped up beside them. "Where's Fuller?"

"Had to talk to the captain about something. Said he'd be here soon." She hoped the captain kept him for the rest of her shift. She was tired of worrying about what her partner was up to. Whether he'd help calm the madness or inflame it.

Said madness exhausted her. During a usual patrol shift, she spent most of the time bored with the sameness of the streets and with Fuller's bull crap stories. There'd be a few minutes of tension during a traffic stop or arrest, but mostly it was tedium. Now, though, every damn second had her tied up in knots.

Another pop. She jumped again, her gaze scanning the vocal crowd for any trace of a weapon. A second bang and she saw a bottle rocket light up the sky.

A skirmish erupted a half-block away. Glass breaking. The shift commander yelled out, "Sanchez! Drake! Branham! Break-ins on Hampton. Check them out."

The three left the line, shields raised, and took Sumter Street east to avoid most of the mob. When they reached Hampton, Mary Beth spotted two men in hoodies bashing in a storefront window with metal trashcans. "There!" she yelled.

"Idiots." Paloma said. "You check the back. We'll cover the front." She and Sanchez climbed through broken glass to enter the cellphone store.

Mary Beth ran to the alley behind the strip of storefronts, used mostly for trash collection, counting doorways until she spotted the one for the electronics store. Just as she pulled on the doorknob, it swung open, knocking her off-balance. The kid that burst through—dressed in dark jeans and a hoodie—eyed her in utter terror as he pushed into the alley.

"Police! Freeze!" Mary Beth yelled, pulling out her weapon. "I said freeze!"

He halted in his tracks and spun around, hands lifted in surrender. "I didn't take anything. Please!" The voice pitched high. This kid was young.

"What were you doing in there if you weren't taking anything?" She took a few cautious steps closer. The kid lowered his hood. It wasn't a boy, but a girl who couldn't be more than twelve, small-framed, with multiple braids in her hair and panic etched on her brown face. She wasn't old enough to be out at this hour. Behind her, an explosion—probably a flashbang—which meant the mob was heading this way. A teargas cannister rolled down the alley, emitting noxious smoke.

The noise startled Mary Beth. Thank God she didn't drop her weapon.

"I just want to get out of here!" the kid said. "Please. Let me go home." She unzipped the hoodie to show she hadn't taken anything.

"Where are your friends?" Mary Beth glanced at the open door, hoping Paloma and Kyle were okay.

"Hey! She's got one cornered!" The voice came from the other end of the alley. A swarm of men—Red Shirts—advanced on them. Three had guns drawn. A pistol. Two automatic weapons that looked like the AAC Honey Badger she'd seen in Fuller's gun magazine. Crap.

When the girl looked at them, Mary Beth could feel her panic. "Take it easy," she whispered.

The tear gas fumes wafted over them and Mary Beth felt the burn in her eyes and lungs. She coughed and sucked in more smoky air. The Red Shirts closed in—a dozen of them.

"Move along, gentlemen. I don't need your help," she said between hacks.

"Looks to us like you do. Caught you a thief, we see." This one looked like he was in charge. Gray-haired. Thin and wiry. Scuffed, dirty chinos. Shaggy beard. Assault weapon held military style, like he was comfortable having it in his grip.

"Move along!" Mary Beth ordered.

The panicked kid took advantage of her diverted attention and took off.

"Hey!" Mary Beth yelled.

She started to run after the girl but noticed the Red Shirts lifting their guns.

"Do. Not. Fire!" She commanded, pointing at their weapons.

"He's getting away!"

Another bang at the corner and she almost dropped her revolver. One of the Red Shirts yelled out, "He's got a gun!" as three weapons leveled at the running girl.

"Stop it!" Mary Beth yelled, her voice lost in the blasts of gunfire.

Chapter Fourteen

Ten minutes later, Mary Beth leaned against the building, fighting to force air into her lungs. Sparks filled her field of vision, images swirling. Her heart fluttered like a frantic bird trapped in her chest. She knew what this was. This wasn't the tear gas. This was a full-on panic attack.

Breathe. In. Out. Her pulse rushed in her ears like some wild river current.

Breathe. Don't let it take over. The fear of the panic could be worse than the panic itself.

She hadn't had one this bad in six years and the timing couldn't be worse. So many eyes on her. She blinked through the fog, spotting Paloma and Kyle where they had two suspects handcuffed. One of the kids kept yelling out, "Where's Annie? Where'd she go?"

Annie? Who was Annie?

"Shut up, you!" An officer replied.

Breathe in. Don't let them see you like this.

"Where is my sister?" the kid yelled. Oh. Annie must be the girl Mary Beth had caught in the alley. She'd disappeared around the corner, but men had shot at her. In the bustle of officers, she heard of a trail of blood drops leading away from the alley. The girl must have been wounded.

If the others would just leave. Let Mary Beth sit here and get her breath and convince herself she wasn't dying. Get her shit together.

"Hey? You okay?" A tall, dark-skinned woman stooped down in front of her. Mary Beth had seen her around the station: Detective Claudia Briscoe.

"Tear gas got to me." The lie came easy.

"Right. Want some water? Need an eye flush?"

They used milk for that, and she didn't relish the idea of splashing her face with the white stuff.

"Should I get an EMT?" the Detective asked.

"No EMT. But water would be good."

The detective motioned at an officer who brought over a bottle. She opened it and handed it to Mary Beth, who spilled it trying to bring it to her mouth. Damn her trembling fingers.

"Slow and easy," the detective said. "Take a few deep breaths." She dropped beside Mary Beth and whispered, "I know what this is."

"Huh?"

The detective sidled in closer. "It's nothing to be ashamed of. You'll be okay. Just remember to breathe. And remember this will pass."

Mary Beth's old therapist had coached her the same way. Or close. *Even when it feels impossible it isn't,* she had said.

"Is this your first panic attack?" the detective asked, her voice low.

Mary Beth shook her head. "Been a long time."

The detective nudged the water toward her, and she took a sip. It was easier this time.

Mary Beth looked over at her. "Are you . . . going to report this?"

"We'll talk about that later."

"Branham! Where the hell are you?" The booming voice could only be one person. The weight on her chest pressed harder.

Just breathe. This will pass . . .

Fuller appeared, looming above like a hawk over prey. Detective Briscoe stood, "Give her some breathing room, Lieutenant. She took in some tear gas. But she got the Red Shirts pinned against the wall there and disarmed."

Mary Beth noticed it then: the five men in red, lined up, answering questions. None were in cuffs.

"I need to check on them. You be alright?" Detective Briscoe asked.

She nodded and the detective moved on.

"They catch the kid?" Mary Beth asked Fuller.

"Not yet. I can't figure out how he got away. You had him cornered, right?" Fuller demanded.

"Her. It's a girl. A kid. She ran. Red Shirts opened fire. I was trying to keep them from slaughtering her."

"Wouldn't have been an issue if you had her cuffed." Fuller narrowed his eyes at her.

Mary Beth wasn't so sure. The Red Shirts might have gunned her down even in her custody. The Red Shirts had a murderous look. Handcuffs would have made her more helpless.

Fuller continued. "We're following the blood trail. Should snag her soon."

Annie was just a kid. Some punk's little sister. Terrified. Wanting to escape. She hadn't taken anything from the store.

After another swig of water, her pulse slowed to a steady, staccato beat. Breathing eased. The sheen of sweat on her face could be blamed on the situation. "What about the shooters? We arresting them?"

"Still being questioned," Fuller said.

"They think they're heroes." Paloma approached them, scowling.

"Shooting a twelve-year-old in the back?" Mary Beth tried to remember exactly what happened. She had seen guns: a revolver and two assault weapons. One of the men—the gray-haired guy—had held a weapon she'd never seen before, at least not in three dimensions. She scanned the men lined up by the wall. He wasn't there. Where'd he go?

She turned to Fuller. "You still have that gun catalog in the squad car?"

"Why?"

"One dude had a fancy AK- type gun. I think it's the new Desert Tech MDRx. Expensive as hell." Mary Beth had been raised with guns. Her father had been an avid collector. Her brother collected hunting rifles. This proficiency about weapons had been the one, single thing she and Fuller had in common.

Fuller looked puzzled. "An MDRx? Really?"

"Really. But his pants and jacket were cheap looking. Worn. He looked like he worked at a garage or mill. He didn't look like someone who could afford a two-thousand-buck assault weapon. Did you see him?"

Fuller shook his head. "Must have gotten away."

"How?" She looked over at the cops questioning the Red Shirts.

"Good question." Paloma turned to Fuller, her dark eyes narrowed with suspicion. "And how'd he get the gun? Local armory?"

"Someone's supplying them," Mary Beth replied. "I think I spotted two Honey Badger weapons earlier. Those guns can do some damage."

Paloma's frown mirrored her own. This was a terrifying thought. Either side armed with powerful assault guns only meant more bloodshed.

Fuller bumped her leg with his foot. "Captain's letting you go early. Report back to the precinct. Guess you're done for the day."

Thank God, she thought, as Paloma helped her stand. She needed to get away from Fuller. From the Red Shirts. From the chaos that had somehow crawled inside her.

Chapter Fifteen

Caleb stopped at the red light on the outskirts of downtown. He'd worked the Monday evening clinic—a therapy group and two individual sessions—and logged in a few notes before leaving the office at nine p.m., mentally exhausted. Sometimes, after long days like this, he felt like he'd run out of words. He craved quality couch time, Shannon on one side, Cleo on the other, a cold beer gripped in his hand.

He'd taken the road north of the Capitol to avoid the protest, but it looked like the whole of Main Street was blocked off. Flashes lit up the sky like a New Year's Eve celebration.

Two police cars, sirens blaring, rushed by him, maneuvering around the barriers, and squealing up Main. He saw smaller glows, low to the ground, like bonfires. Loud pops sounded in the distance. What the hell was happening to his town?

At the next stoplight, a message flashed on his phone from Shannon: *Don't go thru downtown. Looks dangerous.*

No kidding. He replied: *Looking for a way north of the madness.*

Give me a minute. A pause, then she texted him a route that took him five miles out of his way but promised a safe journey.

Thanks. Be home soon.

Be safe.

Twenty long minutes later, Caleb pulled into their driveway and parked. Their cottage—old red brick with beige trim—had been a recent purchase, after Caleb conceded that commuting from Westville was no longer practical. Life in Columbia had its good qualities. He liked being close to downtown and having an easier drive to work. Their neighborhood had giant live oak trees, homes with loads of character, and dogs—lots of various doodles tugging owners down lumpy sidewalks. Cleo had made many friends.

The move made life easier for Shannon, who'd expanded her work with Safe Harbor Homeless Outreach to include statehouse advocacy. She loved helping people who needed her and had no problem confronting legislators who didn't do nearly enough to address issues like homelessness, poverty, and addiction. Shannon could kick ass when she needed to.

As he unlocked the front door, she greeted him, beer in hand, her arms coming around him. "I'm glad you're home. Shit's hitting the fan downtown."

He breathed in the citrussy scent of her shampoo as he took the beer. She took his hand and led him into the den where pizza from Il Buccato, their favorite restaurant, waited on the table. "I see you cooked again."

She grinned. "That recipe never fails."

He shrugged off his jacket, stepped over Cleo, and plopped down on the worn leather sofa. Cleo roused, noticed him there, and bounded up beside him. "Hey, sweetheart." He gave her a pat as she curled into a fluffy, panda-ish ball tucked beside him.

"You keep her young," Shannon said.

"I try." They had talked about getting a puppy, especially after Julia moved to Charlotte with his ex-wife and Shannon had been desperate to offer comfort. He Zoomed with his kid every few days, and she visited every other weekend, but it wasn't the same. He missed all the Julia-sounds and the beloved energy that filled his home and heart when she was here. She was a full-on pre-teen now, with boys and puberty and a whole future looming ahead of her.

He reached for a slice of pizza as Shannon turned the TV on. A local channel covered the downtown unrest. "The protesters are looting buildings and setting cars on fire," she said.

The disturbing images mesmerized him. "Anybody hurt?"

"There's been some shooting after the white vigilantes got there." She turned up the volume. A newscaster stood a few blocks from the bedlam, interviewing a familiar figure: James Saddington, the husband of Caleb's client, Lenore.

"The violence has to stop," the candidate was saying. "People have a right to be angry. To demand justice. But this is not the answer."

The reporter, yelling over boisterous background noise, said, "Your opponent, incumbent Tommy Doyle, was interviewed earlier. He praised the group of counter-terrorists, a group identifying themselves as 'Red Shirts.' He says they are helping law enforcement bring peace to our city. What's your response to that comment?"

Saddington met the question with a look of stunned incredulity. "Doyle said that? Well, he couldn't be more wrong. The Red Shirts aren't helping anything. They aren't police. They aren't National Guard. They're amateurs and they're armed. They're doing nothing but inflaming tensions and making this situation more dangerous."

"Wow," Shannon said. "The guy doesn't hold back."

"He's got a point." He told her about his conversation with Claudia and the link between the Red Shirts and the Ben Tillman legacy.

"Welcome to 1865."

"We didn't lose the war, you know. We just took it underground so it can bubble up every now and then."

"Truth." She took a long swallow of beer.

Caleb finished his second slice and carried his plate into the kitchen. He filled Cleo's bowl and refreshed her water, remembering when Julia was four and sat beside the food dish while her best four-legged-friend ate. There had been so many changes since then.

"Caleb! I answered your cell for you. Some strange woman's on the line."

He returned from the kitchen, grabbing the phone and pressing "mute." "One of my lovers?"

"Didn't think they allowed calls this late from the women's prison." She clapped her hands. "Come on, Cleo. Let's go out."

Cleo ambled off the sofa and trotted after her.

Caleb unmuted the phone. "This is Caleb."

"Hey. This is Quinn Merrick. From the hospital, remember?"

"Sure." But he didn't remember giving her his phone number.

"I had to track you down. Hope you don't mind."

"Everything okay with Laquan?"

"Physically he's progressing slowly. Spiked a fever this morning but they're treating him with antibiotics."

"His mom?" Caleb asked.

"A longer road for her, I'm afraid. I did wheel Laquan into her room so he could see her. She was able to smile at him when he gripped her hand."

"Prognosis?"

"Guarded. Lots of lung inflammation. But I got PT to begin working with her today. At least we can help her with mobility while she's with us."

"Excellent." He wondered what it took to make that happen. Quinn Merrick seemed to be very resourceful.

"Any chance you can come see Laquan tomorrow? He saw the news. Blames himself for the craziness downtown."

Caleb shook his head, picturing a sixteen-year-old boy struggling with guilt and confusion. "I'll try to get there."

"Keep my number and text me when you're coming." She paused, then added "Hold on a second."

Caleb could hear her talking to someone, then she came back on the line. "I gotta run. We have a victim coming in from the riot. Some kid got shot."

"Damn it," Caleb said.

"I fear it's gonna get a whole lot worse before it gets better."

At seven thirty a.m. on Tuesday, Caleb was a man on a mission. He had a cup of coffee in the cupholder and jazz playing over the car stereo as he drove toward downtown. The barricades were gone. No crowd in sight. But the destruction was . . . everywhere. Shattered glass from storefronts glistened in the sunlight. Blackened shells of cars that had been set ablaze lined the streets. Sidewalks had been spray-painted with the phrases "Black Lives Matter" and "Justice for the Harwells."

And trash. Lots of it—strewn on the streets. Littering doorways. He felt like he was driving through some war-torn country, not his town. Caleb made his way past the Capitol building and reached his destination: the site of Sam's art installation. He knew Sam liked to work in the early hours and wasn't surprised to find his van parked in front of the closed garage door.

What did surprise him was the damage done to the building. Graffiti was scrawled all over the cement block walls, the most pronounced being the vivid, black pitchfork that covered the garage door. "Crap," he uttered, anxious to lay eyes on his brother.

He climbed out of his car and trotted over to the building entrance, cellphone in hand. "I'm outside. Let me in," he texted Sam.

A few minutes later, Jace greeted him at the door. "Caleb! I'm glad to see you."

"Everything okay? Where's Sam?"

"He's fine." Jace pointed to the back of the workshop where sawdust made a cloud around a feverishly sanding sculptor. "He's been working like a madman since I got here at six. I'm headed to the hardware store as soon as it opens for paint."

"Paint?"

"To cover that damn graffiti out front. We're both pissed, but he's . . . really riled. He's ready to tear down the damn door if we don't get it fixed."

Caleb nodded, understanding. This kind of thing would affect Sam deeply. He'd view it as an attack against the message they hoped to convey. Justice Be Done.

"There's more." Jace used a quieter tone, glancing over at Sam as though worried he'd overhear.

"Deaf, remember?" Caleb said.

"Come over here." Jace led Caleb to a small desk and pointed to a note. "This was taped to the door we use."

> *We of the South have never recognized the right of the negro to govern white men, and we never will. We have never believed him to be the equal of the white man.*
> *—Governor Benjamin Tillman*
>
> *Do NOT finish this travesty.*

"Jesus." Caleb knew better than to touch it, though he wanted to set it on fire. "Have the police seen it?"

"Not sure we should bother, given all the crap that's going on right now."

Caleb used his phone to snap a photo of the note and texted it to Claudia with the message: *left at Sam's project* with the address. Then he turned to Jace. "I'll talk to him."

"Good luck. Guess I'm heading to the hardware store."

Caleb approached Sam carefully, slipping into his line of vision and waving a hand to get his attention. A fired-up Sam holding a power tool could be dangerous—to himself, mostly. Sam switched off the saw and removed his safety goggles. "Hey."

Caleb signed, "Came by to check on you. See you had visitors."

"Visitors? Vandals. Malicious punks." He wiped sweat and sawdust from his forehead with the back of a hand. A woody smell wafted up around him.

"Happened last night? During the protest?"

"Probably."

"I saw the note. That's a threat. The police need to be involved." Caleb cupped a hand into the shape of a "c" and thumped it against his chest. "I texted Claudia."

"Don't you think the police have their hands full?"

"Frankly, I don't care. This is a priority." Caleb looked at the beam lying across the worktable. "You're making progress."

"I wish it was done. I wish we could erect this sculpture tomorrow so those pricks would see it."

Caleb was glad he couldn't. What would the Red Shirts do to it? To Sam? "You're going to need to be careful, brother. Maybe y'all should move this operation to your home workshop."

"I'm not letting them run us out of here." Anger sparked behind Sam's eyes.

"Even if it's dangerous? You—or Jace or Amanda—any of you might get hurt."

"I know that. But Jace is more adamant than I am. And Amanda—she's fearless."

Caleb stepped closer. "Can you hire some security?"

"It won't come to that. These pricks are all talk."

"At least one had a gun last night." Caleb gave him a long, sober look. He wanted to push harder. To demand that Sam get some kind of protection. But at least he'd told Claudia. She could arrange for extra patrols.

"Don't worry." Sam smiled, placed a hand on Caleb's neck and squeezed. "I can take care of myself."

"So you keep telling me," Caleb mumbled back.

Chapter Sixteen

"Caleb? I'm not calling too early, am I?" Matthew Rhyker asked over the phone.

"Nope. I've been up since dawn. Stopped by Sam's workshop to check on him." Caleb told Matthew about the vandalism and note left at the site. "I drove near downtown last night. Felt like I was in a war zone. What do you think it's going to take for things to calm down?"

"Both sides think they're rebelling against injustice. Black people want to avenge what happened to the Harwells. The Red Shirts seem to think any uprising threatens their way of life."

"They quote Ben Tillman, Matthew. Ben. Tillman. How screwed up is that?"

"Very." Matthew sounded as dismayed as Caleb felt.

"And the match that lit this firestorm is a sixteen-year-old kid who's been mistreated by a racist one time too many and loses his temper," Caleb said.

"But that's just the match. The kindling's been stacked since the Civil War. Just hope we don't have more bloodshed but . . . I'm not optimistic."

Caleb sighed, thinking of his brother. "Me neither."

A pause, then Matthew said, "You have a meeting with Lonzo today?"

Crap. Caleb had seen it on his schedule but had hoped his new boss would cancel. He looked forward to meeting with Lonzo about as much as his annual prostate exam. "I guess so."

"Still nagging you about your notes?"

"I'm doing better. I promise. And if he didn't have that to gripe about it would be something else. He'd micromanage my bathroom breaks if he could."

Matthew laughed. "I doubt that."

"He did get us that nice cappuccino machine. And we have special people who come water the jungle he's got growing in the waiting room. There's even talk of a fountain out front. Soon it will be like working at the Hilton Hotel."

Another pause. Caleb could picture his former boss mulling over what to say. Finally, in a soft voice, he asked, "Are you that miserable?"

"No. I'm okay. The clients are great. The money's good. I can live with the rules. I think. But if he makes me start wearing a tie then you and I are gonna have words."

"Here's the trick when dealing with Lonzo and others like him. He needs to feel important. You're . . . well, you're yourself. People like you and gravitate to you and that's something I suspect Lonzo envies. And I think that makes him harder on you."

"So I need to make him feel important? Kiss his butt, that kind of thing?"

Matthew laughed. "I'd pay to see that! No. But show him respect. And—if possible—ask for his help now and then. That's what I mean by making him feel important."

"Gotcha." Caleb almost ended the call but hesitated. "Hey, how come you're asking me about Lonzo? Has he complained about me?"

"No. He's impressed with your productivity numbers. But he has asked me about how to . . ."

"How to what?"

Matthew laughed. "How to get you to do what he wants you to."

"And you said . . ."

"I said, 'Good luck with that.' And I meant it."

"Thanks," Caleb grumbled, hanging up.

When Caleb got to the office, Janice handed him two messages. The first said his nine a.m. appointment, Lenore Saddington, would be fifteen minutes late. The second was from Lonzo: "Come to my office first thing."

"Great." Caleb stopped for a mug of coffee before rapping on the director's door, mentally reminding himself of Matthew's words: *show him respect.*

"Come in," Lonzo beckoned.

Caleb entered, gestured at a chair and waited for Lonzo to nod before sitting. *Respect.*

"You wanted to see me?"

"I did." He slapped a report on the edge of his desk. "Got a request for us to invoice the Columbia PD. Apparently, you had a second consult with Laquan Harwell."

"Yeah. Visited him in the hospital. I may go back later today. Why?"

"Do you not remember our earlier discussion? I thought I was clear. Any contacts related to the Harwell case were to be cleared through me."

Caleb had a vague memory of that conversation. "I thought you were mostly worried about the media. I didn't see any press outside his hospital room."

"Why did the police want you there?"

Caleb told him about the session, keeping his tone clinical and non-defensive. "Laquan was able to recall some details about the attackers and gave me permission to tell the police. Of course that's all I shared with them."

"And you saw no media?"

"No."

Lonzo sat back in his chair, swiveling it side to side. "That's interesting. Because I got a call from a reporter this morning, asking about a counselor from our agency seeing Harwell at the hospital."

"Seriously? How did they know?"

"Good question." Lonzo's chair stilled. His stare fixed on Caleb.

"Did they mention me by name?"

Lonzo shook his head.

"Good. I'll do my best to be discreet when I go back." Caleb kept his face neutral, though Lonzo's expression was anything but.

"Why would you go back? He's no longer a suicide risk. He's not our patient. The police don't need you to question him. Or maybe you like being close to someone in the news? A local celebrity?"

Caleb took a sip of coffee and tried to collect himself. Where the hell did Lonzo get off making that kind of accusation? Another sip. A deep breath. Finally, he spoke. "You're wrong. Laquan *is* my patient. As long as he needs a therapist and I'm allowed access, I plan to work with him."

"On what? What are your 'therapeutic goals' for this antisocial punk? What can you accomplish before he's locked up again?" Lonzo steepled his hands on the desk.

Caleb looked into his coffee and contemplated how it would look if he tossed it all over Lonzo's desk. He imagined wide coffee splotches across Lonzo's pristine white shirt, staining the expensive silk tie. To curb temptation, he set the cup down.

"Look, Lonzo. It's unprofessional and maybe even dangerous to diagnosis anyone you don't know. And you don't know this kid. He's not antisocial. He's depressed and anxious and dealing with the catastrophic dominoes set in motion by something he did in a rash moment. And if I can help him with that, I will. Because that's what we do. I'm documenting my contacts and the police are paying you for my visits with Laquan, so I don't see what the issue is." He tried not to raise his voice. Really, he did.

Lonzo lifted a pen and held it between his fingers like a cigarette. Former smoker? That seemed odd, given his fitness level. Lonzo always looked like someone who spent hours at the gym. But then, everyone had their contradictions.

"Okay. If you insist that he's still your patient, then I want a chart opened. Here at the clinic. I want consent forms signed. He's a minor, right? You'll need parental consent to treat."

"He's sixteen. Doesn't need consent. And we don't need his insurance info because my contract with the police Department covers my sessions with him." Caleb stood, done with this conversation and not trusting himself to spend more time with this man without getting in trouble.

Respect, Matthew had said.

Lonzo was a long way from earning it from Caleb.

Lenore Saddington had Caleb worried. The khakis and sweater were very casual for her. Her hair made an untidy ponytail, and she wore no make-up. A concern, because even when her depression brought her to her knees, when he saw her daily after her hospitalization, she dressed immaculately, makeup meticulously applied, her outward image contradicting the black storm that raged inside. "Well, Lenore, how are you doing?"

"It's been awful, Caleb. Awful." She gripped a tissue, wrapping it around her fingers.

"Tell me about 'awful.'"

"You've seen the news? James keeps getting calls for interviews about the riots. But that's not what's bad. It's the other calls. And the letters." She hesitated, her voice quaking.

"We're getting threats. I think they're from those Red Shirt people, but James says we can't say that for sure."

"Threats?" Caleb leaned forward.

She looked up at him, her eyes wide and beseeching. "Even Brian! Kids at his school have been calling him names. Saying his dad is 'Antifa' when I'm sure they don't even know what that means. Then he got a letter yesterday." She reached in her purse and pulled out what looked like the scan of a handwritten note, which she handed to him: *Your father is a traitor. You know what we do to traitors?*

"He is nine years old, for God's sake. He's my baby. I kept him home from school today. And James is no help. He said I was overreacting."

"Did you call the police?"

"Of course. They were at our house this morning. Some detective woman. She promised to have patrol cars keep an eye on us and told us to call if anything out of the ordinary happened. There's a truck that keeps driving by the house. Has a Confederate flag bumper sticker so I remember it. It's . . . intimidation. But James downplays everything. He's gotten a dozen calls—maybe more, he wouldn't tell me—men telling him to keep his mouth shut. Calling him—I can't say those words. They're disgusting and vile. But James just laughs it off. Says he's rattling cages and he's glad he's got the platform to do it."

"This has to be frightening for you," he coaxed.

"Terrifying. James tells me to take my anxiety meds. Like that's the answer."

Bitterness leaked through this last sentence. A raw anger he'd never seen in her. "Medicine isn't the answer for everything," he prompted.

"When I'm anxious because of my own damn neurosis, because I'm manufacturing worst case scenarios or self-judging in a harsh, condemning way—then I may need medicine to stop panicking. But having my son threatened. Having my husband receive death threats. That won't be fixed by a pill. And honestly—" She froze, pulling her lips in tight as though preventing words from escaping.

"Honestly what?"

She stared at him, her eyes like twin barrels from a gun. She didn't speak.

He sat back, kept his face neutral, accepting, wanting her to see that whatever darkness she didn't want to let out, this was the place where she could.

"You don't know how it is," she finally said. "With James. How it is to be his wife."

"No, I don't. But I want to."

"He's a good man. I've told you that. A good provider. Supportive of my career. An attentive father."

Another pause, more pursing of her lips. He pictured her internal debate. A war. What she needed to believe versus the truth, whatever that was. Caleb knew not to push, that would just make her more immobile, so he waited, letting the silence do the work.

"I love him," she added.

He said nothing.

"But I don't know that he loves me. I've come to realize . . ." Her hand stroked the arm of the chair. "I've come to suspect that maybe James just loves . . . himself."

Caleb pictured James Saddington, the politician, standing in front of TV cameras. Taking interviews with newspapers. Speaking at rallies full of his fans. Weren't most politicians narcissists?

She continued. "I've watched him these past few months. How he savors the attention. Hungers for it. How he wants to be in front of crowds. And I've felt things change between us. Or maybe they haven't changed, they've just . . . become clearer to me."

"What do you mean?"

"I mean what if it isn't me that he loves? It's the image of who we are. It's James and me and Brian in our lovely home. What if what he loves is how I make him look? It's like I've been married to that man for seventeen years and for the first time I really see him. And . . . and it's—" She paused, looking at Caleb with tear-filled eyes.

He handed her another tissue.

She continued. "What if my marriage has been a lie? He's running for office and expects me at his side and I'm not sure I can do it. Not if . . ."

"Not if you don't think he loves you."

"Exactly. What do I do?"

"What do you want to do?"

A small, fleeting smile appeared. "You always do that. Never have the answer, just more questions. You know what the first thing that popped in my head was? I want to be loved. I want to feel like I matter more than anything. I want things to be the way I thought they were, before I realized it might all be a lie," she said.

Caleb leaned forward. "Only *might* be a lie. How do you determine if it is?"

"What do you mean?"

Caleb had only met the man twice. When Lenore got out of the hospital, James had been the one to monitor her, to make sure she took her meds and made it to her sessions with Caleb. But he'd never been "in the chair," as some of Caleb's clients called it.

"I'm not sure. But I suspect you'll need to have a difficult talk with James."

"Yeah. I'm not ready for that."

"Are you ready to live with your suspicions in the meantime? That might be a harder course, especially given the stress you're under."

She squeezed the tissue into a ball, as though all her stress could be compressed into those paper fibers and tossed away. "You'd have to help me, Caleb. If I'm talking to him about this, I need you in the room."

Caleb smiled. "That's exactly why I'm here."

Chapter Seventeen

Two birds: one stone. This phrase thrummed through Shull's brain like a new mantra that Wednesday morning. Bird one: Get the cucumber reelected. As long as Tommy Doyle followed Shull's instructions, not veering astray, as he liked to do, the election should be in the bag. Or rather, in Shull's pocket.

Recent events had helped. The racial tensions had stirred up Doyle's base, and Doyle was learning how to feed them. "Make your opposition the enemy," Shull had taught him. Vilify Saddington. Make your base loathe him—then make him a threat. *His "libtard" ways will destroy our way of life! And look—his people are rioting in the streets!* Doyle had even learned to pepper each mention with "Antifa!" which always roused the crowd.

The fact that Doyle probably couldn't spell "Antifa" much less define it didn't matter. The base wasn't interested in truth, they thrived on having their fear and rage stoked. It was a thing of beauty to watch.

Which led to bird number two in the two-bird-one-stone scenario: Make himself richer. He could empower the base by selling them weapons. Shull opened the laptop and logged into the dark web site where Butch had set up the Red Shirt chat room. Butch had changed the access code that morning, because he was paranoid that way, which made Shull feel confident that it was safe to post.

It looked like the feed had been busy:

WARRIOR ALPHA: *They destroyed my pickup truck!*

ZION: *The bastards. They had guns last night, too.*

Shull started typing.

PITCHFORK: *Ours are better.* He posted a photo of the new Spectre semi-automatic assault weapon he'd ordered for the store. Had almost to fifty in stock and needed to unload them and the Honey Badgers lining his shelves.

ZION: *I think I'm in love.*

A pause, then:

PITCHFORK: *These are on sale for members of our cause. 25%*

off. Just put "Tillman" in the coupon code at check out.

WARRIOR ALPHA: *We need more explosives, too.*

Shull smiled. Butch could help with that.

ZION: *Saw old man Guthrie last night. Told him about the Harwell house.*

WARRIOR ALPHA: *We didn't know the mother was home. I swear.*

Idiots. They should have checked before tossing the pipe bomb. Shull didn't want the woman killed. He didn't really care what happened to her, but he didn't want any escalation that he or Butch hadn't ordered.

PITCHFORK: *How's she doing?*

ZION: *Our hospital connection says she's gonna make it. Close call though.*

PITCHFORK: *We can't afford any more mistakes.* Shull followed the comment with a GIF of a flaming Pitchfork. His digital trademark.

WARRIOR ALPHA: *We won't, sir. Our mission is too important.*

REBEL SON: *Our mission is EVERYTHING.*

Shull thought for a second, then opted to poke the bear.

PITCHFORK: *Our mission may require sacrifice.*

REBEL SON: *I am ready. Just say the word.* He followed this with a photo of an army with a Nazi symbol emblazoned on the uniforms.

PITCHFORK: *Not yet. But soon.*

Shull smiled. Gun sales would go through the roof. Butch coordinated the online sales on the deep web, assuring that nobody could connect those transactions with Lassiter Munitions.

When Shull heard keys clattering against the back door, he closed down the web browser that accessed the Red Shirt feed. His wife Glenna entered the kitchen, dressed in yoga pants and a top that amplified her very expensive new breasts. Her blond hair was pulled into a knot on top of her head and sweat dotted her face. "Shull, did you eat the tofu scramble I left for you?"

"Every bite." He'd tossed the pale half-burnt mess into the trash and nuked a sausage biscuit he'd hidden in the freezer.

"I'm looking out for your cholesterol like I promised the doctor I would." Glenna lifted a long, lean leg onto a barstool and stretched over it. She had the flexibility of a ballerina, the first thing that had attracted him to her. The second thing had been her complete obliviousness about politics. She identified as neither a Republican nor a Democrat. Though registered, she'd never voted in any election without Shull printing out a pretend ballot and directing her how to vote.

Not that Glenna was stupid. She'd almost finished her third year of nursing school. Shull's daughter, Beryl, commented that Shull married someone to take care of him in his old age and maybe she was right, though he'd never admit it.

As if reading his mind, Glenna said, "Your daughter left a message on the landline. Said she was coming over later."

"Okay."

"Get your checkbook ready. She only comes when she wants money from you."

"That's not fair." Though it was true. Beryl was a Daddy's girl, and apparently, being grown up and married didn't diminish her dependency on him. It didn't help that she'd married a man who barely made enough to cover their mortgage. Al was a decent enough guy, if not the sharpest knife in the drawer. He saw Shull as some kind of beloved father figure which made him easy to manipulate. Al's being a cop had proven useful to Shull, particularly during the unrest. Al joined up with the Red Shirts, believed all the bullshit about the inferiority of the Black race, and delivered messages to the Red Shirt front line that Butch sent via text. While cops were supposed to keep the peace, he was related to one who didn't mind disrupting it. For all Al Fuller's faults, he'd proven to be a great asset.

"Want some more coffee? Or I can pour you some kombucha," Glenna said.

"Coffee." He'd rather drink raw sewage than that brown concoction she downed twice a day. The coffee was probably decaf, another of Glenna's devious tricks to get him healthy. She'd probably snuck some vitamin potion in it, too, God love her.

He stood at the kitchen window as Beryl's Range Rover pulled into the drive. Beryl knocked before letting herself in. Almost thirty now, she still looked sixteen to her daddy. Beryl had Shull's brown eyes, though hers were set wider, accentuated with false eyelashes she'd started wearing earlier this year. Why any woman would want paintbrush bristles on her eyelids, he didn't know, and dared not ask.

"Daddy," she said with a sigh.

"Hey, Peaches." He crossed to her, kissing the top of head, ignoring Glenna's eyeroll. "Everything okay?"

"No, Daddy. Everything is not okay." And the tears began. She dropped into a kitchen chair and reached for a napkin.

Behind Beryl's back, Glenna pretended to open an invisible checkbook and made a writing motion. Shull scowled at her. "How about I leave you two to discuss—" She waved a hand between them. "Whatever this is."

"Thanks," Shull said.

"Good luck," she whispered to him, snagging a banana as she left.

Shull took a seat across from his daughter. "Now tell me what's wrong."

The tears pooled and fell. Her mouth trembled. "I had a big fight with Al."

"A fight?" Shull pictured his son-in-law getting aggressive with his child and thought about which gun he'd use to pay a visit to that son-of-a-bitch. "He didn't hurt you, did he?"

"No, Daddy. He'd never do something like that."

"Good." So Fuller would live to see another day. "What happened then?"

"He was in a bad mood after the fundraiser and the wine incident, which was *not* his fault. Anyway. I had ordered some new clothes. Spring will be here before you know it and I needed to refresh my wardrobe. My package came from Neiman-Marcus and Al was home when it arrived. He saw the invoice and freaked out." She dabbed at her eyes.

"How much did you spend?"

She blew her nose, a boisterous expulsion of snot into the napkin. "Daddy, you know I'm careful. I try to buy sale things but when it's a new season that's harder. I explained that to Al but it's like he didn't even hear me. He just went on and on about our bills and the mortgage and my not working and . . ." She lifted a hand, let it drop.

"How much?" Shull repeated.

"I can send some back. I told him that. I don't keep everything. I try things on and only keep what looks good."

Shull reached over and grabbed her hand. "How. Much. Did. You. Spend."

"Thirteen hundred."

He nodded. This was his fault, he knew. He'd created this monster. When he was married to Beryl's mother, he gave her an allowance of two thousand a month, "walking around money," she called it. When Beryl went to college, he did the same for her.

"You can't spend money like Al's some kind of millionaire, Peaches. He's a cop. He doesn't make that much."

"Don't I know it! He reminds me all the time. Says he risks his life in a thankless job and barely makes enough to put food on the table. And I've made adjustments, Daddy. I've made sacrifices. We don't have any movie channels on our TV cable. I haven't had a pedicure in six weeks. We only have the housekeeper once a month now. It's awful, and I hate cleaning the bathrooms, but I do it. You'd think Al would appreciate it, but nope. Instead he bitches when I order a few tops and jeans."

Shull patted her hand. "Al's a proud man. He wants to be a provider. And it's hard, given his line of work." He had thought about bringing Al into his business, but the man didn't have the personality for sales. Plus, what could Al do? Did he even know how to turn on a computer?

"Maybe I should just . . . get a job." She forced a brave little smile.

Shull watched her gaze flit over to his face, waiting for him to protest, to rescue her. Which was what he always did, but not this time. "Maybe you should. It might be good for you to channel your energy into something besides housework and shopping."

"That's not all I do!" Her voice rose. "I've got my volunteer work at the museum. And I've got my hobbies—I stay busy, Daddy. I'm not some entitled princess."

Glenna would disagree, but he didn't say that.

"Of course you're not. You're my beautiful daughter who's doing her best to be a good wife. But something part-time to help with the bills. I know Al would appreciate it."

"Like what? My degree is in art history. My only work experience is helping you with phone orders in high school."

Shull smiled. "Exactly. Maybe you come back to work for me. I've got a huge sale going on. You can handle the on-line orders. Promise to pay you well," he added with a wink.

Her thick, sculpted brows arched. "How well?"

"I'll pay your Neiman-Marcus bill as a retainer. Forty an hour for . . . let's say. . . twenty hours a week." He paid most of his entry-level workers seventeen an hour. But, of course, she was family.

She looked at the ceiling, clearly calculating the potential earnings. "Can you make it fifty?"

"You drive a hard bargain, but okay. You start Friday. Meet me at the office around ten."

She extended a hand to him. "Deal."

Chapter Eighteen

Mary Beth sat in the waiting area and hoped she didn't run into anyone she knew. This counseling center seemed different than the one she'd gone to as a teen, when she saw Dr. Todd in a restored Victorian home with heart-pine plank floors and tall, rippled glass windows. This had a more corporate feel. Even the art looked generic. The soothing music coming through the ceiling speakers made her feel like she was waiting for the dentist.

Detective Claudia Briscoe had sought her out in the locker room after her spectacular panic event. She'd handed Mary Beth a card with the name "Caleb Knowles, LISW" and a phone number. "He helped me. He's . . . unusual. Smart. Smart-mouthed. But kinda brilliant in a weird way. He can help you. Go see him."

Mary Beth wasn't sure if that was an order, but it sounded like one. So she'd called the number and here she was—wishing she could be anywhere else on earth.

The other people in the waiting area looked more comfortable than she felt. The skinny young woman texting on her cell. The shaggy-beard man whispering to someone on a call. The white-haired woman munching on chips—loudly munching, with chip crumbs tumbling down her blue sweater—like she was sitting in her living room.

Mary Beth had her Kindle with her and tried to read, but moth-wing flutters in her gut kept her from concentrating. When a door opened and an auburn-haired man said her name, she dropped the tablet to the floor, scrambled to grab it and nearly fell out of her chair. Smooth, Mary Beth. Really smooth.

"Can I help?" The man approached and stooped down.

"No. I've got it." She stood, straightening her rumpled blouse and picturing how to flee the building.

"I'm Caleb Knowles. How about we head back?" He cocked a thumb toward the door, and she followed. He had a calm, easy way about him—hands in pockets of his chinos, blue oxford shirt, thick red curls a bit unkempt. When he led her to his office, she wasn't sure where to sit, but he motioned to an armchair. "Care for some coffee? I'm having some."

"No thanks."

"Water?"

She nodded, and he fetched a bottle from a small refrigerator in the corner. She liked the feel of his office. Lots of plants needing pruning. His pictures included a half-dozen Crayola masterpieces framed and filling the wall behind his desk. He must have a kid. Photos lined the credenza: a tall, handsome blond guy in front of a sculpture, the counselor with a red-haired little girl, and a woman pointing at the camera and laughing. She focused on that last picture. There was something about the woman's expression—she looked free and happy—unburdened by the million things that weighed down Mary Beth.

Caleb Knowles sat in a swivel chair and clutched a pottery mug. His eyes were an odd mixture of brown and gold. "How can I help you, Mary Beth?"

Excellent question. Could he reverse time by forty-eight hours? "What do I call you? Dr. Knowles?"

He smiled. "I'm not a doctor, I'm a social worker. Caleb is fine."

"I've been in counseling before. This isn't my first time." She cleared her throat. "But I need a few guarantees."

"Guarantees?" He seemed to be fighting a smile.

"About confidentiality. I mean, I know what I say in here stays in here. And I know needing therapy is nothing to be ashamed of. I mean, people aren't embarrassed about going to the dentist or even the gynecologist, so why should this be something shameful?"

"Exactly."

"But. And it's a big but. I'm a cop. I can't have any of the other officers knowing I'm here. The culture where I work, well, any kind of perceived weakness is a career killer. I wasn't sent by HR, so this isn't mandatory, and you don't need to report my attendance." She forced a confidence in her voice that she didn't feel.

"There's no reason for anyone at police headquarters to know you come here," Caleb reassured her.

"Except Detective Briscoe. She referred me to you, and I'll tell her I came because I'm pretty sure she'll ask. But nobody else."

"That's up to you. Nobody gets info about your session with me without your permission." He sipped, lowered the cup. "Now, tell me what brings you here."

She drew a breath. "I had a panic attack two nights ago. First one in six years. Thought I was done with them. That they were just a part of my miserable adolescence. But nope. I was a full out, hyperventilating mess. Detective Briscoe figured it out, but she was the only one, thank God. I blamed it on the tear gas."

"Tear gas?"

"Yeah. I was working the protest downtown. Or rather, riot. There was a break-in." She went over what had happened. "She was a child. I don't think she had any idea of the trouble she was in. Then the Red Shirts—" she paused, her gaze flitting over to the window. Her memory of that night was a sieve, but she remembered the moment the mob arrived, the weapons gleaming in their hands. Their wild excitement—a fervor to intervene.

"Mary Beth? What about the Red Shirts?" He was watching her with the same expectant expression that Dr. Todd used to wear.

"They were out of control. I couldn't contain them—they opened fire and might have killed that girl. And there was nothing I could do to stop them."

"But you tried?"

"They wouldn't listen to me. Thought they were big heroes. Riding in on their white horses to save the day. But really, I think they're about something else. When they fired at that kid—they were gleeful. Like they just needed an excuse to do it. And I couldn't stop them." That was the thing. She'd been impotent to stop them.

"That must have been terrible for you."

"You have no idea. The kid might be dead—they say she may have been shot, because they saw blood drops in the alley. I pray she isn't."

Caleb nodded slowly. He said nothing.

"It's . . . not easy being a cop. Being a woman cop, even

harder. It's like a battle every day—to prove I know what I'm doing. That I can handle things."

"You used the word, 'prove.' Who do you have to prove yourself to?"

She shrugged. "Everyone. The public. Idiots like the Red Shirts. My fellow cops. My partner."

His brows lifted. "Your partner?"

"Oh yeah. He's been on the force for ten years. Very proud of that fact. He's arrogant. Riding with him is like . . . like being judged every moment of the day." She'd never said that out loud before, but it was exactly how she felt. Every shift. Every moment. Constant judgement. Clearly expecting for her to fail.

"How does that feel? Being judged every moment of the day?"

"It feels like shit." She smiled. "Sorry. Look, he's a good cop. Knows his stuff. Strong. Takes command of situations. At first, I was glad to be assigned to him, figuring I'd learn a lot. But Fuller's—" she paused, as though looking for the right word. "Flawed. Very flawed. And he doesn't see it."

"How so?"

"He's a racist. He treats Black people very differently than whites."

"That troubles you."

She went on to give him several examples. She had a hundred of them.

"Was he with you? The night of the protest? When you had the panic attack?"

She shook her head. "Not till later."

"Okay. Let's go back to that evening. What exactly were you doing when the panic symptoms came back?"

"It's kind of blurry. When it comes on, I lose track of things. I remember flashes—the Red Shirts firing. Tear gas cannisters rolling up the alley. The girl running so fast, like a sprinter, and I was praying they didn't shoot her. But then it gets fuzzier. Paloma—she's my best friend, another cop—she said that when the other officers got on the scene, I had the Red Shirts lined up by the building and told her partner to go after the running kid. I have no memory of any of that, though. The next thing I remember is sitting on the asphalt and feeling like I was choking. Fighting hard just to breathe."

"It's not uncommon to have memory loss during a panic attack. When you had them before, did that happen?"

She nodded. "I was sixteen. And struggling. Really struggling." She paused, not wanting to wade any deeper in those waters. Pressures from school. Dad's drinking. Mom's denying.

"That's a very tough age."

"Tougher for some than others."

He nodded like he understood but how could he?

"Tell me what you were like back then. Introduce me to teenage Mary Beth."

She took a swallow of water, a few drops dribbling off her chin. Her throat didn't allow for smooth passage. "I was fat. More than now. I think I was born that way."

He offered a sympathetic smile.

"And my face kept breaking out. I went to dermatologists and that helped some but—" She shrugged.

"Like you said, tougher for some than others," he said. "How was school for you?"

"I hated it. Never really found a group to belong to. My older brother Thomas was sort of a star. Real popular. Track team champion. Then I come along and I'm . . . clumsy and socially awkward. Didn't make friends easily. I became a target for some of the more popular girls. Bullies, really. It was a miserable time." She hated remembering. The familiar, awful emotions bubbled up as though they'd always been there, waiting.

"I know what that's like. Hard footsteps to walk in."

"You have a brother?"

He pointed at the picture of the handsome blond guy in front of the statue. "That's Sam."

"Sam Knowles? The artist?"

A smile played on his lips. "That's the one."

She'd read all about the successful deaf sculptor who was working on a memorial to Clementa Pinckney. He'd been on the news this week. "Was he always deaf?"

"That happened when we were teens. An accident."

"Wow. Guess that changed everything for him." She imagined what that would be like, to suddenly have the world silenced.

"For all of us. But I wouldn't change who he is now for anything. Don't think he would, either." He sipped again.

"How much older was your brother?"

"Two years. He's a cop now, too. In Charleston. Dad was very proud of him."

"And of you?"

"Not so much." The familiar clutching in her gut came back. Never good enough. She'd become a cop because Dad always talked about how serving others was the highest calling. That was day-Dad. Night-Dad clutched his vodka and cussed at whatever team was playing on the TV.

"You suddenly look very sad." He leaned forward, elbows on his knees, and studied her like he could see through her flesh.

She squirmed under his scrutiny. "I can't fix my family. I never could get my dad's approval and I learned to be okay with that. Besides, he died three years ago. Let's talk about something else."

He looked like he wanted to probe more, but she hardened her expression. Going back in time never solved anything, it just dug up old emotions she'd buried years ago. That crap needed to stay underground.

"What would you like to talk about, then?"

"How to keep the panic attacks from coming back. I can't do my job if I become a basket case whenever there's a little bit of stress. It's . . . dangerous."

"Yes. It could be. But you got in control of them before, right?"

"Dr. Todd gave me breathing exercises. Detective Briscoe did something similar. It helped me not to lose it completely."

"Excellent. We'll build on that. The fact that you had one panic attack after all this time doesn't mean that they're back. You may never have another one. But we'll add to your arsenal of skills, just in case. We'll start with visualization." He had her close her eyes and took her back to the moment in the alley, when the Red Shirts wouldn't listen to her, when the kid ran, and they opened fire. The memory made her breathing shallow, her heart jittering like a frantic moth.

"Okay. I see you're getting anxious. Let's try something." He told her to approach each symptom like a wave rising in the ocean. "It comes, it crests, it moves on to shore. It may feel like you're drowning, but you can swim. You can float and ride out the wave. Just keep your gaze on the horizon. Safety is there."

She felt stupid, at first, doing the exercise, but it helped. His voice, soft and low, soothed her, and soon her pulse steadied, her breathing slowed like the waves she envisioned, in and out, in and out. She opened her eyes.

"How'd that work?" he asked.

"I feel better." She huffed out a breath. Maybe this was the cure. Maybe all she needed to do was picture that ocean and the panic symptoms would never come back. If only it was that easy.

"Excellent. This is just a start, but I'm glad it helped. I want you to practice what you did today, along with the breathing exercises that Dr. Todd taught you." He leaned back, swiveling the chair. "Mind if I change the subject?"

She shrugged. "Okay."

"You mentioned that it was your father who made you decide to join the police force."

"It's a tradition in our family. My grandfather served, too. I'm the first woman, though."

"That's something to be proud of."

"Is it?" She shook her head. "I don't feel proud. I did, at first. When I graduated from training. When I got the uniform. But lately . . ." She wasn't sure know how to finish the sentence. Lately she felt like a fraud? She hated every minute on the job? She'd lost faith in the police? She pictured Al Fuller's face, smug and condescending. Thought about how he misused his power and his badge on a daily basis.

"Lately?" He prompted.

"I'm . . . less enamored. Once I saw how things work—I mean, really work—it's not what I thought it would be. There's a lot of ugliness."

"You mentioned racial issues with your partner."

"And he's not the only one. But he may be the worst. We're handling these awful riots. As far as I can see, both sides are wrong. Black people have a point—what happened to the Harwells was unthinkable—and they must think rioting and looting will force change. But all that destruction can't be the answer. The Red Shirts are worse. They're just there to stir up trouble. And they have weapons—lots of them. And I've seen

Fuller with them twice. Talking off to the side. When I approach, he says he's trying to restore peace, but I don't believe him. I'm scared he's . . . he's with them. A part of that group. And if he is, how can I trust him? Do you know what it's like to have a partner you can't depend on to have your back?"

"That must be terrible. Is there someone you can talk to about him?"

She laughed. "That's not how things work. He's a lieutenant. He has seniority. And he has lots of friends at the Department, including the captain. So no. There's nobody I can go to with this."

Caleb sat back, considering. "What about Detective Briscoe? Could you talk to her?"

She let out a laugh. "Complain to a homicide detective about a problem with my superior? She'd probably tell me to get my shit together and handle it myself."

"That doesn't sound like her." He frowned. "Are you considering other options? Job-wise?"

She thumped her nail-bitten fingers against the arm of the chair. "I'm not a quitter."

"Is that you talking? Or your father?"

The comment startled her. She glared at Caleb, expecting a smirk or a sarcastic glint, but only saw a calm acceptance. "Why did you say that?" she asked.

"Sounds like you've been living by the family script. Joining the force like your brother, father, and grandfather. I wonder, though, if it's the right fit for you. You're smart. Perceptive. And you're seeing things in the force that make you uncomfortable. The recurrence of your anxiety symptoms—I can't help but wonder if it's related to your unhappiness on the job."

She blinked. Wished he would shut his mouth. Wished she was anywhere but in this chair in this office sitting across from the red-headed man.

Wished he hadn't said aloud what she'd been afraid to face.

"We'll go into that more next session. Can I get you back here at the end of the week?"

"That might be good."

Chapter Nineteen

Mary Beth sat in her car, her eyes closed, practicing the breathing technique she'd reviewed in therapy that morning. It worked. For a while. Until she heard the rumble and felt the vibration of Al Fuller's F-10 pulling into the lot. "Another day, another migraine," she muttered to herself, blinking her eyes open.

When someone rapped on her door, it was Paloma, not Al. "Hey, you!"

Mary Beth climbed out. "Hey yourself."

"You okay?" Paloma asked.

"I'm fine. Just hoping tonight's shift is . . . saner than the other day." She'd had three days off and dreaded this return to work.

Paloma shook her head. "Got bad news for you. Shit's hitting the fan downtown. Governor ordered up the National Guard."

"Think they'll help?"

"If they don't make things worse. Never know what people believe or if those beliefs are going to express themselves on the street."

Mary Beth walked beside her friend to the employee entrance of the Police Department. Behind her, she heard Al Fuller on his phone, his voice raised. Great. Her partner was in a mood. "Some days, I just want to call in sick." Mary Beth had almost done it. Had almost called her shift director and said, "My eyes are still burning from the tear gas," but the lie didn't feel right. Back on the horse and all that.

"Me, too." Paloma glanced behind them where Al had stopped and turned away, the phone pressed to his ear. "He still giving you crap?"

"Always." She tried not to wince. "But don't worry. I can handle it."

"I'm not worried about that. I'm worried he isn't going to back you up if you need it." Paloma slid a hand around her shoulder. "Stay close to me if you can. I've got your back."

"I count on it."

Twenty minutes later, Mary Beth sat in the squad car with Fuller driving. He hadn't said much to her, but the way he gripped the wheel and sneered at traffic told her all she needed to know. What had pissed Al off this time? Issues with his wife Beryl? The former cheerleader with the big eyes and too-bright teeth? Mrs. High Maintenance?

The radio crackled out a report of more unrest downtown. Fuller confirmed they'd respond and wheeled the car in the direction of Main Street.

Mary Beth's breath became shallow and fast. And she felt hot—like she was her own oven, sweat beading on her skin and dribbling down. Crap. She did not need another panic attack. She wished they came with a switch she could turn off. She turned to the window, closed her eyes, and pictured the ocean. "Each symptom is a wave. Ride it out," Caleb had said. She imagined herself on a raft, drifting, the sun warming her, a light breeze skimming her skin, cooling her down. Better.

The sound of sirens and sudden bursts of gunfire jolted her. The raft toppled over, and she was underwater fighting to find the surface.

"Some fucker's shooting!" Al yelled, as if she didn't already know that. He squealed into a handicapped spot and bumped over the curb, yelling into the radio: "Do you have a lead on the shooter?"

"Altercation at Hampton and Assembly. BLM protesters against Red Shirts. Need back-up!" came the panic-edged response.

Mary Beth did what she was supposed to. Hurried out of the car. Donned the riot gear. Added pepper spray and stun grenades to her belt. Secured her gun and radio in their holsters. Grabbed the billy club and squeezed it tight. And followed her partner to where the gunfire gave percussion to the night.

The altercation bloomed into a full-out melee. Maybe fifty on each side, with police wedged in between, breaking up skirmish after skirmish. Four Red Shirts stood on the sidewalk in cuffs, and, on the other side of the road, officers had arrested three Black protesters. EMTs worked on several injured protesters. The National Guardsmen remained on the periphery, as though waiting for something to blow.

Mary Beth wondered if it would be her. Her insides felt like a pressure cooker needing release. She mentally counted her breaths. So much for imagining the ocean. If she was at sea, she was surrounded by man-eating sharks and maybe a killer whale or two. She worried she might pass out.

But she followed Fuller through the crowd, blinking against the smoke from a burning car. Numb to the screams and pops from flash bomb canisters. Her brain felt foggy. Blunted. When gunshots blasted from behind her, she hardly registered the body that crashed into her and pinned her to the ground.

"Jesus, Mary Beth. You gotta be more careful," Paloma ground out from on top of her.

"Who's firing?"

"Fucking Red Shirts. Looks like they've got some new assault gun. It fires thirty rounds before you can blink."

Mary Beth pulled herself up, looking for victims. A dark-skinned woman on the sidewalk had blood pooling under her leg. Another officer was pulling her to safety.

Where was Fuller? A minute ago, she was following him and now all she could see was a swelling mob. Why weren't the National Guard intervening?

Paloma was saying something into her radio. Mary Beth kept scanning the crowd, looking for some sign of her partner. The noise—a cacophony—roared through her.

Then suddenly Fuller was there, in her face, screaming, "Branham! I ordered you to stay with me! Keep the fuck up!" He grabbed her sleeve and tugged her to an overhang on the front of a local bank.

That's when a new group of Red Shirts pushed into the crowd. The Black protesters fought against them, but they were mostly unarmed and outnumbered. More popping sounds from guns, but Mary Beth couldn't tell where they'd come from. Fuller had his phone out, reading a text. What the hell? Still fighting with the Barbie-bride in the middle of a riot? Or getting messages from the Red Shirts?

Paloma had moved further north, where her partner was, and Mary Beth wished she could follow. Fuller pocketed the phone. Checked his gun. Eyed the ballooning mob.

Something must have caught his attention because he was off like a bullet. Mary Beth sucked in a shallow—too shallow—breath and went after him. Fuller grabbed one of the Black protesters and, as she approached, she recognized him. He was the kid—Simon—from the university that Fuller harassed the other day.

Simon jerked away from Fuller's grasp, which seemed to enrage him. Next thing she knew, the two had disappeared in the mob. "Shit," she muttered. How the hell could she stay close to Fuller in this craziness? A smoke bomb nearby made everything more difficult. She wiped her eyes and plowed through the swarm of bodies, trying to spot Fuller.

There. She spotted the back of his head pushing through the tumult toward the entrance to a parking garage where some Red Shirts had clustered. Why there? Someone slammed against her—a big guy, his elbow pounding her gut. He turned, apologized, and moved on. She couldn't get her breath. More smoke from a burning pickup didn't help, nor did her escalating sense of panic.

Count the breaths, she told herself. *You are riding a wave.* But it was too big, a tsunami, and what would happen when it toppled her?

No. Get in control. Follow Fuller.

Follow . . . Her quaking legs carried her to the dark entrance of the parking garage. Her vision clouded, colors blurring into gray. Then everything went black.

Chapter Twenty

On Thursday morning, Caleb drove through downtown, headed to the hospital. The first breaths of fall lent the air a dry crispness. Colors began to speckle treetops. Above, the sky was a spectacular, cloudless blue. Yet Caleb hoped it would rain later. Pour. Massive thunderstorms that might dissuade the rioters, because nothing else seemed to be working.

Last night had been the worst. Something awful must have happened, something that had summoned multiple police cars, fire trucks, and other emergency vehicles, according to the late night news, but when questioned, the police commissioner had been vague: "We'll provide details later," he said, which somehow made it sound more ominous.

Ten minutes later, Quinn Merrick, the hospital social worker, met Caleb at the elevator. She wore a denim skirt and the clogs nurses often wore. Her hair hung loose—ample dark curls threaded with gray. "Up for some family therapy?" She asked.

"What do you mean?"

"Maybe my moving Laquan beside his mother wasn't the best idea. We wheeled him in to see her and they got into a big argument."

"He's sixteen. She's a single, stressed mom. Bound to be a loaded relationship."

He started toward Laquan's room, Quinn right beside him. "And he got arrested. Then stabbed. Then their house burned down. So yeah, loaded situation. Can you meet with the two of them? See if you can get to what the problem is?"

"I'll try."

"That's good. Because they're wheeling him into her room right now." She pointed to the wheelchair pushing through a door. Laquan looked small; a skinny kid more scared to face an angry mom than a future in jail. Caleb remembered being that age—but his fear was facing his dad. Of course, big brother Sam usually intervened, absorbing the blows meant for Caleb.

He was so lucky to have a big brother. Now the trick seemed to be keeping him.

"I'll page you when I'm done."

She nodded and left him.

Laquan sat beside the bed, his head lowered. His mother, Pearl, seemed to be sleeping, the drone of oxygen through the canula and the soft beep of a heart monitor the only sounds in the room. She was a small woman, barely a bump under the sheets, her skin a lighter brown than her son's, her gray-streaked hair pulled into a braid. Dark circles dipped below her eyes, and her lips looked dry and scaly, probably from the antiseptic, arid hospital AC.

"Hey, Laquan." Caleb grabbed a chair from the corner and pulled it to the other side of the bed. "How is she?"

He shrugged, not making eye contact.

"How are you?"

"Okay, I guess."

"Much pain?"

"A little. Nothing I can't handle."

"You're a tough guy," Caleb commented.

Laquan's head shot up, eyes narrowed, as though checking to see if Caleb was teasing him. Caleb kept his face neutral. "You are. After all you've been through, it's remarkable that you're sitting here beside your mother. I'm glad to see it."

"She don't want me here."

"Damn right I don't," his mother grumbled, eyes blinking open.

Laquan stiffened. Caleb leaned over her to introduce himself.

"You the counselor?"

"Social worker. How do you feel?"

"Like warmed-over roadkill." As she pulled herself up, Caleb adjusted the pillow for her, noting the limp left arm beside her, aftermath of the stroke.

"Get me some water," she commanded.

Caleb turned to her son. "Think you can fill that cup for her?"

He nodded, snagging the cup and wheeling his chair to the sink to fill it. When he brought it to his mom, she grabbed it without looking at him and sipped. Caleb felt like he'd walked in on a private war.

"Mrs. Harwell, I'm here to see Laquan, but his hospital social worker asked that I meet with the two of you. She was concerned about the tension between you."

"Concerned, huh?" she said with a huff.

"It's normal in families. But y'all are both hospital patients. That kind of stress may impede your recovery."

Her gaze slid to her son. "You okay?"

He nodded.

"You better level with me. I won't have you keeping the truth from me again."

He squirmed. "I said I was okay."

Caleb watched them, the worried look in the mother's eyes, the evasive gleam in Laquan's. "Mrs. Harwell, you mentioned Laquan 'keeping the truth' from you."

"Call me Miss Pearl. Everybody calls me that." She ran her right hand over the sheet covering her. Her left remained immobile. How frustrating that had to be. "The day he went to the store. He come home late, acted like everything was fine. Fixed my soup and crackers for me. I asked him why it took an hour, and he said the store was busy. Didn't bother mentioning that he'd lost his temper and attacked that man. I didn't find out 'til the police showed up at my door and put cuffs on him. Just like a common criminal." She pulled her lips in, narrowed her eyes and leveled a glare on the boy that might have melted cheese.

"I'm not . . . a criminal," Laquan stammered.

"You're not? Then how come you was in jail? I know why—because you beat up that old man so bad he landed here. All for what? What did that do for you, Laquan?"

Another shrug. In this battle of wills, the kid was outmatched.

Caleb said, "Let's back up a minute. Laquan, did you tell your mother what happened that afternoon?"

"He ain't told me squat," she retorted.

"And you have a right to know. Laquan? If I remember right, you went to that store to get your mother some soup. Why?"

"We needed groceries. She had an upset stomach and soup and crackers is what she likes when she's sick."

"You were worried about her."

He nodded, looking sober. "She wasn't able to do for herself ever since she got out of the hospital."

"I told you I'd be fine," she rushed to say. "Don't need you worrying."

Laquan shot Caleb a pleading look. He almost smiled. This kid could be Mr. Tough Guy but not with his formidable mom. "But you do worry, don't you?" Caleb asked.

"It's hard to see her . . . like that. Like this. In a bed. Looking small and stuff. Needing help but not letting me give it to her."

Caleb saw her flinch, caught the subtle vibration of her dry lips. "You're my child. Not my caretaker."

"Except I am your caretaker! Who else is there to do it?" His voice rose.

"Don't you use that tone with me!"

The heart monitor's quiet beep became more manic.

"Miss Pearl? Try to stay calm," Caleb said.

"Calm? How can I be calm? Do you know how hard I've worked to keep him safe? To keep him out of trouble? No, you can't. You aren't a Black man. You don't know the dangers out there for kids who look like him. I've worried that something like this would happen since the day he was born. Taught him to be careful. To not draw attention from the police. To control that temper of his and not tangle with folks like Mr. Guthrie. But he goes off to the store for ten minutes and . . ." Her good hand rose and fell. "And it was all for nothing."

Caleb kept an eye on the monitor, relieved when, after a burst of activity, it slowed to a more reasonable pace. "You're right, Miss Pearl. I don't know what it's like to have a Black son. I can't know. But I do know how it is when you're terrified for your kid."

Her face softened, the lines around her lips and furrowing her forehead smoothed. "Every damn day."

"Every single one," Caleb said. "Laquan is a good kid, Miss Pearl. He went to that store to get you soup. I think he was already wound up—worried about you. Worried what would happen if you didn't get the physical therapy you need. The storekeeper—"

"Mr. Guthrie," she articulated, as though wanting to expel the name from her mouth.

"Yes. Mr. Guthrie. Laquan, what was it he did?"

"He wouldn't wait on me. Waited on everyone around me

but wouldn't even look my way. Pulls that shit all the time."

"Language," she chastised.

"But he does, Ma! And you know he does. He spilled a drink all over me a coupla months ago. Smacked his fist against some chips I bought and crushed them. Laughed when he put them in a bag. Tried to overcharge you once for coffee and you almost let him get away with it."

"I know how to choose my battles," she said.

Caleb answered, "Of course you do. You're older. You've lived a life and learned from it. But Laquan is still a kid."

"I don't feel like a kid," Laquan said, sounding even younger than his age.

She reached for his hand, an unexpected gesture of warmth. "But you are, Laquan. You're my kid. And all I want—all I ever wanted—is for you to be safe."

Caleb felt for her. For both of them. Laquan's bad decision, an impulse, had ruined both their lives. Had Laquan been white, what would the consequences have been? A slap on the wrist? Probation?

"And now the whole damn town's on fire," Miss Pearl said. "I watched the news. I seen the riots. I told that social worker lady—what's her name?"

"Ms. Merrick."

"Right. Ms. Merrick. Told her I'd like to talk to the protesters, tell them that they don't need to make such a ruckus about me, but she said it was about a whole lot more than what happened to me and Laquan. 'Course I know that."

Laquan had grown silent. He looked out the window as though his mind was lightyears away. "Laquan? What's going on?"

"I think that social work lady is right. I think those Red Shirt people were just looking for an excuse to cause trouble."

Miss Pearl looked skeptical. "Why would you say that?"

"Mr. Guthrie. He keeps that bulletin board on the wall behind his register. Mostly people use it to post lost dogs or ads for yard work, stuff like that. But the other day, he had something new on it. A poster. I'd forgotten until just now."

"A poster?"

He nodded. "Red. Glossy. With a black diagram on it. I could be wrong, but I think maybe it was a pitchfork."

"Like what they sliced into your skin?" Anger pealed in Miss Pearl's words.

"Yeah. I think so."

Caleb sat back, considering this. It had seemed that the Red Shirts had organized quickly in response to the protesting Blacks, but what if they already existed? What if Laquan's "victim," Mr. Guthrie, had been one of them?

"Why the pitchfork design? Such a brutal tool." Her mouth twisted in disgust.

"The group reveres Governor Benjamin Tillman. His nickname was 'Pitchfork,' for a threat he made against the president back in the late 1800s. The call themselves 'Red Shirts' after a group he formed. They did . . . they did some pretty terrible things," Caleb said.

"I remember reading about them," she said. "Ugly part of our history. Guess it has a lot of ugly parts."

"Guess so." Caleb couldn't bring himself to remind her that Tillman's group murdered Black people, how Tillman himself bragged about how whites should demonstrate their superiority by massacring as many as they could. What must it be like to be Black and hear something like that? To know that a former governor of your state, a man whose statue has a prominent placement on the statehouse grounds, could be honored for holding such primitive beliefs?

"He was a slave owner, Mama. Did horrible things," Laquan said.

She huffed out a breath. "I've learned it's best not to dwell on that part of the past. It just makes you bitter. Best keep your eyes forward, Laquan."

"But that past is biting us in the butt," Laquan said.

He had a point. Caleb thought about Mr. Guthrie and the interaction that led to Laquan's explosion and subsequent time in jail. Perhaps Guthrie wasn't such an innocent victim after all.

Chapter Twenty-One

"You've seen the news today?" Detective Claudia Briscoe stood in the doorway to Caleb's office, decked out in police blues—pants, shirt, badge on her chest, hair pulled back in an oddly austere style for her. Curious to see her in uniform.

"No." Caleb glanced at the clock. His next afternoon appointment would arrive in ten minutes.

Claudia entered and dropped into a chair. "You need to see it. Bad incident last night at the protest. We lost one of our own."

"Somebody killed a cop?"

She nodded soberly. "No suspects yet. No witnesses either, except someone you know."

Caleb looked up sharply. "Who?"

"His partner, Officer Mary Beth Branham."

"Mary Beth was there?" He chose his words carefully. He couldn't disclose details about his work with Mary Beth, his efforts to help her contain her anxiety, his worry for her on that stressful job. Or about her complaints regarding Al Fuller. "What happened?"

"We don't know. But Lieutenant Al Fuller died in the Hampton Street parking garage at ten p.m. last night. Preliminary findings are someone struck him in the head with a metal pipe. We don't know much else. Branham doesn't seem to remember what happened. She's a mess, Caleb. I know you've seen her, and we need you to see her again. Pronto. This time it's official. If she has information about what happened locked in that messed up brain of hers, we need you to let it out."

"Excuse me? That's not exactly how it works."

Claudia frowned. "Here's the part where you tell me about confidentiality, blah, blah, blah, and frankly I don't give a crap. We have a dead cop. The stupid-ass Red Shirts are blaming it on the Black protesters. The Black Lives Matter group is denying any knowledge about what happened. We're expecting a big escalation downtown tonight, and honestly, we're not ready for it."

She paused, shaking her head. "When we lose one of our own,

we need a moment. A breath. But instead, we gotta keep idiots from killing each other. It's . . . it's more than just exhausting. We're frayed. So you talk to Officer Branham. She promised me she'd call you today. I don't care if you don't have time in your schedule. Work her in. I'll be calling you later for an update."

"Claudia—" He'd work Mary Beth into his schedule, that wasn't the problem. Disclosing confidential information was a different matter entirely.

She stood, shaking her head. "Don't even start with me. Like I said. I'm fried."

He sighed. "This Lt. Fuller. What do you know about him?"

"I know he's dead. Left a wife behind. Oh, and she's well-connected. Her daddy owns a bunch of gun shops and seems to have some politicians in his pocket. We've been hearing from legislators all morning. Like we need the pressure."

"You didn't know Fuller personally?"

She looked away. "I had a few dealings. Not my favorite guy. Redneck jerk kind of dude who wasn't a fan of people that have my skin tone."

Caleb nodded slowly. Her assessment had matched Mary Beth's. Had his racist attitude gotten Fuller killed?

"I'll be calling you later. Have some answers for me." Claudia approached the door but stopped when she spotted someone standing there. Lonzo Petrocelli, looking at Caleb with a displeased expression. Caleb got that a lot from him.

"Sorry to interrupt, Caleb. I assumed you weren't with a client since the door was open."

"Who are you?" Claudia asked.

Caleb introduced them and Lonzo asked, "Are you here about the Harwell case?"

"Among other things. I have a lot of business with Mr. Knowles."

"It's good that we met then," Lonzo said. "I'm happy to work with you on any police referrals or other contract business you have with our firm."

"Right." Claudia shot Caleb an unhappy look.

"Lonzo is our practice manager. And quality assurance guru. He makes sure I dot my i's and cross my t's." Caleb forced a smile.

"Good luck with that," Claudia said to Lonzo. "But FYI—Caleb does great work for us. He's annoying as hell, which you probably know already, but he's saved my butt more times than I can count. Just hoping he can do that again today."

"Bye, Claudia," Caleb muttered, as she left them.

Lonzo remained, looking less than happy. What had Caleb done this time? Forgotten to log in a progress note? Used too much coffee creamer?

"You have a client waiting."

Of course he did. Why was that an issue?

"Another high-profile client. Lenore Saddington."

"Yes. What's the problem?" Caleb glanced at his watch.

"She is a candidate's wife. Don't you think you might have mentioned that to me?"

"Why would I? Her seeing me is confidential."

"Because her husband is in the news every day. Is there anything I need to know about her condition?"

"You can read my notes. Which are up-to-date, by the way." Caleb tried, unsuccessfully, to keep sarcasm out of his voice.

"Yes. I've read them. Do you think Mrs. Saddington is satisfied with your treatment?"

"She keeps coming back. But therapy is work, Lonzo. My job is to support her and challenge her when she needs it. She doesn't always leave with a smile on her face. That's not the job."

"But she returns. Guess that means she's getting something out of it."

"And somehow, that surprises you." Caleb huffed out a breath. "Are we done? Because I don't like to keep my clients waiting."

"How about check in with me at the end of the day."

He'd rather volunteer for a root canal. "Sure thing, Lonzo."

Lenore Saddington looked better than she had on her last visit: dressed in a crimson suit with an off-white top. Thickish makeup. Beige heels polished.

"Nice to see you, Lenore."

"James said he'd come, too. But I got a text that he might be late."

"I suspect he's pretty busy."

"Always. He's doing a press conference this afternoon so I have to stand beside him. That's my job now, apparently. The stand-beside-candidate-wife. Don't I look the part?"

Caleb didn't respond.

"Today's going to be a hard one, though," she went on. "He's issuing a statement about that dead police officer and about the riots. He was up at five a.m. working on it."

"Sounds intense."

"It will be. He's worried there will be Red Shirts at the presser. They love to attack him every chance they get."

A gentle rap on the door interrupted them. Caleb opened it to find the candidate himself standing there, looking polished and trim, a big politician grin on his face. "Hey, Caleb." James Saddington extended a hand. Caleb took it. The handshake was strong and a little too exuberant. "Sorry I'm late."

"No problem." Caleb gestured that he should sit, noting a slight hesitance before James claimed the chair beside his wife. James was a handsome man. Thick silver hair, perfectly styled. Tall, lean, but broad at the shoulders like a former football player. Blue eyes that held a gaze with an almost unnerving intensity.

He was charismatic. The camera loved him.

"We'll have to keep this short, I'm afraid," James said. "I have an interview at ten."

"Ten?" Lenore frowned. "You said you'd be here for me."

"And I am, honey." He reached for her hand.

Her expression tightened, lips paling.

"I want you to know, Caleb, that Lenore has been wonderful during all this. Magnificent, really. I couldn't run for office without her."

"Sounds like you feel well supported."

"I do. And when she's in front of a camera? She's always beautiful. Poised. Smart."

"Smart? I never say anything. I just . . . stand there." She shook her head, annoyance blooming.

"But I feel stronger. More confident when you're with me. And, given what's going on, that's invaluable to me."

"Lenore, you said you just 'stand there.' What's that like for you?" Caleb prompted.

"I don't love being a trophy wife."

"Trophy wife?" James's eyebrows shot up in surprise. "Honey, you are so much more than that. I can't wait to let the public get to know the real you."

She flinched. "The real me? I'm not sure you've even met her."

James stiffened and released her hand.

Lenore's face softened. "I didn't mean that. Not really."

"What did you mean, then?" James asked. "We've been married seventeen years. What don't I know about you? What aren't you telling me?"

Lenore shot Caleb a pleading look, as though backed into a corner and unsure how to escape.

"Have you told James how you feel about his running for office?" Caleb asked.

She shook her head, looking contrite.

James said, "I know it's been stressful. But I try to protect her and Brian as much as I can."

Lenore shook her head. "You try. But you can't. Brian gets threats at school. He's worrying about things no nine-year-old should even have to think about. You've gotten nasty letters addressed to our home. We are being . . . violated."

Caleb nodded, impressed with her use of that word.

James looked shocked. "You're safe. I'd never do anything to endanger you."

"How do you know we're safe? What guarantees are there? The police patrolling by the house? That didn't stop someone from vandalizing our garage door!"

"Garage door?" Caleb asked.

James sighed. "Someone painted graffiti on it last night."

"Someone walked up our driveway in the black of night and spray painted a pitchfork on it. Brian was the one who discovered it." She closed her eyes for a second, as though picturing it. "He came inside and asked why it was there. And we had to tell him."

"That must have been very hard for you," Caleb said.

"But it's fixable. I've hired someone to come later to paint over it," James said. "Nothing to be upset about."

"Nothing? Jesus, James." Lenore looked away.

"What do you want, Lenore? Should I quit the campaign? Would that make you happy?" Something flashed in James's eyes. A spark. More than anger—fury.

Lenore clutched her arms to her chest. She didn't reply.

"Is this what you've been telling this guy? How victimized you are by my running for office?" James's fury gave way to iciness.

Caleb watched, fascinated. He could see James strategizing—trying to stay in control of his wife, of their situation.

"No," she said softly. "But we have discussed how it's been so much harder than I expected. How much more . . . intrusive. This latest incident is a good example of that."

"Talk more about the intrusiveness," Caleb prompted.

"Reporters at the door. Media trucks in the driveway. My son being harassed. The threatening letters and phone calls." She paused, turning to face her husband. "All the ways that it's changed you."

"Changed me?" He glared at her. Caleb expected to see rage but instead saw a woundedness in his eyes.

She nodded. "It used to be that our family was the most important thing to you. At least, it seemed that way. But now . . . now we're just along for the ride. The only thing that matters to you is winning."

James blinked at her words as though they'd struck him. "That's not true."

"That's how it feels."

James looked at Caleb, as though for support. Caleb said nothing.

James cleared his throat. "This campaign didn't happen because my ego needed the attention. It happened because of our beliefs. Yours and mine, Lenore. Doyle has been abusing his power for years. South Carolina deserves better than that self-serving idiot who's in the pocket of every powerbroker. Our state is ready for gun control. An end to police abuse and corruption. For Black people to be treated fairly and justly. That's why I'm running for office. I thought you believed in those things, too."

James Saddington was convincing, Caleb had to give him that. Heartfelt, though practiced. James's hand found Lenore's again and squeezed.

Lenore looked at their joined hands, her face unreadable. "I do believe in those things. But I also believe our family comes first."

"Of course. Always."

She pivoted to face him. "So what if I said let's stop this. You've made your point, but it's not worth the risk to our son.

You'd throw in the towel? Let Doyle keep his damn seat in the senate?"

Something new flashed in James's eyes. Shock? Exposure? Disappointment? All those things?

But then it vanished. When he looked at his wife, his eyes were kindly. "Is that where we are, Lenore? You really want to let fear control us like that?"

She closed her eyes. A tear trailed down her face. James slid his chair closer, his arm coming around her. He whispered, "We just have a few more months. I'll do whatever you need me to so that you and Brian feel safe. I'll quit if that's the only answer. But maybe we can increase security. Let Brian go stay with his grandparents until the election. You can go, too, if that will make you feel safer. I'm just asking that we try some other options before I bail. Others are counting on me. On us. I don't want to let them down."

Lenore swiped a hand across her cheek. She didn't reply.

"Lenore?" Caleb leaned forward. "What are you thinking about what James said?"

"I want to believe him. I always do." She didn't sound convinced.

"I'll keep you safe," James said. "I promise."

She looked at her husband, her head cocked to the side, assessing. "Okay. We'll try it for a few more weeks. Brian can go to my folks' house. But if anything serious happens—and I mean anything—then I'm done. I will not keep living in fear."

James shook his head. "And I would never ask you to." He took her hand and kissed it. "Thank you."

Caleb leaned back, considering. Maybe they'd reached détente. Or maybe James had manipulated the situation to get exactly what he wanted.

Time would tell.

Chapter Twenty-Two

Caleb pulled his Subaru into the dirt parking lot in front of Guthrie Stop and Shop, a squat brick building with signs advertising "boiled peanuts" and "lottery tickets." He'd passed a few dozen clapboard homes, picturing Laquan and his mother living in one of them, Laquan walking the dusty road to this store for soup—and changing his life forever.

To the left of the building, a small girl tossed a stone into one of several coarsely drawn hopscotch squares. She had dirty blond hair, pale skin, and jumped with the agility of a rabbit as she maneuvered between spaces. She looked to be about seven.

He smiled, remembering Julia at that age. Julia had been less interested in hopscotch but obsessed with her Superman cape and magic Harry Potter wand. Now thirteen, Julia had discovered soccer, civil rights and—unfortunately for Caleb—boys.

Caleb climbed out of his car and approached the building.

"It ain't open yet. My daddy's on his way," the girl said.

"Is your daddy Mr. Guthrie?"

She tossed a rock and hopped over a square. "That's my granddaddy. He's not well enough after that boy beat him up. That Black boy."

Caleb flinched at how she leaned into the word "black." "Maybe I'll wait for your father to open up." He leaned against his car, watching her. Why was she here all alone? "You live nearby?"

"I ain't supposed to talk to strangers." She hopped over two squares, nearly lost her balance, and recovered. "But yeah. Right over there." She pointed to a trailer behind the store. An elderly woman sat in a rocking chair, observing them.

"Daddy's late cuz he was up late last night. Downtown with the people standing up for us."

"Oh?"

She reached the end of the scrawled hopscotch board, spun around and hopped back, chanting, "We are the conquerors, we are the patriots. We are the Red Shirts coming for you. We are the Red Shirts getting what's due."

"That's an interesting verse. Where'd you learn it?"

"My daddy's friends like to say it. We ain't letting them take anything else from us. That's what my daddy says."

Caleb swallowed. Hatred wasn't genetic. It was taught. And this child, at about seven, had been fully indoctrinated. What would she grow into? Would she don a red shirt and riot in the streets?

A pick-up truck kicked up gravel and dust as it skidded into the lot. The man who climbed out—thirty-ish, with a scraggly goatee and long blondish hair—fished keys from his pocket.

"Uncle Vic? Where's Daddy?" the girl asked.

"I told him I'd cover this afternoon. You okay, Bean?" He shot Caleb a suspicious look.

"He's waiting for us to open. Guess he needs to buy something." She picked up her rock and came over to the man.

Vic slid an arm around her shoulders and turned to Caleb. "You a customer or just being nosy? We've had a lot of drop-bys lately."

"Shopping." Caleb tried to imagine what the store had inside and spotted the "lottery" sign on the door. "Megabucks tickets."

"Ah. A gambling man." Vic opened the door, which jingled as he stepped inside. Caleb followed as Vic switched on the light that flickered and hummed above a dozen shelves stocked with food items, magazines, and hunting gear. The scuffed linoleum floor looked like it hadn't been scrubbed since the eighties. The place smelled like tobacco and mold. Caleb pretended to browse, grabbed a pack of chips and a six pack of soda, and placed them on the counter. He caught sight of the bulletin board behind it and approached.

"I like your community message board."

"You live nearby?" Vic asked.

"Not far. Closer to downtown." Caleb feigned interest in a hand-written flyer advertising beagle puppies for sale. Above it, red and glossy like Laquan had described, hung the poster: a pitchfork, stark black against the crimson, with the words, *"We have never recognized the right of the negro to govern white men. And we never will." —Governor Benjamin Tillman.*

"Strong words," Caleb tried to keep his tone affable.

"The right words," Vic said. "The governor was prescient."

"Prescient" seemed an odd word for this man to use.

Vic rang up Caleb's purchases. "How many lottery tickets?"

Caleb, who'd never purchased one, stuttered and said, "Five."

"Quick picks?"

He had no clue what that meant but nodded.

"Power up?"

What the hell? Caleb nodded again.

Vic rang up the total. "Eighteen twenty."

Caleb fished out a twenty and wondered how he'd know if he won. And what he'd do with all the money, after paying for Julia's college. It would be fun imagining.

"That was some rally last night," Caleb said.

"Were you there?"

"I stopped by. Got a little . . . scary."

"Price of freedom, brother." Vic handed him his change. "You are a brother, aren't you?"

Caleb drew a breath, unsure how far to take the lie. "I'm . . . exploring my options."

Vic gave him a penetrating look. "Afraid to take a stand?"

"Maybe afraid of the violence. But I respect the cause."

"Violence is necessary in times like this. When an old man gets beaten to a pulp by a thug, it's time for everyone to take a stand."

"That was a terrible thing." Caleb pictured Laquan. "Thug" couldn't be more inaccurate. Or offensive. "Mr. Guthrie is a relative?"

"Not by blood. But we're all family. There will be consequences for what happened to him."

"Already been plenty."

"Some aren't getting the message. But they might tonight."

"Tonight? Something special planned?" Caleb nearly shivered as he imagined what.

Vic shrugged. "Maybe. You grow some gonads and take a stand, you'll find out."

Even from this racist creep, the insult stung. Caleb snatched up his purchases and left the building. The little girl, Bean, sat on the steps.

"You gonna come back here, mister?"

"I might."

Back in his car, Caleb noticed several texts from his brother. *Checking on you. Everything okay?*

We're fine, he answered. *Just tired of the craziness.*

Same here.

How's the project going?

A pause, and then a photo of a large hand made of a beautiful, burled wood, fingers open as though reaching for something, every knuckle beautifully articulated.

Wow. That's incredible, Caleb wrote.

Wait till you see the rest of it. Gotta run. Be safe.

You, too, brother. Caleb replied, remembering the vandalism at the site, and hoping that for once, his brother would listen to him.

Chapter Twenty-Three

Shull held his daughter while she wept into his chest. "Oh, Peaches. I'm so sorry." He and Glenna had come to her house to find Beryl sitting alone in the dark living room, her face pale with shock.

"What am I going to do, Daddy?"

"Shh, now. It's gonna be alright." His heart ached for her. She'd been at his office when she got the horrible call. It had been her first day, and she was making a mess of a spreadsheet and complaining that the accounts "didn't look right," when a police sergeant arrived and smashed her life to bits.

Glenna appeared with a box of tissues and a glass of water. "Why don't you have some water, Beryl? Don't want you getting dehydrated."

Beryl buried her face in her hands. Shull sat beside her. He could never bear to see his child in pain. At age eight, when her appendix had to come out, he'd promised her anything she wanted when she awoke from anesthesia. The pony had cost him three hundred bucks a month to stable.

"Al was a good man, Daddy. I didn't appreciate him like I should have."

"You were a good wife," Glenna said. "He loved you very much."

Beryl peeked at her between fingers, as though assessing her motivation. Glenna offered a sad smile.

Shull was angry about Al's death. The police said he'd been hit with a steel pipe, and they were looking for his killer. Al's partner, some pathetic, whiny novice, was too traumatized to remember, though she'd reported that Al had chased some black punk into the garage. When they got their hands on him, it would not be pretty.

While Shull would never want Al to be killed, he realized how this murder would inflame both sides which would make him money. Butch had texted him that morning that orders for weapons had nearly doubled—Al's murder would be even better for sales. His lackluster month had turned into his best yet. Al's death was tragic, infuriating, and, oddly, lucrative.

He'd need to get with Tommy Doyle soon, work out a statement about the tragedy before the cucumber came up with some nonsense of his own. Some special language that would reach his base inside a rallying cry for justice. Shull could have Butch prime the pump by outreach on the Red Shirts message board. Hell, he'd even tweet it. "#Justice for Al Fuller" would be trending by dusk.

"Beryl is exhausted," Glenna whispered to Shull. "She needs to get some rest."

Shull reached for his daughter's hand. "Peaches? How about you lie down for a little bit."

"Will you stay here for a while?"

"Absolutely. We'll be here when you wake up." He and Glenna helped Beryl stand and guided her to the bedroom.

When Glenna returned, Shull was in the kitchen, laptop propped on Beryl's granite island, checking orders. "You don't have to stay," he told her.

"She's gonna need a lot of support, Shull."

"Don't I know it."

"She's found some old medication. Tranquilizers I think." Glenna shook her head. "Maybe she should come stay with us for a while."

Shull looked up at her, surprised. "Are you serious?"

"I keep thinking about if you'd been the one killed, how I would feel. Nobody should go through that alone. So yes, I'm serious. She's gotta know she has family. We care about her."

Shull grabbed Glenna around the waist and pulled her close. "I'll talk to her about it when she wakes up."

He kept busy during the two hours Beryl slept—making calls, pulling strings. Preparing for what needed to happen. These were the things he'd always been good at. Helping his kid, though, felt impossible. He tiptoed into her room and switched on the lamp beside his daughter's bed. "Peaches, how do you feel?"

She pulled herself up. Her blond-streaked hair made a chaotic mess atop her head. Black lines of mascara striped her cheeks, but the false lashes stayed in place. "I want this to all be a nightmare I can wake up from."

"I know. I brought you some Mountain Dew. Your favorite." He handed her a glass.

"What time is it?"

"Three-thirty." He glanced out her window. Doyle should be on his way over, followed by the media trucks he'd requested.

"Any news? Did they catch that boy that killed my Al?"

Shull shook his head. "Not yet."

She took a loud slurp from the tumbler. "I think I need another pill."

"Not just yet, hon. I need a favor. I hope you don't mind, but I've done something that may help us find who killed Al."

"What?" Her hand trembled as she placed the glass on the nightstand.

"Tommy Doyle is meeting with the press. He's going to announce that I'm putting up a reward for anyone who has a lead about who did this."

"Thank you, Daddy."

"Tommy suggested—and I agreed—that the presser would have more impact if we did it here. If people could see where Al lived. It makes him real. 'Here's where he lived with his loving wife, in a neighborhood just like yours.' People pay more attention to clips like that. So Tommy wants to do the interview on your front porch. We won't come inside. We don't want to disturb you in anyway. And if you don't want this, just tell me and I'll make sure they don't come." It had been Shull's idea. No way he'd cancel it this close to zero hour, but he knew his kid. She'd say yes.

"Will I have to be on camera?"

"No, honey. I'd never ask you to do that. You stay inside and rest up."

"If you think it will help."

"Okay then. I need to go get a few things set up. You be okay up here?"

"Yeah." She didn't sound convincing.

He left the lamp on and shut the bedroom door behind him. When he returned to the living room, the doorbell rang, and he let in Tommy Doyle.

"We good to go?" Tommy had on a polyester suit and silk tie; his sparse hair artistically combed to cover the bald spot that couldn't really be hidden.

Shull nodded.

"I've been working on my statement." Tommy handed him three printed pages.

Shit. Shull carried the speech into the kitchen and pulled out his red sharpie. As expected, Tommy's "statement" was an unmitigated disaster. Why had he included campaign promises about criminalizing abortion, banning medical marijuana, and voter ID?

"You're veering way off message here, Tommy."

"I don't see how. I talk about Al and the riots for half a page."

"And then you turn this into a stump speech. The media won't give a shit about all this." Shull marked through the last two pages.

Tommy scowled. "I've been doing this a long time, Shull. It's important to take advantage of opportunities with the media."

Shull didn't need for Tommy to exert his independence just then. Or anytime, for that matter. "You are standing on my daughter's porch to talk about her husband's death. To scream for justice. To pledge an end to the attacks against our men and women in blue. Don't dilute the message with this other BS."

Tommy's frown deepened.

"Look, I get your point about the media. But this is for Beryl. Also, I need you to say these words at the end of your speech. See it as a call to action." Shull wrote the words "The time is now. Justice for Al." Hell, it almost rhymed.

"I like it." Tommy looked placated.

"This comes at the end, Tommy. This needs to be the last thing you say." This was an important detail. In the Red Shirts chat room, Butch had told the community to listen for those words. They would signal the time to act.

The arrival of the media trucks caused some commotion on Beryl's street. Neighbors came out of their houses to watch. Tommy waved like he was in a Founder's Day parade, all grins and cheeriness, until Shull once again reminded him of the somberness of this occasion.

Not for the first time, he wondered if he could have chosen a more stupid candidate to support.

Microphone cords stretched from the trucks to stands set up on Beryl's walkway. Newscasters conducted sound checks with camera operators. Tommy stood on the porch, smiling as though he owned the world.

"Somber, Tommy," Shull whispered. "Someone died. And stick to the script."

Tommy cleared his throat and adjusted his expression, chameleon that he was. Once all the media had claimed their spaces on the walkway, Tommy approached the microphones. "I have a brief statement." He spoke with more volume than needed, but he got their attention.

"I'm here, standing at the home of Lieutenant Al Fuller, a decorated officer of the Columbia Police Department, a man assassinated last night while doing his job of protecting the good citizens of our community."

Tommy glanced at him, and Shull nodded in encouragement.

"Al leaves behind a widow, Beryl Lassiter Fuller, a family who loved him, colleagues on the force who grieve him, and a myriad of friends and neighbors who already feel this profound loss." He stumbled on "myriad." Shull should have written "a whole lot of" which was more Tommy's speed.

"Al's wife, Beryl, is the daughter of Shull Lassiter, one of our county's most upstanding citizens. Shull, would you like to say something?"

Shit. The last thing Shull wanted was to appear on camera. Tommy was way off script.

"As you can see, he's been traumatized by the death of his son-in-law," Tommy said. "But he wants the city to know that he's offering a reward for any information that leads to the apprehension of Al Fuller's murderer." Tommy took a step closer, eying the cameras like they were his kin. "He's offering thirty thousand dollars to anyone who helps us catch this fiend. That's right. Thirty thousand dollars. So if you know who did this. If it's one of your friends, or someone you saw on the streets last night, just come forward and help us put him behind bars. You'll be doing a great service to the community and to the family."

"Dammit, Tommy. Say the words," Shull whispered.

Tommy blinked, cast a panicked glance at Shull, then returned to the cameras. "The time is now. Justice for Al." Then louder: "The time is now! Justice for Al!"

That would have been the perfect end to the press conference, except the front door opened. Beryl emerged from the house, wearing a pink minidress, her hair a disheveled mess, her makeup looking like it had been applied by a three-year-old. She stumbled over the threshold as she wove her way unto the porch.

"Shit," Shull grumbled.

"Daddy?" She blinked at the TV cameras.

Shull hurried to her, sliding an arm around her and trying to guide her back to the house. "But wait. I want to talk to the news people," Beryl slurred. She must have taken something to settle her nerves.

"She's . . . not well," Shull said to them.

"I'm not well," Beryl repeated. "I'm not well because somebody killed my Al. Please, y'all, help us find the evil person who killed my husband!" She crumpled then, Shull catching her, begging the camera operators to quit filming but this made for excellent television.

Tommy stepped forward, hands outstretched, shielding her. "That's enough folks. You can see the pain she's in. Let's give this family some privacy."

Thank you, Jesus, Shull whispered, tugging his daughter back into the house.

Chapter Twenty-Four

Caleb stared at the TV where the news replayed segments from Rep. Tommy Doyle's press conference. "Let's give this family some privacy," Doyle said.

Following the footage, live shots from the riots downtown aired but to Caleb it could have been a recent report from the Mideast. Smoke. Flash bombs. Fires. Shouts. And, most terrifying of all, gun shots. "Jesus," he whispered.

"Unbelievable." Shannon had her suitcase packed and her knapsack loaded. "I'm wondering whether I should leave right now."

"I don't want you to go, but they need you in DC." The trip had been planned for weeks. Shannon was meeting with funders who donated to Safe Harbor, the shelter for folks struggling with homelessness. Funding was always an issue. "Maybe you should take me and Cleo with you."

At the sound of her name, Cleo looked up from her napping spot on the sofa. Shannon reached over to pat her head. "You won't quite fit in my suitcase, girl." She turned to Caleb. "Promise me you won't do anything stupid while I'm gone."

"Trust my inner cowardice, my dear. I'm avoiding downtown like the plague."

She kissed him. "I love that about you."

On the television, they replayed the scene of Beryl Fuller's meltdown and her father pulling her away from the cameras. It would be seen a million times, Caleb suspected. Fodder for a hungry audience, feeding off the tragedy of others.

"That guy. I hate him. And kind of love him." Shannon pointed to the father.

"Who is he?"

"Shull Lassiter, owner of Lassiter Munitions. You've seen the billboards."

"Damn. He has like a dozen stores, doesn't he?"

"And a huge online business, because we need to make ownership of assault weapons as easy as possible."

"So I see why you hate him. Tell me about the love part."

"He gave fifteen thousand dollars to Safe Harbor last month. We were really hurting to keep the lights on, and it saved us."

"You saved Safe Harbor. If he gave it's because you convinced him."

"More like he needed the tax write-off, but we'll take it. Sometimes I feel like a whore for that shelter." She scowled as though she'd tasted a bad avocado.

"Your work is critically important. I tell everyone that."

"It's sexy, too," she said with a laugh. "Just this morning I got to unload seventy pounds of frozen meat. Then I mopped the kitchen after a package broke. And there was that issue with the toilet in the afternoon . . ."

"That is sexy." He gave her a quick kiss. "What time's your flight?"

"I need to leave soon."

"You sure you don't want me to drop you off?"

"Nah. I'll leave the car at the airport." She reached for his hand. "Promise to stay out of trouble while I'm gone?"

"Absolutely. Knock 'em dead, Shannon." He carried the suitcase out to her car and kissed her goodbye. She'd be gone for five days. Five long days.

"Say hi to your mistress for me." She laughed as she drove away.

Caleb returned inside the empty house, sat on the sofa, and smiled when Cleo laid her head in his lap. "Just you and me, girl."

The news showed more of the riots. On one side, shouts of "Black Lives Matter" resounded. On the other, "Justice for All!" Tempers flared. Violence escalated.

He thought about Mary Beth, hoping she wasn't watching the same footage. The pressure on her to remember had to be daunting, but it would only happen when—and if—she was ready to face it. She'd done good work in their last session, but she remained fragile and traumatized.

When his cellphone rang, he frowned. His ex-wife Margo in Charlotte wanted to Facetime. That only happened when she was displeased about something. He grumbled as he accepted the call.

"What's up?"

Margo's face filled the screen. She'd always been beautiful but her features had hardened with age. Her blond hair cropped short. Angular cheekbones more pronounced. Her forehead and lips unnaturally smooth, probably from Botox. "Julia. She's determined to go to Columbia and join the protest. I caught her trying to reserve a spot on a charter bus heading down there just a little while ago."

"She planned to come by herself?" His voice rose in alarm. His kid was way too young for a venture like that.

"She argued that she'd be with some friends from school who were taking the bus but wouldn't give me any names. I told her absolutely not so of course she's not speaking to me now. Caleb, did you put this idea in her mind? She keeps saying she's talking with you about the protests."

He closed his eyes and swallowed the curse words that tried to come out whenever he talked with Margo. "We did discuss them but I told her, quite clearly, that she should not join them. It's too dangerous."

"I know. She's only thirteen. Going on twenty, though. We've been watching the news. Paul's worried the riots will spread to Charlotte."

"Is he?" Caleb had tried to like Margo's new husband. He really had. Paul was smart (according to both Margo and Julia), had a successful career as an oral surgeon, and gave them a nice home in a safe neighborhood. He attended all of Julia's dance recitals but never tried to usurp Caleb's role in her life, which he appreciated. But he had the personality of a two-by-four. Caleb remembered a torturous fifteen-minute conversation about their late mail delivery while waiting for Julia's middle school Christmas concert to begin. He'd texted Sam, "I wish Margo had married a real boy," and Sam had replied, "Give the guy a chance."

Margo sighed. "Can you talk to her? Please? I need her to calm down before she does something rash."

"Sure. Put her on."

When Julia's face appeared, he saw tears among the freckles. "Hey, Peanut."

"Don't call me that," she said with a furious swipe of a hand across her face. "Did Mom tell you what she did? That I can't come to the protest?"

"Yes. And I agree with her." He winced when he saw the look of betrayal flash across her face.

"He's just a few years older than me," she said.

"Who?"

"Laquan Harwell. Think about it. They're treating him like he's . . . he's nothing. They almost killed him, Dad! Just for being Black."

"It's a little more complicated than that, but I hear what you're saying."

"Do you?" Her voice rose. "Because you're not out there. You're not at the statehouse demanding justice for Laquan."

There was so much he wished he could tell her. That he knew Laquan. That he was doing what he could for the boy. That he'd try anything to keep him from going back to jail. "No, I'm not. And you know why? Because things are getting too violent. I won't participate in anything that leads to people getting hurt."

She seemed to mull that over. Then she asked, "Daddy, are you afraid?"

Oh hell. How to answer that one. He drew a breath and said. "Yes. I'm afraid for my town. I'm afraid for the innocent people who will get hurt in all this. And yes, I'm afraid for Laquan. I know you feel very strongly about this. Why don't you write about it? An essay. A journal. Or even a letter—you could write Laquan if you want. Put your emotions on paper. It may help you feel less powerless."

"I'd feel less powerless if I could come there."

He smiled. "You're coming on Sunday, but we're not going downtown. Not unless the protests are over. Sorry, Peanut, but that's how it's going to be."

She frowned, but then seemed to relent. "I'll try writing something."

"Bring it with you. I can't wait to see it. You're the best writer I know."

She rolled her eyes and it made him smile. "Daaaaad."

"Love you, Peanut."

"I told you not to call me that."

"Sorry. Hard habit to break."

Chapter Twenty-Five

Shull arrived at the diner at ten before nine to meet his friend/confidant/business associate Butch. He tried to summon interest in breakfast, but after the long night with his inconsolable daughter, he had little appetite.

He logged into the Red Shirt feed where *The time is now. Justice for Al* had started trending. It gratified Shull to see so many new members added to the Red Shirt group. REBEL SON was on quite a roll: a two-page diatribe about what he planned to do when they caught the "son-of-a-bitch who slaughtered a man in blue." The dude went off the rails with mentions of dismemberment and "the end of the Negro race once and for all."

But Shull had to admire his passion. He sent a private message offering half off the cost of the new Spectre assault weapon, "to help in your quest for justice."

ZION signed on: *That poor grief-stricken woman on TV last night. I'm praying for her.*

WARRIOR ALPHA: *Gonna take more than prayers.*

VICTORY IS OURS: *Eradicate them all!*

Shull needed to settle them down. Someone going off half-cocked could prove dangerous.

PITCHFORK: *When the time is right.*

VICTORY IS OURS: *How will we know?*

PITCHFORK: *You'll get the signal from me.*

VICTORY IS OURS: *And who the hell are you?*

Shull felt a spark of anger. He wasn't used to being challenged. Few dared to do it. He prepared to respond when Zion did it for him: *Pitchfork is our leader. If you can't accept that, you have no place here.*

A long pause, then Victory replied: *I'll wait for his signal.*

Butch arrived and Shull signed off. This was Butch's favorite restaurant, and Shull suspected he ate most of his meals there. He ordered fried eggs, hash browns, and biscuits so laden with butter that they dripped. Shull settled for toast and jam. He studied his friend, thinking how different they were. While Shull had always been loquacious, Butch could go hours without speaking. Shull finished college, Butch dropped out of tech school. Shull enjoyed living in a 6,000 square foot manor, while Butch lived in a secluded trailer north of town by choice—he worked for Shull and could afford something much nicer. From what Shull could tell, Butch spent most of his money on the most elaborate array of computers and tech equipment he'd ever seen.

He paid Butch under the table because that was where Butch operated. He managed all of Shull's less legal enterprises, including black market arms transactions handled via the dark web. Butch was a ninja at finding his way around the cyber-underground. He left no digital footprint that could be traced and found ways to sell automatic weapons and handguns that made a three hundred percent profit. A deal Shull couldn't pass up.

"New guy in the chat room is a bit off kilter," Shull said. "Handle is 'Victory is Ours.'"

"Oh. Vic." Butch wore a baseball cap that covered a bald spot. His grayish beard grew long and unkempt, and his clothes could have come from the Goodwill store, but Butch couldn't care less. He was a unicorn. A lone wolf. And a freakin' genius. He pointed to the ketchup and Shull slid it over to him.

"Anything I need to know about this 'Vic?'"

Butch tapped his cell and pulled up an invoice, which he showed Shull. Twelve thousand dollars' worth of Shull's guns sold to this "Vic."

Shull lifted a coffee cup and toasted this news.

The server, a plump, elderly woman who had learned to speak "Butch" refilled their coffees. "Y'all need anything else?"

Butch shook his head.

"Leaving y'all alone then. I'll be in the kitchen if you need me."

The two men spoke in code. Or rather, Shull spoke, Butch nodded, made a few grunting sounds of confusion when he wanted something clarified, and nodded at the end of Shull's request. To describe Butch as taciturn was like saying July in Columbia was a tad warm. Shull was pretty sure Butch allotted himself five words a day and didn't want to blow them all at once.

"Any luck finding Al's killer?"

Butch shook his head.

"I want him taken care of, Butch."

Butch's response was a quirk of his eyebrows that spoke volumes. He knew how important this was. His talents extended beyond computers. He had connections in Columbia's underbelly that often proved useful.

"Things still okay downtown?" Shull asked.

Butch took a bite of eggs and lowered his fork. The sun winked through gingham curtains and highlighted the curly threads of white in Butch's beard. "Wondering if we need to escalate."

"Escalate? How?" Shull asked.

Butch added more ketchup to the hash browns. "Bring in more out-of-towners. There's a group in North Carolina that's expressed interest in joining. And the Knights of the Promise out of Georgia would be good additions."

"Not sure I want the specifics." Shull buttered his toast as he considered the suggestion. "But the more the merrier, I guess. Fuel for the fire. Maybe they'll be interested in buying some guns."

After wiping his hands with a napkin, Butch pulled out a small tablet and flicked on a spreadsheet of Shull's sales over the last week. He slid it over to Shull.

"Point made." Shull sipped his coffee and considered the idea.

"We might want to bring in a . . . specialist." Butch leaned in close and whispered, "Someone to take care of Al's killer."

Jesus. Was Butch talking about hiring an assassin? Shull pictured his grieving child: Beryl sobbing in bed. Stumbling into the kitchen with that strange, twisted expression on her face. Staring out the window as though she needed to erase time.

"Up to you," Butch said.

"I can't bear seeing Beryl like this. She's my little girl. You saw her on TV. You saw how she is."

Butch kicked him under the table and cocked his head toward the door. Two men had entered the quiet restaurant. They'd need to be more discreet.

Shull whispered, "I'm fine about other groups joining but

I'm not sure about the other thing. Give me some time."

Butch took a bite of biscuit. Crumbs tumbled into his beard.

"Were you able to dig up any dirt on James Saddington? Or is he still Mr. Perfect?"

Butch swiped a hand across his chin. "You have to decide how deep you want to go."

"Meaning?"

"Meaning I may have something on the wife."

Shull shook his head. If his little girl was off limits, then Saddington's wife should be, too. Unless things got desperate.

Then he'd do whatever the hell he had to do.

Chapter Twenty-Six

Mary Beth sat across from her therapist, sunken in her chair, wishing she could vanish in the cushions and never be heard from again.

Her world had changed seventeen hours ago and she wasn't even sure what had happened.

"Mary Beth?" Caleb looked concerned.

"Sorry. I'm a little . . . foggy." She had finally gotten some sleep when Paloma gave her an Ambien, but it left her mealy-headed.

"I was asking about how you were managing the anxiety," Caleb said.

"Not so well." She ground a hand against an eye that felt coated with sand. Her tongue had become thick and dry. "I tried what you suggested, but things just got too . . . intense."

"I'm sure they did." Caleb stood, crossed to his small refrigerator, and pulled out a bottle of water, which he placed before her. "I'm so sorry about what happened."

"Sorry? I guess I am, too." She opened the bottle and gulped a good bit down.

"I know that you and Lt. Fuller had some disagreements, but he was your partner. This has to be very difficult for you."

She nodded, picturing Al. Puffed up Al, bulging out of his uniform. Scowling Al, displeased at something she'd done. Laughing Al, making fun of a Black kid they once arrested.

Crumpled Al. On the ground. Bleeding out. But what had happened to him? What led to that image? She couldn't reach the memory. It had to be there. That's what the investigating detective had said: *"You were there, Branham. You're the only one who witnessed the murder of a cop. You have to tell us what happened."*

And she'd wanted to, but she had no words. The memories remained out of reach. What could she say? "I had a panic attack that made me hyperventilate. I think I passed out," would not have gone over well.

"Mary Beth? Looks like I lost you." Caleb sounded concerned.

"Sorry. Yeah, it's been hard. Just wish I could remember what happened."

"I think you will, in time."

She swallowed, said nothing.

Caleb tried another tack. "How did you sleep last night?"

"Like the dead. Thank you, Ambien."

Her therapist jotted something down on his notepad. He was always doing that. She wished she could read it. She pictured her name and the phrase, "batshit crazy" beside it.

"When do you plan to go back to work?"

"I think that depends on you. Detective Briscoe insisted I have the week off, but she said I'd need a counselor release before I can work a shift."

He nodded. "Are you anxious to return?"

"No." She felt strongly about that. She wasn't sane enough to wear a uniform, and now all the other cops knew it.

Caleb sat there, asking no questions, just looking kind. Sympathetic.

"You haven't asked me what happened last night. Everybody else has. 'Tell us what you remember. In detail.' Only I don't have much to say."

"Do you want to talk about it?"

She did. And she didn't. She understood how important it was. Al's death was inflaming the Red Shirts. Their numbers on the streets had already doubled, according to Paloma. Many of them armed. Their tone changing, becoming more aggressive. Jesus, it was going to be a bloodbath. "Everyone's saying that a Black guy killed him. But how do they know that?"

"That's an excellent question."

"I remember going into the parking garage. Following Fuller, who was chasing a university student we'd encountered before. I remember being scared for that kid because Fuller was pissed even before we got there. He was looking for a reason to go off. And he had a grudge against Simon."

"Simon?"

"Simon Madigan is his name. He was a smart ass, but he didn't deserve what Fuller dished out. I remember being nervous when I ran into the garage. But there was so much smoke from the flash grenades and tear gas cannisters. It was hard to breathe. Harder to see."

"Sounds frightening."

She nodded slowly, some memories surfacing. "There were some men in red shirts there. Like . . . like they were meeting or something, and Al was approaching them. I don't know where Simon went. Before I got to the structure—the anxiety hit me. I lost my breath. Got a little dizzy. But I pulled it together. At least I think I did. And went to find Fuller." She paused for another swallow of water. Her thirst was unquenchable.

"Was it a panic attack?"

"Yes. I did the breathing thing, and pictured the ocean, and . . . settled down."

Had she, though? She remembered fighting for breath. Trying to focus. Her body not really hers.

"What are you thinking about?"

She gulped again. Capped the bottle. "How it felt. It's happened before."

"You mean the panic attack?"

"The feeling of detachment. Like it's not my body but it is. Like I'm . . . somewhere else."

Caleb leaned forward. "You felt that before? When?"

"A few times. When I was a kid. When things got bad at home. When Dad—" she froze, not wanting to remember. Always trying not to remember.

"When your dad what?"

"Got drunk. Lost his temper." She blinked, not wanting the images anywhere close to her. Dad looming over her, holding the belt. The words he spewed, the fury that fed on itself.

Caleb was watching her with those kind eyes. She saw him wince, as though he could see what she was trying not to.

"I'm so sorry, Mary Beth."

"For what?" she whispered.

"For the abuse. No child should have to deal with that." He kept his voice low and gentle.

She closed her eyes. She never cried. Never let herself. But now the tears forced themselves out, dribbling down her cheeks and off her chin. Her tears, unshed for so many years.

"It's over now. Done," she said.

"Sometimes the trauma stays inside us and resurfaces when

something triggers it. I think that's what you're feeling now. And maybe what you felt last night."

She blinked, wanting to stop the tears but they kept coming. A fountain of them.

One evening came to mind, as it often did. She'd been nine, or ten. The family watching Roseanne on TV. Sodas and popcorn on the table. Dad in his La-Z-Boy. Mom in the upholstered chair she'd gotten when grandma died, crocheting. Mary Beth and her brother, Thomas, stretched out on the scratchy plaid sofa, fighting for space because they fought over everything. Thomas kicked her. She kicked back.

Roseanne said something that made Dad laugh.

Thomas threw popcorn at Mary Beth. Dad yelled, "Stop that."

Mary Beth kicked him again and he replied by shoving her off the couch. She nudged the table, their glasses toppling the floor. Sticky soda spilled everywhere.

Dad propelled himself up, eyes wide with rage. His hand was huge as it struck her, fast as a hornet's sting.

"Mary Beth?" Caleb sounded concerned. "What are you thinking about?"

"One of the bad times. I spilled something and Dad . . . Dad got mad. It hurt."

Caleb watched her.

"But the thing I remember most is so weird. It's not Dad and what he did to me. It's—" She hesitated, stumbling on the image that so often flashed in her mind.

"It's what?"

"It's Mom. Sitting in her chair, crocheting. Not stopping. Not looking up. Dad's pounding me over something stupid, Thomas is begging him to stop, and Mom's just . . . there with her yarn. Don't think she even dropped a stitch." Mary Beth drained the bottle.

"When you remember that, how do you feel?"

"Desperate. Or that's how I felt then. Why was she just sitting there? Why didn't she do something?"

"She was your mother. She should have protected you."

Mary Beth stared at him, but in her mind, she was staring at Mom. The needle in her hand, the long strand of blue yard ending in a ball of it beside her. She didn't even look upset.

Not worried or frightened for her child. Indifferent.

"Mary Beth? You keep drifting away from me."

She blinked, his face swimming into focus. "Sorry. I keep picturing her. Sitting there. Doing nothing." She spat out the last word.

"That makes her complicit."

"Yes. She was a co-conspirator. Never crossed him. Ever." She twirled the bottle in her hand. "I don't remember anything else about that night. Except his hand coming at me. Her hands working the yarn. Then it all goes blank. Next thing I remember is the following morning. Looking in the mirror at the bruises."

Caleb's nod looked sorrowful, as though he truly understood what she'd been through.

"She gave me the throw," Mary Beth said.

"What?"

"The blue and white throw she was crocheting. When she finished it, she gave it to me. I still have it."

Caleb stared, something churning behind his eyes.

"What?" she demanded.

"How do you feel about that throw?"

"Honestly? I hate it. Loathe it. Want to burn it. I shoved it up in a closet, so I don't have to see it. Now I can't stand to see anything that's been crocheted. Sweaters. Doilies. Anything. It repulses me."

"Why don't you get rid of it?"

"Honestly? I don't know. Loyalty, I guess."

"We keep things that have sentimental value. I'm not sure that throw conjures up the right sentiment," Caleb said.

Maybe he was right. Maybe she should toss it out. Maybe that would help her get her shit together because God knew, something had to help. She couldn't keep living like this.

Caleb's desk phone dinged. She checked the clock above it. "I can't believe I've been here a whole hour."

He smiled. "You did some good work today."

"I did?"

He nodded. "I know this is frustrating for you. Not remembering what happened to your partner. And you're getting pressure to remember, which doesn't help. My guidance is to tell them you're doing all you can because you are. If they get obnoxious, you can send them to me. Also—our psychiatrist, Dr. Rhyker, has a clinic day tomorrow. I'd like to get you on his schedule. He may want to prescribe something to help you manage the anxiety."

"No."

"Mary Beth—"

"I know you mean well, but I need to manage this on my own. No meds." If she was prescribed something, it might interfere with her ability to do the job. She couldn't risk it.

"Okay." Caleb sounded frustrated. "We'll hold off on that for now."

"Thanks, Caleb."

Chapter Twenty-Seven

Caleb finished a session with a nine-year-old boy whose divorcing parents were engaged in endless conflict about child custody. Both wanted Caleb to testify, to choose them as the better parent, and the kid wanted nothing more than for the legal proceedings to be done. He used the sessions with Caleb as a place of sanctuary. No sides chosen except his. No ulterior motives. Just fifty-five minutes of playing Jenga and letting out his frustration, grief, and anger in tumbling hunks of wood. When the session was over, Caleb requested to meet with both parents the following week, hoping to help them see what their conflict was doing to their son.

"See you next week," the boy said, his face a little sad as he left.

Caleb sighed as he headed to the waiting area to collect his next client. Lonzo stopped him midway.

"Caleb. I need to see you for a second." Lonzo's expression got him nervous. What had he done this time? He was a little behind on his notes, but no more than usual. He'd clocked out for lunch yesterday. He even wore the damn name tag.

When he got to Lonzo's office, Claudia Briscoe waited in the doorway. She looked off. Clothes a little disheveled. Hair out of place. Her usual heels replaced with black gym shoes. Worst of all was her expression—worried. It was her very concerned face.

"What's wrong?" He demanded.

"Two explosions across from the Capitol this morning."

"Across?"

She nodded. "They blew up Sam's workshop."

His breath caught. "Sam?"

"Injured. On his way to the hospital."

"Okay." Caleb spun around and hurried to his office for his car keys. He said nothing to Lonzo about leaving, assuming he'd have Caleb's sessions canceled. Before Caleb reached the exit, Claudia intercepted him.

"You're riding with me," she said. Not a request.

He didn't argue.

She filled him in on details as she drove. Two pipe bombs. The first struck the new sculpture, exploding it to splinters of wood and shards of metal. Projectiles that injured a man walking by. The second targeted the workshop. Sam had run inside where another artist had been working. The ceiling collapsed on him and knocked him unconscious. He'd inhaled smoke. Firefighters got him out before more damage was done.

"The other artist is fine, by the way. A woman named Amanda Stockdale. She ran out the rear of the building as soon as she heard the first explosion."

"Thank God for that," was all Caleb said.

Claudia used lights and sirens, weaving through traffic with the experience of a twenty-year veteran police officer. Caleb gripped the dashboard and tried not to imagine how bad Sam's injuries might be. Catastrophizing came too easy to him.

When they reached the hospital, social worker Quinn Merrick waited at the entrance, offering him a sympathetic smile. "Hey Caleb."

"My brother—"

"Is on his way for a CT scan. He was conscious when he arrived. Oriented."

Caleb savored these nuggets of information.

Quinn introduced herself to Claudia and said, "They told me we had a VIP enroute. Had no idea your brother was the famous artist."

"VIP?" Caleb had never thought of Sam that way.

"Yep. That's a good thing. It's why he's already getting scanned." She walked with him to the waiting area. Claudia said she needed to get back to the site.

"Thanks for getting me," he said to her.

"Text me when you have news."

News came an hour later, when Quinn returned with a doctor in tow. He was a small, bald guy with round wire-frame glasses and a harried expression. "He's doing okay," the doctor said. "Scans looked good except for the concussion. And his lungs are little inflamed, but all in all, he's a very lucky guy."

"If he was lucky, he wouldn't be here at all," Caleb answered.

Quinn stepped closer. "We're going to keep him overnight, but that's more of a precaution than anything. Part of that VIP service."

Caleb was relieved that they'd keep a close eye on him, something he planned to do as well.

"We've got him set up in a room if you want to go see him," Quinn said.

For the next two hours, Caleb did not move from his spot by Sam's bed. Even when the nurse came and said visiting hours were over. Even when the tech took vitals. Even when Quinn suggested he get some rest, promising to let him know if anything changed.

Not even when the nurse assured him that Sam was just sedated, that they hadn't found any significant brain injury despite the nasty bruise blooming on his forehead. "The oxygen cannula is to help his lungs heal from the smoke. He's strong and his vitals are good." But Caleb knew he belonged at his brother's side. When Sam awoke, he would need someone who could communicate with him. No hospital staff on the floor knew sign language, Caleb had checked. And he wanted to be here when Sam opened his eyes, because Caleb had a *lot* to say to him.

The vigil brought back hard memories—the worst being Sam's motorcycle accident at sixteen, Caleb waiting for him to regain consciousness, only to find himself in a completely silent world. And it stayed that way.

Caleb had been here, in this same spot (different room, different hospital, different circumstance but so very much the same). Had seen the confusion on Sam's face, the grief filling his eyes when he realized what he'd lost. Had held Sam's hand like a tether, chanting "we'll figure it out" to ears that couldn't hear.

He blinked back unexpected tears at the memory. Hospitals often made his emotions raw. Trauma seeking an outlet to resurface. Stupid feelings. God, he hated having them.

Sam looked pale. The lines that highwayed his face deepening. Caleb's gaze traveled the long length of him, fixing on his leg. Cancer hid in that bulging muscle. Stupid cancer.

If Sam had gone ahead with the surgery to remove it, he wouldn't have been at the studio when the explosion happened. He wouldn't be here in this bed, looking so . . . vulnerable. He may have even gotten good results instead of the awful news that Caleb feared waited for them. But no, Sam had refused.

Caleb stood abruptly, the chair scraping back, and moved to the window.

"Caleb?"

He spun around at the female voice. Amanda Stockdale stood at the foot of Sam's bed, staring down at the sleeping man. "How is he?"

Caleb approached. "He's going to be okay. Just sedated right now."

Tears appeared in her soft brown eyes. "It's my fault. He thought I was still inside the workshop."

"Not your fault. Sam's just . . . like that."

She crossed her arms as though chilled. She wore a peasant top over jeans, her long brown hair hanging loose. She was more attractive than Caleb remembered. "He's so damn brilliant. It's raw talent—I mean, he's had the training and all, but his instincts are incredible. And his ability to envision forms, to see beyond the materials—I've worked with a lot of artists but nobody like him. He's . . . he just has to be okay."

Caleb wondered if she knew about the cancer. It wasn't his place to tell her.

She sighed and stepped closer, touching Sam's hand as though reassuring herself that he was alive. "I'm learning how to sign."

Caleb's brows lifted. "You are?"

"Sam doesn't know. I want to surprise him. I've taken an on-line class and now I'm working with a tutor. It's not easy, but I love it." She signed the last sentence, a fist skimming her chin and flicking outward.

"He'll be touched that you're learning. It means a lot. People are always relieved that he reads lips so well, but it takes tremendous concentration, and he still misses stuff."

"I know. I don't want him ever missing anything."

"Me neither." Caleb wondered if someone had yelled out when Sam entered the exploding building. Words of warning he hadn't heard.

She stepped back from the bed. "He's a very special person,

isn't he?"

Caleb searched her face, seeing unexpected affection there. Did Sam even know?

She approached the door. "Tell him I stopped by. I'll be back later."

"I will."

She started to leave but turned back. "Are you okay, Caleb? You look . . . stressed."

"I'm good. Be better when he's out of here."

"You and me both."

It was a few minutes after she left that a weak voice uttered, "Hey."

Caleb looked up to see blue eyes—open eyes—watching him. "Hey," he signed.

"You look like shit."

"You're a beauty yourself. But the doctor says you're doing good," Caleb signed, then detailed his injuries: smoke inhalation from the fire. Hematoma on his head from where the ceiling crashed in on him and sent him careening into the sawhorse.

Sam nodded. "The others?"

"Everybody is good. You were the only one stupid enough to run into the building after the first bomb went off."

"Amanda was inside." Sam jerked up, eyes wide with panic. "I couldn't get to her."

"She got out on her own. Turns out, she didn't need some idiot hero coming to save her. She was just here checking on you."

"I'm glad she's okay."

Caleb could see the wheels turning in Sam's head slowly pick up speed. "Our work?"

The question he'd expected. "Total loss. I'm sorry, Sam."

Sam blinked as the dark truth set in. "We're alive. That's what matters."

"No shit." Caleb was surprised by the surge of anger clipping his signs.

Sam looked confused. Caleb cleared his throat, wanting to push the unwanted emotion down, but it wasn't going anywhere. Finally, Sam said, "What's wrong?"

Caleb leaned forward, glaring at him.

"What?" Sam repeated.

He knew he shouldn't say anything. Should just let it go, but he couldn't. "What you did was incredibly stupid. You could have been killed. Do you even get that?" His brother couldn't hear his voice quake but caught the tremble in his hands.

Sam watched him. Didn't reply.

Caleb huffed out a breath, grabbed a plastic water cup and filled it from a pitcher. "Want this?"

Sam nodded, took it, drained the cup in a few quick swallows. Handed it back. Watched him.

"I need to go check on the dog. I'll tell the nurse you're awake. Need anything while I'm out?" Caleb asked.

"My phone? It was in the truck. Is my truck okay?"

"It didn't blow up if that's what you're asking. I'll fetch your phone. Be back in an hour or so."

Chapter Twenty-Eight

Caleb didn't need to return to the hospital. After leaving Sam, he'd Ubered to the office to get his car and received a text from his brother: *Amanda just brought my phone. I'm fine. See you tomorrow.* It was just as well. Caleb needed a little time alone to get his shit together.

Those plans were interrupted when someone rang his doorbell. Cleo thumped her body against the door in apparent glee over whoever was on the other side. With reluctant steps, Caleb answered the door.

The man on his stoop—tall, lean, hair whiter than it used to be, wire-rim glasses and frosted eyebrows that matched his mustache—held a six-pack of Allagash White.

"Matthew?"

His unexpected visitor smiled. "I'm only following instructions." He handed Caleb his phone. Caleb read a series of texts:

Any plans this evening? From Sam.

Nothing that can't wait. What do you need? Nice to hear from you, BTW.

Can you buy some beer and go talk sense into my idiot brother?

"Sam even Venmo'ed me the money for the beer."

"Sam's an asshole," Caleb said.

"Well, obviously." Matthew held up the beer. "Can I come in?"

Caleb gripped the door as Matthew entered and greeted an enthusiastic sheepdog. "We're both showing our gray, aren't we, old girl?"

They moved to the living room. Matthew handed him a bottle and opened one for himself, setting the rest on the table between them. "I hear work's been pretty crazy," Matthew said. Interesting that he knew that—given that he now spent most of his time at the research center several blocks from the clinic.

"Crazy? That's an understatement." Caleb gulped his beer. It tasted like heaven. "Lonzo loves me, by the way. I have all these high-profile cases and he's just waiting for me to screw one up and make the headlines so he has to clean up after me, so that's going just great."

"He didn't say that."

"Subtext. It's in the subtext of everything he says to me, around the 'you're behind on your notes' and 'don't be late again' comments."

"He's the one who told me about Sam. He's not always a jerk, you know."

Caleb let out a breath. "Good to know."

"Fill me in on the Harwell case." Matthew sipped from his own bottle.

Caleb told him about his visits with Laquan and Pearl, his worries that with the escalation in the violence, something else would happen to them.

"I feel for that kid. A stupid impulse ruined his life. And his mom's," Matthew said.

"If he were white, he'd probably get a stint in the juvenile facility or head straight to probation. Instead, they toss him in county jail where he almost gets killed. And it won't get easier for him."

"No, it won't." Matthew sipped again. "But media attention may help him. So many Black youth end up in prison unjustly. Perhaps with the right pressure, he'll be treated more fairly."

"And I could win the lottery!" Caleb didn't mean to sound so bitter, but he'd reached critical mass. The violence. The posturing on both sides. The people ruled by beliefs so skewed that they couldn't see the humanity in each other. The loss of innocent lives.

His brother almost a casualty.

Matthew stroked Cleo's fur and said, "Your human's in a funk."

"Sorry."

"Sam's going to be fine, you know."

Caleb looked into his bottle. "Is he? Yeah, he'll get over the injuries, but the cancer's still there. Cancer he won't have removed yet."

"And he's getting treatment for it. Caleb, this was his decision. And this is going to blow over."

"What is?"

"All of it. The riots. Sam's situation—he's strong. Relatively young. He's got an excellent chance of full remission."

"It would be more 'excellent' if he'd have the damn tumor removed now instead of later." Caleb sighed, drank more beer, and thought about smashing the bottle. "Guess I'm not in the most social mood right now."

"Want me to go?"

Caleb averted his eyes and let silence answer for him. Matthew nodded. Stood. Left his half-finished beer on the table. "I know you'd love to control everything, especially when it comes to your family. But you can't. You need to cut yourself some slack."

Caleb scowled. "What the hell is that supposed to mean?"

Matthew sighed. "Nothing. Call me if you need anything."

Caleb felt guilty when Matthew drove away. He'd been a shitty host. Matthew deserved better.

He drained the beer, fetched another, turned on his laptop, and clicked the news bookmark. Live coverage from downtown Columbia filled the screen. Two people had been shot, the newscaster said. The National Guard had taken control of Main Street. Any violators of the mandatory curfew would face arrest and prosecution.

The next footage was from Sam's project, filmed soon after the pipe bombs detonated. Smoke billowed from the rubble. Firetrucks and other rescue vehicles flashed strobe lights. An ambulance blared a siren as it sped away, probably holding Sam.

Caleb gulped from the bottle; the beer cooled his dry throat. Then he started reading the comments posted below the news footage.

Always, always a huge mistake. Idiots mouthing off. Racist diatribes. He'd had enough of all it. He finished the beer and grabbed a third one.

Fueled by liquid courage, he began to type.

That next morning, a hungover Caleb poured a cup of coffee, downed two Tylenol, and scooped food into Cleo's bowl. Thank God it was Saturday so he could spend the day with Sam. Hopefully, he'd be released from the hospital soon.

He pulled out his phone and texted his brother. *Coming your way. Need anything?*

Sam's response: *I'm fine. No rush.*

I'll be there soon, Caleb answered.

The knock on his back door made him dart to the bedroom for a shirt before answering. An unfamiliar dark-skinned man stood on the stoop, wearing a denim shirt and black jeans. Cleo immediately assessed him as "no threat" and pressed her wiggly butt against him.

"Hey, fella." The stranger scratched Cleo's head as he handed Caleb a business card. "Mark Frierson, WJBW News. Are you Caleb Knowles?"

"Yeah. Can I help you?"

"I read your comments on our website last night. I don't usually, but when one statement gets so many responses, it gets flagged. You started quite a debate."

Crap. He vaguely remembered ranting into the keys, a stupid, ill-advised beer-tainted decision. "I can't help you." He tried to close the door, but Mark Frierson flattened his hand against it.

"Just hear me out. You have a unique perspective. You're the brother of an important victim, a famous artist. You're a social worker, with a good insight into the systemic issues behind all the chaos. Let me interview you. I promise I'll be fair. Mr. Knowles, I think you can be helpful to a lot of people who are struggling with this."

Lonzo Petrocelli's face flashed in Caleb's mind, his adamant warning about not talking with the press. What an idiot he'd been to comment on the news site—especially while drinking. "I don't think that's a good idea."

Frierson cocked his head, looking like Cleo when she didn't understand something which was, frankly, most of the time. "You might want to rethink that. What you published online is ours to use. The editor plans to quote you in Sunday's broadcast. The entire segment is devoted to the riots.

"You might want to clarify some of what you said." His smile looked like a weird cross between warm and predatory. "If you let me interview you, you can expand on some of your comments. You probably don't want them taken out of context."

Caleb blinked, trying to remember what the hell he'd written last night. How much beer had he drunk? How much trouble had he gotten himself into? "Look, I'm headed to the hospital right now to check on my brother. This will have to wait."

"Okay, okay," Frierson said. "But I'll be back. Let's say three o'clock? That way I'll make my deadline."

Caleb might, or might not, be there.

As Frierson drove away, Caleb hurried to his laptop and opened the WJBW "sound off" page. There was his epistle. Not as bad as he feared. He'd written about getting the terrifying call that his brother was in an explosion, waiting at the hospital. Watching the news that showed more violence erupting.

He argued that the Red Shirts clung to Benjamin Tillman because they were threatened by the multiculturalism that Caleb believed enriched their state. Maybe most of the Red Shirts didn't feel entitled but believed they hadn't gotten their chance. Other whites—the wealthy, the lawmakers, the elite—had profited from years of discrimination against the Black people and Hispanics and reaped rewards not available to them. Poorer whites hadn't had their turn to partake of the American dream, and now Black people were demanding—rightly—a piece of it.

That was the injustice the Red Shirts believed they must fight, he summarized. The Black people, Caleb argued, had centuries of mistreatment and unjust discrimination motivating them. That conflict came to a head when Laquan Harwell had been attacked. The perfect storm.

Had he really been so stupid as to mention his client by name? But at least he hadn't disclosed anything confidential or described his connection to the boy.

The commenters had a lot to say about his stance. Caleb was called a "libtard" and "Snowflake" by Red Shirts. They argued that they fought against Black people because they were an inferior race that must be suppressed, referencing disgusting quotes from Tillman—the ultimate racist himself. The vitriol worsened as more climbed aboard, including personal threats against Caleb.

What an idiot he'd been for starting this discussion.

He flipped the laptop closed, tucked it under his arm, and headed out the door.

On his way to the hospital, he phoned Lonzo Petrocelli to warn him about his post and Frierson. No answer, so he left a message, relieved for the delay in that uncomfortable conversation. Caleb put his chances at getting fired next week at fifty-fifty.

When he reached the hospital, he found Sam with a visitor: Jace, the artist overseeing the Clementa Pinckney project, sat hunched over beside Sam, the two of them peering at a sheet of paper. Sam looked good. His color less yellow, his face clean-shaven. The bruise on his forehead looked less ominous.

"Am I interrupting something?" Caleb asked and signed.

"Damage assessment," Jace said.

"And?"

"Not much to assess," Sam answered. "Nothing salvageable."

Jace lifted a hand. "We have one of the scales. It's salvageable."

Caleb liked how Jace spoke directly at Sam, clearly articulating so that Sam could read his lips. Caleb signed what he said just to be sure Sam got everything.

"And the plans," Jace added, thumping the sheet of paper. "We can start over. The question is, is it worth it?"

Caleb expected his brother to argue, to assert that the work was too important to walk away from. Instead, Sam said nothing.

Jace looked puzzled. "Nothing we need to decide right now." He turned to Caleb. "I see you're getting yourself famous."

"Huh?"

"Amanda texted me to check the WJBW site. Damn, way to poke the bear."

"I didn't mean to." Caleb felt his face flush with embarrassment. "At least, not to that extent."

Sam looked perplexed, so Caleb fired up the laptop and showed him the site. Sam read, shook his head, read some more. "Jesus, Caleb."

"I know, I know. It was stupid. Beer may have been involved. Beer you paid for, by the way. And a reporter showed up at my house this morning. Wants to interview me later."

"People are threatening you," Sam looked appalled as he pointed at the screen.

"It's easy to mouth off when you're anonymous. I should

know. But I'm sure it's nothing to take seriously," Caleb said.

Sam sighed. "Shannon left town, what? An hour ago? And you get into this mess?"

"It'll be fine. Don't worry."

Jace positioned himself so that Sam could see him better as he said to Caleb, "You have an interesting take on those Red Shirt pricks. But you didn't say much about the Black side of things."

Caleb shrugged. "I didn't feel it was my place. I'm not Black. I'm not living the experiences they are. You are."

Jace wiped his lips where perspiration had appeared. "Still. Would be good if you balanced the two sides better."

"I hope you don't think I was siding with the Red Shirts. Because from the hate messages posted, they sure didn't think so."

Jace shook his head. "No. I know that. But the media doesn't cover the Black side of things. They air footage of burning police cars and broken storefront windows without listening. We need people to listen." His voice had a frustrated edge to it. Rightly so.

Caleb signed Jace's comments and felt them deep inside. Jace was right. The Black perspective had mostly been ignored in favor of the sensational: the violence. The rage. Fires and destruction got the ratings. Listening to the truth required patience most viewers didn't have.

"I have an idea. That reporter is coming back to my house at three. Why don't you come over then? You can tell him what you need to say," Caleb said.

Jace's eyes widened in panic. "I don't think—"

Caleb interrupted him. "You are a well-respected artist whose work was destroyed—your perspective is a lot more important than mine."

Jace looked at Sam as if seeking reinforcement. "I . . . I don't do that kind of thing well. I'm not the person to express this stuff."

"You're talking to a man who ranted on-line after drinking two—make that three—beers. You *have* to be better at it than me," Caleb said with a smile.

"I agree," Sam said. "Jace, you lost months and months of hard work. Think about what we were trying to say with the sculpture. And now it's in ruins. You have the chance to tell people what this means to you. You deserve to be heard."

Jace looked unconvinced.

Caleb scribbled down his address and handed it to him. "Three p.m. When you get there, you'll be greeted by a mammoth dog that looks like an overgrown bedroom slipper. She's going to love you."

Sam grinned. "That she will."

Chapter Twenty-Nine

Beryl was napping again in her old bedroom, which Shull had kept as it had been when she was a teen: flowered bedspread and curtains. Large chest of drawers bulging with clothes she'd never wear again but he couldn't part with. Paintings she'd done at camp, which he'd had framed, hanging on every pink wall.

Shull approached the bed to find her tucked on her side, the cotton sheet pulled up to her ears like when she was eight and he'd tried to awaken her for school. The memory made something clench inside. His little girl who'd wrapped him around her finger at birth. After the divorce from Beryl's mother, he'd had his girl on weekends only. Overindulgence became his pattern. There was nothing he wouldn't do for this child.

And that might be his downfall.

He closed the door and tiptoed down the stairs. Glenna had the TV on in the den and shushed him when he started to say something. He went to the bar and poured himself a bourbon before joining her on the sofa. She sat bent forward, some disgusting green smoothie thing gripped in her hand, mesmerized by the evening news being broadcast.

He turned up the volume. A Black reporter was interviewing two men: a white guy with auburn hair, dressed in jeans and a blue denim shirt, and a man with neck-length dreadlocks, wearing a white polo shirt that practically glowed against his dark skin.

"He's one of the artists whose work got destroyed by the pipe bomb," Glenna explained.

"Who's the redhead?"

"A social worker. Brother of the other artist. The deaf one who's still in the hospital."

The interviewer asked, "Mr. Bennett, you say that the Black protesters aren't just dealing with recent events. That the attack on Palmer Guthrie was simply a catalyst."

"Mr. Bennett" nodded. "We've dealt with this racism for

years. Centuries. Laws change, but attitudes do not. Some whites' hatred towards us doesn't go away because the Civil Rights Act passed. And my people have had that hate directed at them for too long. Something finally burst open."

"And that's what's creating the riots?"

He shrugged. "That's part of it. We say, 'enough is enough,' but the whites—the white supremacists I mean—answer 'don't you step out of line, boy.' That's what happened to Laquan. That's what happens to so many of us every damn day. And maybe we can't take it anymore." He had that layer of rage in him, just below the surface. Shull could see it in his eyes.

"Mr. Knowles? What's your perspective?"

The redhead looked surprised by the question. "My perspective? When it comes to what Black people are feeling and experiencing, my perspective is irrelevant. What do I know about facing the negativity and oppression that you've had to deal with for generations? My perspective is I need to listen. I need to try to understand. And most importantly, I need to respect and honor their pain."

"Give me a fucking break," Shull muttered. Everything about that liberal nut job made him want to punch something.

"Shh," Glenna said.

The interviewer turned back to Jace Bennett. "You heard Mr. Knowles's comments. Is there something else that he, as a white man, should be doing?"

Shull watched closely as Bennett gave the red-headed man a long, sober look. "We all have a part to play if we're going to fix this."

Focusing again on Knowles, the interviewer asked, "Do you believe that?"

Knowles nodded. "Absolutely. My brother could have died because of this sick racism that plagues our state. I'm truly grateful Sam's injuries weren't more serious. But the real issue is why the explosion happened in the first place. Jace and Sam—my brother—are artists. They are creating an incredible project to honor the spirit and memory of Senator Clementa Pinckney. That work has been destroyed. Why? What does that accomplish? What do the Red Shirts gain by attacking an art project and nearly killing a man? What the hell kind of statement are they making?" Knowles's voice grew louder, his eyes widening.

"There's been considerable violence on both sides," the interviewer said.

"And we're no closer to a resolution," Knowles replied.

Jace Bennett shook his head with an angry vehemence. "You don't get it. Neither of you. It won't resolve. We—us Black people—aren't going to be passive anymore. We've had enough. The Red Shirts are doing all they can to put us in our place, but it won't work. We won't go back to the 1800s. So things will just keep escalating."

Shull hoped the Red Shirts were watching. They'd have a lot to say about Mr. Jace Bennett's perspective.

"So you're saying we're at some kind of stalemate?" the interviewer asked.

"I'm saying Black Lives Matter. I'm saying Laquan Harwell shouldn't be in a hospital bed with a racist insignia sliced into his skin. His mother shouldn't be wondering where she's gonna live because somebody burned down her house. If that happened to a white family, can't you just imagine the cries for justice? Well, that's what we're trying to do. We're crying out for justice."

The interviewer lifted a hand. "But what about Lt. Al Fuller? What about justice for him?"

Bennett sat back. That question seemed to take the wind from his sails for a second, but then he said, "His killer should be found. And tried in court, but not on the streets. What scares me is that the vigilantes will do their own form of justice. And what if they carry it out on the wrong person? What happens then?"

The camera cut back to Knowles who sat there nodding, like some kind of plastic puppy on the dashboard of a car.

"Wow," Glenna muted the TV as it cut to a commercial.

Shull slurped his drink and thought about the interview. Bennett was annoying, but that Knowles fellow made him physically ill. Liberal snowflake ass.

"What do you think, Shull? What's it going to take to end the violence?"

He'd pay good money to keep the fight alive, but he didn't say that. Instead, he said, "I think I'm tired of listening to bullshit."

After the commercial, the two men had gone, and the news anchor sat across from James Saddington himself, dressed in a green polo shirt that made him look like an everyday joe, except better looking. "What did you think of that conversation, Mr. Saddington? You've been a strong supporter of Black Lives Matter, correct?"

Saddington replied, "Yes. I support much about that BLM movement, but I abhor the violence, which is happening on both sides. Take a look at this." He pointed to what looked like a beach towel spread out on the floor. On it were five guns: two pistols and three assault rifles, including the Honey badger and the same model of Spectre that Shull had on sale.

"The police kindly agreed to bring these weapons to our interview. They were taken from rioters last night. Look at them. Look at the lethality here." He lifted the Spectre Mark Ten.

"This gun is fully automatic, meaning it can fire twenty bullets with one pull of the trigger. Get that? It can shoot twenty people in a few seconds. This weapon belongs on the battlefield, not on the streets of Columbia." He placed the gun back on the towel, then gestured to the other arms. "We have armed vigilantes on both sides thinking they're in the right. Thinking the answer lies in a bullet. That kind of thinking is deadly. It leads to bloodshed and death, and we have to stop it. A good start would be a bill to outlaw weapons like this." He pointed at the larger, menacing looking weapons. "My legislation will also make it harder for anyone who isn't properly screened and trained to buy any gun. I promise to introduce it my first day in office. I will do all I can to make Columbia a safer, kinder place to live."

The anchor nodded thoughtfully, then turned to the camera. "Viewers, in the interest of fairness, we reached out to Representative Tommy Doyle, the incumbent and Mr. Saddington's opponent in the upcoming election, but he was unavailable for comment." A shot of Doyle in a mint green shirt holding a golf club appeared.

Shit. Shull punched the power button on the remote. How dare Saddington put his weapons on camera? And threaten to outlaw them? And where was the stupid cucumber?

He pulled out his phone and texted Butch: *Send me everything you have on Saddington's wife. And find out everything you can about a social worker named Caleb Knowles.*

Will do. One more thing. A grainy photograph of a Black man in a Gamecocks ballcap appeared.

Who is this?

Simon Madigan. Person suspected of killing Al.

Shull glared at the photo, fury roiling like lava inside him. Simon Madigan, the man who'd ruined his child's life.

Find him for me.

Already on it, Butch replied.

Chapter Thirty

Mary Beth awoke just as the sun began its climb above the horizon. The sleeping pill from Paloma made her feel disconnected from her body. Her head felt so fuzzy it was like thinking through a marshmallow. And her tongue was as dry as talc. She wanted to close her eyes and go back to sleep. To escape into the blackness again.

Yoga jumped on her bed. He was ostensibly Paloma's cat—a small black panther with a purr that could wake the dead—who made himself at home wherever he chose. Which was, more often than not, right beside Mary Beth.

"Move over," she commanded as she fumbled for the remote and turned on the news. And immediately wished she hadn't. The riots had intensified. Two stores downtown burned beyond repair. Cars set ablaze, random gunshots that injured half a dozen people.

Shouts of "Justice for Al" countered with "Defund the Police."

Her town, her responsibility. Now bedlam.

"Why the hell do you have that on?" Paloma stomped into the room, holding a steamy cup of coffee, and flipped off the TV. "Seriously. You'll give yourself an ulcer watching that."

Mary Beth took the coffee and slurped, wishing it was a caffeine IV. Yoga blinked lazy yellow eyes at her.

"How are you feeling?" Paloma asked.

"Okay. Blurry. Ready to hibernate."

"That was one helluva a nightmare you had."

"No kidding." It had become a recurring dream, a nocturnal visit to the parking garage where Al lay dying on the ground and she looked on, helpless to do anything. Her screams had awakened Paloma.

Paloma patted Yoga. "Wish I could stay here with y'all."

Mary Beth tossed back the covers. "Climb on in. Yoga will make room."

"Can't. Have to report in soon."

Guilt washed through Mary Beth. Her friend would be stepping into the quagmire, while she was home on medical leave. How violent would things get? Would Paloma be safe? All while Mary Beth lazed around in bed and waited for her therapy appointment.

"Stop it!" Paloma said.

"Stop what?"

"Stop with the wallowing. You've been through a terrible trauma. You can't work right now; it would put you in danger. You have one job—get yourself better."

"Yes, boss."

"You better believe it." Paloma swatted the sheet. "Oh, and I have news."

"What?" Dread filled her.

"It's not bad. It's about that kid in the alley. Annie was her name, right?"

"Yeah." Mary Beth remembered the terrified girl trying to escape, the Red Shirt vigilantes gunning for her.

"She's okay. Turns out, the bullet just nicked her thigh. Bled a lot but no permanent damage. She saw her pediatrician and, unfortunately for her, a nurse at the clinic called the police. The captain will want to talk to you about charging the kid, but she's so young, and she didn't take anything."

"I'm glad." Mary Beth pushed the covers off her and tried to imagine herself on her feet. She should get dressed. Begin her day. For what? She felt paralyzed by her own weakness. If only she could just remember what happened. She could help her colleagues at the PD find the person who killed Al, before someone got falsely accused, before some eager-beaver cop got revenge on the wrong person. Before the bedlam became a war.

It all depended on her, and she couldn't answer the question everyone kept asking. Caleb said to give it time, to not pressure herself. He said the memory might return when she was ready. When she was strong enough. That felt impossible. She wasn't strong. She was weak. Pathetic.

"You gonna be okay?" Paloma peered at her, concern flashing in her dark eyes.

"I should be asking you that. You be safe."

"I will." She hesitated, then said, "The night Fuller died—you told me to check on someone. You whispered it like you didn't want the others to hear."

"I did?" Everything from that evening was a black blur. Now and then a shape emerged, but it always vanished if she looked too closely.

"Yeah. You thought he might be hurt. A guy named Simon Madigan. Anyway, my partner's been looking into him, sort of off the record. Kyle found him on the law school enrollment, but it doesn't look like he's been to class this week. Kyle checked the hospitals—hasn't been treated. My guess is he's lying low."

"Al was chasing him into the parking garage. They'd tangled before. Al bullied him. I was scared, but I don't know . . . I can't remember what happened." One thing she was sure of: she didn't want this kid's name blasted in the media. Some overzealous cop or citizen avenger might administer some impromptu "justice." "If anything turns up on him, let me know."

"I'll text you later."

Mary Beth watched as Paloma left and considered what to do with her day. She'd see Caleb on Monday, something she both looked forward to and dreaded. Why was she so screwed up? Therapy was supposed to make her better but instead she seemed to be slowly crashing. Where was the bottom? Would she end up in some psych facility, catatonic and staring out the window?

No. That would not be her destiny. She'd get her shit together. She had to. And she had a good idea where to start.

She went to the closet and reached up to the top shelf. There, buried under old T-shirts and pants that no longer fit, was the afghan her mother had made.

Clutching it brought back memories. The day her mom gave it to her, wrapped in a bundle, a yellow bow on top. "For your bed," she had said.

"Thank you," had been Mary Beth's reply, as she fought a tangle of emotions. Did Mom not know what the throw meant to her? Maybe she did, and this had been her apology. It wasn't enough. It would never be enough.

Mary Beth put on some jeans and a sweater and carried the blue and white throw outside. She gripped it tight, her fingers knotted in the crochet, remembering her mother working the needle and yarn, ignoring the violence right in front of her. The memory sickened Mary Beth.

She approached the dumpster at the back end of the parking lot. Her mind pictured her mom, now in a retirement village with her sister in Florida. She rarely came to visit. If she did, and she asked what happened to the gift, Mary Beth would tell her the truth. "I couldn't bear to have it anymore. It reminded me of what you let happen to me," she would say, and Mom would deny it. She'd always created her own version of truth.

Mary Beth hurled the afghan into the trash.

Why didn't she feel something? Relief? Victory? She wanted this to be an important step in her recovery, but she all she felt was a void, a grayness that filled all of her. She wondered if there would ever be color again.

She returned to the apartment. After a quick shower, she put on her uniform, which she wasn't supposed to wear when she was off-duty, but left her gun secured in the locked drawer. She wasn't ready for that yet.

A bagel eaten in her car served as breakfast as she drove downtown. No rioters filled the streets, thank God. Late afternoon was when they gathered like a storm brewing. After dark, tempers ran hot. She'd be long gone by then.

When she parked on Sumter Street and climbed out, memories came in bursts, like photographs flashing on a screen. Fires. Smoke. The noise—the relentless pops, shouts, and bangs. The sirens howling like wolves in the night.

Following Fuller into the garage. It had been closed for repairs for weeks after a flooding incident.

Now she retraced her steps, freezing where the police tape secured the scene. The crime scene. The murder scene.

More photographs clicked inside her brain. Fuller saying something to the three Red Shirt men. But then they were gone, and Simon was there, and Fuller yelled at him, so full of contempt that it frightened her. Simon's hands were outstretched, trying to reason with him, his gaze shifting all around as though looking for a route of escape. There was no escaping Fuller when he got like that.

Simon spotting her, yelling, "He's crazy," as though she didn't already know that. Fuller turning to glare at her.

And a shadow. Dark, looming, a new presence without a face, swooping over her like a massive raven but not a bird, a man. Who was it? Why was he there? Her body feeling like a block of ice—immovable. Not even alive, really, though she was. Wasn't she?

The images stopped. No more clicks. The memories dissolving like vapor.

She whispered a curse. Why couldn't she remember what happened next? Who was the shadow? It felt like someone slammed the door shut.

A cement-floored space beside the construction dumpster had tiny orange cones marking where they'd found Fuller's body. She didn't remember that, either, but had clear recall of the gurney, the body bag, and the hordes of police filling the place after. Where had she been? She glanced around, spotting the area beside the wall. She'd been on the floor there, leaning against the cold concrete, Detective Claudia Briscoe bending over her, speaking softly, kindly, offering her water and assuring her she was safe. Mary Beth holding on to her hand like a frightened child, which was exactly how she felt. Paloma arriving, taking over, keeping others away from her. When the captain demanded answers Paloma told him, "She's in shock. She can't talk right now" with enough force that he backed away.

She remembered the officers filing behind the gurney as they wheeled Fuller away, hats tucked against their chests, in a makeshift funeral procession.

Mary Beth wiped sweat, or tears, from her face that she hadn't realized was there. This little experiment had gotten her nowhere. She could only hope her session with Caleb would break down the wall that she'd apparently constructed between herself and what happened that night.

She had to remember.

As she drove away from the garage, Paloma called.

"Bad news. We got an alert on your Simon Madigan guy."

Shit. "What kind?"

"Person of Interest. Someone's connected him with Al the night he was killed. I'm afraid they're going to put it in the media."

Mary Beth slapped her steering wheel. They could get Simon Madigan's photo from the school and blast it all over the TV. How many vigilantes would scout him out? What would they do to him?

Chapter Thirty-One

Sunday afternoon, Shull found the address that Butch had sent and parked up the block from it under a live oak tree. This was a neighborhood with bumpy sidewalks and older brick homes. He had an old hunting buddy who lived on this street. When he bought the bungalow, it had closets the size of refrigerators and bathrooms with olive green fixtures. His buddy spent a fortune renovating it, converting a bedroom to a master bath and knocking down walls to open up the main living area. The exterior was beautiful now. Charming. What did it look like inside the idiot Knowles's house? Cheap furniture? Floors covered with shag carpeting? Did he have hippy posters on his walls?

Butch had dug up other info on this Caleb Knowles. A social worker in a private practice. No criminal history. Decent credit score. Not active on social media. Divorced, one kid. Registered democrat, of course. Drove a Subaru, naturally. Textbook.

The Knowles house did have some character though. Old red brick. Green shutters. A front porch like Shull's grandma once had, with white rockers. He could picture the old woman swaying back and forth, iced tea glass in hand, telling Shull stories from her childhood. Happy memories he hadn't visited in a while.

Caleb Knowles stood in his small front yard, tossing a softball to a tall, spindly pre-teen with wild auburn curls and a mean curve ball. Caleb's kid, Shull supposed, immediately picturing his own child who'd never played ball, but had won awards on the cheer team. His child who might not recover from a tragedy that should never have happened.

A message came in from Butch. *See the news?*

Yes.

Working hard on the escalation. A few were injured though.

Shull knew that. Three hospitalized, one in serious condition. He wanted no deaths.

Butch texted: *We should take advantage. Fear is mounting. Maybe boost the ad campaign?*

Shull smiled. *Excellent idea. Target small business owners, especially downtown. They need handguns to protect their property.*

We have that shipment of Springfields in the warehouse. Wanna put them on sale?

Do it.

How about I put some out on the streets? Might generate sales.

Keep track of them. Shull clicked off the phone and returned to watching Knowles and the auburn-haired girl. He tossed a ball over her head, and it landed in the bushes of the neighbor's yard. The two didn't seem to know where it was as they searched next door, rustling through boxwoods and azalea bushes nowhere near where the ball had landed. It was kind of funny how the girl seemed all frustrated and Knowles looked apologetic. Finally, Shull decided to help.

He climbed out of his SUV and trotted over to the ball. "This what you're looking for?" He offered it to the girl.

"Thank you." She peered up at him, her eyes a disquieting light brown, freckles a constellation on her face.

Knowles immediately came to her side. "You live around here? Don't remember seeing you before."

"No. Visiting a friend, but I saw your mean pitch land in the wrong spot."

"Accidental knuckleball, I'm afraid." Knowles smiled. He had the same eyes as the girl and slipped his arm across her shoulders. "She's better at softball than I am."

"I have a daughter, too. Older than you," Shull said to the child.

"Is that your car?" The girl pointed to his SUV.

He nodded.

"I noticed the NRA sticker. And the gunrack. Are you a hunter?"

Knowles said in a cautioning tone, "Julia."

"Are you?" she demanded.

Shull didn't like her attitude. She seemed entitled, like she had the right to judge him. Punk kid. "I am. Deer mostly. The occasional rabbit. Bagged a wild boar two years ago." He forced a smile as if he didn't mind her questioning him.

The girl honest-to-God scowled at him.

Knowles said, "Julia has decided she's vegan."

Of course she was. "And you? You a vegan, too?" If he said yes, Shull just might barf on his shoes.

"God no. I love cheeseburgers too much. You look familiar. Have we met before?"

Crap. Shull didn't want to be recognized. "I have one of those faces, I guess."

Knowles tugged at the girl. "Come on. We need to feed Cleo."

They wandered away from Shull, back to their yard, then through the front door.

Shull returned to his car, the one with the gunrack and NRA sticker. Knowles didn't look like much of a problem. His daughter would grow up to be one, he guessed, if she didn't change her tone.

She was nothing like his Beryl, who'd never been that kind of sassy when she was a girl. Though she was changing. Grief seemed to be hardening her edges, and it hurt him to see it. All he wanted was for Beryl to get on with her life. It had turned out to be a good thing, having his girl work for him. When she returned to the job, he could keep a close eye on her.

Chapter Thirty-Two

On Monday morning, Mary Beth dragged herself into the building where the counseling center was housed. She needed Caleb's help to remember what happened, but she hated the thought of dredging up more of her screwed up childhood. Part of her just wanted to run away. Maybe move to Tibet or Antarctica and live there for the rest of her life.

She signed in at the front desk, and the receptionist with monochromatic blond hair grinned in welcome. She looked like someone who'd stepped out of the 1980s, but Mary Beth liked how her smile stayed genuine even when people were bitching at her. Would be nice to have that kind of chutzpah.

When Caleb came for her, she had to make herself follow him. He held the door to his office open, and she reclaimed the same chair she'd used last time, always a creature of habit. She accepted his offer of a bottle of water, watching as he sat across from her.

He looked a little different. Eyes more shadowed. A hint of beard dusting his chin. She'd heard he was on the news, but didn't watch it, not wanting to picture his life outside of this sanctuary.

"How are you, Mary Beth?" When he asked this, it wasn't like when others did. The question scratched deeper than the surface.

"Still a wreck. Still can't remember shit."

"How are you sleeping?"

"Paloma gave me another Ambien. Appetite's a little better," she added, anticipating his next question. "But I did something stupid. I went back to the place where Al died."

Caleb leaned forward, expectant.

"I'd hoped it would trigger a memory. And it did—but not enough. What actually happened is still a great big blank and I'm getting scared."

"Scared?"

"Not for me. For Simon." She went on to tell him about

Al's encounters with the law student. "I don't think the guy killed Al. I don't. But I have no proof. And now that he's a person of interest, I'm terrified some hothead will carry out some vigilante justice if I can't stop them. And the only way to do that is to remember. It's so damn frustrating!" She pounded a fist against her own thigh, savoring the tiny throb of pain. She'd use a hammer on herself if it would help her recall those hours.

"I know you want to force the memory, but honestly, I don't think that's a good idea."

"Is it possible? I mean, could you use hypnosis or something to make me remember?"

He shook his head. "I'm not trained in that, and I wouldn't if I was. Like I said before, you've blocked the memory for a reason. Respect that. As you get . . . stronger, you may recall more. When your mind is ready for it."

"That sounds like bull to me." It came out harsher than she meant, but he didn't get it. He didn't seem to understand how critical the issue was. The riots might become a full-out race war over Al's death. Simon Madigan might get lynched if the wrong people found him.

"I understand why you're impatient." Caleb used his soft, therapizing voice. "But you need to let things unfold as they should."

"Nope. I can't. This is too important. If you don't do hypnosis, can you refer me to someone?"

His sigh was loud enough to be heard two offices away. She didn't want to disappoint him, but then again, he'd disappointed her. He wasn't helping her get what she needed. He sipped from a coffee cup and swiveled his chair side to side, then said, "Tell me what happened that afternoon when you went to the crime scene."

She recounted how she'd seen the spot where Al died, the blood stain still there, the yellow police tape wrapping the area like a twisted Christmas present. "But something weird happened. I remembered this . . . shadow there. A person, but I couldn't make out the face. He was big, dark. Menacing. I remembered being so terrified.

"This may be the person who killed Al. Don't you get it? I have to be able to remember more. I need to see his face. I'm getting closer, but not close enough."

"Tell me more about the shadow."

She shrugged. "It was standing over Al, then . . . then it moved. It . . . this is going to sound strange, but . . . it kind of floated towards me. Like a bird but not. Like a figure in a nightmare or something."

Caleb didn't say anything, just sat there, watching her.

"Do you think I'm going crazy?"

"No, Mary Beth. You're not going crazy. You're simply reaching for something that you're not ready for. Like I've said before." An edge of impatience leaked out.

She felt a niggle of guilt, but it wasn't her job to make him comfortable. "Then how do I get ready? Because I'm serious. I will do whatever I have to. I'll google 'hypnotherapists' till I find one. You can help me or not."

She leveled a glare at him. A dare. She wanted his help. If he couldn't hypnotize her, he had to know someone who could. She'd rather it be someone he trusted, but she'd go to a freakin' psychic if she needed to.

She would remember, one way or the other.

Chapter Thirty-Three

Before Caleb could get his next appointment from the waiting room, Janice let him know he was being summoned to Lonzo's office. He'd been expecting it. Lonzo would want his hide for the weekend press exposure. Best to face the music.

Lonzo didn't rise from his desk chair as he motioned that Caleb should sit. He didn't speak, but handed Caleb several sheets of paper still warm from the printer. "What's this?" Caleb asked.

"The transcript of your weekend diatribe. Thought you might need a refresher." His silver brows pinched together. His lips pressed into a pale, angry line.

"That's not necessary. I know what I said."

"Do you? Note the highlighted section. Page two. Where you mention the name of your client."

Caleb swallowed his shame and embarrassment. "I know. I should never have done that. I can't tell you how sorry—"

"You're sorry?" Something dark flashed in Lonzo's eyes. "I suppose I'm glad that you're 'sorry.' That at least you know you did something wrong."

"I know. I really messed up." Caleb gripped the chair, fighting a tide of panic. This was turning out as badly as he feared. Was he about to lose his job?

"Were you intoxicated?"

"Yes. I had a few beers. I was mad. I messed up. But it's not something I usually do. Don't know what else to say." He lifted a placating hand, wishing he had a better defense, and wishing he hadn't been such an idiot.

Lonzo watched him. Snagging a pen and tapping it against the desk. His silence made Caleb squirm. What if he did get fired? They counted on his income. His health insurance covered all of them, including Julia. How would he tell his family? It could get worse—Lonzo could go after his license. Caleb might not get hired anywhere.

A knock on the door interrupted them. Matthew let himself in, coffee cup in hand. "Hope you don't mind if I join you."

Caleb wanted to hug his old boss.

"Go ahead, Lonzo. Don't let me interrupt," Matthew said.

"Okay." He turned back to Caleb. "Then you were on the news. You accepted an interview without clearing it through me."

"Yeah. Not exactly what I wanted, but . . ."

"But what? You could have said no. Turned the reporter around when they showed up at your door."

"I tried to refuse but he didn't take 'no' for an answer." Caleb told him about the reporter's threat to air his comments if Caleb didn't accept the interview.

"So you're claiming the reporter blackmailed you?"

Caleb felt pinned. He looked at Matthew, hoping for a rescue. Matthew sipped his coffee.

"No. I was really mad about what happened to my brother, Sam. But mouthing off on the site was beyond stupid and the interview was my attempt at damage control. And I tried to call you, Lonzo. To give you heads up. To maybe get some guidance about what I should do."

"I was out of town. Cell reception wasn't good."

"I didn't mention working at the clinic. They didn't say anything about it on the broadcast. This wasn't a professional thing. This was personal. It was about my family." Family. The word resonated as he spoke it. Family. His brother/best friend could have been killed by the sons of bitches that bombed the studio. He blinked, anger blooming afresh.

"Caleb?" Matthew's voice was soft. "Tell Lonzo a little bit about Sam."

"Like what?"

"Like you have a very close relationship with him, don't you?"

"Yeah. He's my brother. A royal pain in the ass sometimes but . . ." he drew in a long breath and continued: "He's deaf. He's a brilliant artist. He's braver than I'll ever be. The idea that someone would hurt him . . . it makes me a little irrational."

Matthew smiled. "I can attest to that."

Lonzo watched him, those lines crinkling the edges of his eyes deepening. "The other guy on the interview—Jace some-one?"

"Jace Bennett. He's Sam's partner on the project."

"He mentioned Laquan Harwell. Does he know Harwell is your patient?"

"No!" Caleb turned to Matthew, anger surfacing. "I would never disclose something like that."

Lonzo glanced at Matthew. He didn't say anything.

Caleb said, "Look, I admit I screwed up. If you're going to fire me, go ahead, because I'm done here." He stood.

"Caleb," Matthew used his soft, steadying voice. The one he'd probably use on a toddler. "Sit, please."

Caleb sat, because he never defied his friend. Well, rarely defied him.

"Nobody is getting fired today. We just wanted some clarification," Matthew said.

"I'm glad. Because I like this job. Most of the time."

"It's good that you tried to reach out to Lonzo, especially after the comments you posted."

"Where you mentioned your client by name," Lonzo added with a bite.

"But he didn't identify him as a client. Caleb never mentioned where he worked or what he did. Sadly, Laquan has become a public figure. Several others had already used his name on the site before Caleb did. Caleb's interview got a lot of people thinking. Having Bennett with you was especially smart." Matthew spoke kindly, as though softening a blow. "But that kind of media exposure may still cause some repercussions. Your clients may have seen it. They may have questions about your perspective. Some may disagree with you and that can disrupt the therapeutic relationship. I'm not saying it's wrong, but I'm saying it may have consequences you didn't expect."

"I understand," Caleb answered, sobered. Matthew was right. He usually was. "I'll handle whatever comes up."

"I'm sure you will," Matthew said.

"And this won't happen again. I'm not a fan of being in the media."

Lonzo spoke up. "I'm sorry about what happened to your brother. And I can see how you might need to . . . vent. But we can't afford this kind of exposure. I hope you get that, Caleb. I hope you get it that whatever you do can reflect on our clinic, whether you mean for it to or not."

Lonzo was asserting himself as alpha, that was clear. Caleb had no interest in challenging him, but wondered if somehow, his very existence did just that.

Chapter Thirty-Four

Caleb hadn't expected Mary Beth's hypnosis session to happen so soon, but on Tuesday, he entered the unfamiliar office and took a seat in the empty waiting area. "Dr. Ferrante will be with you in a moment," the young receptionist with blue-streaked hair told him. He didn't want to be here, but after two phone calls from Mary Beth, he'd asked Matthew for a referral, so here he was. He would not let his client go through this session alone.

This was a smaller practice than where he worked: just two psychologists, according to the sign on the door. They were clearly successful, given the downtown address and the opulence of the restored historic home that had been tastefully converted to offices. Caleb wondered if they had a Lonzo Petrocelli in their practice.

He leaned back in the cushy leather armchair and thought about the past weekend. The time with Julia had been wonderful, once they got past her insistence that they at least drive by the protests. She'd shared the letter she planned to submit to the editor of her Middle School newspaper about racism and what had happened to the Harwells. They'd had fun with Cleo and tossing around the softball, though that interaction with the strange man who found their ball had gotten Julia ranting about guns for nearly a half hour. "Did you see his license plate? 'Gunzzzz.' Like it's his religion!" she had said. He hadn't told her that for many, it was. Nor that the guy had seemed familiar to Caleb, though he wasn't sure why.

Sam was right, Julia was becoming quite the radical, but she'd likely move on to other passions before she hit fourteen. Last year it had been soccer and musical theater. Before that, the K-pop group BTS. He loved every iteration of her. Saying goodbye when her mother came for her always made him feel half empty.

Ten minutes later, he sat across from Emily Ferrante and tried not to let his impatience show. The office felt odd, with its single lamp, thick red carpet, and leather fainting sofa—like something Freud might use. Emily Ferrante looked younger than Caleb, with brown hair that reached her waist and a silver hoop in her sculpted eyebrow. She eyed him with the same look of skepticism Caleb was showing her. Mary Beth hadn't yet arrived.

"I don't usually allow witnesses for these sessions," she said.

"Don't think of me as a witness. Think of me as Mary Beth's counselor. I'm just here to support her. To make sure she's okay."

Emily cocked her head. "And why wouldn't she be?"

He didn't know how to answer that. He didn't want to say, "Because I don't believe in this hokum" or "I think it might cause her harm" because he'd promised Matthew he wouldn't. Matthew had referred him to Dr. Ferrante, a psychologist who worked with him on the research project about addiction and depression. "She knows what she's doing," Matthew had promised. "So please don't antagonize her."

Caleb had no plan to antagonize anyone, but this whole thing had him squirmy, especially after Claudia Briscoe called, urging him to find a hypnotherapist so Mary Beth would remember what happened, and they could "prevent an effing race war." He didn't bend to that kind of pressure but worried when he got the last call from Mary Beth: "Please, Caleb. I have to move forward, and I can't, until I remember what happened." It resigned him to the inevitable. So he'd talked to Matthew and agreed to meet Mary Beth here, with eyebrow-pierced Emily.

"She's very fragile, Dr. Ferrante. I worry this process will push her to remember things she's not ready to face."

"It doesn't work that way. Her subconscious won't allow her to do anything that is harmful. Nor will I." She had a calm, easy manner, her voice melodic and soft. "I'll want you to sit over there." She pointed to a chair in the corner. "Please don't speak. If something raises a concern for you, write it down and hand it to me. Pen and paper are beside you."

He suppressed a sigh. Her office, her rules. He'd have to comply.

Mary Beth entered the room, dressed in a frumpy sweater and jeans. Comfort was important, Dr. Ferrante had explained to Caleb. She guided Mary Beth to the sofa, instructing her to lie down. Mary Beth kicked off her sneakers and complied, clearly eager to get underway.

After a few minutes of introduction and explanation, Emily Ferrante gave their client a sleep mask and instructed her to put it on. Mary Beth glanced at Caleb before complying, then listened as the hypnotherapist began.

Soft, soothing music streamed from a speaker as Ferrante guided Mary Beth to relax her toes, fingers, arms, legs, chest and head, her tone calming. Next came a guided visualization: she described a staircase winding down and had Mary Beth envision descending it, each slow step taking her deeper into unconsciousness. Ferrante spoke in a gentle near-whisper—soothing. Oddly mesmerizing. Caleb himself felt a little sleepy.

"Mary Beth, I want you to picture something from your childhood. A toy. A blanket. A favorite piece of clothing. Something that brought you joy. That made you feel comfortable. Nod when you have the image."

Mary Beth's nod was almost imperceptible.

"Hold onto that image. Let yourself feel a warm connection to it. Let it comfort you."

A small smile appeared on her face.

"Tell us about the object."

"It's a red sweatshirt. Carolina. Has the mascot Cocky on it. My best friend gave it to me when I was ten. I used to wear it all the time."

"Excellent," Ferrante said. "Now place the sweatshirt in the corner. It's your safe place. If anything makes you anxious or uncomfortable, return to the sweatshirt. Nod if you understand."

Mary Beth nodded.

Ferrante assured her she would remember everything from their session, then took her back to the day of the shooting, walking her through the streets of downtown, asking questions about what Mary Beth saw, heard, and smelled. Mary Beth answered calmly, as though describing a walk on the beach: "A lot of smoke. Cars set on fire. The sound of windows shattering. People shouting. Chaos."

"Where is Lt. Fuller?"

"He's ahead of me. Following a Black man. Simon Madigan."

"Where are they going?"

"The parking garage, I think. The one the city's doing work on. It's abandoned, but there are lots of building materials there. There are men waiting at the entrance."

"Tell me about the men."

"Three of them. Red Shirts. One has a long scraggly beard and wears a tattered ball cap. Al stops to talk to them. I can't hear what they're saying, so I try to sneak closer. The bearded man seems to be in charge. It's odd because he was chasing a suspect, but he stops to talk with those men? Then the men are . . . gone. And Al goes into the parking garage."

"Do you follow him?"

"Yes. My footsteps are loud on the concrete though I'm trying to be quiet. I don't know what I'm walking into. Then Simon is there. Fuller spots him. Yells out his name. Fuller's face is red and contorted—he's mad. He's always mad. He gets in Simon's face, screaming about . . . I can't quite make out the words. Simon's frightened. Simon sees me and gives me this helpless look, like he wants me to do something. To keep Fuller from . . . hurting him."

"That's good, Mary Beth. Remember the sweatshirt. It's there if you need it." Emily paused, then continued: "What happened next?"

"Someone else is there." Mary Beth's face changed, paling, lips trembling just a little.

"You're safe, Mary Beth. Take a deep breath for me. That's good. Now, can you see a face?"

"No face. A shadow. Dark. I don't think it's human at first."

She'd said something similar in her session with Caleb and he'd found it disturbing.

"But it is. A man. Big. Looming." Her voice grew louder, a hint of terror ringing through it.

Caleb leaned forward, concerned. Emily raised a hand to still him. "Take another deep breath. Remember, you are safe. Nod if you understand."

A soft nod.

"He's pulling back from me. Turning towards . . . the other person."

"The other person? Simon Madigan?" Emily asked.

A hesitation, then Mary Beth said, "No, it's someone else. There, in the shadows. Someone smaller."

"Can you see who it is?"

She shook her head. "It's a girl. She's hiding. Afraid. It's her. But it can't be her." Her brow knit in confusion.

"Can't be who?" Emily asked.

"The girl from the alley."

Emily looked over at Caleb, who was equally perplexed. The girl from the alley had to be the girl Mary Beth had tried to protect from the Red Shirts. How could she be there?

"Annie. She's there but she's not. She's . . . blurry. Not in focus." Mary Beth shook her head, her lips twisting as though disturbed.

"Take your time. This seems to upset you. Remember to go to the sweatshirt if you need to," Emily instructed.

"Why is Annie here? I see her look at me. She's so scared. She wants me to protect her. They both do. I . . . I don't know what to do. The big man stomps towards her. He's going to hurt her! Annie, look out!" Desperation and panic echoed in her voice.

Caleb shot forward, ready to intervene if Emily didn't do something. She lifted a hand, and said, "Mary Beth, it's time to leave the garage. Turn away and find the exit. Remember you are safe." Emily reviewed the "steps" again in her soft, soothing voice, having Mary Beth ascend them in her mind, the journey from the hypnotic state to full consciousness. She removed the eye mask and blinked her eyes open. She looked calm, but very tired.

"Mary Beth? You okay?" Caleb asked.

She nodded.

"How do you feel?" Emily asked.

Mary Beth scanned the room, as though searching for something she'd lost. Then she turned to Emily and said, "Relieved. Like I'm getting closer to the truth."

"Do you remember what you experienced?"

She nodded. "It's very confusing. Annie . . . Annie wasn't there, but she was. Or I think she was."

"Give it some time. It will start to make sense. Remember, what you experience in hypnosis comes from your subconscious."

"Then I need . . . can I have another session soon?"

"Of course. I'll work with Caleb to get it scheduled."

"Thank you." Mary Beth stood.

After Mary Beth left, Caleb stood to follow, but Emily lifted a hand to halt him. "I hope you're less suspicious of the process now."

"You're accomplished. I can see that. And I do trust that you won't let Mary Beth get herself in any trouble."

"But?"

"But I'm concerned about what she said. I'm not sure it's possible that Annie—the kid from the alley—would have been in the parking garage."

"Sometimes the unconscious speaks in symbols. If she wasn't an actual memory, then what's her role in Mary Beth's life? What does she represent? We may have more answers after the next session."

As Caleb drove away from Emily Ferrante's office, he used the voice command to call Detective Claudia Briscoe's number. "How did Officer Branham's session go?" was her version of a greeting.

"Do you know everything?"

"I do. You should know that by now."

"It went fine. Still no real answers though. We'll see what happens in the next session." He drummed fingers against the steering wheel and wondered how to proceed. "Claudia, the kid in the alley that the Red Shirts shot—Annie was her name, right?"

"Annie Suffolk. Why?"

"How's she doing?"

"She's good. They treated the injury—which was mostly superficial, thank God. I actually met with the parents the other day. The older brother is facing some charges for vandalism but the girl's not being charged."

"That's good," Caleb answered.

"Why do you ask?"

"Just curious. Where is Annie now?"

"They sent her to stay with an aunt out of town right after the incident. Said she needed some time away from the brother. Plus I think they're concerned about the kids the brother hangs out with. They have him under parental house arrest until the unrest dies down."

"Unrest?" he said with a sardonic edge.

"Okay. Chaos. Riots. Race war. That better?"

"It's more accurate." He paused, then asked, "Is there an end in sight?"

"Excellent question. I think so—but things might get worse before they get better. Stay away from downtown after dark."

He laughed. "Don't worry. Shannon would kill me if I set foot in that craziness."

"I like it that you're scared of her."

"I'd be foolish not to be."

Chapter Thirty-Five

Mary Beth sipped a cup of chamomile tea at her kitchen table and wondered when Paloma would return. These moments alone sometimes made her morose, especially at dusk, but since the hypnosis session earlier that day, she found herself feeling more energized. Almost hopeful. The answers to her questions—to everyone's questions—hid in her subconscious, and she would get to them. Maybe even in the next session.

Caleb didn't like the process, which was clear. He thought she was pushing too hard, but he didn't understand the stakes. He didn't see the potential for more destruction, more fatalities, if she couldn't remember.

Paloma had texted that Simon Madigan was still a person of interest and hadn't been spotted yet. She wished the guy would either present himself at police headquarters so that he could be questioned and released or let them know that he'd escaped to New York or Timbuktu—anywhere out of reach of the Red Shirts. That they might get their hands on him before the police did terrified her.

She took another sip. The tea had cooled. She considered turning on the news but couldn't bear the thought of more coverage of the riots. Every violent image from downtown piled onto her sense of failure.

The doorbell ringing surprised her. She wouldn't answer if it was the media, but curiosity made her approach the peephole and peer out. She opened the door.

"Beryl?" Al Fuller's wife—his widow—stood in the hallway. Mary Beth had met her once before in a parking lot when she dropped off Al. Now she looked awful: blond hair in a fraying ponytail. Makeup attempt a patchy mess. A pilly cotton knit sweater that would have benefited from a lint brush.

"I hope you don't mind. Al had your contact info in his phone and . . . and I should have called. That would have been the polite thing, but I was out driving and . . . and found myself here."

"Come on in." Mary Beth had never imagined having this woman in her apartment. Never pictured socializing with the Fullers. But here she was, looking too tragic to turn away. "Would you like some hot tea?"

"Got anything stronger?" Beryl asked.

Mary Beth shook her head. "Sorry."

"Tea will do then." Beryl followed Mary Beth to the small kitchen area. Mary Beth poured hot water from the kettle into a pottery mug and added the last chamomile tea bag she had. If anyone needed calming chamomile, it was her partner's widow.

"How are you doing, Beryl?"

"Not great. I never thought . . . I mean, I know police work is dangerous, but I never thought Al would get killed. He was always so strong, you know? I guess I thought I'd have him forever. That he was invincible."

He'd thought that, too, Mary Beth almost said. Al liked to escalate things. To step into business that wasn't his. He was pompous and full of bluster, but he didn't deserve to die. Not like that—in a cold, empty parking garage. "It's very unfair," Mary Beth said.

"Daddy says I should move in with them. That it's best if I get away from the house where I lived with Al. Away from his clothes and his CD collection and workout gear and other stuff. But I wanted to sleep in my own bed last night. I used his pillow so I could smell his aftershave on it. Is that . . . crazy?"

"Of course not. You should do whatever you need to do to help you through this."

"I guess that's why I'm here." She paused, bringing the mug to her lips. "You were the last person to see Al. I mean, besides his murderer . . . you were the last to talk to him. Can you tell me what he said?"

The last thing Mary Beth wanted to do was let this pathetic woman down. "I'm having problems remembering. I do remember Al chasing a suspect, but not much else about his death."

"Are you sure? I mean, you probably saw his killer." She leaned in closer, her voice taking on a dark edge. "Are you sure you can't remember? Maybe there's something . . . you don't want the public to know?"

Mary Beth startled at her tone. "I'm not hiding anything,

Beryl. I promise."

Beryl's poorly outlined lips sagged. "I just want to know. It's all I can think about."

"The memories will come back. And when I remember more, I'll tell you."

The new widow nodded, though her disappointment deadened the air between them. "I want to know what his last words were. His last thoughts. I want to know . . ." Her voice trailed off.

Mary Beth felt even more sorry for her. "You know what I do remember? A conversation with Al a couple of days ago. He was telling me about his niece's dance recital. How proud he was of the kid. It made me laugh to think of big old Al cheering a seven-year-old ballerina. And sitting through a few hours of really bad dancing."

Beryl smiled, her eyes tearing up just a little. "They were bad! I mean, some were so awful it was funny. But Al sat through the whole thing and cheered like crazy when Josie performed. We always wanted kids. I think he would have been an amazing daddy."

"I'm sure he would have been," Mary Beth commented, though she couldn't stand to think of the racist ideology Al would have imparted to his kids.

Beryl gripped the mug. "I hear it was a colored person who killed him."

The statement took her by surprise. "Why do you say that?"

"My daddy has connections. He knows some of the Red Shirts and they say it was some Black guy who hated cops. Who wanted revenge for what happened at the jail to that Black kid, when Al had nothing to do with that."

Did this mean there were witnesses? "Who are these Red Shirts? Did someone see what happened?"

She shrugged. "Just people talking."

"I think talk like that is dangerous. The death of a cop is a serious thing. I have no doubt we will catch his killer. That person should be punished, period. But we don't need vigilantes doing our job for us. That will only lead to innocent people being hurt. Or worse."

Beryl scowled. Mary Beth wondered what she was thinking.

"I want the person punished, too," Beryl said. "Sometimes,

it's all I can think about. I watch the news and see the destruction and . . . and I'm okay with it. Go ahead and burn all of downtown for all I care. I can't have Al back. He's gone. So go ahead and set fire to everything."

The comment seemed extreme, but grief did funny things to people. Beryl spoke calmly, almost matter-of-factly, about destroying their hometown. "You don't mean that," Mary Beth said.

"Maybe I do." Beryl pushed the cup away. "Daddy says there will be justice. That whoever took my Al will pay."

"Of course! Al was a police lieutenant. The death of one of our own is something we take very seriously."

"Yeah, well, we take it seriously, too."

"You mean your family?"

"I mean all of us fighting for what's right. Daddy says we can't always trust the justice system to work our way."

It sounded like "daddy" was a vigilante like the Red Shirts. What was it Al had said about him? He owned a couple of gun stores. Had a fancy house and a trophy wife. Al seemed to really look up to him.

Mary Beth leaned forward, looking Beryl straight in the eye. "You can trust the justice system. We will find Al's killer. You worry about taking care of you."

She set the cup down and stood. "Thanks for saying that. And for talking to me. Everybody's walking on eggshells and you . . . you treat me like I'm a normal person. That's what I want to be. Normal again."

"I understand." Mary Beth did, because she wanted the very same thing.

After Beryl left, Mary Beth considered what she'd said. It worried her to think of what the vigilantes might do. Beryl's father sounded like a powerful man, and he was a gun dealer. Did the police have him on their radar?

She called into the station and asked for Claudia Briscoe. If nothing else, the detective needed to hear what Mary Beth had learned.

Chapter Thirty-Six

After difficult afternoon sessions with a teen struggling with OCD ("can you listen to me without counting my words, Corey?") and a woman with poorly managed bipolar disorder ("actually, Miranda, it might not be wise to explore on-line shopping opportunities at three a.m. Do you think the drill bits can be returned?"), Caleb drove from his office to the Columbia Medical Center where his next client waited: Laquan Harwell.

The hospital elevator smelled like old lunch and rumbled as it climbed floors. A Beatles tune played through a speaker, no vocals, just massacred instrumentals. At the second level, the door opened, and a man stepped inside. He wore a wool hat, an oversized hunting jacket, and kept his head down as he moved to the back corner. He seemed to be whispering something unintelligible.

Caleb wondered if he was on a phone call but saw no earplugs. Whiskers shadowed the man's pale complexion. His lips kept moving, but his words were inaudible. Was he hearing voices? Could be. With the deinstitutionalization of folks with mental illness, symptomatic people could be found just about anywhere. Caleb glanced at him again and caught a flash of something metallic beneath the jacket.

"Elevator sure is slow," Caleb said.

A delay, then a quiet response: "Always is."

Caleb turned a little for a better look. He was a little shorter than Caleb, but fuller across the shoulders, and probably in his twenties. His thin brown hair trailed below the hat and brushed his collar. His close-set eyes kept shifting sideways to check him out, the way people struggling with paranoia sometimes did. His right wrist looked pink, with skin peeling around a design; the guy had recently gotten a tattoo.

Of a pitchfork.

Crap. Caleb pointed to it. "Did it hurt to get that?"

"A little. Worth it, though." Pride smugness crept into his

voice.

The door dinged open at Laquan's floor. The man pushed forward and stepped out, the flap of his jacket scraping against the door. The hidden gray object came into focus.

Caleb moved fast. "Excuse me, but they don't allow guns here." He stared at the weapon: dark gray, larger than a pistol, tucked in a holster close to the stranger's chest.

The younger man continued to whisper something, ignoring him. He started to move up the hall.

Worried, Caleb rushed to step in front of him. "It's just that there are signs posted that say no weapons allowed. I'd hate for you to get in trouble."

The man stared ahead at the closed doors up the hallway, a slip of paper gripped in his hand.

"What's that?" Caleb asked.

The guy looked at him then, his eyes dark and deadly as bullets. "None of your fucking business."

Without even thinking, Caleb snatched the slip of paper from his hand. Room 314. That was Laquan's room.

"Why—" It hit him then. The man was there to shoot Laquan. "Help! Security!" Caleb yelled at the officer stationed outside Laquan's door as he grabbed the man by his jacket.

He pulled away, slamming Caleb against the wall, and charging up the hall.

"Police!" Caleb yelled, lunging after him. "He's after the Harwell kid! He's armed!"

Caleb reached him before the officer did. He grabbed the back of the man's jacket just as he pulled the gun from its holster.

The would-be assassin made guttural sounds like a captured wolf, fighting hard to pull from Caleb's grip. Caleb kept an eye on the weapon, terrified of the damage it could do. The officer finally got to them and snatched the gun from his hand.

Caleb knew nothing about guns, but this one looked deadly. Like a pistol mated with an assault weapon.

The officer secured the safety and searched the gunman. He found a revolver tucked in the back of his waistband and two magazines filled with bullets. He spun the man around. "What the hell are you planning here?"

Caleb pointed to the new tattoo on the man's arm.

"You're with the Red Shirts? They sent you to kill Laquan?" Caleb demanded. He turned to the officer. "Check for an ID."

The officer looked unhappy that a stranger was issuing orders but did a pat down. "None on him."

"Of course not." Caleb stepped closer, his face inches from the now unarmed man. "You were here to kill Laquan Harwell. Or his mother. You're an assassin."

The restrained man glared at the dark skin of the officer. "The white man is supreme."

"What?" The officer demanded.

"The white man is supreme. The white man is supreme." He said it like a chant, over and over, as he stared at the floor.

"Ignore him." Caleb bent down, trying to make eye contact with him. "What's your name? Who sent you?"

The suspect seemed to gather himself. He stood taller, blinking his eyes at the officer. "You have no right to detain me."

Caleb held up the scrawled room number. "Why did you have this?"

The assassin moved with the speed of a viper, snatching the slip of paper from Caleb's hand and shoving it into his own mouth.

"Spit that out!" The officer yelled, but he just chewed and swallowed. And smiled.

"There goes our evidence," the officer grumbled.

Caleb said to him, "Get him out of here. And call Detective Briscoe."

The officer cuffed the man and radioed for support.

Caleb fell back against the wall and took in a few deep breaths. His heart hammered in his chest like it wanted to escape. What the hell was happening in his town? Killers in elevators? What next?

A few minutes later, Quinn Merrick, the hospital social worker, emerged from the elevator and hurried over to Caleb. "Just heard what happened. Are you okay?"

He offered a weak smile. "I'm fine. Laquan was the one in danger."

"Jesus." She approached the officer and, in a hushed but enraged voice, blasted him on the security he was supposed to be giving the Harwells. It amused Caleb to watch the man hang his head, utter "yes, ma'am," and "we're increasing security" only to be berated some more: "Anything happens to Laquan or Pearl and this town becomes even more of a dumpster fire. I hope you get that."

"You don't need to worry about that, Ms. Merrick. I get it. We all do." With that, he exited with his cuffed suspect, just as two other officers arrived to take his place.

Quinn walked over to Caleb. "You seen Laquan yet?"

"Heading there now."

"Good. He was asking about you." She walked with him towards his young client's room. "Administration is eager to discharge him. I'm trying to hold on to him, though. It's gonna be very dangerous for him to return to the jail."

"How do you hold on to him?"

"Right now I'm exaggerating his mental health issues. Guilt and trauma, etc. But that's only going to buy me a few days. The kid needs a good lawyer."

"Excellent point." Maybe he could help with that.

She opened the door to Laquan's room. "Thanks for coming. The kid needs a friendly face."

Caleb found Laquan sitting by a window, wearing a hospital gown that left twig-like arms exposed, a sheet of paper in his hand. He looked better. He had more color to him. The bags that had drooped beneath his eyes were gone. He resembled an almost healthy adolescent kid. "How are you doing, Laquan?"

"Hey, Mr. Knowles. I'm okay."

"Glad to see it."

"Mama's better, too. They got her up and using a walker now."

"That's wonderful."

"She's going to have help when she leaves here, too. That social worker lady set up physical therapy. Even got a van to pick her up and everything."

Thank God for Quinn. "Your mother is a force of nature. Nothing's going to hold her back."

"You got that right."

Caleb sat back, remembering the man with the gun he had confronted, wondering if he should tell his client. He knew truth was important to build on Laquan's trust in him. "I need to tell you something."

Laquan listened intently, saying nothing, hands gripping the cotton of his hospital gown. "He came here to shoot me?"

"I think so. But they got him. And they're increasing security." Caleb nearly shuddered, picturing what might have happened, and what still might when Laquan returned to jail.

"People I don't even know want me dead."

Caleb heard the pain behind his words and wished he could erase it.

Laquan shoved the slip of paper at Caleb.

"What's this?"

"A note Mama wanted me to write. I was hoping you could get it to Mr. Guthrie."

"The man at the Quick Mart? Okay if I read it?"

Laquan looked embarrassed as he nodded.

Caleb unfolded the sheet and read:

> *Dear Mr. Guthrie, I'm very sorry for what I did to you. I shouldn't have lost my temper. I shouldn't of hurt you. I'm very, very sorry. Laquan Harwell*

"This is a nice letter, Laquan. Are they your words?"

He shrugged. "Sort of."

"Sort of?"

"Mama said I gotta apologize. Only way I'm gonna be right with Jesus is if I tell old man Guthrie I'm sorry."

Caleb scanned the letter again. "But is it how you feel?"

He heaved up a shoulder in a half-shrug. "He's a mean old dude. But I feel bad that I hurt him like I did. And I feel worse about all that's happened since."

"We've talked about that before. I hope you understand that the riots, the violence, and the craziness are not your fault."

Another half-shrug.

"You don't quite believe me?"

He tossed a thumb toward the TV suspended from the wall. "I seen the news. Saw about that cop that got killed. All the other shit that's going on." He sighed. "Sorry. I'm not supposed to say shit."

"That's okay."

"None of that would have happened if I hadn't beat up Mr. Guthrie."

"If you hadn't beaten up Mr. Guthrie, there would have

been another catalyst. Some other match to light a fire that was destined to burn. We've been laying the kindling for generations."

Laquan squinted at him, clearly confused by a metaphor Caleb took too far for a sixteen-year-old.

"People have been mad for a long time, Laquan. Sooner or later, things were going to blow up. You couldn't prevent that."

Laquan turned back to the window. The oppressive day was tinted gray. Pregnant dark clouds hung low, laden, as ready to burst as Columbia itself.

"I gotta go back to jail soon. The guards told me." He no longer seemed young.

"Yeah. I hate to hear that."

"It's okay. Probably where I belong."

"I don't believe that."

"You don't? Most white folks round here want me locked up forever. Or killed." Laquan turned to face him. "I'm worried about Mama. I mean, she's gonna get help and all, but if something bad happens to me when I'm locked up—it'll kill her."

Caleb wanted to assure the boy that nothing bad would happen, that he'd be safe. That soon he'd be out of jail and could move on with his life. But all that would be a lie.

"Would you mind—I mean, you don't have to, you don't really even know us—but would you mind checking on her? Especially if . . ." He didn't finish the sentence. He didn't have to.

"Of course, Laquan. I'll check on her. Until you come home."

Laquan spun around to face him. "You'll mail that letter to Mr. Guthrie?"

"If you want me to, sure."

"They aren't my words, exactly, but they need to be said. It's important to Mama."

"You're what's important to her, Laquan."

His smile vanished as soon as it arrived. "I know but—" He lifted a hand and dropped it. "I wish I had money to pay for the postage."

"Don't worry about that. I'll make sure he gets the message." Caleb would. Even if he had to hand carry it to the man—which actually might not be a bad idea.

"Thanks, Mr. Knowles."

"No problem, Laquan." He only wished there was more he could do for the kid. And that there was some way to protect him from all the creeps out there who wanted him dead. Laquan deserved a future that he may not live to see.

Chapter Thirty-Seven

They busted Rebel Son.

This was the first comment that greeted Shull on the Red Shirts message board that evening as he sipped his bourbon at the kitchen table. Glenna had a private client in her backyard yoga studio. Pizza delivery was running late, so Shull had signed onto the Red Shirts site to monitor activity. The arrest of "Rebel Son" was bad news. The kid had always been active on the site, and he was one of Butch's favorites because of the number of guns he purchased.

What happened? Shull typed, donning his "Pitchfork" persona.

He went to the hospital to take out the Harwells. Got stopped when he stepped off the elevator, Zion replied.

"Damn it," Shull said into his drink. They didn't need this exposure.

Charges? Shull typed.

Illegal possession of a weapon. They want to get him for attempted murder but can't prove intent, Victory said.

What weapon? Could that be traced back to Butch? To Shull?

He's a dedicated soldier, but this was too big an assignment for him, Victory added. Shull remained curious about this newcomer, Victory, but he liked it that this guy had good connections with the police. Now that Al was dead, that could prove useful.

They posted bail yet? One Plank joined in.

"Huh," Shull whispered to himself. "One Plank" was Butch's Red Shirts username, a reference to his very favorite Tillman quote: "We reorganized the Democratic Party with one plank and only one plank, namely, that this is a white man's country and the white men must govern it." While Butch monitored the chat with the vigilance of a hungry raptor, he rarely spoke up like this. Even online, Butch lived in the shadows.

Hearing is at ten tomorrow, Zion said.

We can fund bail, but he needs to be released ASAP, One Plank said.

Butch's strong interest amped up Shull's worry. He texted Butch off-line: *What's the deal with the kid in jail?*

Might cave during interrogation. Don't want the cops digging into this group.

Did someone tell him to take out the Harwells? Seems like a stupid move, Shull typed.

We'd been discussing it. Rebel Son volunteered. Others egged him on. Idiots.

Should I be nervous? Any links to me? Like through his guns? Shull asked.

Butch posted an emoji of a bearded man laughing. *You're using the security measures I set up on the computer?*

Of course.

Then I got your back.

Satisfied, Shull returned to the chatroom where Zion was making arrangements to post bail.

Rebel Son's not the sharpest knife in the drawer. Stupid to let him take this on, Victory commented. *We can't afford mistakes like that.*

The kid's one of our most fervent followers, Zion said.

Exactly. He's a follower. For something like this, we need a leader, Victory said.

You that kind of leader, Victory? One Plank asked. A challenge. Butch must have issues with this particular vigilante.

We wouldn't be cleaning up this mess if it had been me. Or Zion, Victory said. *Next phase will require better planning. Our work is too important to screw up.*

Follow orders and everything will be fine, One Plank answered. *That's all for now.*

As the chat window closed, Shull dialed Butch's number and asked, "What's the story on this Victory guy?"

"'Victory is Ours' is his username. Moved here from Charleston. Joined us several months ago. Has climbed quickly through the ranks. Smart. Buying lots of your product."

"Then I like him."

"Just secured a case of Spectres for him," Butch added. "The expensive ones with the scope. But he's gotta be reined in. He wants to take over."

"And leadership is your job, right?" Shull liked this about Butch. He controlled the group without the member even realizing.

"I have lots of jobs. By the way, I'm sending you the info

you asked for about Lenore Saddington. It should help Tommy with his campaign. Check your email."

As soon as they hung up, Shull accessed his secured email. The file Butch sent contained notes from a medical record from Columbia Memorial Hospital. Included were psychiatric sessions from when Lenore Saddington was hospitalized for depression the year before.

"Well, well, well," Shull whispered. This was wrong, and he knew it, but it was also a little delicious to read about the woman's struggles. She felt "unheard" by her workaholic husband. "Overwhelmed" by her teaching job and the duties of being a mother. "Emotionally exhausted" from trying to please everyone.

A drug overdose led to the admission. She remained in the hospital for six days and was referred for outpatient treatment upon discharge. Those records weren't yet available.

"How did you get this?" he asked Butch. "I thought hospital records were well secured."

"They are. I found a back door to the insurance company's files." Ever-resourceful Butch. But it brought up difficult questions for Shull: what should he do with the info? Go to the press? They'd probably accuse Shull or Doyle of playing dirty pool, but they'd want to put the information out there. It could be a fitting end to Saddington's campaign. Still. It seemed too low a blow. Too big an invasion. This Lenora Saddington's life would be ruined if he leaked the record to the press.

"I need to think about this. I'll get back to you." Shull hung up the phone.

What if he didn't have to take it that far? What if the threat of publicizing the hospitalization was enough? If James Saddington loved his wife, he'd want to protect her from public exposure—maybe enough to drop out of the race. Shull would have to be careful, though. Saddington must never connect any threat to Shull or Tommy Doyle. Again, he texted Butch. When it came to acting and leaving no fingerprints, nobody did it better than his friend.

Their James Saddington problem might evaporate as soon as tomorrow.

Chapter Thirty-Eight

The next morning, Caleb arrived early to work, determined to catch up on his notes before Lonzo felt the need to comment again. Or worse. He liked the quiet of the office before the rest of the staff brought in their bustle: the younger clinicians eager to describe their evenings. The older ones griping about the number of new intakes expected. The psychiatric nurses prepping medications for med-check sessions in morning clinic. Silence helped him get more done.

He was in the middle of his third progress summary (and fourth cup of coffee) when Janice appeared in his office door, wearing a pink sweater that matched the tiny pink bow in her very blond hair. "You're here early," she said with her usual perky smile. "Everything okay?"

"Ha. Just being a super-duper productive employee like always."

She laughed. "Uh oh. Did you forget your medication again?"

"Maybe. Just hoping to get off Lonzo's shit list for a while. If that's even possible. What's up?"

"Dr. Rhyker's asked if you can join him in the conference room. You don't have an appointment until nine."

Odd. Normally Matthew would drop by his office, not summon him. "Guess I'll see what he wants."

Caleb refilled his cup before entering the conference room, a plush executive-style space with a massive oak table surrounded by a dozen leather chairs. To his surprise, Matthew wasn't alone. Claudia sat beside him, her expression taut, leaning towards him and speaking too quietly for Caleb to hear.

"Hey," Caleb said, puzzled. "What's going on?"

"Have a seat." Claudia eyed Matthew. "I won't keep you long. It's about what happened yesterday at the hospital."

Matthew spun a coffee mug in front of him as he looked up at Caleb. "You okay? I was surprised to hear you stopped a potential assassination."

"And that may be overstated. But I'm fine."

"I don't think so," Claudia said. "He had the weapons, the motive, and the intent. He's beating himself up for not succeeding. Saying he 'let down' his brothers."

Caleb pictured the guy—a kid, really—chanting about white supremacy. The dark focus in his eyes. "Who is he?"

Claudia went on. "Name's Boyd Holiday. Twenty-three years old. Dropped out of high school at seventeen."

"Criminal history?" Matthew asked.

"Sealed juvie record. His father has a long one, though. In and out of prison most of Boyd's life. Doing twenty now for assault and battery."

"So mostly absent father with violent tendencies," Matthew commented.

"That might explain his son's connection with the Red Shirts," Caleb added. "Needing to belong to something. Seeking connection."

Claudia rolled her eyes. "Or . . . and I know this is a stretch for you two . . . he's a murderous asshole. A bad guy. The kind I lock up every day."

"Or that," Caleb said.

"He was armed to the teeth," Claudia said. "Mostly legally-procured weapons because we live in South Carolina and love our guns. Anyway. We were curious about where he got the money to buy the artillery. Turns out his mother died in an accident five years ago. He got a bundle in the insurance settlement, and he's spent most of it on weapons. We think Holiday was on a mission to take out both Harwells."

"Both? Jesus." Caleb remembered the size of the gun in Boyd's hand. The abundance of bullets. He could have killed everyone on that floor.

"He hasn't lawyered up yet. And he's talking. A lot. Mostly about Ben Tillman. Talks about him like he's still alive and issuing orders."

Caleb pondered it. "He was talking to himself in the elevator. You think he's hearing voices?"

"I don't think Holiday's crazy. Not your kind of crazy, anyway, but what do I know? Which is why I'm here. We need a mental health assessment on him." Claudia drummed her fingernails on the table—red, with lethal points.

"I can fit him in tomorrow I think," Caleb said.

Claudia gave Matthew a long look.

"What?" Caleb asked.

"Claudia and I discussed it and that's why we wanted to see you. While the contract with the police department is for you to do these kinds of consults, it's not appropriate for you to see him, because you're involved in this," Matthew said. "He'll remember you from yesterday."

Caleb nodded. That made sense—Holiday might not trust Caleb after their altercation. And Caleb's own issues with the man might make him less than neutral. "So what then?"

"The captain wants Dr. Rhyker to do the interview. But we'll need him to do it in the interview room at the station. The one with the one-way mirror. So we can observe the session."

"And Matthew agreed to that?" Caleb didn't hide his skepticism.

"Well, no. Not yet, anyway." Claudia cleared her throat. "But it's what the captain wants. And the mayor, if that matters. We're doing everything we can to get a handle on the power structure of the Red Shirts and Holiday's our best clue so far. There's somebody pulling the strings with this group. And they're buried. They operate in the deep web and they're frankly brilliant at covering their tracks. If we don't get the leader to surface—and arrest him—he'll continue to engineer all the destruction we're seeing. What happened at the hospital will continue. The violence—we can't let it get worse."

"But you said Holiday's talking to you. Why do you need to invade Matthew's assessment?" It seemed the ultimate violation of client-doctor confidentiality to have police watching the interview.

"He's talking, but it's more of a babble. Maybe Dr. Rhyker can determine how wacko, sorry, I meant mentally ill, he is. And, if in the process, Holiday discloses something useful about the Red Shirts, we'll be on it like white on rice."

Caleb looked at Matthew, who wore an uncharacteristic granite-hard expression.

Claudia cleared her throat. "Well, Dr. Rhyker?"

Matthew didn't even hesitate. "No."

She sighed. "Look. I understand your personal and professional ethics. But don't they also apply to the safety of our citizens? If you can help us save lives, aren't you obligated to do it?"

"Jesus, Claudia. Don't lay that on him," Caleb muttered.

Matthew clearly wasn't swayed. "Of course I want to save lives, but not at the expense of my medical license, detective. Not at the expense of the sanctity of the doctor-patient relationship. When we do jail consults, you're entitled to know if the patient is a threat to himself. Your medical staff is made aware of treatment needs. But that is all. You know this, Claudia."

Caleb hid a smile. Matthew's words were measured but his tone could slice a diamond in two.

Claudia's eyes widened. "Sorry, Dr. Rhyker. I didn't mean—"

It was like watching a tennis match: two strong Alphas with competing agendas. His money was on Matthew.

"Perhaps we can find a compromise," Claudia said. "I'm not sure what, but there must be an answer that works for both of us."

"If you come up with one, I'd like to hear it. In the meantime, I'll give your proposal more thought. I'll be in touch later." Matthew stood, effectively dismissing Claudia, who frowned as she rose from her chair.

"Thank you, Matthew. I wouldn't ask if we weren't desperate."

After she left the conference room, Matthew shut the door. "What do you think?" he asked Caleb.

"I think she was crazy to think you'd agree. And in typical Claudia fashion, she pushed too far."

"She has a job to do. For that matter, so do we. If he's mentally ill, we need to get him into treatment."

"So what do we do? It's like she's blackmailing you. 'You wanna see the kid? You have to let us watch.'"

He looked thoughtful. "Suppose I comply, under a few conditions. One, Holiday knows we're being watched so he doesn't incriminate himself. We make clear that anything he says can't be used against him—except for assisting in their investigation. Two, I end the session if I think he's getting himself in more trouble."

"Three, you suggest he gets himself a lawyer. I don't love

the guy, but he needs legal guidance," Caleb added.

"Four, and this involves you. You sit in the observation area with the police. You can keep an eye on them. And if you have any ideas re: my line of questioning, knock on the door. You do these jail consults all the time. I'm a newbie."

Caleb almost laughed. Matthew didn't need his help any more than he needed a pet alligator. But still, the idea of watching the interview held appeal. He wanted to understand this Boyd Holiday and hoped understanding him might offer insight into the whole Red Shirt phenomenon.

"I'm in."

Chapter Thirty-Nine

As soon as Caleb returned to his office, Janice put through a crisis call from Lenore Saddington. "I have to see you right away. I don't know what to do. James's is furious. Please, can I have a session today?"

It hadn't been easy fitting her in, but he managed to carve out thirty minutes between late morning appointments. She arrived early and, according to Janice who phoned to notify him, "paced the waiting room like a caged cheetah." When Caleb finished his eleven o'clock session, he fetched her back.

Lenore wore sweatpants and a wrinkled cardigan, her hair pulled back in a clumpy ponytail. He'd never seen her look this unkempt. She hurried to the chair and sat, her foot bobbing up and down as if it was possessed, her gaze skittery. She gripped an envelope in her hand.

"Lenore? What's going on?" He leaned towards her, concerned.

"This. It came today." She thrust the manila envelope at him. "Read this."

Caleb pulled out nine printed pages and a billing form: progress notes from when Lenore had been hospitalized eighteen months ago. The notes included her diagnosis, her treatment, and even transcripts from a family session held with Lenore and James. "Did you request these from the hospital?"

"No. They came to James in this envelope. With this message attached." She gave him a printed note: *The media will be interested in this.*

"Do you know who sent it?" he asked.

"We don't know. James called Tommy Doyle, his opponent, and asked if he was responsible but Tommy acted like he had no idea what James was talking about." She scowled. "But Tommy Doyle's full of crap."

Caleb didn't say he agreed with her. The state representative had always seemed lacking in intelligence and scruples, relying on his good-ole-boy status to keep him in office. So far, it had worked.

"I'm so sorry. This is a serious violation of your privacy." He skimmed through the sheets again, reassuring himself that there were no copies of his clinical notes in the mix. "Did they hack the hospital records?"

"Sure looks like it. Can you imagine if they did? What else they might get their hands on?"

That thought was terrifying. So many secrets lay hidden in medical records.

Tearful eyes met his. "I don't know what to do. James says he'll pull out of the race if I want. And at first, I did. I mean, if this information gets in the newspapers, my life is ruined. My principal might fire me. And Brian, our son—how humiliating it would be for him." Her speech accelerated, pressure building up.

She continued: "But then I think—no. We're not caving into blackmail. James's not giving up what he's worked so hard for because someone is pulling this crap!"

Already, she sounded stronger. Caleb wasn't surprised by her resolve. She'd clawed her way out of the bowels of depression. But if this information hit the press, it could be disastrous for her. "Have y'all gone to the police? Blackmail is illegal."

"James mentioned that. But I'm not sure he should. I mean, what if he shows it to someone on the force and that person decides to post it on Facebook?"

"I understand why you'd be nervous about that. Does the hospital know there's been a breach?"

"James yelled at them for twenty minutes. They're probably terrified he's going to sue."

"They should be." Caleb couldn't imagine how this could happen. Lonzo had put multiple levels of security on the clinic's medical records and the hospital would be even more vigilant.

Lenore pointed at the envelope. "It was on our doorstep this morning. Whoever did this was at our house, Caleb. Honestly, I'm scared." She looked it. Her brown eyes wide and beseeching. A slight tremble to her lips.

He wished he could reassure her that nothing would come of it, but one simple post on social media might derail her life.

She stood and walked over to the window that looked out

on a patch of grass and a small sandbox, the one Caleb had insisted they add before he'd join the practice, because sometimes play therapy required an outside setting. Caleb moved to stand beside her, not too close, in quiet support.

"If they threatened to leak medical records of my appendectomy, or James's hernia repair, I wouldn't be upset like this," she said to the window.

"No, I suspect not."

"I've worked hard to not be ashamed about my depression. To see it as a medical issue like high blood pressure or psoriasis or . . . or whatever. Our son knows his mommy has it and that she takes medicine to feel better because I wanted to normalize it for him. I pray he never has to battle it, but you've explained it can run in families. God knows my mom was a depressed wreck. So I don't want to feel . . . the way I feel right now. That I have something to hide. To be ashamed of. But I do feel it. And it's sickening."

He said nothing as he stood there beside her.

"And there's no answer that's right. James could quit the race, but that would be letting them win. Or he could stay in, and we pray this is a bluff, and I live with the anxiety of knowing that at any second my mental health can be splayed all over Facebook and Twitter and the front page! James's leaving it up to me and I appreciate that. But I also hate it that I have the responsibility. And I'm mad that I'm in this situation and wouldn't be if he'd never decided to run for office. Which is childish, I know, but still." Tension radiated from her.

"You didn't expect this level of disruption to your life."

"Exactly. And there's Brian. God, what would it do to him to have this get out?"

"I can see how that worries you. But people have a different attitude about needing help than they used to. Most do, anyway. You were very brave to go into the hospital when you needed to."

"Of course you'd say that." Her shoulders heaved up in a sigh. "You see things so differently than the rest of the world. Do you know that?"

Caleb smiled. "That's been said before."

"I want you to tell me what to do, but you won't. You can be maddening that way." Just the slightest edge came out in her voice.

"It's because you don't need me to."

Her cell phone rang. She glanced at her purse, then returned to the chair and opened it. "James's calling."

"You can take it."

She shook her head. "Whatever I decide—he's going to have a press conference to announce it."

Caleb took a long look at her. "This is a lot of pressure. You doing okay?"

She shrugged. "I'm mad. I'm scared. But yeah, I'm okay. I'd be better if I could spend five minutes with the anonymous person who sent that envelope, but I'm okay."

"I believe you are. And whatever you decide, it will be the right thing."

She gave him a long, heartfelt look. "Dear God. I hope you're right."

At noon, Caleb signed out for lunch and stepped outside into an oppressively warm day. Fall might be coming, but not soon enough. He pointed the Subaru east of town and ten minutes later, pulled into the Guthrie's Quick Mart parking lot. He had a note to deliver.

The little girl wasn't there. "Bean" had been what her "Uncle Vic" called her. Was she in school? Was she learning anything that might counteract the racist views she'd internalized? He wanted to think there was hope for her, but so much could get ingrained in a kid still forming an identity. He prayed it wasn't too late. Where would she hear other perspectives? How many new generations would be taught the vitriol of racism?

An old green pickup idled in the gravel lot. The bed was covered with a black shell, no windows, and the exhaust pipe puffed out a pale cloud. The man in the driver's seat had out-of-style sideburns and a beard that might have housed rodents. He looked almost cliché.

A red SUV backed in beside the truck. Windows opened; the drivers conversed. Caleb climbed out of his car and entered the cement block building, bells on the glass door jingling. A man stationed at the register looked up. He had short-cropped brown hair and a youngish face, sparse hairs making an anemic mustache over thin lips. He asked, "Can I help you?"

"Just grabbing some snacks."

"We just restocked. Knock yourself out."

Caleb selected a soda and a bag of chips. Behind the register, the bulletin board remained, the same poster with the pitchfork that had become too familiar to Caleb prominently displayed. Below hung an article about Laquan's attack on Mr. Guthrie. The match that lit the fuse.

An older man with bright white hair came from a room in the back. An ace bandage secured his right wrist and a purple bruise blossomed on his left eye. He was smaller than Caleb had pictured, a little hunched at the shoulders, wearing faded khakis and a Clemson sweatshirt. Caleb remembered he was close to seventy but somehow, he looked even older.

"Need something, Pop?" the younger man asked.

"Got the orders in." He moved behind the counter and sat on a stool.

Caleb pointed to the news article. "Are you Palmer Guthrie?"

"In the flesh. The bruised flesh, I reckon."

"You're so much better though, Pop," the other man said.

"I am. Thanks to your mama's good cooking."

"Glad to see you up and around." Caleb placed his purchases on the counter.

"Thank you."

The younger man looked out the door at the two vehicles idling in the parking lot. "You okay by yourself for a while?" he asked Palmer.

"Good Lord, son. I've been running the place on my own for forty years. Maybe running it into the ground, but I get by."

The young man chuckled and left them. Through the window, Caleb saw him trot out to the trucks.

Palmer rang up his purchases. "Need a lottery ticket?"

"No, thanks. My last one didn't pay for my kid's college like I'd planned."

Palmer laughed. "The gods didn't smile on you, huh? Ain't that the way it goes."

Caleb had expected to loathe the man. To see him as the symbol of the bigotry he hated in his home state. But he was hard to hate somehow. He seemed humble. Friendly.

But then, Caleb wasn't Black.

"Mr. Guthrie, I have something for you." He pulled out the note. "I've gotten to know the young man who hurt you. Saw him yesterday at the hospital. He wanted me to get this to you."

Guthrie took the note, squinting his gray eyes as he read it. Caleb watched, curious to see his reaction.

"Laquan Harwell sent this?"

"Yes. He's upset about what happened. And about all the fallout since." Caleb realized he needed to be careful. He was dangerously close to violating Laquan's confidentiality, a knife edge that had cut him before.

Palmer placed the note on the counter. "Well I'm glad he's sorry. That's something, at least."

"You do know what happened to him, right? Why he's in the hospital?" Caleb felt himself pulled closer to the knife edge.

Palmer smoothed the note with crinkled hands. "Heard someone attacked him in jail."

"He was beaten and stabbed. Had a pitchfork design sliced into his torso. Just like that one there." Caleb pointed to the poster.

Palmer looked up, eyes narrowing. "Not my fault. I was in the hospital myself when that went down. Recovering from the beating he gave me."

The sound of a car door slamming took their attention. The bearded man from the truck had climbed out to open his tailgate. The young man from the register and another man, wearing a hunting cap, eyed something in the truck bed.

"You know how many times I been robbed?" Palmer asked Caleb. "Truth is, I don't even know myself. Been held up at gunpoint twice. But people steal other ways. Sneak in here, leave with my merchandise tucked in pockets or under shirts. A kid looks just like Laquan has hit me a half dozen times. My son caught him in the act last week. Had two pounds of meat under his jacket, two sodas in his pockets, and a bottle of Gallo wine stuffed in his waist band."

"What happened to him?"

"We called the cops but he ran off before they got here."

"You said he looked like Laquan?"

"Yup. Same skin color. Same haircut. Same sneaky way of

moving around my store like he's up to something."

"So when Laquan was here that day—you thought he was the kid who'd been shoplifting?"

"If I said, 'they all kind of look alike,' you'd say I was a bigot. But yeah, I didn't know if it was him or not. I kept my eye on him."

"But it wasn't Laquan who stole. Laquan was here to get soup for his very ill mother. He had money to pay for it."

Guthrie offered a slow nod. "Pearl Harwell is a good woman. Been a decent customer. Knows how to be polite. To wait her turn. Her son could learn a lesson or two from her."

Caleb heard the entitlement between his words. Palmer Guthrie wanted Black people to know their place, subservient to whites. Pearl's generation tolerated it better than Laquan's, but at what cost? "Pearl Harwell lost her home. She almost died in that fire. She's still recovering. All because you thought Laquan was a shoplifter and treated him like he'd robbed you."

A crooked finger pointed at Caleb. "Because that young hoodlum attacked me. I had nothing to do with what happened to Pearl because I was half-unconscious so don't you go blaming me for that." His voice rose. The men outside took notice.

The son came hurrying back. "Everything okay, Pop?"

Guthrie tossed Caleb's purchases in a bag and thrust it at him. "He's just leaving."

Caleb lifted the sack and tossed money on the counter. He started to leave but turned back around. "I'm sorry you were hurt. Laquan is, too. He's young and, well, most kids his age don't have the best judgement or self-control. But given what he'd been through, I hope you can try to understand. That's all I ask." He lifted a hand in a beseeching gesture.

The son stepped closer. "Want me to toss him out, Pop?"

Guthrie shook his head. "Only if he tries to come back here."

Caleb nodded and exited, eager to leave them both.

The two trucks remained in the parking lot. The bearded man stood beside the old green one. The younger man beside the red SUV looked vaguely familiar: brown hair, trim goatee, and a scowl on his pale face. Vic. The man who had waited on Caleb the last time he was here.

The two seemed to be in serious negotiation. Bearded guy

reached in the back of the green pickup, slid a brown case up to the tail gate, and opened it, pulling out a gun—larger and thicker than a handgun, but not as long as a rifle. From this distance, it looked similar to the one Boyd Holiday had at the hospital. Vic took the weapon, removed something else from the case, and snapped what looked like a curved magazine into place, then raised the gun as though preparing to shoot.

He didn't.

Bearded guy slid more cases to the front of the truck bed—maybe a dozen. Vic opened the back of his SUV and began transferring the cases into it.

This was a gun sale. Someone was selling what looked like automatic weapons to a member of the Red Shirts. To use in the riots? To gun down more innocent people?

Caleb needed to tell the police. But he needed proof. He pulled his cellphone from his pocket, wanting to snap pictures, but caught the bearded man looking his way. He'd need to be subtle. Not exactly his strength.

"Hey! I was hoping I'd hear from you today." Caleb spoke into the phone as though he'd gotten a call but kept the screen in front of his face. "I have news about the sale. They took our offer . . ." as he continued the phantom conversation, he pressed the button on his camera, catching shots of the gun cases and the two men.

Who were now both watching him closely. Caleb kept the prattle going as he walked to his car and climbed in, picturing what might happen if they realized he'd taken photos. They were armed. Heavily armed.

He dropped the phone onto the passenger seat and backed out of the spot. As he tried to exit the parking lot, the bearded man approached his car. He said nothing, merely stared, arms crossed, his leathered face void of expression.

The dude looked soulless, like someone who could kill without giving it a second thought. The idea that a guy like that had a stack of high-powered weapons in his truck was nothing short of terrifying. Caleb waved like they were old friends and maneuvered the car around him, glad to be escaping these men.

Chapter Forty

At three the following afternoon, Caleb entered the police station where Claudia greeted him by the glassed-in reception area. "I got the photos you sent yesterday," she said.

"Recognize anyone?"

"The task force is working on it. But you need to be careful. If those idiots saw you taking pictures of them, things might have gotten ugly. Where were you, by the way?"

"I paid a visit to Guthrie's Quick Mart—the place where Laquan was arrested."

Claudia looked incredulous. "Are you insane? Why the hell would you do something like—"

"Anyway," Caleb interrupted her. "I saw them in the parking lot. The guns looked kind of terrifying."

"It is some serious weaponry." She opened a folder and pulled out prints of what he'd sent her. She pointed to one weapon. "That one's the Spectre Mark Ten—like one on a guy we busted last night at the protests."

"I think the green truck guy was selling them to Vic, the guy in the red SUV. About a dozen of them." He sorted through the pictures and pointed to one of Vic. "I don't know his last name, but I know he's a Red Shirt. Calls himself a 'brother.' He's pals with Palmer Guthrie. You might want to check into that," Caleb said.

"We will. But there's a lot I can't talk about right now. You understand, I'm sure." She glanced at the door. "Matthew on his way?"

"Right behind me."

When Matthew arrived a few minutes later, Claudia said, "We've got Holiday in the interview room. Follow me."

She led them down a linoleum-floored hallway past the records room, the canteen, and the briefing center. Officers hurried by them with an air of rushed seriousness. A Hispanic woman in animated conversation with a red-headed man almost bumped into them. "Perdón," she uttered, and hurried on.

"Things are a little crazy around here," Claudia commented.

"I'll bet." Caleb could only imagine the pressure they all felt, the violence escalating with no end in sight.

A guard stood outside one of the interview rooms, which was just across from two detention cells. Claudia passed it and entered the observation area. "We'll watch from here."

Caleb took a seat beside the window. A man in chinos sat in front of recording equipment, and Claudia took the remaining chair.

"Dr. Rhyker, while we're not wild about your stipulations, we're accepting them. But we do hope that if Holiday gives you any information about the Red Shirts, you'll pursue it with him. We need any help you can offer."

Matthew's response was a non-committal shrug. Caleb could see he was in a tough spot—clinically, he needed to focus only on Holiday's symptoms, but he'd also want to do what he could to end the violence. Matthew would be walking a familiar tightrope.

"Here," the audio guy handed Matthew a tiny earbud.

"What's this?"

"We can feed you questions. We can't make you ask them, but . . ." Claudia shrugged.

He wasn't happy, Caleb could tell, but Matthew inserted the device into his ear.

The guard opened the door and Matthew entered the interview space where the inmate waited. In the observation room, the audio guy turned on his equipment.

"Mr. Holiday? My name is Dr. Matthew Rhyker," Matthew began, extending a hand. His voice sounded tinny over the speaker.

Holiday ignored the proffered hand. He remained seated, his fingers laced together on the steel table. He looked different than he had at the hospital. No hat, longish brown hair in a greasy tangle. Splotchy whiskers on his cheeks and chin. The orange jumpsuit looked too big for him, or perhaps he just looked shrunken without his guns.

"I'm here to see if you need mental health care," Matthew went on. "But we're not alone."

Holiday looked up at him as Matthew explained the audience behind the one-way mirror. "I want you to understand two things. One, we're being recorded and two, there are police behind that mirror. Be aware that anything you say to me, they will hear."

"Dammit," Claudia grumbled. "What's he doing?"

"What did you expect? He'll play by your rules but he lives by his," Caleb answered.

Holiday said, "I don't need mental health care."

"That's good to know. But I need to ask you some questions." Matthew went on to do a mental status exam. Holiday was oriented to time, place, and person, though his answers leaned towards the concrete and his capacity for abstract thinking seemed limited. He didn't hear voices, didn't have visual hallucinations, but mention of the Black race sent him into a tailspin: "They are destroying America," became a common theme, and led to animated, fiery outbursts.

"I need to ask you about two days ago, when you went to the hospital," Matthew said.

"What about it?" A defiant glare matched his tone.

"Why were you there?"

Holiday shrugged. "To visit a friend."

"A friend? Who?"

"None of your business." He swept the table with his hand in a dismissive gesture.

"You arrived there with several concealed weapons."

"I have the right to my guns! I have a permit. Things are so crazy these days—I'm allowed to protect myself."

"But they aren't allowed at the hospital. There are signs that say that. You had the weapons for protection?"

"Damn right. So many nut cases out there."

"He's right about that," Claudia muttered. "I'm looking at one of those 'nut cases' right now."

Matthew continued. "What confuses me is that you had a slip of paper in your hand with the room number for Laquan Harwell. Was he the 'friend' you went to visit?"

"What slip of paper?" He flashed a self-satisfied smile. "You got it with you?"

"You destroyed it."

"Did I?" A wider grin. "Seems to me that without that slip of paper, you got no reason to assume I was there to see that

Laquan fellow. Like I said, I was there for a friend."

Matthew leaned back, said nothing. Holiday met his stare. After several long moments, Matthew spoke. "What are your thoughts on Laquan Harwell?"

"He's the punk who started this madness. He attacked an innocent old man, nearly killed him, and now people treat *him* like he's some kind of martyr. Guess you could say I'm not a fan."

"You seem to have some strong feelings about him." Matthew kept his expression gentle.

Holiday gave him a long, hard glare. "I have strong feeling about what's right for America."

"I don't doubt that. And you see Laquan as a threat to America?"

"Don't you see where we're heading? We let people in from anywhere. We treat colored people like we *owe* them something. And where does that lead? It leads to what happened to nice people like Palmer Guthrie. It leads to scumbags like Laquan Harwell."

"So Laquan Harwell is symbolic for you."

"Yes. Yes, exactly. He's what's fucking wrong with the world today. We'll continue to take this short path to hell if we don't stop people like him."

"So you wanted to stop him, which is what you tried to do at the hospital?" Matthew kept his voice even, which couldn't have been easy.

"I . . . I didn't say that. I didn't go there to hurt anybody."

Matthew paused for a moment, then glanced up at the mirror. He said, "I've been hearing about this group, the Red Shirts. You know about them?"

His eyes widened. "Why do you ask that?"

"They sound like a very interesting group."

Holiday let out a sarcastic laugh. "Interesting? You think they're 'interesting'?"

"How would you describe them?" Matthew asked.

"They know how to fix the country. We've strayed down the wrong path too long, but we can turn back. My brothers will make it happen."

"The Red Shirts are like your brothers," Matthew repeated.

"Family doesn't just mean blood."

"Exactly. I would do anything for my brothers." He leaned forward, his eyes intense. "Anything."

"It feels good to belong to a group like that," Matthew said. "That connection can be so powerful."

Claudia looked at Caleb. "Matthew's doing my job for me."

"He's just trying to get a handle on how much control Holiday had over his own actions. He suspects the guy is a sheep being led."

"And I'd kill to get my hands on the shepherd," she replied.

Caleb had an idea. "Hey, can I say something to Matthew?"

"Sure." The audio guy clicked on a smaller mic beside them.

"Matthew, ask him if he knows a guy named 'Vic.'"

Matthew smoothed a hand across the table, giving Holiday a pensive look. "You mentioned your brothers. Is Vic one of them?"

Holiday's eyes widened. "How do you know about Vic?"

"You do know him then."

"I don't . . . know him. I mean, I haven't met him in person yet, but . . ." His demeanor had changed. Sweat beading on his forehead. Cheeks reddening, as though he'd been exposed.

"What's he like?"

"He's . . . he's the best. He's strong. He's committed. And smart—probably smarter than all of us."

"You respect him a great deal," Matthew said softly. "Did he know about your visit to the hospital? Is he the one who told you to kill Laquan Harwell?" Matthew asked.

"Jesus," Caleb whispered, never expecting Matthew to push this hard.

"No!" Holiday smacked a hand against the table. "I wasn't there to kill anybody. I think we're done here."

Matthew didn't move but glanced up at the one-way mirror. "You're worried about Vic. You don't want him implicated in what happened at the hospital."

"He had nothing to do with it! And nothing happened! I don't even know why I'm here—like I already told you, I didn't do anything. I didn't hurt anybody!"

"Damn," Claudia said. "I was hoping he'd confess."

Matthew seemed to switch strategies. "Vic is lucky to have a loyal friend like you."

"He's a brother. I mean, Zion and Alpha—they're great

guys and all, but Vic—he's different."

Caleb looked at Claudia. "He's got some serious hero worship going on."

Claudia's response was an odd smile.

"What?" Caleb asked.

Claudia pressed the button connecting to Matthew's earphone. "See if he'll say more about the others—Zion and Alpha."

Matthew frowned. Caleb knew he didn't want to be a puppet for the police. It wasn't his role, and Matthew was not one to be manipulated. He leaned forward. "Boyd, listen to me. I see how important the Red Shirts are for you. I think they've filled a need you've had for a long time. A need for family. But the violence, the destruction—the Red Shirts are at the center of it."

You don't understand." Boyd Holiday's eyes widened. "Sometimes the violence is necessary. Sometimes a revolution is necessary, and that's where we are right now."

Caleb saw Matthew glance at the mirror. Holiday's fervor was alarming. This was the same passion, the same zeal that put him in the elevator with Caleb. That drove him to try to kill the Harwells.

Boyd sat back, a wide, strange smile on his face. "We are the true sons of the South. We're reawakening Benjamin Tillman's legacy."

Matthew replied with a slow nod. Caleb could almost see the wheels turning in Matthew's brain. "What would Tillman want to happen?"

"The Blacks put back in their place! The Red Shirts will get us back on track. We understand our mission. We'll do what we must to restore our country." He sat back, a self-satisfied smile on his face.

Caleb noticed a change in Matthew's expression. A small lift of his chin. Eyes crinkling just a little. This was the look Matthew had when an insight came to him. Caleb stood and approached the window.

"Did your parents hold the same beliefs?" Matthew asked Boyd.

"My pa sure does. Not mama, though. She was a strong Christian. Said God loves each of us equally. Of course, she's dead now. And why? Because of them!"

"I understand you lost your mother a few years ago. An accident, I believe."

"An accident," Boyd spat out.

"Am I missing something?"

"My mom worked at a grocery store. She was driving home after a long shift. A colored asshole driving a tractor-trailer swerved into her lane. Clipped her car. She lost control and crashed into a tree."

"I'm so sorry." Matthew spoke softly.

"Guy said the sun was in his eyes and he couldn't see, but I don't think that's what happened. He was drunk. Or stoned. Or talking on his fucking cell phone. He killed my mother. Murdered her."

"Did you ever meet the driver?"

"I saw him once. Older Black man named Zachary Matthews. Pretended to be all repentant."

"Jesus," Caleb whispered. "This could be what it's all about for Boyd. He's after Blacks to avenge his mother."

"That man shouldn't have been behind the wheel. That's why his company settled—they didn't want the publicity of a civil trial. My lawyer said it was for the best. Settle it. Move on with my life. That's what he told me." Boyd sounded young, an orphaned kid.

"But it's not easy."

"I live with it every moment of every day. It almost destroyed me, that pain. But then I found the Red Shirts. I found my purpose."

Matthew nodded slowly. "Boyd, I need you to listen to me. You're in some serious trouble. The Red Shirts can't help you now, and you need help. You have to hire a lawyer. There's going to be a bond hearing in a little while—you have to have someone there to represent you."

Boyd wiped his nose and nodded.

"You don't have to be alone in this. Let a lawyer help you." As Matthew ended the interview, he handed Holiday his card. "If you get bonded out at the hearing, and want to talk some more, you can give me a call."

Holiday took the card. Caleb hoped he used it.

As Matthew ended the interview, he joined them in the

small surveillance room just as the audio guy exited. Claudia closed the door. "Well?"

"He drank the Red Shirts' Kool-Aid," Caleb said. "A whole bucket of it."

"Lot of that going around," Claudia replied.

Matthew stood with his back to the door, looking pensive. "He's a needy kid. Someone's pushing his buttons. Maybe it's this Vic guy. Maybe someone else. But he's the perfect target for them. Would be good if we found out who it is."

"If we don't, we'll see more casualties. I fear for our town," Claudia said.

Chapter Forty-One

Mary Beth Branham's name appeared on Caleb's schedule. It hadn't been there that morning. A note from Janice in the "comments" section of the digital calendar explained his four o'clock had canceled, and when Mary Beth called, she sounded "very upset", so Janice made the right call and urged her to come in. Emergency appointments had become the norm that week.

"Mary Beth? It's nice to see you." Caleb motioned to the usual chair, and she sat, a knapsack gripped in her arms as though it held some precious secret. Once again, she looked . . . burdened. Hair needing a brush. Pilled sweatshirt and faded jeans, as though she'd just climbed out of bed and thrown on these clothes. Caleb worried that she'd gotten much worse. What prompted it?

"Thanks for working me in. I really needed to see you."

"It's okay. Tell me what's going on." Caleb could feel the tension radiating from her.

"Nightmares. Really brutal nightmares since that hypnosis session. Paloma said I woke up screaming. Scared the hell out of her."

"Sounds awful."

"It is. Last night was the worst one. I'm getting scared to go to bed."

"Did something happen yesterday? Something that might have triggered it?" He hoped she hadn't returned to the parking garage.

"Nothing. Except—except Beryl came by."

"Beryl?"

"Al's wife. His widow, I should say. She surprised me when she came over. Had no idea she knew where I lived." Mary Beth picked at a cuticle.

"What did she want?"

"She wanted me to tell her about Al's death. Said I was the last person to talk to him, but of course, I can't remember it.

She's having a rough time. Rough as in she could use your services." A bright drop of blood oozed from her finger where she tugged skin loose. He handed her a tissue.

"Tell me more about your nightmares."

"I've been having them ever since the hypnosis session. I can't remember much detail. Just a series of images. Blurry images. The parking garage. Al's body. The . . . the other person that I can't see clearly—the shadowy person.

"In the dream, I'm running. I'm desperate to get out of the garage but wherever I go I hit a wall. I can't find the exit. The shadowy person is chasing me, and I feel him getting close, looming over me. I'm terrified. I can't escape. I know . . . I know he'll kill me."

Caleb took in her rapid, panicked breathing. The sweat on her splotched face, as though she was living the nightmare right there in his office. "Mary Beth? Slow your breathing."

"Sorry." She obeyed, sucking in a deep, measured breath, then slowly releasing it in a hiss.

"Better?"

She nodded. "It's like I'm being haunted. The dream keeps coming back. I'm forever trapped in that damn garage."

"And you hit a brick wall," he said.

"Exactly. I can't get out. I can't figure out who's chasing me. But he keeps coming back, over and over. That's not all. There's the girl. Annie. She's suddenly there. The figure turns away from me and lifts a hand to her. She's scared, cowering, begging me to save her, but I'm paralyzed. I can't move. I can't intervene. His hand comes down to strike and that's when I wake up. Screaming, apparently."

Caleb moved to the small refrigerator and pulled out two bottles of water, handing one to her. She opened it and took a loud gulp.

Caleb sipped from his own.

"But Annie wasn't there," Mary Beth said. "She's in my dream—nightmare. Every. Single. Time. But she wasn't in the parking garage the night Al died. I know it. She's in North Carolina. It makes no sense. Why do I keep dreaming about her?"

Caleb wondered how far he should probe about the nightmare. He didn't want her to push herself too hard—something she had a pattern of doing. But mostly, he wanted to help.

"There's a technique to help with nightmares called deconstruction. It involves taking three or four important images from the dream and analyzing them down to their core—their symbolic meaning for you. It can be a hard process, but it's effective. It removes the power of the nightmare. It puts you in charge so you can control it." He spun the bottle in his hands. "It's completely up to you, Mary Beth. We can try it or not."

"Will it help me remember more about what happened?"

"Honestly, I don't know." Caleb leaned forward again, closing the distance between them. "Dreams aren't usually replays of actual events. They distort. They take an emotion—especially strong emotions—and give them images. I think it's the mind trying to make sense of what might be beyond logic. Your trauma from what happened is very real. Very present inside you. And your mind is trying to sort it out."

"This . . . deconstruction . . . will help that happen?"

"It should."

"So when I see Annie in the parking garage—that's not really a memory. It's an image my brain conjured up. That makes sense."

"If you want to try this, we can start with Annie as the first image."

"Okay. Let's do it. I'll do anything if it will help."

Caleb lifted a pad and pen and told her to describe what she remembered about Annie from the dream—every little detail. He wrote down what she told him, encouraging her with questions about how she looked, what she said, and where she was positioned.

"She wasn't wearing the hoodie in my dream," Mary Beth said. "That's what she had on in the alley, but in my dream, she wore a sweater. Pink. It reminded me of one I had as a kid."

That was interesting. "Tell me more about the sweater."

"It was a birthday present when I was nine. Pink was my favorite color back then, and I wore it all the time. But not later. Later I hated that sweater."

"Why?"

"I don't know. I just did."

"So Annie had on a sweater like the one you used to have," Caleb prompted.

"And she was younger than I remember her being. Anyway,

she was running, and the dark figure was after her, and I wanted to protect her. That was my job, keeping her safe, but I couldn't get to her. I couldn't save her from him."

"You wanted to protect her. You saw her as vulnerable."

"Exactly." Mary Beth looked at him with clear, focused eyes. "That was my role, but I failed."

"In your dream, you couldn't get to her." Caleb wanted to clarify that this hadn't really happened. Annie was not in the parking garage. "You wanted to shield her from the shadowy guy, but you couldn't. How did that make you feel?"

"Helpless. Frozen. Terrified—for her and for me."

He noted how she connected herself with Annie in the dream. "Helpless is a terrible way to feel. Can you think of another time in your life that you felt that way?"

She replied with a hesitant, "Yes."

"Can you tell me?"

"When . . . when things got bad with my dad. When he got mad." Her voice quieted. She sounded young.

"Can you remember a specific time?"

She nodded.

"How old were you?"

"Around nine, I think, when it first happened."

Nine. She'd received the pink sweater on her ninth birthday. Annie wore that pink sweater in her dream. Did Annie represent a young version of Mary Beth? As puzzle pieces clicked in place inside Caleb's mind, a sense of alarm spread inside him. "Can you tell me about the dark figure?"

"I can't see his face. It's like he's a villain from a cartoon or something. But he feels real. He's huge. And . . . menacing. He's after Annie. He wants to kill her."

Again, her breath became shallow and rapid, panic taking hold.

"Slow down," Caleb spoke softly, reassuring. "It's okay. You're safe."

"This happens whenever I think about him. I get kind of crazed."

"Deep breaths." He watched as she slowly calmed. "Better?"

"Yes. There's something else about him. Something glowing. It's gold. On his chest. I stare at it when he comes after me."

Something gold . . . a badge? Her father was a cop. So was Al. "What else do you remember?"

She blinked at him. "Something rushes through me. An energy. Maybe even strength—I don't know where it comes from. I'm not going to let him hurt her. But . . . but then it all went blank. And I woke up when Paloma shook me."

Caleb sat back, his mind whirling as a theory formed. A theory with terrifying implications.

He cleared his throat. "I think that's enough for today. You've done some important work." He hesitated, then said, "You've been resistant to seeing our psychiatrist, yet you're taking medicines from your roommate."

"Just to help me sleep."

"I understand. But Dr. Ryker is very good at his job. I'd like you to see him. I'd much rather you take medicines that have been prescribed for you."

She shook her head. "No. Not yet, Caleb. Just give me a little more time."

He sighed. So many clients were just like her. Stubbornly refusing the medicines that could make therapy much more effective. "Okay. I can't force you to see him. But please—give it some thought."

"If I'm not better soon, I'll see him. I promise."

As soon as Mary Beth left, Caleb texted Dr. Matthew Rhyker: *I need a consult. Today, if possible.*

It took a few minutes for the response to come. *Stop by the house at 5:30.*

I owe you one, Caleb replied.

Just one?

Kidney. I meant kidney, Caleb replied with a smile.

Chapter Forty-Two

Shull Lassiter stood beside Butch Miller and marveled at the number of words coming from his mouth. They were important words, no doubt about it, but Butch never talked this much. Ever.

They leaned against Shull's SUV in the parking lot by the Riverfront Park. The evening had brought a cool breeze over the Congaree, gray clouds hanging low. There were not many cars near them this time of day because suppertime in the South was a sacred hour.

"Rebel Son's out of jail," Butch talked around the toothpick wagging from his mouth.

"That's good, I guess. He talk to the cops?"

"Says he didn't. Says they brought in a shrink to try to get him to confess, but he didn't bite."

"A shrink?"

Butch nodded. The toothpick wiggled. "He's a good kid. A good soldier. Maybe not the sharpest knife in the drawer, but he's eager to please."

Shull wanted to say that most of the men on the Red Shirt's message board were dull knives but didn't want to get Butch defensive. Butch took pride in the digital universe he manipulated. He loved being the puppet-master. "Eager to please, huh?"

"Yup. Which might make him useful to us."

"I'd be careful with that. Cops are gonna keep an eye on him," Shull said.

Butch flicked the toothpick away. "I got other news for you. We found that Black guy they think killed Al. Name's Simon Madigan. He's been hiding out in an apartment off Saint Andrews Road."

Shull turned to stare at him. The man who killed his son-in-law. The man who ruined his daughter's life was still in Columbia?

"I've got a tail on him," Butch said. "What do you want to

do?"

Shull drew a staggered breath. He wanted the guy brought to him. Wanted to tear the miserable assassin limb from limb. But no—he shouldn't act on impulse. Best to plan. Be methodical. But still have his revenge. "Has his location been put on the message board?"

"Not yet. Want me to leak it?"

"No. Need to be strategic about it. Timing is important."

Butch shot him a puzzled look. "I thought you'd want quick resolution. For Beryl."

Shull frowned. He never like being questioned.

"He's gotta pay for what he did, Shull." Butch's tone changed. Quieter, yet somehow deadly.

"He will. When I say it's time."

Butch hesitated, then answered, "Sure thing, boss."

"What else you got for me?"

Butch continued. "The gun sale's going well. Thirty Spectres, Fifteen Springfields already sold. You're making a killing."

"Glad to hear it." He checked his watch. He was supposed to meet with Tommy Doyle in ten minutes. He'd had enough of Tommy's excuses for recent poor showing in the polls. Leaking the dirt on Saddington's wife would probably cinch the election for Doyle but damn, it left a sour taste in Shull's mouth.

Butch let out a sigh. "One more thing. Might be nothing. But I was selling the Spectres yesterday and some guy was watching us."

"What guy?"

"A red-headed dude. Ran his license plate. Turned out it was the same guy you had me check out—Caleb Knowles."

Jesus. Maybe Shull had underestimated that liberal idiot.

"Want me to handle him?" Butch asked.

Shull answered, "We'll let the Red Shirts have at him."

"They'll enjoy that." Butch saluted, climbed into his old truck and drove away, two dozen assault weapons secured behind the driver's seat.

Shull started to leave, too, but hesitated. He used his phone to log onto the Red Shirts message board.

Caleb Knowles is a problem, Pitchfork typed.

What do you need us to do? Cobra asked.

He hesitated, then typed, *I trust you to take care of this.*

Glad to, Cobra replied.

Sounds like fun, Zion joined in.

Be discreet, Pitchfork warned.

Tommy Doyle needed a new suit, Shull thought for the hundredth time. His stomach bulged over his waistband and the lapel had a small mustard stain that annoyed the hell out of Shull. How hard would it be to take the damn thing to the cleaners? Or buy something that fit him? Given what Shull gave to his campaign, he could afford a custom-made suit, but Doyle was too clueless to bother.

"What's the good word, Tommy?" Shull closed the door, shutting out the chatter from the volunteers stuffing envelopes and making cold calls in Tommy's cramped campaign headquarters.

Tommy looked red-faced and rattled sitting behind his giant desk. He seemed to be doing all he could to avoid looking at Shull.

"Judiciary committee met today, right Tommy?" Shull didn't sit but stood over him, arms folded.

"You know it did."

"And my bill?"

Tommy continued to avoid his gaze. "We rebranded it like you suggested. It's officially the 'Keeping Families Safe' act. But there's still a lot of resistance. Especially now."

"Now? Now's the perfect time for it. People are scared. Having their own firepower should make them more secure."

"True." Tommy loosened his paisley necktie. "But the assault rifles—they're a tough sell, Shull. Especially when we got James Saddington out there saying that the only reason we want the guns approved for open carry is so we can use them in the riots. Like we plan to gun down every Black person we see or something."

"So who do we have to bankroll on the Judiciary committee to make the bill pass?" Shull had deep pockets, and bribing came naturally to him.

"Meyers from Rock Hill. And the whole Charleston contingent. And that feisty woman from Lancaster."

"I can hit up Meyers. A donation to his reelection campaign might sway him. Norman is impossible. Damn do-gooder. The Charleston folks want the harbor dredged. You can threaten to have that removed from the infrastructure bill if they don't support you on this."

"Yeah, that should work. I'll check with them later and see if it flies."

"You do that." Shull paced the office then spun back around. "I'm taking care of Saddington. You damn well better take care of everyone else. I need that bill passed, Tommy. What affects me, affects you."

Doyle's eyes darkened. The muscle over his jaw poked out. "Yeah, look. I need to win this reelection. If the bill is going to sink me, I may need to let it go."

"Let it go?" Stupid cucumber. How dare Tommy act like he had a choice in the matter. "There will be no letting it go. We need this bill. *You* need this bill."

Tommy swiveled in his chair. "I wish you'd told me what you were going to do to Saddington. That was a low blow."

Shull didn't have to defend himself to an idiot like Doyle. He moved to the window and looked out at the small parking lot. Dusk had come and gone, leaving a black moonless night. God how he wanted all this done. Doyle reelected. His bill passed. Al's killer in the ground.

Beryl on the mend.

Tommy cleared his throat and wagged his phone at Shull. "Just got a text alert. James Saddington's having a press conference tonight. Think he's dropping out of the race?"

"If he's smart, he is. I gotta get going. You go to work on the Charleston delegation. Let me know when you've got their votes."

"Will do."

"We're almost to the finish line. Don't let me down."

Chapter Forty-Three

Caleb finished up with his last evening clinic client at eight thirty. Days like these always exhausted him: they began at nine and ended twelve hours later. Lonzo gave him compensatory hours to bank but finding a way to take time off while still managing his demanding caseload was a challenge. Today's two therapy groups and six individual sessions had him wrung out, and he still had a stack of progress notes to tackle. He could picture Lonzo monitoring the electronic records, waiting for Caleb to fall out of compliance yet again.

After completing two notes, a gentle knock surprised him. Janice, holding her purse and jacket, stuck her head round the door. "Let's go home, Caleb." She looked tired but as cheerful as always. The blue scarf frothing at her neck brought out her eyes.

"Why are you still here?" he asked.

"Because you are. I don't like to leave anybody alone. You working on your notes?"

"Yep. I just need another thirty minutes. I'm a big boy now. Go. Home." He stood, towering over her, arms crossed like a defiant child.

"If you're sure." She scanned his face, concerned. She was a mother to everyone who worked there, always bringing in treats, circulating the birthday cards, and starting the coffee before the first appointment arrived.

"I'm very sure." He walked her to the exit and watched as she approached her car. His was the only other vehicle in the lot. As she drove away, he returned to his office and pounded out four notes before deciding he'd had enough. He needed supper. A beer. And the bed.

He locked the office and stepped out into the night. A cold breeze promised the coming of winter, and he wished he'd remembered to bring a jacket. A truck idled in the parking lot, a few rows away from his car. Caleb gripped the keys as he hurried to the Subaru, eager to get on his way.

The truck pulled up closer and the driver climbed out. Before Caleb could unlock his door, the man approached. "You Knowles?"

"Yes. Who are you?" Caleb wished he'd parked near a streetlight. And wished the man wasn't so close.

"That's not important." He stood as tall as Caleb—six feet—but had more breadth, especially across his shoulders. A black mustache drooped around his lips like a swag and matched thick, unkempt brows. He wore jeans and a gray sweatshirt that had something bulging under it. A gun? Caleb flashed back to his encounter outside the hospital elevator. "Look, I need to—"

"You need to keep your damn mouth shut. I saw you on the news, mouthing off about my brothers like you think you know us. You don't know us." He moved closer, his face inches from Caleb's.

"What do you want?"

"Just here to give you a message."

A shiver ran down Caleb's back—he had a good idea what that message would be. The man's hand moved to the protrusion under the sweatshirt.

A rumbling noise drew their attention to the road where three cars pulled into the lot. Good. Maybe someone would help, or maybe the presence of witnesses would defuse this guy. The cars wheeled right up to Caleb's and the three men who climbed out did not look friendly. "This him?" one asked.

The man nodded, his gaze still fixed on Caleb. Four of them now, probably all armed. Caleb had no way to defend himself. That hard reality gripped him like a fist.

There had to be something he could do. "Look, I understand that you're upset about what I said, but—"

"Upset? We ain't upset."

The other men drew closer, swarming him. As he scanned their faces in the dim light, he recognized no one. Three looked to be his age. The others were younger. All wore the same expression: blank stares. Cold antipathy.

Caleb stepped back, his butt against the car door, hands outstretched. "Please. I just want to go home."

"Yeah. That's not going to happen," one of the men said.

"Zion, check him for weapons," the first man instructed.

Zion—that name was familiar. Boyd Holiday had said it at the jail.

Rough hands shoved Caleb against the fender and frisked him. Caleb jerked away from the violation and one of the men punched him in the jaw. Pain lanced through his head. "Think about this. I don't know what you have in mind, but whatever you do to me, you're only getting yourself in a lot of trouble."

"We should get out of here," Zion said. "Take him to the country."

"Agreed. Open your trunk," the first guy replied.

A click and the trunk of a black Oldsmobile yawned open. Zion reached in and pulled out zip-ties.

Crap. Caleb closed his eyes, willing someone—anyone—to drive up, to interrupt what might be his murder.

As if on cue, a fourth car arrived, a black SUV that somehow looked especially menacing. The man who climbed out immediately took control.

"What do we have here?"

"Pitchfork wants him taken care of," the mustached man said.

Caleb turned to the new arrival, who stood in the shadows.

The man came a little closer. He looked familiar: blondish hair brushing his shoulders. A goatee that needed pruning. "Vic?" Caleb asked.

Vic scowled at his name being voiced. He turned to the other men. "Brothers, what's the plan?"

Zion held up the zip ties. "A trip to the country."

"That what Pitchfork ordered?" Vic asked.

The man with the mustache shrugged. "He said take care of him. That's what we're doing."

Vic smiled, pulling a handgun from his pocket. "How about you leave him to me? Knowles and I have unfinished business."

The others pulled back, though Zion didn't look happy about it.

"What are you going to do to me?" Caleb wasn't sure why he even asked. The answer rested in Vic's hand. Vic gave him a long, inscrutable look. Caleb took in his untrimmed goatee, the small scar between his eyes. He looked as deadly as a timber rattler. Vic was too big for Caleb to wrestle. Too lethal to show mercy. And his Red Shirt friends were there to back him up.

The rumble of pounding bass notes took them by surprise. A van pulled into the lot, emblazoned with the sign: Columbia Industrial Cleaners. It was the janitorial crew Lonzo had hired to clean the building.

Vic eyed the intruders as they clambered out, armed with mops and brooms and buckets. Caleb felt an urge to hug them, especially when Vic holstered his gun.

"Hey there!" Caleb yelled out to them. "I need some help over here!"

"Shit," Vic muttered. He turned to the others. "That's too many witnesses. Let's get out of here."

And they did. The four men climbed into their vehicles and sped off. Caleb fell back against the metal, relief gushing through him.

Vic dropped into his driver's seat. "I better never see you again. If I do . . ." He gestured with the gun.

"You won't," Caleb whispered, as Vic drove away.

The janitorial crew approached, and Caleb waved them off. "It's okay. Thanks anyway."

Caleb climbed in his car, locked all the doors, and exhaled. Something manic was happening to his heart. His hands shook as they gripped the steering wheel. He fumbled for his phone and dialed Claudia's number to tell her what had happened.

"Jesus, Caleb. You got any names?"

"That dude Vic. And someone they called Zion. Remember Boyd Holiday mentioning them? And someone they called 'Pitchfork.' Sounds like he's a leader. Guess they're not real names, are they?"

"No, but I'll run them and see what turns up. How about you avoid empty parking lots for the next few days. Or anybody who looks like they might love the color red. Come into the station and make a report first thing tomorrow."

"No problem." After ending the call, he drew a deep breath, and started the car.

Twenty minutes later, Caleb found himself pulling into Sam's long driveway and parking in front of his house. Lights glimmered through the floor-to-ceiling windows of his brother's living room, which meant he was still up. Caleb climbed the steps and punched the door button three times—the signal that identified the nighttime caller as his annoying brother.

Sam opened the door. He had on sweatpants and a T-shirt, his feet bare. He guided Caleb inside and positioned him under the light. "What happened to your face? Who did that?"

Caleb signed all of it, describing the men who encircled him, who threatened him in that cold parking lot.

"Jesus," Sam said. "And you were all alone."

"I was until the cleaning crew showed up. I need to send them flowers or something," Caleb signed with a sick little laugh.

"Have a seat," Sam said, then disappeared into his kitchen. When he returned a few minutes later, he had a bag of frozen peas, which he placed against Caleb's jaw, a beer, and a small plate with crackers, fruit, cheese, and pepperoni slices. He had bottled water for himself. "I figured you hadn't had supper yet."

Caleb placed his fingers against his chin then extended the hand: "Thank you." The beer tasted wonderful. The peas did their job. He didn't have much interest in the food but did his best. Chewing wasn't fun.

Sam sat across from him, hands knotted together. "I want the guys who did this to you caught," Sam said. "I want them locked up forever. Right beside the ones who destroyed Justice Be Done."

Caleb nodded. He knew how much the sculpture meant to Sam—it was like his child. He probably cared more about its demise than his own injuries.

"Yeah," Caleb signed. He saw that muscle throbbing over Sam's jaw, as if holding back unspoken words. "What, Sam?"

Sam let out a sigh. "I don't like feeling like this. The rage. It kind of eats at me."

"I get it." He knew Sam was a gentle guy. A gentle giant. He could get angry, though. He could, on occasion, let down his tight control, and then heaven help anyone standing in his way. That hadn't happened in several years. Still. "It's a lot to process, and you already have plenty going on."

"We both do." Sam sipped his water. "Maybe I should hire some security. To keep an eye on you."

Sam would do it, too. He had the funds and the overly-protective instinct.

“I don’t need a bodyguard.”

“You need a keeper,” Sam retorted. “How about this? You stop working the evening clinic until the craziness stops. Or if you do, you text me when you’re about to leave and I come see you to your car.”

Caleb suppressed a smile. “Yes, Mom.”

“I’m serious. And . . . and there’s something else.”

Sensing a change in Sam’s tone, Caleb set down his beer, extending both hands and moving them back and forth, signing, “What?”

“Stop. Doing. Stupid. Shit. I mean it. You have to be careful now. When you’re driving, make sure nobody’s following you. If they are, call Claudia or head straight to the police station. Leave your porch light on and scan your surroundings before entering your house. Do you have a Taser? If not, I’ll get you one.”

“Yes, to being more careful. No to the Taser. I’d just zap myself and you know it.”

“True.” Sam seemed to relax a little.

Caleb sipped more from his beer, snagged another cracker, then stood, feeling better. “I should get home. Cleo will be worried.”

“Text me when you get there,” Sam said, and Caleb smiled.

Chapter Forty-Four

Caleb pulled into his drive behind Shannon's car. A much-welcome surprise—apparently, she'd come home a day early. Caleb donned a game face and entered the house, securing the door behind him.

"You're home! Finally!" Caleb dropped his knapsack on the floor to wrap his arms around Shannon. She looked travel-weary: hair springing free of its clip, jacket rumpled, new bags sagging below her ice blue eyes.

"Finally. I missed you." She kissed him, and he tried not to wince.

She pulled back, then guided him under the light, frowning when she spotted the reddening bruise. "What the hell happened to you?"

He told her all of it, and about the visit with Sam. "He's ready to hire me a bodyguard."

"Not a bad idea." She gave his face a thorough study. "Maybe I should take you to the E.R. to get that checked out."

"I'm bruised and sore, that's all."

She looked skeptical. "You called the police?"

He nodded. "Claudia. She said to go to the station in the morning and file a report." He pulled her into the living room, eager to change the subject. The two of them snuggled close on the sofa. "I didn't think you'd be back till tomorrow. How'd it go with the funders?"

"Okay. But I'm so tired of being nice to people I may need to spend the next three days growling and being ornery."

"Fine with me. You're hot when you're ornery," he answered with a smirk. Shannon curled up beside him—even a growly one—made him feel content. She made their home warmer somehow. She'd picked out most of the furniture: the overstuffed sofa "perfect for napping." The two rockers by the fireplace. The art over the mantel. But it wasn't the "stuff" that mattered. It was the little Shannon noises she made, her scent on the pillows. The sight of her making any room a happier place.

Shannon reached for the remote to turn on the news. The face of Caleb's client filled the screen. He stiffened.

The news camera pulled back to take in the small family sitting in what looked like a living room: Lenore Saddington, James, even young Brian on a large leather sofa. Behind them was a stone fireplace with a photo-ladened mantel and flowers blooming on the hearth. A golden retriever rested at Lenore's feet. Mark Frierson, the now-familiar newscaster, sat across from them holding a hand mic. "Mr. Saddington? I understand you wish to issue a statement."

James shot a quick glance at Lenore before he began: "This race has challenged me in ways I never expected. I knew it would be a tough campaign. I expected attacks from my opponent—that's how politics works. But I didn't realize how low people would go. I didn't expect this type of attack on my family."

"I understand you received some sort of threat in the mail?" Frierson prompted.

Lenore eyed the camera, then looked down as her husband took her hand. "My husband received an anonymous package this morning. Yes, it was a threat. We had a choice: give in to the blackmailer and pull out of the race or do this. Confront the truth head on."

She looked at James whose gaze on her was oddly intimate, even adoring.

"And this truth is mine to share. So here goes." She drew in a breath, releasing it slowly, lips parted slightly the way Caleb had taught her to help control her anxiety.

You got this, Lenore, he mentally said.

"Last year, following a very difficult time . . . I was hospitalized for psychiatric treatment. I have depression. It's an illness that I now control with therapy and medication. But before I got help, I was in a bad way. It was James who took me to the hospital. He visited me every day. He attended family counseling sessions. He's supported my recovery in every way possible." She laid a hand on Brian's shoulder. "As has this little guy."

Brian smiled at her. His blond hair had been carefully styled. The polo shirt almost matched his dad's, as did the angle of his cheeks and jaw, but the green eyes had definitely come from Lenore. He'd lost a front tooth and poked a pink tongue through it.

"Your mental health issues were something you kept private?" Frierson asked.

"Of course! How is it anybody's business? Except now it is. Someone found out and threatened to tell the press. They want James to withdraw from the race." She sat up straight, glaring into the camera as though she was addressing whoever sent the damn package. "But he's not pulling out. I don't want him to. We're not giving in to blackmail."

"I see," said Frierson.

"I don't think you do. Yes, our privacy has been violated. Horribly violated. But I want to use it as an opportunity. One thing I've learned is this: mental illness is not a flaw. It's not something to be ashamed of any more than having heart disease or skin cancer is. I have depression. It's not who I am. It doesn't define me."

Frierson looked a little taken aback by the strength of her words. Caleb wanted to throw his hands in the air in victory. She had come so far.

James spoke up. Did he need the attention focused on him again? Typical politician. "When I'm elected, my second order of business—after introducing the ban on assault weapons—will be to improve funding for our public mental health system. I want this to include an anti-stigma campaign, focusing on schools. Like my lovely wife has so beautifully articulated, mental illness doesn't need to bring shame. It should bring out our empathy and concern."

Again, Lenore addressed the camera: "So I want to say to whoever the coward was who sent the package: it didn't work. We're not dropping out of the race. Instead, we're going to win it."

James looked surprised by her tone, her confidence. Little Brian stuck his tongue through the hole in his teeth again.

James spoke to the camera. "There will be a rally on the statehouse steps tomorrow evening at six p.m. I will be speaking about how it's time to end the hate and the violence. About my proposed gun safety legislation. And about how Columbia can get back to who she really is—a place of warmth, a place where we care about our neighbors, no matter the color of their skin."

Shannon clicked off the TV and ran a hand through her long, somewhat frazzled hair. "I need a shower."

Caleb sighed, not wanting her to leave the room just yet. It felt like she'd been gone for weeks.

"There's room for two," she said over her shoulder.

Caleb grinned as he stood. Indeed there was.

Chapter Forty-Five

"Shit," Shull muttered at the TV. The damn press conference was everything he didn't want to happen: Saddington announcing he was staying in the race and actually getting mileage from the released medical records. And bragging about that stupid legislation he planned to introduce that would screw over Shull's business. He poured himself a bourbon and wished he could drown in it.

"Everything okay?" Glenna eyed him over the novel she was reading—some feminist crap she'd bought online.

"Yep."

"You look wound up."

"The news always does that to me. Saddington and his BS gun safety bill."

She closed the book and placed it on the side table. "We need to talk, Shull."

Well crap. This day just got better and better. "I'm not in the mood—"

"It's not about us—that's a topic for another day. It's about Beryl. I'm very worried about her."

Shull was, too. "She's grieving."

"No, she's not. She's too stoned on the pills to process Al's death. It's not healthy."

Glenna had a point. Beryl stumbled through her day, drifting from one medication to another. Valium daytime. Ambien night. When she'd left that morning in her car, Shull worried she'd crash it or get a DUI. "What do you suggest?"

"She needs professional help. I know that's not your favorite thing. I know you think therapy is BS, but your kid is suffering and it's only going to get worse if we don't help her."

He shook his head. No way he was sending Beryl to a shrink. Wife number two had gone to therapy and that had led to an ugly, expensive divorce.

"We have to move forward with the funeral arrangements, too. Even if they can't release his body, we can do a memorial service. I keep trying to get her to make plans, but she won't. Al's family is very worried, but I guess it's too hard for her to face it."

Right on cue, Beryl shuffled into the room. She wore sweatpants she'd had since high school and a white cardigan she had buttoned incorrectly. "Daddy?"

"There's my girl!" He patted the space on the sofa beside him. She drifted over and plopped down. She could have smelled better.

"How do you feel, Beryl?" Glenna asked.

"I took another nap. I like napping. It's the waking up that sucks."

"I know, honey. It'll get better, I promise." Shull tried to sound convincing.

"You say that. You want it to be true. But the only thing that makes it better is what's in the medicine cabinet," Beryl mumbled.

Glenna arched her brows at Shull, her patented "I told you so" look.

"That's just a temporary fix. Pills aren't good for you, hon," he said.

Beryl eyed the drink in his hand as though she wanted to snatch it from him. He tightened his hold.

She said, "I keep thinking that once they catch the killer, I'll be okay. Maybe then I can . . . I don't know. Move on?"

"You want closure," Glenna said. "That's understandable."

"I went to see his partner. Thought that would help. Al never liked her much. Said she was soft. Unreliable. Said she'd probably get kicked off the force. She was nice though. Tried to make me feel better. Everybody wants me to feel better, don't they?"

"Of course!" Glenna said.

"But there's only thing that will help. When they catch that Black son of a bitch who killed him. It's not fair that Al's killer gets to walk around, living his life, while Al's . . . Al's gone."

"I know, honey." Shull placed the drink on the table, out of her reach. "But I promise you this—we're gonna find him. And we're going to take care of him. Before you know it, Al's killer will be brought to justice."

Glenna cocked her head, her "are you out of your freakin'

mind" look. "I'm sure Shull is right, it's just that these things take time."

"Well I'm out of patience!" Beryl's voice rose, sharp as a blade.

"It won't be much longer. I promise." Shull ignored his wife's incredulous glare. Glenna didn't know he had the culprit under surveillance.

Beryl grabbed the remote and turned on the TV, surfing until she found the Hallmark channel—some romantic movie that made Shull want to stab a fork into his eye. He left the women to the film and went into the kitchen.

He used his cell to text Butch: *We still have eyes on Madigan?*

A took a minute for the response to come: *They moved him to an apartment off Broad River. He moves around a lot.*

We need to act.

Absolutely. Just say when.

This time it was Shull who hesitated. He needed the Madigan situation resolved. But maybe they could do it publicly, to make a statement.

Bring him to the statehouse tomorrow night. Send word to the Red Shirts that Al's killer will be at the Tillman statue at 8 p.m.

A pause, then Butch replied: *This is the moment we've all been waiting for.*

Chapter Forty-Six

Mary Beth moved through the world like a ghost. It was a crisp Friday morning, the sun a golden orb in a cloudless sky, but she had little appreciation for it. Her drive to the clinic had been mindless, and as she entered the building and sat in the familiar waiting room, she looked around at the other waiting clients: a mother with a little boy who didn't want to be still. An older woman on her cellphone, berating someone for not doing what she had asked. A pimply teen in the corner texting with his thumbs, laughing at the response, and texting again. All these people with their own lives, their own families. Their own reasons to exist.

Mary Beth felt like she'd lost hers.

Would she say that to Caleb? He might think she was suicidal and slap her into a hospital. She didn't want that. She just wanted to . . . exist. Be more than a vapor—because that's how she felt. Did Caleb have a cure for that? Could he give her substance?

Maybe it was the nightmares that wrenched life from her. The shadow man who swooped in like a vampire, who filled her with so much terror that she lost her voice, even in sleep. She couldn't even scream anymore. He couldn't be a memory; she knew that now.

She'd done the nightmare deconstruction thing. She couldn't write "shadow man" on the paper without feeling like an idiot so she drew a sketch. She was supposed to record every detail she remembered. She used the sketch to do that, too, but nothing made sense. The black coat he wore had blurry edges. He changed in size—massive sometimes, smaller and more agile other times. She could never see his face.

The hand though. That always came in clear. Wide, with long fingers. A chunky gold ring on his left hand. Wiry dark hairs on the knuckles. That hand swooping toward her face.

Annie's face.

"Mary Beth?" Caleb appeared in the doorway and motioned

her back. She stood, feeling oddly wobbly, and smiling when she saw the look of concern on his face. He was nice to be worried. "You okay?" he whispered.

"I'm fine." For a ghost. She clutched the notepad to her chest as she walked, focusing on putting one foot in front of the other so she wouldn't stumble into the wall. Maybe she'd evaporate one day. Simply dissolve into mist.

It would be a blessing.

Caleb held the door to his office and watched her very closely as she took a seat. She didn't want to cause him to worry. She took the bottle of water he handed her—liking the familiar routine of this. The water. The comfortable chair. The plants climbing the window like they wanted to escape.

"Tell me how you are," Caleb said.

"Fine."

"I don't believe you."

She looked over at him, surprised by the confrontation. He simply shrugged. "You look . . . different. Is this a bad day?"

"They're all bad. This one is no worse than the others." This was a lie of course. This was the day she began to disappear.

"Yet something is off. I can't put my finger on it, but something."

Smart man, that Caleb. She held up her pad. "I did the deconstruction like you suggested. I'm not very good at it."

He smiled. "You can't be good or bad at it. It's a journey. It's to help you learn what your dreams are telling you."

"Nightmares, you mean."

"Right. Sorry. There's nothing pleasant about what you're experiencing." He reached out a hand. "Can I see what you did?"

She felt reluctant. He'd see the picture she'd drawn and realize how crazy she was, but she gave it to him anyway.

He sorted through the pages, stopping at the one with her drawing. "This is interesting."

"I tried to write about him, but the drawing worked better. I'm not an artist or anything."

"He looks menacing. Sinister."

"But I still can't see his face. I try. Hard. But . . . I can't. I just . . . can't." Her voice quaked and it embarrassed her.

Caleb's head cocked to the side as he watched her. After a moment, he said, "Maybe you're trying too hard. Maybe the figure is like your memory. Neither will become clear until you're ready. I don't think it's good for you to push yourself."

Of course he'd say that. He meant well, but he didn't know what she knew. If she didn't remember, she'd fade away into nothingness.

"Mary Beth?"

"I keep thinking about his hand," she said. "Why do I recall it with such detail, when everything else is kind of blurry? Do you have any ideas?"

"We'll get into that in a bit." Caleb smiled encouragingly. "First, I see you're not sleeping well, thanks to the nightmares. How's your appetite been?"

She let out an exaggerated sigh. "Not great. But I can stand to lose a few pounds." Al had often chastised her about her weight. *"You're too soft, Branham. Inside and out. You need to toughen up and slim down if you're gonna make it as a cop."*

"This is not the way to lose weight." Caleb softened his voice. "How's your mood been? How's the anxiety?"

"Not too bad." She didn't tell him how she felt like she'd left herself. That she'd become a ghost, because he'd know how crazy she was then.

"Tell me more," he prompted. He was always doing that.

"I'd rather get back to the hand." She pointed to her sad little sketch. "It's a big hand. And he's got a ring on his finger. Big. Chunky. Gold."

Caleb leaned back, watching her.

"What's weird is sometimes I think it's a wedding ring. But other times, it's different—like a class ring from college."

Again, silence from her therapist.

She studied the drawing, a memory sharpening into focus. "Al wore a ring like that. He was a Citadel grad." He was so damn proud of that and brought it up every chance he got: "Back when I was a cadet" or "My professor back at the Citadel" worked into almost every conversation. Mary Beth had been to college, too, but Al had never even cared enough to ask her.

"Al wore a class ring," Caleb reflected.

She blinked at him, picturing the ring. Al's hand in front of her face. Fear crawled up her throat like a spider.

"Mary Beth? What's going on?"

She couldn't answer. She didn't know. But the hand was there, big, in front of her face, ready to strike. Like her father used to hit her. She closed her eyes, desperate for the vision to clear.

"Hey," Caleb whispered. She felt him move. Heard the crack of his knees as he crouched in front of her. "Tell me what's going on."

She shook her head, trembling now. Her whole body quivering. The hand. It would hit her. It would knock her to the ground and then what would happen? She felt frozen.

"Open your eyes, Mary Beth." Caleb's voice was stronger now. "Look at me."

She obeyed, blinking until his kind face came into focus.

"Excellent. Now take in a long, slow breath. Like I taught you."

The breath stuttered coming into her, but she let it fill her chest, pictured the oxygen sliding into the alveoli in her lungs.

Caleb handed her the water bottle. Her hand vibrated as she held it to her lips and drank.

"Better?"

"Getting there."

"Good. Want to tell me what happened?"

No, she didn't. She wanted to hide under the chair. To flee the room like it was on fire, but she'd never to do that to Caleb. He'd always been kind to her. "Just another panic thing. But I'm okay now."

"Triggered by the drawing?"

"Yeah."

He reached for it. "Let's stop doing the nightmare deconstruction for now. Let's focus on getting a better handle on the anxiety symptoms. We've talked about you seeing our psychiatrist. It's time I make that happen."

"Meds?"

"Not long term. Just till you have your sea legs back."

She'd resisted this. Needing meds meant she was more screwed up than she had wanted to admit, but now she knew. Maybe a prescription would keep her from disappearing.

He didn't wait for an answer. He got on the phone and

asked for the next opening on Dr. Rhyker's schedule. This time she didn't argue.

"He's got an opening this afternoon at four. Can you come back then?"

"Okay." She'd try anything to feel better.

Absolutely anything.

Chapter Forty-Seven

Caleb hurried through the crowded entrance of the hospital and smacked his hand against the elevator button. He hoped he wasn't too late.

Quinn Merrick, the hospital social worker, had called him. "They're transferring Laquan back to the jail this afternoon," she had told him. Bad news piled onto an already sucky day. He wasn't even sure why he'd come here. He couldn't stop the transfer, as much as he wanted to.

The metal doors parted and he stepped inside. He could smell the annoying tang of disinfectant. A dark-skinned mother and little girl entered behind him. The mother, so pregnant he wondered if she might deliver between floors, gripped the hand of the preschooler who stood on tiptoes to press the button for the fourth floor. Caleb hit the "three" button and forced a smile for the child. The last time he'd been in this elevator he'd been with Boyd Holiday—the Red Shirt would-be assassin who was now back out on the streets.

The mother leaned against the wall, stroking her immense middle, eyes closed. She looked ill.

"You okay?" Caleb wondered if he should call for help.

She flashed an exhausted smile. "Six days overdue. Carrying Shamu."

The little girl reached a hand over her mother's stomach. "That's my brother."

"Yes, it is," the mother said.

Caleb thought the child was probably biracial: the amber skin. Gold-flecked brown eyes. He wanted a better world for her, a world where Black people and biracial people and everyone else would be safe. He glanced at the mother, a small smile sliding onto her face as she looked at the girl.

And he thought about Laquan, preparing to return to jail where he might get killed.

The world was a long way from safe, especially for people of color.

As he stepped off the elevator, he spotted Quinn talking to an officer. She motioned him over. "They're sending transport for Laquan. Should be here in ten minutes."

"How's he taking it?"

"Like it's a death sentence, which it may be." She scowled at one of the officers. "Surely you can do something. You know what will happen when he goes back there."

The officer squirmed under the intensity of her glare. "I don't control the jail, but they'll do all they can to keep him safe."

"Yeah, right. That worked so well last time." She cocked her head at Caleb, who followed her to the door outside Laquan's room. "Do you have any ideas? I'm scared about what they'll do to him."

"I wish I did."

"His mom's been crying all morning. Laquan's more worried about her than his own safety."

"How's he doing medically?"

"He's better, but not great. Still has stitches. One punch and we're looking at serious internal injuries, not that the cops care about that." She shook her head.

"I have an idea." He pulled out his phone and called Claudia.

Miraculously, she answered. "What do you want?"

"Do you greet everyone that way?" He pressed the speaker button so Quinn could hear her.

"Just you." She huffed out a sigh.

"I'm visiting Laquan." He filled her in on why he'd been summoned. "There has to be a way to keep him safe. Anything happens to him, this town will explode."

"Like it hasn't already?" She sounded tired. No worse—demoralized.

"Laquan is still on the mend. Seems to me it would be wise to transfer him to the jail infirmary," Caleb said.

A pause, then, "He's that bad off?"

"He will be if he goes back to general population. You know it, too. If he's in the infirmary, there's staff twenty-four seven. Will be harder for anyone to get to him." Harder, but not impossible. He glanced at Quinn who was texting someone on her phone.

"That might be an okay short-term solution, but we can't keep him there indefinitely. And we'll need doctor's orders."

Quinn flashed her phone at him. "Just did the request. Should have the order in a few minutes."

"Excellent." He said into the phone, "At least this buys us some time until we can get him out of jail."

"Not sure how that's going to happen, but okay. I have to run." Claudia clicked off.

"Thanks," Quinn said. "This helps. Why don't you go tell him?"

Caleb rapped lightly on the door and entered when he heard a weak "come in."

Laquan stood at the window. He wore the jail-issued orange jumpsuit, an ominous reminder. "Remember what you promised," Laquan began. "You said you'd check on my mama."

"I will. I understand she's doing better."

"Moving around okay with the walker. She's going home tomorrow."

"That's excellent news." Caleb added hesitantly, "And where is 'home' now?"

"A duplex off North Main. It's handicap accessible. Some nice people got it for her and paid rent for an entire year." He smiled, a kid recognizing the goodness of people even after he'd seen so much evil.

"Wow. That's incredible. I have some news for you, too." Caleb told him about the plan to move Laquan to the infirmary. "That should keep you safe for a few days, at least."

"That's good." He didn't sound enthusiastic, but who could blame him. "What happens then?"

"Then we get you out of jail." The voice came from behind Caleb. Female, unfamiliar.

He spun around to find a roundish, short woman with reddish black hair styled in a thousand short braids. She marched up to Laquan and extended a hand. "I'm Tasha McDowell. Your attorney."

"Attorney?" Caleb introduced himself.

Laquan shook his head. "I can't afford to pay—"

"That's taken care of. I'm working with a civil rights group that's taken an interest. Sit down, Laquan. I have some things to discuss with you." She pointed to a chair, looking like someone unused to being defied.

Laquan sat.

She turned to Caleb. “I’ll need time alone with him.”

“Okay. But before I go—how do you plan to get him out of jail?”

She turned to her client. “Do you mind if I share my plan with your—”

“Social worker,” Caleb supplied.

“Social worker?” She asked.

Laquan nodded at her.

She shot a frown at Caleb but opened a folder she pulled from a bulging satchel. “We’re suing the jail for allowing a hate crime to take place. That should motivate them to keep you safe.” She flipped through some long, legal sheets. “And here’s a petition for a bail hearing. My plan is to hit the media tonight. A little public pressure should help us.”

Caleb liked her confidence. He suspected Tasha McDowell would be a formidable opponent in court.

“You got one job here, Laquan. You stay out of trouble. Keep your head down. Stay alive until I can get you out of jail.” She turned to Caleb. “And you. I may want you to testify. How do I get your notes?”

Caleb hated court. Hated sharing confidential information in a trial setting. The exposure always—without fail—sabotaged his relationship with the client. “I’ll need written consents from Laquan and his mom. And a court order. Also, there’s something you need to know.” Caleb went on to tell Tasha about Palmer Guthrie’s disclosure that he’d mistaken Laquan for a shoplifter.

Tasha shook her head. “Well damn. That stupid mistake started all this B.S.” She smacked the folder closed. “And now, you give us some privacy.”

Caleb stood and approached his client. “I think Ms. McDowell will take good care of you. And I promise to check on you at the jail.”

“And Mama . . .”

“And Pearl. I promise.”

Chapter Forty-Eight

Everything echoed in the parking garage. The shouts. The clatter of dropped metal. The scrape of boots against the concrete. No sound came from Mary Beth though. She tried to scream, to summon help, but words froze in her throat, just as her feet froze in place, preventing her from running.

Al was there. His voice boomed like a cannon. Simon Madigan winced under the looming bulk of Al spitting out words nobody should ever hear.

Then the gun appeared, gripped in Al's hand. He always loved to hold his weapons. The barrel pressed under Simon's chin.

The dark figure appeared then, a shadow, a presence, black and cold in the night. Watching her. A specter.

She gathered all her will, her courage, and moved, approaching Al. "Don't!" she yelled. "Don't hurt him."

He shot an annoyed glance at her, as though she were a pesky mosquito he'd like to swat.

"I mean it Al. Don't. Hurt. Him." She pushed all her strength into her voice as she reached for a metal pipe that rested on the cold concrete floor. Not her gun. She wouldn't shoot her partner, but the pipe might pose enough of a threat to make him stop.

Al turned to glare at her. "Put that down."

She eyed the gun, still pressed against Simon's throat, and the hard lines of Al's face. A man who could kill and feel nothing.

The figure came closer, his shadow darkening everything. She could hardly see, but suddenly Simon wasn't there. It was Al, and the figure, but then Al was the figure, and she was so confused, her thinking a tangle of threads. On fire.

It changed again. As it turned to stare, the face was different. Familiar.

Her father. Standing there in the parking garage, a hand raised, the hand she'd dodged a hundred times and failed to dodge even more often.

Why was he there? What did he want? She knew the answer. It was in the way the hand swooped at her, smacking her face, the familiar sting biting deep inside her, his voice resounding "you worthless, lazy, bitch," words she'd heard too many times, slicing her into pieces.

So she swung the pipe. Summoning every ounce of energy she had, she smashed it into him, knocking him down, prepared to hit him again when she noticed the pool of blood seeping across the gray floor.

She bent over him, the side of his face concave from where the pipe had struck, only it wasn't her father. It wasn't the dark figure.

It was Al's body crumpled on that cold concrete.

Mary Beth shot up in bed, her face doused in sweat, breath gone from her lungs. She gasped, starved for air, for relief from the terror of the nightmare.

The images remained. Simon. Al. The dark figure. Her father.

Al's body.

She blinked again and again, wanting her eyelids to erase them. Bile climbed up her throat. She fought the sheets that imprisoned her, her feet scrambling to reach the floor. She stood, staggered into the bathroom, and threw up in the toilet.

She moved to the sink next. Cold water on her face and rinsing the vile taste from her mouth. She thought she might be sick again, but nothing remained in her stomach.

She dropped onto the toilet seat, gripping her middle, and wishing she could pretend she'd never dreamed it. The images flashed in her mind, solidifying into memories. Her dad hadn't been there of course—he'd been dead five years. The dark figure—also not there. Al was. And in her panicked state, she'd confused Al with her father.

And she had killed him.

She bent forward, retching again. Dry heaves. This new reality changed everything.

From outside the bathroom, Yoga meowed, wanting attention.

"Not now," she muttered.

When her cellphone rang, she stumbled away from the toilet, snagging a towel as she reached for it. Paloma.

"Hey." She almost didn't recognize her own scratchy voice.

"Are you home?" Paloma's voice yelled over a cacophony of noise.

"Yeah." It was so hard to focus, a piece of her still tangled in the dream, but something in her friend's voice raised alarm. "Where are you?"

"At the big rally in front of the Statehouse."

The rally. It must be evening then. "You okay?"

"So far. It's so damn crazy I can't even describe it. It's . . . bad. I don't know when I'll be home. Can you feed Yoga for me?"

"Of course." She should be there with her friend. She should be working the riots, but she wasn't well. No, she wasn't well at all.

Paloma said, "Things are about to pop. We caught word that the Red Shirts got their hands on Simon Madigan. They're bringing him here. We're hearing something about an execution."

Execution? They would be killing the wrong man. Madigan wasn't the murderer—she was. Mary Beth thought she might throw up again. She couldn't let this happen.

Paloma went on: "The National Guard is sending more troops, but they may not get here in time. It's going to be a bloodbath."

Mary Beth shivered at Paloma's tone. Her friend didn't scare easily, but fear reverberated in her voice now. "What can I do?"

"Stay home. Stay safe. Take care of Yoga." A pause, then, "And if something happens—make sure he has a happy home. If you can't keep him, find him someone who will love him."

"Stop it. You'll come home to him. End of story." Mary Beth felt a new fear—for the safety of her best friend. For all the officers in danger from this chaos. It was her fault, all of it.

Another pause, then Paloma said, "We can't let them execute him."

Mary Beth closed her eyes. "No. That can't happen." And she was the only one who could stop it.

"Gotta go. Text you later." Paloma clicked off.

Mary Beth stared down at the phone. She knew what she had to do. Armed with the truth, she had only one option. Only she could do it.

After brushing her teeth and washing up, she returned to the bedroom and put on the uniform, buttoning and smoothing down the front and donning the belt but not her gun. She wouldn't need the gun. The hat came next. Her hair pulled back, she positioned the hat carefully so that the bill was in perfect alignment with her face. She studied herself in the mirror, memorizing how she looked.

If she survived this night, she would never wear this uniform again.

She fed Yoga an extra helping—just in case—and scooped his litter box for good measure. He wound between her legs, his purr rumbling, and she wished she could gather him close and crawl back into bed, but that wasn't an option.

Instead she drew a deep breath, closed her eyes, and focused on her mission, because that's what it was. Probably her last.

The drive to the Statehouse took longer than she expected. Cars inched along Sumter and Main Streets. Not a parking spot in sight. She ignored the "no parking" sign and pulled into a bank lot, noticing other cars planting themselves haphazardly, drivers climbing out with signs. A few opened trunks to remove guns.

Paloma was right about the potential for a bloodbath. Mary Beth attached the billy club to her belt, felt the empty holster. She would not be shooting anyone tonight.

She had a fleeting thought of her brother and his family. Should she call and tell him . . . what? Goodbye? What was there to be said?

But there was someone she needed to talk to. Someone who deserved to know. She reached into her wallet for the business card and punched in the emergency number for Caleb's office.

Chapter Forty-Nine

The text from Sam asked Caleb to stop by. It was a good day for a drive. The highway to Sam's lake house wove through forests and fallow cotton fields. Autumn had brought early flames of color on the maples and oaks, and the dome of sky overhead was a brilliant blue.

He turned off the highway and onto the long, winding drive that led to Sam's house. Caleb could see him in the workshop with someone else. Jace was in there, too, the two of them bent over Sam's drafting table looking at some kind of sketch. Caleb walked in and flashed the lights to signal his arrival.

"You two look like co-conspirators," Caleb said and signed, letter spelling the last word.

"Nope. I'm just a consultant this time," Sam said.

"Not if I get my way," Jace argued, articulating carefully as Caleb signed.

Sam motioned Caleb over to the drawing labeled "Justice Be Done."

"What's the plan? You're going to redo the sculpture even after what happened?" Caleb's voice rose, his signing crisp with fear.

Jace nodded. "The funders want it. The city needs it. I just need to get your stubborn brother on board."

"I'm glad Sam's being stubborn." But it didn't sound like his brother. Quite the opposite.

Sam shook his head. "That's not the issue."

"What is it, then?" Jace thumped the drawing spread out between them. "It's a great project. This time around, it'll be even better."

"It will," Sam agreed. "You and Amanda should finish this. I'm around if you need a consult on the wood sections."

"I don't get it." Jace pursed his lips like he'd tasted an unripe grapefruit. "You've been a part of this from the beginning."

Sam let out a loud sigh and shot Caleb a "help me" look.

"What's going on, Sam?" Caleb signed.

His brother ran a hand through his hair, looking frustrated, then said, "Okay. Here's the deal. I'm having surgery next week."

"You're having the tumor removed? Finally?" Caleb blurted out.

Sam nodded.

"Wait—what?" Jace looked alarmed.

Sam told him all of it—the mass, the radiation sessions, and the ultimate plan of removing the tumor. "My little brother's been pestering me to get it done so I'm getting it done."

"You are?" Caleb asked, not quite believing.

"I always do what you tell me to do."

"Huh?" Caleb felt like he'd stepped into an alternate universe. "Are you on something?"

Sam ignored him and turned to Jace. "I'll be out of commission for . . . well, we don't know how long. Hopefully just six weeks or so. I don't want this project delayed."

"Jesus, Sam. I had no idea." Jace looked at Caleb, perplexed.

"I didn't want you to worry. But when I've taken the afternoon off the past few weeks—that was the radiation treatment."

Jace looked back and forth between the brothers as if trying to take it in. His eyes softened. "I had no idea," he repeated, his voice low.

"This isn't something to worry about," Sam said, and Caleb wanted to believe him. "I'll have the mass removed and, if the margins are clear, I should have an easy recovery. But climbing around on a ladder isn't a good idea. Not for a while, at least."

"You'll be coming to our house to recover," Caleb said, expecting a fight.

"Okay. You don't have stairs. That has some appeal."

"And Cleo will be your fulltime nurse. We got you covered." Caleb's relief sounded in his voice and maybe showed in his signing hands. He wanted that tumor out of his brother. He wanted clear margins.

He wanted—needed—Sam to be whole and healthy for another fifty years.

Jace waved a hand at the plan. "I can't believe I bothered you with this."

Sam slapped a hand against the drawing. "Jace. This. Is. Important. I'm so proud of our work. You know everything you need to know about the wood components to this piece. Amanda knows almost as much as I do. So you won't have any problem finishing it. I cannot wait to see it completed." Sam gripped Jace's arm, a sign of their friendship. Jace nodded, his eyes misting a little. He looked relieved when his phone rang.

He carried it outside, leaving Caleb alone with Sam. "Is that why you wanted me to come over? To tell me about the surgery?"

"And to make sure the timing worked for you."

"It's fine." Caleb would make it work, no matter what. Hell, he'd quit if he needed to. Sam mattered a hell of a lot more than his job.

"Are you nervous about the operation?" Caleb signed.

"A little. But also relieved that I'm getting it over with. Dr. Simm thinks that the radiation may have shrunk it some. That's good, right?"

Caleb winced at the vulnerability in Sam's question. It wasn't like his brother. "Absolutely. This will be a piece of cake."

Sam nodded slowly. "I like cake."

From outside, they could hear Jace's voice rise in pitch. He paced outside the open garage door, his boots crunching on fallen leaves. When he clicked off the call, he turned to them. "I gotta go."

"Everything okay?" Sam asked him.

He shook his head as he approached. "Shit's about to hit the propeller blade."

Caleb struggled to sign that, but Sam seemed to be doing okay reading Jace's lips.

Jace eyed each of them, then continued. "You heard of Simon Madigan?"

Caleb tried not to react to the name.

"The guy they think killed the police officer?" Sam asked.

"Yeah. Only, he didn't do it. I've met him. Talked to him. He's just a kid who wants to be a Civil Rights attorney, not a killer.

"There's a small group of us trying to keep him safe. The Red Shirts have been looking for him—they'll kill him if they get the chance. So we've been moving Simon around, just trying to keep him safe. Except—"

"The call?" Caleb asked.

"One of my friends was moving Simon to a safe house in the country. A truck ran him off the road. They took Simon."

"Oh, God," Sam said.

"They plan to kill him." Bleakness resonated in Jace's voice. "They're gonna bring him to the Capitol and execute him."

Caleb didn't wait for permission before calling Claudia. When she came on the line, he pressed the speaker button and filled her in. None of his information seemed to surprise her. Caleb asked, "Did you know about this? Is he even still alive?"

An impatient exhale preceded her usual, "I can't disclose what I know. But I will say this—things are going to get more volatile tonight. Stay the hell away from downtown."

"No problem there. But Claudia, y'all have to save the Madigan kid. Don't let the vigilantes win." Caleb looked over at Jace, who was busy texting someone.

"Preaching to the choir, Caleb." Another loud sigh. "We're trying to get James Saddington to cancel his rally tonight, but he's stubborn. Says he won't be controlled by fear. Apparently, he won't be controlled by common sense, either. Stay away from the Capitol. And say a prayer that things don't go nuclear. I fear they might." She clicked off.

Jace rolled up the drawing and inserted it in a cardboard tube. "I have to go."

Caleb held up a hand, relaying the concerns from Claudia, but Jace merely shook his head. "You don't get it. Hell, you're white. How could you? The Red Shirts are out of control. They want to make an example of Simon. God knows what else they'll do. They want their racism on full display on CNN."

As Caleb signed Jace's comments, he noted the concern forming on Sam's face. He felt the same way.

"My people are convening. We can't let them kill that kid." Resolve echoed in his voice, and a conviction that worried Caleb. Jace might get himself killed.

He snagged a slip of paper from Sam's table and scrawled down a number, which he handed to Jace. "This is Detective Claudia Briscoe's cell number. You can trust her. Let her help you."

Jace looked skeptical but pocketed the slip.

"Please, be careful," Sam said.

Jace approached, placing a hand on Sam's shoulder. "You worry about getting yourself well. I'm gonna be fine. I have nine lives like a cat."

"I hope you're right," Caleb replied, watching as Jace left the studio.

Sam leaned against the drafting table, arms crossed, lines of worry etched on his face. "I should follow him."

"I'll put you in a headlock if you try."

Sam looked out the door as Jace's jeep sped away. "I'm worried about him."

"And I'm worried about you. Though less so now that you're having the surgery." Caleb felt his phone vibrating—a page coming in. He glanced at the number: his work emergency line. He signed to Sam that he needed to make a call.

"This is Caleb Knowles. I got paged?"

"Caleb! Thanks for calling in." Janice was on the line. "One of your clients called. I know this isn't your weekend to be on call, and if you prefer, I'll forward it to the on-call person."

"What's going on?"

"It's Mary Beth Branham. She called asking for you. Wanted me to give you a message that worried me. I have her phone number and can text it to you."

"Please do. What was the message?"

"She said 'tell him thanks for trying to help me.' Then she apologized for 'being a bother.' It was her tone, Caleb. She sounded so despairing."

"You did the right thing in phoning me." He hung up and punched the number Janice texted him. Mary Beth took her time about answering, and when she did, sounded breathless. "It's Caleb. I got your message."

"Hey." He could hardly hear her over background racket: shouts. Rumbles. Pops like fireworks.

"Where are you?"

"Doesn't matter," she practically yelled into the phone.

"I think it does. What's going on, Mary Beth?"

"I know the truth. And I think maybe you know it, too."

"What truth?"

"I wondered why you held me back. From the hypnosis. From the dream deconstruction. I wanted to understand the nightmare, but you said not to rush it. You knew, didn't you?"

He did not want to discuss this over the phone. It was far too dangerous. He'd hoped he was wrong, but as insights had come to Mary Beth, his realization of the truth solidified. He'd met with Matthew to discuss his fears and gotten guidance to back away from the nightmare deconstruction. "The truth will come to her, but it's best not to rush it," he had said.

Booms sounded in the distance. "Are you downtown?"

Mary Beth continued: "You figured out that it was me. I was the one who killed Al, not Simon Madigan."

Crap. "Mary Beth, we need to talk through this. I can meet you at the office—"

"It's too late for that." She hesitated, her breath audible through the phone. "Why did I dream about Annie? Why did I think she was there?"

Mary Beth could implode any moment. This all felt too volatile.

"Tell me." She demanded.

He sighed. Maybe if he kept her talking, she'd change her mind. "I think she represented you when you were a child. She symbolized the vulnerability you felt back then. I think something happened in that garage that triggered a flashback of the abuse you experienced."

Quick, panting breaths came through the phone. "I dreamed about him last night. My dad. It's all so confusing."

"It is. That's why we need to talk. Tell me where you are."

"I told you it was too late to talk. What the hell good is talking, anyway? I killed someone. And now more people will die if I don't stop it."

Caleb closed his eyes, dreading what would come next. "Are you downtown?"

"Simon Madigan is innocent. I have to do something—"

"I understand why you think that, but this situation is too dangerous. Go to the police station. Or call Detective Briscoe. She'll understand and she'll help you figure out what—"

"There's no time for that and you know it. I just called to tell you thanks. You helped me, Caleb. You helped me get to the truth." Her breath quickened—was she moving? "I want you to know that I'm okay with this. I feel . . . right. Strong. I'm doing what I have to."

"Mary Beth—"

"Goodbye, Caleb. And thank you for believing in me."

He heard her click off. He redialed but it went to voicemail. He didn't bother leaving a message.

"What's wrong?" Sam watched him, eyes soft with concern.

"A client in danger." Caleb ran a hand through his hair, feeling a little frantic.

"Anything you can do?"

"That's an excellent question." He let out a weird little laugh. He had to do something. He couldn't let Mary Beth complete this suicide mission. "I have to go."

Sam stepped closer. "Where?"

"I have to go see a client."

"Where?" Sam sounded almost confrontational.

He thought about lying, but that wasn't how it worked with him and Sam. "Downtown. I have to get my client somewhere safe. But I'll keep an eye out for Jace."

Sam glared. "You promised me you wouldn't do stupid shit."

"I know. But this client—it's life or death, brother."

Sam reached for a jacket that hung on a hook. "Then I'm coming with you."

"No, Sam." Caleb snapped two fingers against his thumb and shook his head for emphasis.

"My car or yours?"

"You're just out of the hospital—"

"I'm fine. And staying here while you're doing something incredibly stupid by yourself would not be good for my blood pressure. So if you're going, I'm going."

Caleb sighed, pulled his keys from a pocket, and pointed to his car.

Chapter Fifty

You coming tonight? Butch texted Shull.

Shull was already in his truck, barreling toward the city. He'd told Glenna to keep an eye on Beryl. That he had to run an errand and would be back soon. Yeah, he had an errand alright. He pulled over and texted Butch: *Yes. Are we ready?*

Chomping at the bit.

I want no mistakes, Shull replied.

Gotcha.

Shull merged back into traffic. When he encountered the mass of cars headed toward the rally, he had to smile. The Red Shirts would do him proud tonight.

And they'd take care of Simon Madigan, who was on his way to the Capitol, bound and gagged in the back of a van. Shull couldn't wait to face him. To look him dead in the eye, the man who had killed his son-in-law. The scum who ruined Beryl's life.

His phone buzzed and he pressed the answer button on his steering wheel.

"Shull? It's Tommy. You hear about what's going on?"

Yes, Cucumber. Shull had heard. Shull had made it happen. "It was bound to explode sooner or later."

"Saddington's holding a damn rally on the Capitol steps! The Red Shirts are rallying on the other side. I'm headed there now. They'll want me to speak."

"That's the last thing you should do." Shull tried not to laugh. Tommy Doyle had no idea what was about to come down. "You stay away. Issue a statement tomorrow. Believe me, there will be a lot to talk about."

"What's going on, Shull?" Again, that demanding tone.

"Tommy. Do as I say. There's more to all of this than you know. I'll explain everything tomorrow. For now—you need to trust me."

Silence. Shull tightened his grip on the steering wheel. He could not afford for Tommy to complicate things.

Finally, Tommy relented. "I do trust you, Shull. I have to."

Shull didn't bother with goodbyes before ending the call. Traffic had slowed to an anemic crawl, which pleased him. Filled him with pride. He had the power to cause this. Him. Shull Lassiter. Moving in the shadows, pushing the buttons. Pulling the strings on hundreds of puppets.

He used the car's voice command to dial home. When Glenna answered, he asked, "How is she?"

"I've told you a million times. She's a mess."

He sighed, not appreciating her tone. "She up?"

"She was for a bit. Couldn't get her out of her pajamas. She needs a shower but wasn't interested in my advice on the subject."

That wasn't like his Peaches. Even as a girl, she'd been fastidious about her appearance. He remembered her in kindergarten, how a spilled drop onto her dress from an ice cream cone led to a meltdown. How she never set foot in the sandbox he'd built for her because "no dirty, Daddy."

"I'm worried about her," Glenna said, softer now.

"She back in bed?"

"Yep. Glued to the news again. Says they're going to get Al's killer. Says that's what will make her better. I tried to tell her revenge isn't going to bring Al back. She needs therapy. You're going to have to get her there, Shull. You're the only one she listens to."

He hated Glenna's berating tone. Like she knew what was best. She didn't understand Beryl and what she needed.

"Order her some pasta from Café Divino. Tell her she can have it after she showers. That ought to work. See you in a while."

He didn't wait for her smart-ass answer.

He parked in front of a dumpster behind a café, not exactly legal, but that didn't matter. The Red Shirts had agreed to convene behind the old tire store on Gervais Street and march to the Capitol. As he reached the sidewalk, two buses passed him, windows open, passengers chanting from inside.

The buses parked, and the crowd spilled out—mostly Black people, some whites, all carrying signs with bullshit messages on them: "Justice for Laquan." "Hate won't win." "End the Violence." Saddington's people, the idiots.

Shull lifted his jacket collar and kept pace with the marching mob, eavesdropping. They had come from Charleston—two AME churches and an Episcopal parish joining forces. Their tone was festive, the chanting now an off-key song: "We Shall Overcome."

Oh no you won't, Shull thought with a smirk.

He turned down the alley and found a large white crowd gathered behind the old hotel, all sporting the red shirts with the pitchfork across the front. Shull didn't wear his. Nor did Butch, who stood beside a brick wall, watching. Shull worked his way to him, weaving through the festive throng. "How many are we expecting?"

"Hard to say." Butch's voice was so low that Shull almost didn't hear him. Another cluster of men arrived, these carrying their own placards. One had a Tillman quote: "White Domination or Extermination" that would surely get media coverage. It wouldn't be hard to work this crowd into a frenzy. Let the fervor take hold. Let loose their hatred of Blacks. Then when Madigan arrived . . .

"We got him!" One of the men proclaimed, holding up his phone. "We got Madigan!"

This created quite the stir among the other protesters: "Where is he?" "What's the plan?" "We'll make our own justice!" The energy picked up, a nervous enthusiasm building. Good. Shull needed them amped up.

"There's a problem you need to know about," Butch whispered, motioning that they should step away. Shull followed him to a quieter spot near a streetlight where Butch lit a cigarette.

"What?"

"The guns I sold the protesters—the Spectres—they're not here. We sold sixty, but I don't see a single one in this crowd." He motioned to the mob with his Salem.

"Who did you sell to?"

"Vic. He placed a massive order and I hand-delivered to him. But he's not here either."

"What the hell?" Shull frowned. "Maybe he's running late?"

"Not like him. Nor is not replying to my texts." Butch took another long drag. "We got the numbers here, though. And most are packing."

"They need to conceal their weapons when we reach the Statehouse grounds. Make sure they know it." Shull peered over at Saddington's rally just across the street on the Capitol steps. Security was sparse. No way they could adequately monitor this mob when they made their move. Good.

"We got everything set for the fire. Told capitol police it was part of Saddington's stage set," Butch said with a chuckle.

Shull nodded. If anything pulled the cameras away from Saddington, it would be that. And what followed.

Butch took another puff then dropped the cigarette, grinding it out with the toe of his scuffed boot. "It's almost go time."

"Any second thoughts, Butch? Should we wait for Vic?" Shull asked.

"We don't need him." Butch eyed him with a strange intensity. "I've been waiting for this moment for years."

Chapter Fifty-One

Mary Beth wondered if the uniform was a mistake. She didn't want people to think she was here in an official role. She wouldn't be stopping to deal with drunks or combative protesters. She had only one purpose.

Still, the uniform gave her access. The giant crowd parted as she passed through. She liked the energy around her: hopeful songs chanted offkey. Signs calling for peace and justice. A large group close to the stage holding hands and swaying, Blacks and whites in unity. It made her think that maybe, just maybe, her town would recover from this insanity. She might not live to see it, but that was okay. What mattered was the truth.

The candidate, James Saddington, took the stage. His wife stood beside him. Mary Beth had seen her on the news, talking about her own mental health issues. A brave disclosure, and Mary Beth had felt profound admiration. She wished she could be that open about her own struggles. Maybe if she had been, things wouldn't have gone so far. Too far.

Too late now.

She spotted a cluster of approaching police officers on the sidewalk and ducked behind a tree. Paloma and her partner led the pack: the odd couple. Paloma with her glistening dark skin. Lanky, pale Kyle in step beside her. They would keep each other safe.

She wanted to say something. To hug her best friend and tell her thanks for everything, but knew she couldn't. Paloma would stop her. Kyle would help. They wouldn't understand how critical it was that she carry out what she'd come to do.

Noise erupted from the street behind her. She turned to see a large group of men, all dressed in the red shirts she'd learned to dread, marching up Main Street. Their chants had a more aggressive, angry edge. When they reached the grounds, they pushed through the larger crowd, jostling and shoving, some protesters pushing back. The police officers rushed to intervene, but it wasn't needed. The Red Shirts kept moving, pushing through the friendlier crowd at Saddington's rally and marching to the other side of the statehouse.

Two rallies. One explosive night.

She moved through the garden to follow them, like a panther stalking prey. Some red-shirted men waited on the steps. They'd erected a large wooden structure, crude, but its shape inescapable. A ten-foot tall pitchfork.

A white-haired man stood at a microphone reading words that clearly weren't his. They weren't even from this century: "We of the South have never recognized the right of the negro to govern white men, and we never will!"

The Red Shirts screamed their agreement.

"Governor Benjamin Tillman spoke the truth!" The man said to more shouts of assent. Their hate speech sickened her. Why did they worship a man so full of hate?

Another protester approached—younger, with a dark goatee and purple baseball cap. He piled kindling at the foot of the structure. Another brought a match. Soon, a blaze erupted, flames licking the wood as they climbed, smoke billowing up to the heavens.

This was highly illegal. They may have gotten permission for a rally, but there was no way they had permission for that. She spotted Kyle on his radio, hopefully summoning the fire department, as other officers moved to intervene.

Another flurry of activity distracted them. A black SUV parked, hazard lights flashing, and a second truck rumbling up behind it. The men who climbed out hurried to the back of the SUV and opened it. It took three to haul out a man they had bound and gagged; he stumbled when they pulled him to his feet.

It was Simon Madigan.

Chapter Fifty-Two

Caleb approached the growing crowd with trepidation. How would he find Mary Beth in all that chaos? Sam walked stoically beside him, his gaze skimming the mob, probably looking for Jace.

A short line of police officers flanked the periphery. Caleb wished there were more of them. The protesters north of the statehouse looked like a mostly peaceful lot—singing songs, waving posters and signs promoting justice and an end to gun violence. A younger Caleb would have been in the thick of it. But the throng of Red Shirts pressing through them had a different tone. Hostile. Bullying. Shoving their way through the mob as though looking for a reason to fight.

More buses arrived, people pouring out. The volume grew, the pressure mounting as the two groups encountered each other.

Sam nudged him and pointed to a cluster of Black men standing by a lamp post. Jace stood among them. Sam led the way, muscling through the crowd like Moses separating the Red Sea. "Jace," he said.

"Sam? What are you doing here?" Jace asked.

Sam cocked a thumb at Caleb. "I'm here to keep him out of trouble. Any sign of Simon Madigan?"

"Not yet. But I'm not liking this crowd." Jace pointed at another group of Red Shirts hurrying by.

Caleb didn't like it, either. What would they do to Mary Beth if he couldn't stop her? He reached for his phone and called Claudia.

"What?" she demanded when she answered.

"Are you at the protest?"

"Why?" She sounded pissed, which wasn't unusual. "Are you?"

"Yes. I'm . . . looking for a mutual friend."

"Branham? Is she here? Why?" Shouts bellowed in the background. Claudia was definitely on site.

"There's been a development." Caleb had to scream if she had any chance of hearing. "She's not well. I'm trying to find her, so if—"

"I'll keep an eye out. Stuff is about to go down."

Before he could ask her, "What?" she ended the call. Caleb stared out at the swelling throng. Along the perimeter, scuffles erupted. How would he find his client in all that? And what did Claudia mean when she said, "stuff was about to go down?" Her tone had scared him. He looked at Sam. If gunfire sounded, he wouldn't hear it. Maybe this wasn't a great idea.

Caleb tapped Sam's arm and signed, "We should go, Stay close."

Sam eyed Jace, then Caleb, and nodded.

Chapter Fifty-Three

Shull remained in the shadows, watching, the phone gripped in his hand. Butch sent texts to update him: *Van enroute. Fireworks about to start.* A few fights had broken out, the police intervening, but there had been few arrests so far. Good. Shull needed as many as he could get for the final act. It would be spectacular.

Van is here.

Shull felt a rush of adrenaline. Excitement? Anxiety? Both. He texted Butch. *Our people in place?*

Waiting for your signal.

Someone had lit a torch. The flaming pitchfork summoned more Red Shirts. Hundreds swarmed the grounds of the statehouse as the man at the microphone, who introduced himself as "Zion," continued one of Governor Tillman's most famous speeches: "We deny, without regard to color, that 'all men are created equal:' it is not true now, and was not true when Jefferson wrote it."

The crowd ate up the words as though they'd been written that day. Tillman's spirit seemed alive and well.

Ready for Madigan? Butch texted.

Shull had a moment of hesitation. Maybe this was enough. Maybe they should turn in Al's killer to the police.

He has to pay for what he did, Butch texted. *We all need this.*

Things might get out of hand.

They already are. Butch was right. *This is what they're hungry for.*

The crowd needed the sacrifice of Simon Madigan. And he needed them.

Shull moved closer for a better view. The throngs pushed in. The man at the microphone raised his hands and began the chant: "White Power! White Power!" The words sliced through the night air.

Chapter Fifty-Four

"What the hell?" Caleb signed, pointing to the smoke billowing from behind the statehouse. Sam tugged Caleb in the direction of the fire. So much for leaving. The size of the mob, the noise they made, the glow from the burning structure was overwhelming. Caleb kept close to Sam, who used his size to push like a battering ram through the throng.

Suddenly, the crowd parted, the chants of "White Power" silenced. An SUV idled on the street as a group of Red Shirts dragged a stumbling Black man, his hands bound, his mouth gagged, up the sidewalk.

"What are they doing?" Sam asked.

"I think that's Simon Madigan," Caleb signed.

The kid looked awful. A cut over his eye barely scabbed over. A reddened lip bulged under his nose. His T-shirt torn and dirty. He stared at his feet as though unsure where to place them. What else had been done to him? And what would they do to him now? Caleb glanced at Sam, desperate to help but unsure how he could.

As the men led Simon to the stage, Caleb recognized one: Boyd Holiday, the guy from the hospital. Crap. The horde pushed forward, grabbing at Simon, pulling at his shirt like they wanted to strip him bare. He didn't fight. He looked too weak to do it. The speaker stepped back, microphone gripped in his hand, as Boyd shoved Simon up to the platform.

"Here he is, brothers. The man who killed Lt. Al Fuller."

"Boyd! Stop this!" Caleb shouted, but couldn't be heard. The Red Shirts erupted. Shouts of "Justice for Al" pealed through the night air. Boyd raised a hand in front of him. Just like Hitler.

"Jesus." Caleb pulled back, scanning the faces for his client. Sam remained beside him, looking as desolate as Caleb felt.

A single gunshot split the night.

Chapter Fifty-Five

Mary Beth closed her eyes and pictured the ocean. She tuned out the screams, the pushing from people rushing to get closer to the tower of fire in front of the Capitol. She floated on her raft, letting the waves lift her, lower her, as she took in slow breaths of smoky air. Inhale to the beat of five, exhale seven. Just her and the ocean. A calm slid through her. Purpose. She knew what she had to do.

When she opened her eyes, she saw him. Simon. Bloodied. His eye swollen, scrapes on his face. He looked lost and defeated. Someone hurled him to the stage, others screamed words she didn't want to hear. She longed for silence. To be back at the ocean. But she had work to do.

She felt no fear as she approached. She thought that odd—she cut through the crowd, ignoring their insults, making eye contact with nobody. Her hand felt for the gun that wasn't there. An instinct, but she didn't need it. Her weapon was her voice.

And she was strong enough to do it.

She pushed through a group of men in some kind of intense discussion and reached the metal steps leading to the platform. The man with the microphone was talking about Al. "A hero in blue." "One of our brothers. "A loving husband." "A martyr for our cause."

"Al died at the hand of this man. And now he'll know our brand of justice!"

A blast from a gun made her jump. She cast a panicked glance at Simon, but he looked uninjured, but ashen in the firelight. The shot must have been fired into the air. More guns appeared, pulled from pockets, removed from backpacks. Assault weapons extracted from the folds of coats. So many of them, and she felt like a civilian caught on the battlefield in some massive war.

"Don't hurt him!" Mary Beth finally reached the stage and attempted to ascend the steps. "It's not his fault. He didn't kill

Al!" she screamed.

A hand grabbed her shoulder.

She tried to jerk away but it held tight. She spun around, prepared to fight, and found Caleb Knowles standing there. "Mary Beth," he said. "Don't do this."

"I have to. They'll kill him." She wouldn't be stopped. Not even his soft, caring gaze, his hand gripping her arm, or the taller man beside him who kept his stare fixed on the stage.

"They won't listen to you!" Caleb pleaded. "Look at the mob. Do you think they care about the truth? They just want vengeance."

The taller man nudged him and pointed beyond the platform. A large group of men approached—mostly Black, probably from the other rally.

"Jace," the taller man said.

"This is going to get a lot uglier." Caleb released her arm to sign what he'd said. So the tall man must have been his deaf brother.

Another gunshot echoed, this one close. She used the distraction to pull away from her therapist and scramble up the steps.

"Mary Beth!" Caleb shouted, but she'd moved beyond him. He would never understand why she had to do it—that even if she failed, she had to try.

Shull counted the weapons. Six Spectres. Nine AKs. A dozen or so handguns. One idiot even had a short sword. And probably more firearms Shull couldn't see.

This should do nicely.

The Black kid, Simon Madigan, squirmed like some trout on a hook. No way he'd get free, not with three rabid Redshirts containing him. And with this armed, rowdy crowd: no way he'd survive.

Butch slipped up beside him, cell phone gripped in his hand, texting someone.

"We good?" Shull asked.

Butch's smile was unexpected. His eyes seemed to glow with excitement. "We're ready."

Shull spotted a new man on the stage. He had long blond

hair, a goatee, and wore a revolver strapped in a shoulder holster. "Who's that?"

"Finally. That's Vic. About time he showed." Butch texted again. Vic glanced at his phone then pocketed it. "He better not be ignoring me."

But Vic looked to have his hands full. He strode across the platform to where the Madigan kid stood, head bowed, looking broken, like he knew what was about to happen to him. Vic said something to him then yelled at the man with the microphone.

Shull spotted another person who appeared there—a police officer. A plumpish white woman. She made a grab for the microphone, but the man wouldn't release it. He shoved her, knocking her down.

That's when all hell broke loose.

Chapter Fifty-Six

"You can't reach her," Sam shouted at Caleb over the tumult. Fights broke out. The man who'd been speaking was no longer alone. Up on the stage, Mary Beth had reached for the microphone, but someone knocked her down. In the middle of the bedlam, the flames rose from the wooden pitchfork, fingers of fire reaching for the sky. Red-hot sparks showered on the crowd below.

Someone checked Simon Madigan's shackles. Below, a group of men pointed their weapons.

Jesus Christ. This was a firing squad. They were going to execute him right there on the steps of the state house.

One of the men on stage looked familiar. Vic. The guy who'd been involved in the arms deal at Guthrie's store. The venomous man who had threatened Caleb outside his office.

"Damn it," Caleb uttered. He looked at Sam, saw the same helplessness on his face that Caleb felt.

Mary Beth managed to stand and move closer, to move in front of Simon Madigan and yell out, "He is innocent. I know who killed Al Fuller!" but her words were drowned out by a crowd that didn't care.

She'd be executed, too, Caleb realized. Collateral damage. He had to get to her. "Shit," he shoved through the bustle of Red Shirts to ascend the steps when Sam grabbed him. "No, brother. You can't help her."

"I have to—"

Sam's grip tightened. "No."

Loud booms blasted behind them. Smoke billowed from canisters tossed at their feet. The men with guns coughed, some doubling over. It became hard to see, to breathe.

"Caleb? What the hell?" Claudia Briscoe had a handkerchief over her face. "Come with me."

He hacked and struggled to breathe, letting her lead him away from the smoke, gripping Sam's sleeve to keep him close. Claudia wasn't alone. It looked like fifty officers, decked out in full riot gear, dispersed into the crowd. Behind them, National Guardsmen pointed weapons as though waiting for someone —anyone—to make the wrong move.

"Get Madigan," Caleb said between coughs. "They're going to kill him."

"Not on my watch they're not." Claudia gestured for him to sit and hurried away back to the platform. And walked straight up to Vic. Did she not realize he was heavily armed? But she seemed unafraid. Stood there talking to him like he was a regular person instead of a terrorist.

Caleb stared. Vic removed what looked like handcuffs from his pocket and was helping to arrest the rioters.

What the hell? Vic was a cop?

It all went to shit.

Shull watched in horror from his station in the trees. The men who were supposed to shoot Simon Madigan all doubled over, hacking, the smoke billowing all around them. Police moved in—an army of them. Or maybe the army was the National Guard troops assisting them. One Red Shirt after another was led away, cuffed, gagging. On stage—he could barely see through the fog—someone freed Simon Madigan.

He clutched his phone and yelled to Butch, "What now?"

No answer. Where was he? Why were people running away instead of shooting? A second later, Butch appeared at his side, his face reddened, tears running from his inflamed eyes. "Damn smoke," he mumbled.

In that second, with the screams and the smoke and gunshots, someone released Al's killer.

No. He couldn't allow it. He thought about Beryl. He turned to Butch. "What do we do?"

Butch had a wild look about him, but the smoke had him coughing. "You have to finish this."

"How?" All was bedlam.

Butch flicked the flap of his jacket and snagged the handgun he always had strapped under his arm. He pressed it into Shull's hand. "I can't . . . see well enough."

Shull gripped the gun and considered what to do. He never expected to be front and center. He preferred lurking in the background. But if he didn't take charge now, Al's killer would likely escape. He had no faith in the justice system.

Butch gripped his shirt. "This is what we've been waiting for. You can do it. You *have* to do it."

Beryl's tearful face filled his mind. Her devastation had to be avenged. Shull fished a bandana from his pocket and tied it around his nose and mouth. Still hard to breathe, but at least the fumes weren't filling his lungs. He just needed to get a little closer. He'd always been a good shot, but Madigan was a moving target, shielded by that traitor Vic and a Black woman in what looked like a bulletproof vest. He had to be precise, but that was his specialty. Guns were his life, after all.

Shull snaked through the crowd, the gun hidden until he was close enough to fire. His hours of target practice had led to this moment. He would complete what he couldn't trust others to do.

The certainty of this drove him forward, filled him with purpose and intent. Nothing would stop him. Not the smoke bombs. Not the National Guard. Not the police.

As he approached the platform, tears blurred the scene in front of him. Smoke seeped through the cloth of the bandana, making it hard to breathe.

There. Now he was close enough. Madigan being led down the stairs, the Black woman to his right. Shull had enough bullets for both. He raised the gun and aimed it.

"Claudia!" A man with auburn hair screamed out, pointing at Shull. It was Knowles.

It shook him, just for a nanosecond, but his finger tightened on the trigger.

Caleb stared in horror at the man pointing the gun and screamed a warning. Everything seemed to happen in brutal slow motion. Vic hurled Madigan to the ground just as Claudia spun around, gun in hand. Four quick blasts exploded from her weapon.

The man she shot looked dazed. He stumbled back, collapsed to his knees, then his torso hit the ground. A dozen officers swarmed him, guns drawn, blocking Caleb's view.

A noise drew his attention back to the stage. A sickening thud as Claudia crumpled onto the platform.

It took a second to register. His friend, gunned down. A

bloodstain blooming in her side, just under her twisted left arm. The noise, the chaos, the world seemed to stop. He blinked, gathering himself, and yelled, "Claudia? Claudia!" as he rushed to her. "I need EMTs!" The bullet had found the arm opening of her bulletproof vest. He pressed his hand against the seeping wound. The warmth of the blood surprised him. So much of it, red sliding through his fingers and puddling around them. "Claudia," he whispered again.

Sam appeared, holding a paramedic's arm, and dragging him up the steps. Soon emergency personnel pushed Caleb out of the way so they could work on Claudia, shouting out orders to each other, screaming into a radio. Worried police officers stood sentry around them, a wall of blue. Claudia's family. Caleb scanned the anxious faces, grateful for the solidarity. Maybe they could will Claudia to be okay. When a gurney arrived, she was hoisted onto it.

"Caleb?" her weak voice cut through the chaos.

He bent over her. "I'm here. You're going to be fine." He needed to believe it. How close was the bullet to her heart?

"Did I get him?"

"You did."

"Racist bastard," she whispered, her eyes drifting shut.

He wanted to follow her to the hospital, but he couldn't leave. Not yet. He signed to Sam to stay put and returned to the platform. Mary Beth sat on the top step. She looked dazed as she scanned the chaos around her. "Mary Beth?"

"Caleb? Is Simon okay?"

"He's fine. Bruised, but safe and very much alive."

"Thank God."

"How about you. You doing okay?"

She looked him in the eye, hers softening. "I will be. I have to turn myself in. I know it's what I have to do."

He didn't argue. Maybe he could help. Maybe her mental health issues would spare her a criminal sentence. His next thought disgusted him: at least his patient was white.

A Black person would face the death penalty for this crime.

Chapter Fifty-Seven

"I could punch you, Caleb Knowles. Right in the face." But instead, Shannon ran a cool, damp cloth across his eyes, which still burned from the smoke at the riot.

"I'd deserve it."

"No shit. You went to the protest without me. Without even telling me. What if something had happened to you? There were guns there. A sea of idiots with guns. What would I have said to Julia? Do you have any idea what might have happened?" She'd gotten herself worked up now, tears spilling from the corners of her eyes.

"I'm sorry, babe. I mean it. It was a client—I didn't know what else to do."

"And you dragged Sam into it!"

Caleb grabbed her hand. "I didn't drag Sam anywhere. I couldn't stop him from coming. He's my self-appointed keeper."

"So am I. And apparently, we're not enough to keep you safe." Her voice broke a little, and it broke something in him.

He stood, wrapping his arms around her. "I'm safe. Sam is safe."

"And Claudia?"

He pulled her closer. "They said she was stable. Quinn promised to call if anything changed." He'd stayed at the hospital until this word came, waiting with anxious officers, watching the minutes click by. God, he hated hospitals.

Shannon sunk against him, her head against his chest. He breathed in the scent of her, lavender from her shampoo. "We need for all this to be over. All of us."

He wondered if it were possible. If Mary Beth's arrest, and Simon Madigan being set free, would change things. He wanted to be hopeful, but fatigue and fear for Claudia still weighed him down. He buried his face in her hair, grateful for this tiny bit of sanctuary.

Two mornings later, Caleb sipped coffee as he scanned the news on his iPad. The man who'd tried to assassinate Claudia turned out to be Shull Lassiter, the local gun shop owner and major contributor to the homeless shelter Shannon managed. From the photo, Caleb realized he was also the man in the truck who'd been in front of his home when he played ball with Julia. If Lassister survived his injuries, he'd spend the rest of his life in prison. He deserved it.

Caleb's cell buzzed. "Hey," a weary female voice said over his phone.

"Claudia?" He exhaled in relief. "Damn, it's good to hear from you."

"Good to be heard from."

"How do you feel?"

"If you ever say 'just a flesh wound' around me, I'll kick you in the nuts. Bullet nicked a rib but otherwise I got off lucky. Going home today."

"You're unstoppable. Need anything? I can run to the store or drop off some lunch."

"Nah. What I need is for you to go check on your client. I cleared you to visit her. She hasn't hired a lawyer and she needs one. There's someone else who's asked to see her—I think it's best you're there when that happens."

"Who?"

Static obscured her words, then, "Gotta go. Can you stop by the station later this morning?"

"Will do."

They'd brought Mary Beth from the jail to the police department for his conversation with her. Professional courtesy, Caleb guessed. When he entered the small interview room, she sat at the metal table, wearing a jail jumpsuit, her hair frizzing around her blotchy face. She didn't look up when he dropped into the seat across from her. "Mary Beth? You okay? Has bail been set?"

It took a minute. She drew a breath, pulled her gaze up to him, and forced a smile. Her eyes looked crusty. "Bail hearing is this afternoon. Everybody says I need an attorney."

Caleb said, "Absolutely. You need someone looking out for you."

"Why? I confessed. I did it. I'll tell anyone and everyone. I killed Al. No lawyer is going to change that fact." Her words sounded leaden, weighed down by dark truth.

"There may have been extenuating circumstances. I know you feel responsible for what happened but honestly, I don't think you were."

"Of course I was. It was my hand on the pipe. I swung it and hit him. I did that, nobody else. Me." She closed her eyes.

"You're a trauma survivor, Mary Beth. You were in the throes of a flashback and it caused confusion and the blackout. This didn't happen because you meant for it to. It happened because you were sick."

Somebody knocked on the door. An officer opened it and told Caleb he was needed in the hallway.

Caleb stepped into the linoleum hall to find Jace waiting there with, of all people, Simon Madigan. A cut on Simon's chin had been bandaged. Swelling around his right eye looked purplish. His left hand was wrapped and secured in a sling.

Jace spoke. "He wants to talk to Officer Branham."

"Is she okay? I know she's been in jail," Simon said.

"It's been rough."

"Simon may help with that," Jace said.

"How so?"

"You'll see." He motioned Simon into the interview room, Caleb following.

Simon took the chair across from her and began, "I read that you confessed to killing Al Fuller."

She nodded.

He replied with a slow nod, then said, "I was there. I saw what happened. I don't think you remember, but I was there. And I'm here to set the record straight. When Fuller found me in the parking garage, I knew what would happen. I'd seen it in his eyes. He was a monster. He planned to kill me."

Mary Beth's eyes widened. Was she remembering now?

"You believed him, too. That's why you tried to stop him." Simon leaned closer to make her look at him. "I don't have much faith in cops. People like Al Fuller destroy a person's trust. But you . . . you stepped up. You were determined to protect me, and he turned on you. The things he said . . . the way he held the gun . . . we both knew what he was going to do. He would have killed us both without blinking an eye. You did what you had to. You grabbed that pipe and swung as hard as you could. He wasn't expecting it. I remember that stunned look on his face before he collapsed."

Mary Beth didn't blink, just stared.

"Do you understand what Simon is saying, Mary Beth? He's saying you acted in self-defense," Caleb clarified.

Simon thumped the table. "She was protecting me and herself. If she hadn't done it, you'd have found two bodies in that garage. And Fuller would have gotten away with it."

Caleb looked at Mary Beth. "This may change everything."

Mary Beth wiped a tear that fell down her cheek. Caleb sensed her confusion and fear. He turned to Simon. "Can you give me some time alone with her?"

Simon nodded and approached the door, where he hesitated. "I wasn't sure I'd get the chance to thank you, Ma'am. Hell, I wasn't sure I'd survive this thing, but I did. So thank you—for saving my life." He shut the door quietly behind him.

Caleb let silence settle in the small room. On the wall, a clock clicked the passing seconds. Mary Beth stared down at the scarred metal table.

He waited. Finally, she looked up at him. "I remember," she whispered.

"Everything?"

"Yeah. When Simon described what happened, it came back. All of it. One domino after another. Al wanted to kill us both. Simon for being black. Me for being . . . me."

"You for being a witness," Caleb clarified.

"I wish I hadn't killed him. Ending a life—it's hard to live with."

"I can see how it would be. But if you hadn't—"

"I know." She smoothed a hand across the table.

Caleb leaned forward, holding her gaze. "Your memories are coming to you because you're ready for them. You're strong enough. That's important."

She looked at the closed door.

"What's next for you?" Caleb asked.

"I get a lawyer. See if they can get me out of jail. If I don't go to prison, I'll need to find a job, because I'm not cut out to be a cop. Especially not after what I did."

"What do you think you'll do?"

She shrugged. “I don’t know. Maybe you can help me figure it out?”

He smiled. “I’d be honored to help you see what your next steps are. You have a lot to give the world, Mary Beth, once you figure out who you want to be.”

Chapter Fifty-Eight

Shull drifted. It felt like he stood on a raft on a stormy ocean and couldn't find his balance. The movement of the raft had him nauseous. Each movement—each tiny movement—brought on searing pain in his chest and stomach. If only he could find calmer waters, somewhere he could rest. But people kept trying to wake him. Ask him questions.

"Daddy? Daddy!" Beryl's urgent voice filled his ear.

He should go to her. He always answered when his Peaches needed him, but the effort to open his eyes felt impossible.

"Daddy! I only have a few minutes. We have to talk."

He blinked his eyes open. Overhead, stark fluorescent lights blinded him. Around him: machines, tubes, and an electronic beeping sound proved too much to take in. He closed his eyes again.

"Where is Butch, Daddy? Where would he go?"

Butch? The memories emerged, like a cascade of playing cards. The rally. The noise. Simon Madigan. Vic—Vic's betrayal. Butch slapping the gun into his hand.

Shull firing at Al's assassin.

The Black policewoman spinning to shoot him.

Then as he lay on the ground, terrified, Butch bending over for those first few seconds and whispering something before vanishing like a vapor.

"Daddy!" Beryl sounded exasperated. He felt her hand squeezing his and looked at her. "They said we only have ten minutes."

We? He glanced behind her. Glenna was there, against the wall, arms crossed. She looked furious.

"Daddy, the police need to find Butch. He stole a bunch of weapons from your store. And . . . and I don't know how it happened, but there's money missing from your accounts, too, and the police think he took it."

"Took it?" he struggled to comprehend.

"Like close to a million. And three hundred thousand worth

of guns. And they can't find him. If you can help, they might go easier on you."

He tried to move his hand and found he was handcuffed to the bed. "Butch . . . stole from me?"

"Worse than that!" Beryl exclaimed. "The police say he's behind everything. He's been controlling the Red Shirts through some dark web site. Selling them guns and pocketing a chunk of the money. He's been stealing from you for years. Hell, Shull. He's been controlling you."

"No, that can't be right." Butch was his oldest friend. He trusted him.

"It's the truth." Glenna's voice cut through like a razor. "They found all kinds of radical shit on his computer. He's a neo-Nazi. He wants to eradicate the Black race. And he's. Your. Friend." She practically spat out these last words.

He tried to make sense of it. He could almost feel Butch's breath against his ear that moment when Shull was bleeding and fighting to stay alive on the Statehouse grounds. What was it Butch said before he vanished? "This is a white man's country. We're taking it back."

Butch. His friend. His betrayer.

Beryl sighed. "You gotta help the police. We have to get that money. And maybe they'll let you go on probation or something."

Glenna laughed. It sounded ugly. "They'll never let you go. You shot a police detective. You did that. You. You ruined our lives."

"I was after Al's killer. For Beryl." For his kid. He'd do anything for her.

"Oh, Daddy," she said. "That man didn't kill Al. Al's partner did it."

"Huh?" It was too much. All of it. He wanted to pull the sheet over his head and return to the raft, even if the ocean claimed him.

The door pushed open and a police officer yelled out, "Time's up!"

"We have to go." Glenna moved to the end of the bed. "And don't count on your so-called friend Tommy Doyle to help. He's telling everyone that he barely knew you. You're not getting out of this mess you've created. Neither are we." With that, she exited.

Beryl lingered for a second. "Don't worry, Daddy. I'll do what I can with your business. What's left of it, I mean." She leaned over and kissed his cheek.

"Time to go!" The officer demanded.

She obeyed, leaving Shull alone, cuffed to the bed, trying to make sense of all he'd lost.

Chapter Fifty-Nine

Caleb gripped Shannon's hand in the quiet hospital waiting room. He savored it, needing the anchor. Sam had been in surgery for an hour. Sixty endless minutes. Caleb checked his phone for messages. *Let me know how it goes* from Matthew. *We're all thinking about you* from Janice back at the office.

And one from Lonzo: *Leave approved through Monday. Prayers for your brother.* Odd how Lonzo had changed his tune since the Capitol incident. Caleb's photo had made the front page of the newspaper, with the headline "Midlands Social Worker Gives Aid to Officer." Lonzo loved the free publicity for the practice, even mentioning using the photo for brochures and billboards. Over Caleb's dead body, but that was an argument for another time.

Soft music played through the sound system. Some instrumental crap ruining an Elton John song. The upholstered chairs, a mauvy pink pleather, looked more comfortable than they felt, but at least he and Shannon had the small room to themselves. Caleb wasn't planning to freak out, but if he did, he wanted no witnesses.

He felt oddly naked sitting there. He'd wanted this all along—for Sam to have this surgery. Insisted on it. As though if he pushed hard enough, Sam would make the right choice that would save his life. How arrogant Caleb had been, to think he knew what was best. He flashed back to Matthew's visit to his house, beer in hand, when Caleb had been an awful host. What was it Matthew said as he left? *You'd love to control everything, especially when it comes to your family. But you can't.*

He got it now. He could be a pushy twit, doing his best to manipulate everything, but it accomplished nothing. This situation—like so many—was not in his to control. Sam's fate lay in hands that weren't his.

It was damn humbling. And maybe, just maybe, a little freeing.

Shannon squeezed his hand. "You okay?"

He nodded. "Just coming to terms with the fact that I don't rule the world."

She tugged harder. "Honey, you don't even rule your closet. But we love you anyway."

The laugh felt cleansing. Almost purging. He stood to move closer to the clock. Only twenty minutes had passed.

"Caleb?"

He spun around to find Jace and Amanda entering the room. "How is he?"

"Still in surgery. They said it would take a few hours."

"And how are you?"

"About to jump out of my skin." He introduced them to Shannon. "How's the project going?" Caleb asked.

"New plans are approved," Amanda said. "Wanna see the design?"

He could definitely use the distraction. Before, they'd been so protective, the sculpture a secret mission not to be unveiled until completed. But that was before the pipe bomb ruined everything.

Jace unfolded a large sheet of paper and placed it on the small table by the loveseat. Shannon and Caleb crowded close to study it.

It was magnificent. The scales of justice, suspended on chains, in minimalist metal. Beneath each of the two plates, giant hands—one Black, one white, carved from wood, supporting the sides, kept them balanced. "Justice Be Done" was carved below the hands, with Senator Clementa Pinkney's face etched beside it.

"You won't believe it, but there's actual talk of installing this on the statehouse grounds," Jace said. "They're drafting legislation to make it happen. Might be a longshot, but still."

"Wow," Shannon said. "That's fantastic."

"Right?" Caleb agreed. "No wonder Sam's been so excited."

"He wants us to finish without him. But that ain't happening. I'll work on the scales, but I need him for the hands. No matter how long it takes for him to get well enough to tackle this, we'll wait," Jace said.

The symbolism wasn't lost on Caleb. A Black artist and a white one, joining creative forces to honor the man who died at the hand of a racist coward. South Carolina needed this message, especially now, even though much of the state would refuse to receive it. "I hope he can get back to his work soon. But if things go south . . ."

"They won't." Amanda said, her eyes tearful.

"They won't," Shannon repeated. "We're getting good news from the doctor. I know it."

Caleb didn't know it. What Caleb knew was that fate had screwed Sam over too many times. The accident that left him deaf. The murder of his fiancée.

"Can we get y'all some coffee? A sandwich?" Amanda asked Shannon.

"That would be good. I'll join you. Caleb, we'll be right back, if that's okay."

He nodded, grateful for a few minutes alone. He really needed to get it together. For Sam. He'd be there for Sam, however Sam needed him to be. If the worst case happened—it might mean more treatment. Chemo. Radiation. Even amputation. Whatever it took to beat this damned disease, he'd help Sam through it. He owed him that. Sam would never have to deal with this alone. Caleb drew a breath, letting the resolve fill his lungs. *You got this*, he had signed to Sam.

We've got this, he signed to himself.

Four hours and seventeen minutes later, Caleb sat beside a very stoned brother who was doing his best to climb through the fog of anesthesia. Caleb had ice chips for him. Shannon sat in the chair in the corner, saying nothing. A quiet support for which Caleb couldn't be more grateful.

The bandage on Sam's leg looked gruesome. A tube snaked from the gauze to a pouch below where blood drained. "To ease the swelling," a nurse had said.

He'd said little else, even after Caleb begged for more info. "Dr. Simm will be here soon," was his lone reply. Annoying bastard.

Sam blinked at him.

"Wanna try more ice?" Caleb signed.

Sam nodded, so Caleb slid a few chips between his lips. "More," Sam whispered.

"Okay but take it easy. Don't want you barfing on me."

Sam closed his eyes as more ice tumbled into his mouth. Caleb had a thousand questions, but they would have to wait.

Just as Sam drifted off to sleep, Dr. Simm appeared.

Caleb tapped his brother's good leg to rouse him.

"Can you interpret?" Dr. Simm asked Caleb.

"Absolutely."

"How are you feeling, Sam?"

"Uh . . . altered."

She smiled. "I'll tell you all of this again, in case you have questions."

Caleb moved closer, positioning himself so that Sam could see him clearly. *We got this,* he signed, and Sam nodded.

"We did a wide resection of the mass including the margins so we could test for cancer cells. The pathology report just came in." She lifted her tablet and skimmed through a few screens.

Caleb held his breath. Steeled his expression.

"I'm pleased to report no sign of spread. Your margins are clear, Sam. That's excellent news."

Caleb signed "clear" three times, each with more exaggerated emphasis.

Dr. Simm went on to describe his recovery, the home visits from a physical therapist and nurse to help with the wound over the next week or so, and Caleb signed it all, but in his mind one word resounded.

"Clear."

Sam would be okay.

When the doctor left, Shannon excused herself. Caleb dropped in a seat, ice chips gripped in his hand.

Sam's rheumy eyes studied his face. "You okay?"

"I'm . . . excellent." Caleb felt a moisture building behind his eyes. Relief. Profound, utter relief.

"Well that's good. Because I plan to be the most annoying house guest you've ever had. Get ready, brother."

"Because you're an ass," Caleb signed with a wide smile.

"Gonna be fun." Sam slid down, pulling up a sheet, a goofy, drug-induced grin on his face.

About the Author

Carla Damron is a social worker, advocate and author whose novel, *The Orchid Tattoo,* won the 2023 NIEA Award in suspense, the Winter Pencraft Award for Literary Excellence, the Literary Titan Gold Award, and the Firebird Award for best suspense. Her work *The Stone Necklace* won the 2017 WFWA Star Award and was the One Community Read for Columbia, South Carolina.

Damron is also the author of the Caleb Knowles mystery series, each of which deals with social issues. This fourth installment, *Justice Be Done*, explores the brutal Impact of unresolved racial tensions on a southern community. Damron holds an MSW and an MFA and lives in South Carolina with her husband and large family of poorly behaved shelter animals.

www.carladamron.com

Printed in the USA
CPSIA information can be obtained
at www.ICGtesting.com
LVHW051751121123
763661LV00067B/2370

9 781622 681815